praise for jerusha agen

"Jerusha Agen's masterfully written *Special Target* will wrap around your heart and not let go from the first page to the end. It's a story that will stay with me a long time."

Patricia Bradley, ECPA, Parable, and *USA Today* bestselling author

"*Special Target* is suspense with soul—a novel that grips you, breaks you a little, and then puts you back together with a deeper understanding of strength and faith. It's the kind of book you'll think about long after you close it, and one that reminds you why stories matter."

5-Star Reader Review

"Jerusha Agen once again delivers top-level suspense and thrilling action. Fast-paced suspense at its best."

DiAnn Mills, bestselling author of *Concrete Evidence* on *Covert Danger*

SPECIAL TARGET

books by jerusha agen

GUARDIANS UNLEASHED SERIES
Midnight Clear (prequel novella)
Rising Danger (prequel)
Hidden Danger
Covert Danger
Unseen Danger
Lethal Danger
Terminal Danger

WINDY CITY WESTONS SERIES
Waylaid
Wasted
Watched (2026)
Wanted (2027)

SECURITY LEAGUE SERIES
Protected (prequel novella)
Introverted (second prequel novella)
Rescued
Trapped

SISTERS REDEEMED SERIES
If You Dance with Me
If You Light My Way
If You Rescue Me

JERUSHA AGEN

SPECIAL TARGET

SDG Words, LLC

© 2026 by Jerusha Agen
Published by SDG Words, LLC
www.JerushaAgen.com

All rights reserved. No part of this publication may be reproduced, stored in a retrieval system, or transmitted in any form or by any means—for example, electronic, photocopy, recording—without the prior written permission of the publisher. The only exception is brief quotations in printed reviews.

Library of Congress Control Number: 2026900030

ISBN 978-1-956683-65-3

Scripture quotations are from The ESV® Bible (The Holy Bible, English Standard Version®), copyright © 2001 by Crossway, a publishing ministry of Good News Publishers. Used by permission. All rights reserved.

This book is a work of fiction. Names, characters, places, and incidents are the product of the author's imagination or are used fictitiously. Any resemblance to actual events, locales, or persons, living or dead, is coincidental.

Without in any way limiting the author's [and publisher's] exclusive rights under copyright, any use of this publication to "train" generative artificial intelligence (AI) technologies to generate text is expressly prohibited. The author reserves all rights to license uses of this work for generative AI training and development of machine learning language models.

To Joni Eareckson Tada. Your fight for the value of every human life inspired this story.

Soli Deo Gloria

*Why did I not die at birth,
come out from the womb and expire?*

Job 3:11

chapter
one

For a child, home should mean chocolate chip cookies in the oven, the sound of her mother's laughter, lullabies to dream by. Home should be heaven.

Not a living hell.

Ashley Sorenson stared out her car window at the house that would've been white if not for years of dirt and weather damage that had painted and battered the siding. She'd give her right arm to see through those decaying walls.

"Ashley, no. Stay where you are. I'm almost there."

Ashley ignored Tina Griffon's protests over the cell phone as she shoved open the car door and stepped into humidity thick enough to slice. "Two minutes. Then I'm going in."

"Ashley, don't." A tremor belied the sharpness of Tina's tone.

Ashley rounded the car and paused, her muscles coiled like nervous springs. "He could be doing anything to them in there."

"The police must be close by now. At least wait for me. I think I'm like five minutes away."

A shriek came from the house. A smash. Then another child's scream.

Ashley took off, pocketing the phone as she homed in on the deep voice that yelled curses between pounding and smashing.

She yanked open the gashed screen door and slammed through the unlocked wooden one behind it.

A tall, scrawny man held a bat in midair, mouth hanging open as he stared at Ashley.

Two of the children dashed to her. They hid behind her—small, hot bodies pressing close as they gripped her T-shirt.

A smaller girl huddled on a pile of trash in the corner under the man with the bat. She whimpered. The little hands that covered her head were spattered with blood.

"Put the bat down." The fury that boiled in Ashley's throat powered the order.

The monster's lips curled to reveal teeth that looked like a stack of blackened rubble. "Ain't you a cute little thing?" His beady eyes slid up and down her body.

Ashley didn't need to hear the slur in his words to know he was drunk. The odor was as obvious as the smashed beer bottles at her feet. "I'm a social worker, and the police are almost here. Drop the bat and get away from her."

"Why would I do that?" He kept watching her with that sleazy grin.

"Kids," she kept her voice calm for the little ones behind her, "a nice lady is coming for you outside. Go out front and stay there until she comes. You'll be safe."

The boy and girl, no older than eight, reluctantly let go of her shirt and started to back toward the door, watching their cruel excuse for a father with wide eyes.

"No, you don't." He took a step toward them and raised the bat again. "Get over here, you—" He launched a string of foul words no children should hear. "You do what I say!"

"Go!" Ashley pushed the kids toward the door and whipped around to face the charging monster. She planted herself in his path. He'd have to kill her to get to those kids.

He stopped inches from her. Spittle and his repulsive breath dropped on her face. "Them's my kids."

She stared up at him, unblinking. "Not anymore."

He grabbed her arm and flung her into the wall.

She crashed to the floor. Pain seared her shoulder, and her head throbbed. How could somebody that drunk move so fast? She hadn't even had time to use her self-defense moves.

The sound of sobbing cleared the fog in Ashley's head.

She looked up in time to see him stomp over to the crumpled victim in the corner.

No. He was not going to touch her again.

Ashley scrambled up, blinking away her blurred vision as she rushed to the girl. She dropped, covered the child with her body as he raised the bat over them with that horrid grin.

"Freeze! Police!"

Ashley let out her held breath.

Two officers stood just inside the door, guns trained on the madman.

"Aw, man." His arms sagged. The bat dropped to the floor at his feet.

The officers moved in to secure him and take him away.

Ashley ignored the commotion of the arrest and the man's yelling as she turned her attention to the youngest victim.

Ashley sat back from the girl.

She was so tiny, probably only four unless she was extremely small for her age. Her dark hair clung to her face, skin tight from malnourishment and wet with tears and blood.

So much for carrying the girl out right away. Ashley would have to find the source of that blood first. "Hey, sweetie. You're safe now." She gently wiped back the pretty black strands of hair, guiding them off the girl's face to reveal large blue eyes that watched Ashley.

The blood came from an angled gash across the girl's forehead—the highlight of her bruised face. Her little hands also sported several cuts, but her arms looked worse. The many bruises that covered them left patches of deep purple. What other injuries hid under the surface of the little girl's body? More than one bone was likely broken.

Ashley swallowed the bile that rose in her throat. There should be another word for fathers who were the polar opposite of what the name should mean. Perverted loser came close, but there had to be something stronger, something more meaningful that she could apply to the sorry excuses for human beings she encountered nearly every day.

She looked away from the girl just in time to catch a hateful glare from the abuser the officers took out the door, cuffed as he should be. He shouted a few curses, at her this time, as he left the house. Better her than the kids. People like him should never be allowed to have children in the first place.

"Ashley?" Tina touched her shoulder as she crouched down to see the little girl. Tina's gaze shifted to Ashley, sickness in her dark brown eyes. She had as much on-the-job experience as Ashley, but even social workers never got used to seeing stuff like this. "The ambulance is on its way."

Ashley nodded as she stroked the girl's hair.

The little victim's sobbing had stopped, but shock now set in. She sat frozen and pale, her body trembling.

Ashley moved closer to the wall and the tiny girl. She gently wrapped her arms around the small form, careful not to apply any pressure or move her. She held the girl until the ambulance came and the nightmare, for this child, ended.

A quick walk into the emergency department was enough to remind Ashley why she tried to avoid hospitals. It was as if all of Chicago's pain and dysfunction were gathered in this one place filled with hurting, crying people. And death.

"Ashley Sorenson, the social worker?"

The odd question brought her attention back to the nurse behind the desk. "Yes."

"I had a message to call you, but it's just been so steady for the past hour."

Ashley braced herself. This day was not happening. If this was for another emergency placement, she was calling it a record.

"Let's see." The nurse searched behind the desk until she found a chart. "Oh, yes." She looked up from reading it. "We have an accident situation with a minor. His parents just died, and the police haven't been able to locate any relatives or guardians."

"How old?"

"Uh..." She checked the chart. "Sixteen."

"Is he injured?" Ashley fished in her oversized purse for a scrap of paper, pushing back the wave of auburn hair that fell in front of her eyes.

"Just some minor scratches and bruises. He can leave at any time."

"Do you know his name?" Ashley wrote the age on the back of a gas station receipt.

"Matthew Haase."

"Okay. Let's wrap up the registration for Olivia, and I'll go find him." Ashley shoved the paper into her bag, trying to ignore the fatigue and throbbing bruises on her forehead and shoulder that were starting to get to her.

She had already caught one lucky break today in finding immediate placement for the two older Richardson kids, now on their way to a temp foster home. Olivia, the battered little girl, would need to stay in the hospital for several days. Which meant Ashley had only that long to find her a foster family. At least she was young and cute. Placing a sixteen-year-old would not be so easy.

"Miss Sorenson?"

The nurse's voice broke through Ashley's internal strategy session.

"I said you won't have to look for him. He's right behind you."

Ashley turned around to see where the nurse pointed.

Across the waiting area, a thickly built young man wearing a red and blue baseball cap sat next to a lady cop. He jerked his hands up and down repetitively while the officer perused a magazine.

"Is he in shock?"

The nurse checked the all-knowing chart on the desk, then shook her head. "I don't think so."

Ashley glanced at the boy behind her as she finished Olivia's registration. The teen kept up the odd motion with his hands for five minutes straight.

"That's all then." The nurse took the forms and looked past Ashley's shoulder. "I'll call Dr. Lewis while you meet the boy. She performed surgery on his mother before she passed. I'm sure she'll want to talk to you."

Ashley headed across the room. Just had to be a teenager. Little ones were so much easier. Teens more often wanted a punching bag than a warm shoulder. She braced herself for a sixteen-year-old's attitude as she stopped in front of him. "Matthew?"

He kept swinging his hands, not looking up.

The officer lowered her magazine. "Child Protective Services?"

Ashley nodded.

The woman glanced at Matthew and reached to still his hands.

He lifted his head. Beneath the crooked brim of the Chicago Cubs cap, small eyes stared out at Ashley through angled slits in an unmistakable face.

Down syndrome.

Her heart clenched.

"Ma'am?"

Ashley closed her mouth, pulled her gaze to the officer. "I can't take him."

The woman's thinly shaped eyebrows lifted. Was that judgment in her eyes?

Ashley folded her arms across her chest and raised her chin. "We're not equipped to take him right now. A condition like his requires a special foster situation. I can't offer that on such short notice." She'd already stuffed the two Richardson kids into the only home she had that would even think of fostering a Down syndrome teen.

The cop stood, annoyingly taller than Ashley. "You'll have to take him. We haven't been able to locate any living relatives." She glanced at the boy and lowered her voice slightly. "If you don't take him into foster care, he'll be sent to a public mental institution."

Ashley swallowed, letting her gaze drift to the teen who watched her with those oddly shaped eyes. She'd seen institutions before. Seen what they did to people. She wouldn't put her worst enemy in one of those.

The leering face of the man who'd beat five-year-old Olivia sprang to mind, challenging the declaration. Actually, Ashley had met plenty of creeps she would put in an institution and throw away the key. But this teen didn't deserve that. Wasn't his fault his parents chose to bring him into this world, knowing he would never be happy.

She swallowed back a sigh. "I'll take him."

"Thought you couldn't."

"I'll figure it out." Ashley met the cop's superior smirk with a confident stare. Though where she was going to put the boy, she had no idea. "What's his functioning level? Does he have any health concerns?"

A flush of embarrassed color replaced the smug smile on the cop's face. "I—I don't know."

The nurse from the desk appeared at Ashley's side. "Dr. Lewis is with an emergency case. I can tell you what you need to know. Let's see..." She studied the omniscient chart she'd brought with her. "We couldn't locate a medical history, but our examination shows that he appears to be fairly high-functioning, except verbally. He can handle the bathroom himself and feed himself."

Thank goodness. Ashley tried to keep her expression neutral. Not that it mattered, since the nurse never tore her gaze from that chart.

"He hasn't spoken at all since he got here, but the doctor says it's possible he's quiet because of shock and unfamiliar surroundings. He follows instructions well and does as he's told. He doesn't seem to have any of the potential health side effects of Down syndrome at this point. His thyroid appears normal, as does his heart." The nurse finally looked up. For a second. "He could have behavioral issues, but we haven't seen evidence of any yet. He's shown no signs of aggression while he's been with us."

Aggression? Great. Ashley hadn't even thought of that. The kid looked maybe about an inch taller than Ashley's five feet and five inches, but a lot thicker and heavier. What would she do if he turned out to be aggressive?

An image of the round-faced teen, locked up in a white-walled cell flashed in her mind.

She couldn't live with herself if she did that to any kid. She'd have to find another way. One that had very little to do with her directly. She was in this business to give miserable children happier lives, not to get involved in hopeless cases.

The teen started jerking his hands in the air again as he stared at his lap.

She couldn't give this boy a life anything close to happy. No one could. He had been doomed by his parents when they decided to have him. Now she was the one who had to pick up the pieces, as usual. Only this time, she wouldn't be able to make something beautiful out of these pieces. She couldn't fix a life Down syndrome had already ruined.

"I'll need you to sign this." The cop held out a clipboard. "If you're still taking him."

Ashley pulled the clipboard from the woman's hand and signed the form.

Special Target

The officer exchanged the clipboard for a file when Ashley handed it back. "This is all the information we have about him so far."

Ashley opened the file. Just one sheet lay inside, sparsely filled out. "No family information at all? Other relatives? Address?"

The cop shook her head. "Only his parents' names. Kevin and Jane Haase."

The boy didn't react to the names. Did he not understand anything that had happened?

"How did they die?"

"Plane crash. Their private plane went down just after takeoff."

"And the boy wasn't hurt?" Ashley raised an eyebrow.

"He was in the back."

"I see. You'll keep me informed if you find out anything more?"

"Sure."

Ashley's gaze went to the teen. "Let's go."

He jerked his hands up and down without looking at her.

The cop tapped his hand, and he stopped moving. "Time to go, Matthew. You're going with this lady here."

The boy looked at Ashley, almost like he had understood.

She beckoned with her hand. "Come on."

He stood. Great. He was another inch or two taller than she'd thought. What if he threw a fit or something? Ashley had only defended herself against normal people. He'd probably be completely unpredictable and out of control.

"Follow me." She turned away from him and shook her head at herself as she headed for the hospital doors. *No more fear.* She hadn't broken that promise to herself in fifteen years. She wasn't going to let an orphaned kid with Down syndrome make her break it now.

Something touched her hand.

She jerked to the side.

Matthew's chubby hand reached for hers.

What was he doing? He was sixteen, not six.

"Let's go." She kept walking, the boy now at her side.

He reached for her hand again.

She pulled away. *Calm down.* Her rapid pulse was slow to obey her mental order. He must want to hold hands in a childlike kind of way. She hoped. Whatever the reason, it was inappropriate. He looked like a grown man from a distance.

She folded her arms in front of her and gave him a firm glance as she kept moving. "No."

He stopped, dropping behind her.

Ashley sighed and turned to look at him.

He covered his ears with his hands, and his lower lip stuck out in a five-year-old pose.

You've got to be kidding. She might have spoken a little sharply, but this was ridiculous. "Pouting won't do you any good. It's not appropriate for you to hold my hand."

No reaction.

She took a step toward him, trying to ignore the people giving them strange looks as they walked around the stalled teenager. "Look, you have to start growing up now. Sixteen-year-olds don't pout." Well, not like that anyway. She looked into his round face, made herself glance at the slitted eyes that watched her.

Did he understand a word she said? She wasn't exactly practiced at talking to people like him. Never had to before. Never thought she would.

He made a noise.

Was that a whimper?

His lip pushed out even farther.

Ashley spun around with a frustrated grunt and stalked a few steps away. She couldn't do this. She didn't know anything about people like him. How was she supposed to see that he was cared for when she couldn't even manage to get him out of the hospital?

She took in a long breath and slowly let it out. She was just exhausted. The day was getting to her. But she needed to keep her head if she was going to find a solution to this problem.

Like it or not, she was the boy's only hope right now. She inhaled another bolstering breath and turned back.

He was gone.

chapter **two**

Ashley scanned the people passing through the hallway. She'd only looked away for thirty seconds, tops. Where could the kid have gone?

She stalked back the way they'd come, retracing their steps to the front desk in the waiting area. There was no need to get excited. He must have simply wandered back this way. He had to be fine. He didn't seem to move very fast.

Ashley stopped at the desk.

The same nurse stood behind it.

"Did you see the boy come back here?" Ashley waited for the woman to check her chart.

She shook her head instead. "No, but I was busy."

Ashley turned away and scanned the room. The same people who were there minutes before sat in the same chairs, leaning their heads in their hands, some crying softly, others staring into space or at their smartphones.

No boy in a Cubs cap.

Maybe he'd somehow snuck past her out the doors instead of coming back this way. Ashley's heartbeat picked up speed as she hurried through the hall to the exit.

She'd never lost a child. Never.

Special Target

This one couldn't even think normally. If she lost him, he wouldn't have a chance. Sick people targeted kids like him.

A bitter taste surged up her throat as she brushed past an entering man and shoved through the glass doors.

She looked right.

Nothing.

Left.

A figure with a red baseball cap lumbered away from the hospital.

"Hey!"

He kept walking.

Ashley jogged after him and called again.

The boy stopped and turned around just as she reached him. His mouth stretched into a wide smile.

Something tightened in her chest. Just a reaction to her sudden sprint. She pushed away any other explanation. She had a job to do. She glared at the sunny smile. "You can't run off like that, do you understand? It's not safe."

He still smiled.

"You're a bad boy." Maybe talking down to him would get through. "You have to stay with me, got it?"

A frown reversed the curve of his lips until the bottom one started to push out again.

Not another crying fit. "It's okay now." She tried to soften her voice and waved at the boy to follow her. "Come with me, and let's get in the car. I'm going to take you somewhere safe." If she could find anywhere to take him at all.

She purposefully stayed in front of him so he wouldn't try to take her hand as they walked to the car. But she checked back every other second.

"This is it." She went to the passenger door of her little white car and unlocked it with the key. She opened the door for Matthew since he probably couldn't do it himself.

Took him longer to get in the seat than her boyfriend's grannie.

Ashley's gaze wandered as she waited to shut the door.

Something moved in the shadow of a tall bush next to the hospital exit.

A man. He looked away.

That meant he'd been watching her. Why?

The hairs on the back of her neck perked.

Even from this distance, his Hispanic features with wavy dark hair and broad cheekbones were obvious, reminding her of Eddie. Except this guy was taller. And he did not give her the same warm feelings as her boyfriend usually did.

Ashley's stomach clenched as she shut Matthew's door and went to her side of the car. She got in fast and pressed down the lock that had stopped working the day she got the clunker. Best lesson she'd learned on the streets—a good bluff could save her life.

She looked to see if the man had bought it.

He was gone.

She started the car. Tried to. The engine choked, as usual. She tried again. Third time was the charm, and she cast a last glance at the exit as she pulled out of the stall.

No one was there except a woman who pushed through the doors. Maybe the guy had been checking Ashley out. Though in her oversized, bloodstained T-shirt and old jeans, she doubted that was the explanation.

She glanced at Matthew.

He stared out the window, his hands jerking up and down again. At least he didn't seem to have noticed anything wrong.

She forced out her pent-up breath. She shouldn't care about one random guy among the twenty-some people she'd seen go in and out of the hospital since she'd arrived.

But for some reason, her gut cared. And her gut never lied.

Ashley fiddled with the cord where it connected loosely to the base of the lamp. The bulb flickered on again, shifting the shadows that crept in through the uncovered office windows.

"Whoa. Did you see it's dark out already?" Tina moved from the window to pick up the small pink clock on her desk. "No wonder." She showed Ashley the clock face. "It's a quarter to nine. I have to get home."

"No, wait." Ashley looked away from her glowing computer screen and rubbed her weary eyes. "You can't leave me alone with this mess."

Tina plopped in her desk chair again. "Okay, but I'm out of ideas. The foster homes are full, including the only one in our system who would take a sixteen-year-old with Down's. The group homes are all filled."

Ashley shoved her fingers into her hair. "St. John's is the only one equipped to handle someone with his needs anyway."

Tina nodded. The beads on her countless slim braids that were gathered into a thick, black ponytail clinked together as she twisted her swivel chair back and forth in short motions. "I could try St. John's again and push for a spot, but we'll have to wait until morning to have a shot at reaching anyone high enough up to give the okay."

"A lot of good that does us now." Ashley glanced at Matthew, who sat quietly in a chair near the door. "He has to go somewhere tonight."

Tina stared at Ashley.

Her stomach clenched. "No way." She shook her head. "He is not going home with me."

Tina's dark brown eyes narrowed as she lowered her volume and angled away from Matthew. "Why are you treating him differently?"

Ashley pulled back like she'd been slapped. But heat crept to her face, almost as if she deserved the smack. She turned to her computer screen and swallowed. "What are you talking about?"

"I heard your tone of voice when you brought him in here and had him sit down. Like you were scolding him when he didn't do anything wrong. I've never seen you like this with our other kids."

Ashley's throat tightened. Had she really been sharp with him? She hadn't meant to be. But she was never good with people who made her uncomfortable. How was she supposed to act around him?

Tina stood and walked to the front of Ashley's desk, probably trying to force Ashley to look at her. "I know how you feel about this, but you shouldn't take it out on him even if you think his parents made the wrong choice."

"I'm not." Ashley's voice rose with her gaze. Tina should know she'd never do that.

But Tina's eyes held only confusion, not judgment.

Ashley tucked her hair behind her ear and glanced past her friend to Matthew. "I can't help him, Tina. He's suffering. He'll suffer as long as he lives, and I can't do anything about it." She met her co-worker's softened gaze. "He isn't like the other kids. He isn't even...normal."

Tina surprised Ashley with a laugh. "Normal? Girl, none of the kids we see are normal. You know that."

"You know what I mean."

Matthew started up his weird hand swings, as if to prove Ashley's point.

"I don't know how to talk to him, let alone how to handle him if something goes wrong. I'm not the right person to take him."

"Sure you just don't *want* to be the right person?"

Ashley pointed a glare at Tina. "You know we aren't supposed to take kids home."

Tina snorted. "I don't think the manual covers a case like this one. When you're removing a child from the home is one thing. This is something else."

"I notice you're not sticking your neck out. You just want me to."

Tina shook her head. "I really don't think anybody's going to call you unethical in a situation like this."

Special Target

Ashley picked up a pen and tapped one end of it on the desk. Either way, she couldn't take him home.

"Why don't you just call upstairs and get the okay?"

Their supervisor's office was actually about ten miles away, but Tina insisted on using that phrase anyway. "Julie is on vacation."

"Yeah, but she has a sub."

"Who?"

"Dean."

Ashley wrinkled her nose. "Dean 'do-it-yourself' Kendall?"

Tina flashed a smile, her perfect white teeth contrasting beautifully with her copper-toned skin. "The one and only."

"He's never worked in CPS."

"Seriously, woman?" Tina's eyebrow lifted. "How many people do you know who are even in the right department after the cutbacks?"

"Good point."

Tina nodded to the phone on Ashley's desk. "So are you going to call him or am I?"

Ashley sighed. "Get me the number, and I'll call."

Her first attempt got kicked to an answering service. After insisting the call was a real emergency, Ashley was finally transferred to Dean himself.

"Hello?"

"Dean?" Was the guy at a party? Loud music and laughter from more than one woman nearly drowned out his voice.

"Who is this?"

"Ashley Sorenson from CPS."

"CPS?"

Could he not hear, or had he actually forgotten about their department completely? "Child Protective Services."

"Oh, right. You're after hours."

Like she didn't know that. "Sorry, but we have a strange situation. I have an orphaned teenage boy with Down syndrome. The foster homes are full, and we can't get a group home to take him right away. We were, uh..." She glanced at Tina, who nodded.

"We were considering the possibility of taking him to one of our personal homes. Just temporarily until we can place him."

"What? Sure, yeah." More laughter in the background. "Look, you need to handle things like this yourself. I can't be your babysitter. Don't bother me outside the office again."

Ashley opened her mouth to give him the reply he deserved, but the noise on the other end cut off. He'd hung up on her.

"Feel better?" Tina watched Ashley with a knowing grin.

"I suppose you knew what he'd say."

She shrugged. "For once, I agree with Dean."

"Okay." Ashley leaned back in her chair. "Then why don't you take him?"

"Me?" Tina raised an eyebrow. "Have you ever raised twin toddlers? Boys? I don't think so." She chuckled as she faced her desk and started gathering papers like she was going to leave. "And speaking of the twins, Javon is probably going crazy right now trying to get them to bed, late as usual. I'd better get home, or he won't let me come to work tomorrow."

Ashley rolled her eyes. "And you tried to talk me into getting married? You make it sound like a prison sentence, and your husband's the warden."

"You could've been happily incarcerated yourself by now if you and Eddie weren't so afraid of commitment." Tina stuffed the last of the papers into her tote bag.

"Hey, we're committed. We can have love and commitment without a ring."

Tina looked up. "Mm-hmm. He probably won't propose because he wants kids, and you don't. Which I do not understand because you're amazing with them." She glanced at Matthew. "Present company excluded."

"Thanks a lot. I think."

Tina grabbed her other two bags and slung her purse over her shoulder before pinning Ashley with a serious gaze that meant trouble. "For real, you should think about settling down and being a mom. Look how Olivia took to you today. All kids do that with you. I've never seen anyone so naturally gifted with children."

Ashley dropped her attention to the piles of forms on her desk, her throat thickening. "There's no way I'm bringing another person into this world to suffer. The world is cruel to children. You know that. We see it every day."

A heavy silence stretched between them.

Then Tina drew in an audible breath and pushed out a teasing tone. "Well, I'm going to go home while I still have *my* marriage."

Ashley lifted her chin with a smile. "The warden might let you out, huh?"

"No way, girl. I already threw away that key." Tina paused by the doorway and glanced at the boy. "Goodnight, Matthew. Don't let Ashley fool you. She's a softy at heart." Tina ducked out before Ashley could respond.

Ashley's gaze fell on Matthew. Wait a minute.

She launched out of her chair and darted through the doorway, stopping at the top of the staircase that led to the exit. "Wait! What about the boy?"

Tina shrugged from the base of the stairs and reached to open the windowless door. "You have more experience than I do. You'll figure it out."

More experience by six weeks. "Thanks." Ashley crossed her arms over her chest, hoping Tina caught the sarcasm in the word.

"Nightie, night!" Tina waved as she disappeared into the darkness outside.

"Right." Ashley glared at the closed door.

A sound came from behind.

She spun around.

Matthew. He stood there, watching her with squinting eyes. Had he said something?

He pushed out a noise again.

Was he trying to talk? The attempt was slurred nearly beyond recognition.

"What?" Ashley listened closer as he repeated himself.

"God good."

She blinked at him. Had she heard that right? What kind of sixteen-year-old walked around spouting motivational poster slogans? Or mini sermons.

"God good." His mouth angled into a little smile that matched the irritating slant of his cap.

She sighed. A teenager with Down syndrome who'd just lost his only family in the world was preaching about a mythical being who was supposedly good? The irony could've made her laugh if the circumstances weren't so grim. "Let's go back inside."

She shook her head as she passed Matthew into the office and went to shut down her computer. This day kept getting weirder and weirder. But it looked like the only way out at this point was to go home and go to bed. A new day couldn't be quite so bizarre.

Ashley gathered Matthew's documentation together and shoved the papers in a file folder to take along. Maybe at home she would see something in them that she'd missed. Maybe his parents hadn't really left him without anyone to take care of him. But the most irresponsible people always seemed to be the ones who chose to be parents.

"Let's go." Ashley was careful not to use a scolding tone as she picked up her purse and pointed to the office door. She'd tell the boy he was going home with her, but he wouldn't understand anyway.

He waited until she went through the doorway, then followed her as she carefully walked down the dark staircase.

Somebody should put a light in the stairway. Maybe she and Tina were the only ones who stayed late enough to notice. The other employees in the building seemed to keep such nice, normal hours.

She opened the door at the bottom of the staircase, and

surprisingly cool air touched her face as she stepped outside. Maybe that meant tomorrow wouldn't be such a scorcher. She checked to be sure the door locked behind Matthew before starting down the sidewalk to the car.

The well-lit, permit-only parking lot had cleared out now, of course. Somehow it was always too full for her to park there when she arrived. She peered around the dumpster as she turned and took the sidewalk along the back of the building to the street.

So much for her new pact with Tina that they would leave together at night. Tina was the one who'd insisted on the idea after she had heard about the homeless guy hanging around after dark.

Ashley checked behind her for Matthew.

He followed about two feet back, his head down as he stared at the ground.

"Watch your step." She pointed to the spot where the sidewalk dropped to a cracked, sunken section. She had never understood how the street at the front of the building could be so beautifully kept while the street behind boasted disintegrating sidewalks and a flooded, empty plot of land across the road.

Ashley watched to be sure Matthew navigated the rough portion okay, then glanced up and down the street to be sure no suspicious characters lurked.

Looked clear. She got Matthew into the car and kept an eye out as she sat behind the wheel. The car started on the third try, and she pulled away from the curb, her mind moving ahead to where she was going to put Matthew at her house.

A scraping noise broke into her thoughts. Why did the car feel unbalanced? She stopped, only a few feet from where she'd started. She drove ahead again, slowly.

Yep. Lopsided. Like the car was running on the rim in the rear. Terrific. She pulled back to the curb and killed the engine. What else could go wrong?

She shoved open her door and marched to the back of the car.

The tire wasn't just a little flat. The rubber was practically gone, the rim nearly in direct contact with the ground.

Cool air blew tendrils of her hair, tickling her ear as she lifted her gaze. A crawling sensation crept up her neck.

She scanned the empty street, the parking lot. The night was eerily quiet.

A dog barked somewhere in the distance.

A door creaked far away. Or was it close?

She ducked into the car and pretended to lock her door. She watched out the windshield. She was no chicken, but her instincts knew a dangerous situation when she was in one.

"God good."

She jumped at the sound of Matthew's voice. She glanced at him, trying to calm her breathing. Were those the only words he knew? It was going to be a long night.

She sighed, her uncharacteristic paranoia leaving with the air. "I have to change the tire. I want you to promise you won't get out of the car while I'm doing that." She met his slanted eyes.

He nodded.

Not that he actually understood a word she had just said, let alone the concept of a promise. But it was the best she could do. She reached across his lap and pressed down the lock on the passenger door. At least one worked.

She held up a finger. "Do *not* touch the lock, okay? I'll be right back."

She turned to get out.

Her gaze collided with a face.

chapter
three

The shadowed man outside the window thumped his knuckles against the glass.

Ashley's teeth pinched her bottom lip as she bit back a scream.

"Hey, there. Need some help?" The man's voice sounded oddly normal.

Adrenaline pumped through her veins, washing out the fear. She narrowed her eyes at the face cast in darkness. The guy would have a fight on his hands if he was up to no good.

She could go for the knife in her purse, but she better not yet. He might try to get in if he saw her make a sudden move. She inwardly cursed the broken lock that would make that too easy.

She peered at the man. If only she could see him better.

His body blocked the light from the streetlamp as he looked in, placing his features in deep shadow.

She could tell he had tanned white skin—a surprise in this neighborhood—but couldn't see much more than that.

"I said, do you need help?" He seemed to have a wide smile that he kept flashing. He held up his hands. "Tell you what, lady. I'll change the tire while you stay in the car. I just want to help."

His speech wasn't slurred or sloppy. Maybe he was okay. But how would he change the tire without getting to her spare?

"I'll even use my own spare, okay?"

Why would he do that? She nodded anyway. She wasn't about to let him in her car to get the spare or step out herself and have him try any funny business. In this neighborhood, she'd get spectators before she'd get any help.

She breathed more deeply as he walked away. Where was his vehicle with the supposed spare? She craned her neck around to watch his progress behind her car. Turning forward to use the rearview mirror instead, she spotted a black car parked far behind hers at the other end of the street. How had she not seen that before? The street had been empty, she was sure of it.

It's fine. You got this. Ashley reached into the outer pouch of her purse and clutched the folding knife she kept there.

The car suddenly moved.

Her gaze jerked to the side mirror.

The man was jacking it up. Was he really going to change the tire or was he just trying to put the car out of play?

Matthew made some murmuring sound and gripped the armrest on his door.

"It's okay." Ashley pushed confidence into her voice. "He's just changing the tire. He'll be done in a minute." She hoped.

She watched the guy in her side mirror. She could see him better now in the light from the streetlamp. Still couldn't get a good look at his face, other than in profile, but he had short, light brown hair and a lean build in dark jeans and a fitted leather jacket.

Before she started to like the look of him too much, she redirected her thoughts to the question she should be asking. What were the chances of meeting an honest-to-goodness nice guy in this neighborhood at this hour? Zilch. There had to be a catch. And since it hadn't come before the tire changing bit, it must be going to come after.

She kept her breathing calm as she watched him lower the car and putter with the tire. Checking it or killing time?

Her fingers clutched the key in the ignition. If he would just step away...

He stood.

She quickly turned the key. *Start for once, you junk heap.*

It did.

She didn't have time to marvel at getting her wish as she pulled the car away from the mystery man, hoping she didn't drive over his toes.

She didn't look back to check. Just being able to breathe normally again and put the knife back into her purse were enough for her. She rubbed a clammy palm against her denim-clad leg, the grit of dirt and blood there reminding her how badly she needed to get cleaned up.

"God good." Matthew pushed his hands against the dash like she was driving crazily as he said his only two words.

She clenched her teeth. More like *she* was good to get them out of there alive.

At least Eddie was working the night shift and wouldn't be home when she showed up with Matthew. She could deal with Eddie's reaction to their visitor in the morning, after she'd had a shower and rest.

Ashley glanced at her man-sized passenger. He hadn't shown any signs of aggression yet. But she wouldn't let her guard down until she was sure he wasn't a threat.

The idea he could be dangerous seemed like a stretch, given his docile behavior so far. Even so, she couldn't shake the premonition that this kid was going to cause her trouble. Big trouble.

She felt the presence before she awoke, somehow sensing he was there in the darkness of her dreams. Just as she always had.

Ashley opened her eyes, her gaze meeting the patterned gray and blue fuzz of a couch cushion.

She wasn't in bed. Not in her childhood room. She was a grown woman in her living room.

But the feeling of being watched was unmistakable.

Someone stood behind her.

She wasn't a helpless girl anymore. She flexed her fingers, readying for action. They brushed against something cool and hard under the afghan that covered her.

The memory of last night emerged from her sleep-induced fog. She'd found a broken chair leg in the garage and kept it close in case her house guest turned out to be more dangerous than he appeared.

Was the teen behind her now?

She slowed her breathing, closed her grip on the table leg as she rolled over and sat up in one quick motion.

Matthew stood inches away, his outline tinged in glowing sunlight that pushed through the thin curtain covering the living room window. He looked down at her with his lips flattened into a smile.

She shifted to the side away from him and stood, willing her pulse to slow back to normal. "You shouldn't sneak up on people."

He rubbed his eyes that were even more squinted than yesterday, his smile holding steady.

She turned away to tuck the chair leg between couch cushions. And to digest the shock of seeing him again. She'd already forgotten how strange—how different—his face looked.

Maybe she just needed coffee.

"What's going on here?"

She jumped at the man's yell behind her. Eddie.

She let out a long breath, suddenly feeling tired all over as she turned to face her boyfriend.

"Care to explain this?" Eddie's thick, dark eyebrows nearly touched in the middle as they drew together.

She yawned and ran her fingers over the top of her crown to pull her hair away from her face. "What time is it?" Far too early for him to pick a fight, judging from her level of exhaustion.

"Six." He crossed his arms over his skinny chest. "And I'd like to know why you're with another man in my house." Each word grew louder as red tinged his tawny cheeks.

"*Your* house?"

"I want to know what's going on."

His slight Mexican accent usually charmed her. Before coffee, it grated on her raw nerves.

She turned her back on him and started folding the afghan. "He didn't have anywhere else to go."

"Oh, and that makes it okay for you to bring another man into my house when I'm gone?"

Ashley threw down the afghan and whirled to face him. "It's not your house, and he's just a boy. An orphaned teenager." She spewed out a curse, her tired voice rising to a yell as anger shook off the fatigue. "Just what kind of person do you think I am?"

"Hey." Eddie clamped a hand on Matthew's shoulder and stared at his face.

"Don't touch him." Ashley grabbed Eddie's wrist.

His eyes widened as he dropped his hand. "What's wrong with him?"

She nearly rolled her eyes. She certainly wasn't with Eddie for his intelligence. "Obviously, he has Down syndrome." She turned away and finished folding the afghan. She had to admit Matthew's face wasn't the most pleasant thing to look at first thing in the morning.

A twinge of guilt followed the thought. Wasn't his fault he wasn't normal. And it wasn't her fault she was cranky. Waking up to Eddie's shouting would put anyone in a mean mood.

"You said you don't like children like him."

"I don't dislike them. I just think..." She glanced over her shoulder at Eddie's accusing stare. "Forget it. I help kids for a living. I can't pick and choose only the healthy and normal ones."

"But why would you bring him into our home?"

She faced him. "Why wouldn't I?"

He narrowed his eyes. "You don't want children. You said so. Now you want to adopt this boy?"

So that was it. "We both agreed on no children."

"No." He shook his head, a shock of black hair bobbing with the motion. "*You* said so. I want children."

She swung her hand toward Matthew. "Then what's the problem? He's a kid."

Eddie took a step toward her. "A stranger's child. I don't want a stranger's child. I want my own. You can't keep this boy."

"I don't want to!" Ashley's shout brought Matthew's lower lip out. Great. She toned her voice down, shooting daggers at Eddie with her eyes instead. "Not permanently. I just couldn't find anything else for him right away. His…special needs make him hard to place, okay?"

"Is he wearing my pajamas?" Eddie scanned the boy up and down, his square jaw tightening. "He's wearing my pajamas."

"So what? He didn't have any other clothes."

Matthew whimpered, his lips sagging even lower.

"Matthew," she looked past Eddie, "can you get dressed?"

The boy grunted and went into the bedroom. He didn't shut the door behind him, but at least he was out of sight.

Eddie took a step after him. "Don't touch any of my clothes!"

Ashley glared at Eddie. "What is your problem?"

His dark gaze turned to her, and he closed the distance between them. "No, what is *your* problem? It was your idea. No children, no marriage. You remember?"

"Yeah, I do. I also remember you agreed to that. Then you spent the last year changing your mind and trying to get me to change, too. I'm not going to."

"You just did. I see now the truth. You didn't want my child. No baby of mine." He pointed to the hallway. "You want him instead. A boy who isn't even normal. You think he's better than my child?"

A foul taste reached her mouth as she stared at him. "Are you drunk? You must be drunk to be saying these things to me." She crossed her arms in front of her. "Get this through your head. I am not keeping Matthew. I'm going to find a home for him. But until I do, he'll have to stay with me. *Comprende?*"

"*Si.*" His eyes flashed. "Only I won't be here."

She lowered her arms. "What?"

"I'm not going to play papa to a boy who is not my own."

"So that's it then?" She pressed her lips together. "You say you're committed to me and then walk out because I have to care for an orphan?"

"I agreed we didn't need a wedding to stay together because that's what you wanted. I didn't know you wanted to start some kind of ..." he waved his hand like he always did when looking for an English word, "orphanage in our home. You think you can trick me into liking him. You think I'll say you can keep him." Eddie gripped her arm. "You send him somewhere else, or I go."

She shook off his hold. "You can't tell me what to do. No one tells me what to do."

"*Si.*" Eddie backed away, shaking his head. "That's the problem. No one can tell you what to do. You're so perfect. But maybe you aren't always as right as you think." He turned away and swaggered out of the room like he'd won the argument.

She took a few steps, following his retreat to the side door. "I know it isn't right to take orders from someone who'd throw an orphan out on the street!"

He stopped at the door. "I didn't—"

"You'd be running a dictatorship if I let you. I've had enough of that. It's a good thing you're leaving, or I'd have to kick you out myself." At least she'd had the sense to put the house under her name alone.

"Call me when you start thinking straight again."

"Like you'd know anything about that." She sneered at him. "I wouldn't take you back if you came crawling on your hands and knees."

He slammed the door on his way out.

Good riddance. She would not give in to the painful sinking feeling in her chest. He didn't deserve it. To think she'd wasted three years on that jerk.

"Like him."

Ashley startled inwardly.

Matthew again. Why did he have to sneak up on her like that?

She turned to see him standing behind her, just outside the bedroom door.

He wore one of Eddie's Texas T-shirts, backwards, the cotton squeezing the boy's bigger torso. "Like him."

So he could say something else. Was he telling her to like Eddie? Now the kid with Down syndrome was telling her what to do, too. Unreal.

She pointed at the backward clothing. "Go back in there and turn the shirt around. You have it on the wrong way."

He looked down at the shirt, running his hands over it like that helped. His lips pulled up into a smile, and he went back into the bedroom.

He better get it right. He was too old for her to dress him.

How in the world had she gotten stuck surrounded by so many clueless males? Eddie would come back. He always did after their spats. But this one was the worst they'd had. She was tired of it. If Eddie knew what was good for him, he'd wait a while before crawling home. The way Ashley felt right now, she wasn't sure she wanted him back this time.

Matthew came out of the bedroom, the T-shirt on correctly, but he'd added his Cubs baseball cap. The crooked angle of the cap on his head accented the oddness of his features.

"Can you straighten your hat?"

He tilted his head, which just made the cap's slant worse.

Whatever. "Do you want breakfast?"

He just watched her.

"Can you eat breakfast on your own?"

Nothing.

She sighed and headed for the kitchen. "Come on." She dug the children's cereal Eddie loved out of the cupboard and filled a bowl for Matthew.

The boy smiled when she held a milk jug over the cereal, so she took that as a sign he liked it that way.

At least he didn't talk as much as Eddie. The silence as he munched cereal at the table gave her time to think. Though that wasn't always the best thing either.

She poured herself a bowl of plain flakes and crunched them as she leaned back against the counter. There had to be somewhere she could place this kid. A list started to formulate in her mind of foster options they hadn't tried yesterday.

Stacey Gerneke had mentioned a couple weeks back that she might have an opening soon at the group home she directed. Maybe Tina hadn't called her.

Ashley had to find a place for Matthew soon. For his sake and hers. Still no signs of aggression, but from what she'd heard, it could show up anytime without warning.

The broken table leg still lay stashed between the couch cushions. She should probably hide it better or put it away during the day. Or should she keep it handy?

Matthew breathed a watery giggle as milk dribbled down his round chin. Hard to imagine him becoming aggressive.

She looked at her watch. Only ten minutes until she had to leave for work. She glanced around for yesterday's mail. Don't tell her Eddie forgot again.

He only had two simple chores to do during the day before

he left for the night shift—bring in the mail and feed the fish. Probably hadn't fed the fish either.

Ashley dropped her bowl on the other dirty dishes in the sink. "I'll be back. You finish your breakfast."

The boy didn't look up from stirring the colored cereal balls in the milk.

Ashley sighed and went to do Eddie's jobs. She fed the fish and changed clothes in six minutes flat, leaving four to grab the mail and leave. She jogged out to the mailbox at the end of the short driveway.

The morning air was humid, but not quite as sticky as the day before. Probably would get worse by noon. She pulled the small stack of letters from the box and turned around.

A man stood a foot away.

Her breath caught.

Matthew. He must have followed her out of the house.

"I told you to finish your breakfast." Her irritation sharpened the words. "What are you doing out here?"

The pouting lip again.

She pointed to the house. "Go back inside."

He turned around and started for the door. At least he listened so far.

She started to follow the boy.

"Hey, Ashie."

LeBron Smith. At least that's what he claimed his name was. Ashley hadn't seen her neighbor standing there, watching them from the side of his house. But then, she tried not to notice him in general. He was the kind of guy that made a person not want to think about what he did in his basement. Judging from the regular junkie traffic he got to his side door, she could take a good guess. Ironic that she'd thought buying a house here was a step up from the last neighborhood she had lived in.

LeBron looked particularly mean today, the way he kept staring at Matthew. "What's with the retard?"

She barely bit back the urge to ask if he meant himself.

"Gotta keep the neighborhood nice, you know."

She gave up trying. "Oh, so you're leaving?"

"Cute, Ashie." His stoned gaze turned on her.

"If you call me that one more time, I'm gonna call the cops on you, okay? Bet they'd love to see whatever you have in your *nice* place."

"Watch yo'self." His menacing tone and the nasty name he tacked on to his warning didn't bother Ashley nearly as much as the jerk probably wanted.

But there was no point in hanging around for a long chat. She caught up to Matthew and gently grabbed his arm to speed up his progress to the house.

"Don't want retards here!"

Ashley didn't grace LeBron's shouted smear with so much as a glance as she pushed Matthew inside and shut the door.

She checked her watch. Thanks to the neighborhood jerk, she was now late. She finished getting ready in a rush and hurried Matthew through the side door to the car.

At least LeBron must have crawled back under his rock somewhere.

The undersized rear tire on her side of the car caught her gaze. She'd forgotten she'd have to go to the garage later today to get her flat tire fixed.

Wait a minute.

She went to the trunk and opened it, looking at the boxes of thrift clothing she was going to drop off at the free store for foster families like her stare would make her old tire appear.

She blew out a breath as she closed the trunk and got in the car, calmly sitting behind the wheel, though she'd much rather punch something...or someone. The guy hadn't put the damaged tire in her trunk. Though, she was the one who'd driven off before he'd had a chance to. And she hadn't wanted to leave the car to open the trunk anyway.

She began the three attempts to start the engine. Better to be alive and need to buy a new tire. But the cost would hurt. Especially if she was out Eddie's income to supplement hers.

She forced out a loud breath as she looked behind to back the car down the driveway.

"God good."

Wonderful. The boy was back to the religious stock phrase from last night. First things first, she had to get rid of this kid.

chapter
four

Ashley barely stopped herself from slamming down the phone receiver when she hung up. Wasn't there anyone to take this kid?

"Good morning." Tina's cheerful voice blew into the office ahead of her as she squeezed through the door, turning sideways to accommodate her tote bags of various sizes. What they were all for was one of the great unsolved mysteries of the age.

Tina somehow made it through the opening and smiled at Matthew in the corner as she went to her desk. "Find anyone to take our boy yet?"

Our boy. She'd adopted him already. Why couldn't Tina have taken him home if she liked him that much? "Oh, sure." Ashley tapped a pencil against the papers in front of her on the desk. "Every foster home in the county's just begging to take him. Didn't you see the line outside the door?"

"My, my." Tina laughed as she plopped down the last bag and took her laptop out of its bright orange case. "Somebody got up on the wrong side of the bed."

"Try the couch."

"Ouch." Tina winced sympathetically but looked at Matthew instead of Ashley. "So no takers?"

"None."

Tina sat in her swivel chair and rolled it up to the desk, opening her computer and turning it on. "I guess you'll just have to keep him a little longer." She narrowed her eyes at the screen of her laptop. "I don't know why this thing takes so long to boot up. Maybe Javon's right—I need a new one."

Ashley stopped fiddling with the pencil and stared at the person she had considered her friend seconds ago. "So that's it?"

Tina looked at Ashley. "What's it? My computer?"

"Stop it, Tina. We were talking about Matthew."

"Mm-hmm. Was it really so bad last night?"

"Do you have to ask me that? You know this boy shouldn't even have to face this kind of a life. What kind of people would choose to let the pregnancy go full-term knowing about the suffering he would have if he were born?"

Tina shrugged, her toned brown shoulders lifting under the straps of her fluorescent pink tank top. "Maybe they didn't know he had Down's."

"Oh, they knew. They owned their own private plane. They were rich enough to have medical care." Ashley tossed her pencil onto the desk. "They knew, and they still had him anyway. Now he has to face life as an outcast." She gestured to the boy sitting in the chair, obsessively jerking his hands. "It's almost like he's a living vegetable that can feel just enough to suffer."

Tina turned her head toward Matthew. "He doesn't really seem miserable. Aren't people with Down's happy all the time anyway?"

"That is a ridiculous misconception."

Tina appeared undeterred by Ashley's correction. She pressed her full lips together as she watched Matthew. "That's the same spot he was sitting in last night." She narrowed her eyes at Ashley like she'd done something criminal.

"I swear I took him home."

"Why haven't you given him anything to do?"

So that's what she was getting at. Ashley looked at her computer screen for an excuse not to meet Tina's accusing stare. "I don't know what he can do, if anything. Besides, he wanders off, so I can't leave him alone to get...whatever he might be able to use."

"What about blocks?" Tina had that fix-it look in her big eyes.

"What are you talking about?"

She stood and pulled out the lower desk drawer. "The blocks I keep here for the boys when they come to work with me." She took out a small plastic bin.

"Blocks. Isn't that a little young?"

Tina paused on her way to Matthew and shot Ashley a chastising look. "First you think he's incapable of doing anything and now you think he's too old for blocks?"

Ashley leaned back in her chair and crossed her arms in front of her. "I don't know what's right for him. That's the point. That's why he'd be much better off with someone else. Like you, Supermom."

Now it was Tina's turn to roll her eyes, but her usual smile returned with the gesture as she reached Matthew and showed him the blocks, setting the bin on the coffee table beside him.

He stopped his hand motions and reached for them, a smile curving his mouth as he took out the squares and rectangles one at a time and stacked them.

"You know, the way you're talking makes me wonder if you're thinking of keeping him." Tina cocked an eyebrow as she made her way back to her desk.

Ashley gaped.

Tina sat in her chair. "You sound so concerned about him."

Ashley closed her mouth. "I don't keep the kids we rescue. You know we're supposed to draw the line at personal involvement."

"You have our supervisor's okay."

"Dean?" Ashley lifted her eyebrows as high as she could.

Tina nodded as if his identity didn't matter. "You're off the hook."

"You know you've never kept a kid." Why did Ashley feel like she had to make a case for something so obvious? "Besides, Eddie already walked out last night because of Matthew."

Tina's smile dropped as lines crossed her brow. "What? Why?"

Ashley glanced away. Probably shouldn't have told Tina that. "He wasn't comfortable with Down syndrome either." Not exactly true, but she wasn't going to tell Tina she had refused to have children when Eddie wanted them. She could do without the psychoanalysis and lecture that would follow.

"You mean he walked out on you because you brought home a child who wasn't perfect."

Ashley jerked her gaze to Tina. "Eddie's a very nice guy. He just wasn't comfortable with Matthew…and I don't blame him." For that part. She certainly blamed him for walking out because she had the good sense to know the world didn't need more innocent victims and lousy parents. At least now she had no doubt what kind of parent Eddie would be.

She shook her head. "I can't do it, Tina. I can't keep Matthew any longer." She pushed away from her desk and stood. "Among other things, I can't get work done because of him being here. I had a potential foster home to spot check today and a follow-up on a report I was supposed to do."

"Why can't you take him with you?"

Ashley lifted one hand in exasperation while she rested the other on her hip. "How? I don't even know if he's safe to have around kids."

"You could leave him in the car."

Ashley shook her head. "He walked off the other day when I looked away for a second. I can't risk leaving him alone."

"He's sat here for what…" Tina glanced at the pink clock, "two hours before I got here? And I bet he's barely moved an inch. I don't think he'll interfere if you take him along." She got to her feet, picking up her purse and only one other bag. "I'd do your meeting for you, but I'm supposed to do three follow-ups, and then I'm in court the rest of the day."

"I notice you don't offer to take Matthew yourself."

Tina fished some envelopes from her purse. "You know we're not supposed to handle each other's cases."

"Interesting how you only like the rule book when it suits your purpose."

Tina tossed her clacking braids over her shoulder with a grin as she walked to Ashley's desk. "You make me sound so evil."

"If the shoe fits."

She laughed, and Ashley couldn't stop the tug of an answering smile. She always had a hard time staying mad at Tina. Probably why the woman got away with everything.

"You're funny, girl." Tina handed Ashley two letters and grinned as she turned away.

Ashley's gaze hit the first envelope. She froze.

That handwriting.

A shudder shifted through her body. Ashley forced her trembling hand to hold on to the paper. "Are these from today?" Her voice was so calm. Like it came from someone else.

"The letters?" Tina bent over to flip through files in her desk drawer. "Yeah. Grabbed them from the box on my way in."

How did he find her here? She figured he'd learn her new last name from Veronica, thanks to the mistake of visiting the woman at the hospital. But moving and keeping her address unlisted was supposed to prevent this. Now he knew where she worked. He could—

She tried to force air through her closing throat. *Stay calm. You're strong now. He can't hurt you.*

Her gaze darted around the room. She had to get rid of the letter. The paper burned against her fingers like it was singeing her skin.

The shredder.

She darted out of her chair and stuffed the letter in the machine.

Air filled her lungs as the shredder sucked the envelope inside and sliced it into a million shreds.

She took in another deep breath, then stopped herself. Had Tina noticed the big scene? "Junk mail." Ashley spit out the explanation with a glance at her friend.

"Hmm?" Tina rummaged through one of the deeper tote bags with her back to Ashley. Hadn't noticed a thing.

Relief coursed through Ashley's body. Until she saw Matthew.

He watched her from across the room.

For one silly, unnerving second, she thought he might have seen, might have understood. Everything.

chapter
five

Hot sun beat down, giving the humidity help it didn't need in making Ashley uncomfortable as she left the office building, Matthew in tow.

She checked around the corner as they turned.

The boy touched her hand, making her jump.

"Will you stop that?" Guilt hit her when his eyes doubled in size. "I didn't mean to snap, but you have to stop trying to take my hand. It's inappropriate." And way too weird for her already frazzled nerves.

That envelope had really done a number on her. She thought she'd learned to be tougher than this.

Her gaze roamed the full parking lot and jumped ahead to the street. Everything looked clear. A few not-too-dangerous-looking people strolled on the sidewalks.

She had parked two cars down from her spot on the street the night before. She scanned the area where her car had been last night—something she'd done that morning when she'd arrived, too. Still couldn't see an extra tire or tire-changing equipment left there. Though if the things had been left, someone probably would've swiped them by now.

All traces of her nighttime savior or attacker, whichever he'd intended to be, were gone. At least the sunlight and additional cars parked there now made the atmosphere less unnerving.

As she stepped onto the pavement and walked to the driver's door, her gaze fell on a person sitting in a parked, navy blue car across the street with a newspaper over his or her face. Whoever would sit in a parked car with their face covered around here, even during the day, had to be at least a little crazy.

"Hey, I forgot!" The shout probably would've startled Ashley again if it'd been anyone but Tina.

Ashley waved to her co-worker, who trotted toward them on the sidewalk and stopped by Matthew on the other side of Ashley's car.

"I forgot our new rule to walk out together when we can. Should've done that last night. Sorry about that."

"No worries." Ashley smiled across the car's roof. "I was fine." Unless she counted nearly getting murdered by some random thug.

Tina thumbed to the parking lot behind her. "Can you believe I snagged a stall today?"

Ashley shook her head. "I've said it before. You've got a charmed life."

"Well, be safe on your runs, okay?"

"Always."

"At least you have Matthew for backup." Tina sent a teasing grin Ashley's way. She gently touched his arm. "Do you need help getting in, sweetie?"

"Oh, he's fine." Actually, Ashley had always helped him get in the car before. But there was no need for Tina to think Ashley had been neglecting the boy.

She fought to keep the surprise from her face when Matthew tugged open the door himself and got in, slamming the door behind him.

Tina met Ashley's gaze. "I guess he is."

Ashley gave Tina a wave and a forced smile as she ducked

into the sweltering car and worked on getting the engine started.

She barely noticed when it finally kicked in, and she navigated the twenty-five minute drive to the wellness check on autopilot.

Dark memories clutched at the edge of her consciousness as she fought the mental battle to keep them away. To breathe.

She focused on the sweat trickling down her temple. The hot, humid air the car's joke of an AC couldn't beat. The computerized voice on her phone's GPS that told her where to turn next.

She flexed her fingers on the steering wheel, the cramp in them telling her she'd been holding a tense grip. She had to stop thinking about that letter. The first stop this afternoon was going to be tough enough. Possible sexual and physical abuse. The little girl needed her full attention.

The child's grandparents' report of their suspicions was helpful, but unfortunately lacked hard evidence. That meant Ashley had to do a house call. Stupid requirement. Like any parent was ever going to admit letting such a thing happen to their child. But that didn't mean it wasn't happening.

Ashley took in what she hoped would be a calming breath as she pulled up in front of the apartment building.

She should probably tell Matthew to stay in the car. She scanned the run-down building and the street types going in and out. Then again, the car was not a safe place in this neighborhood. And he could wander off.

Ashley tried not to notice the stares of the people they passed on the way up the walk to the building. Not like any of these jokers had a right to look at anyone that way. Gangbangers, druggies, and prostitutes most of them. No prettier than the kid walking at her side.

Ashley had to announce her arrival in the intercom so the parents could buzz her in through the outside door. Gave them too much time to get their cover story right if they needed one.

Matthew walked beside her in the hallway when they got inside.

She was ready for him when he reached for her hand. She pulled away and shook her head with a gentle, "No." Though she couldn't really blame him this time. The building was old and dirty, with a smell that reminded her too much of places she'd once lived and tried to forget.

She reached into the outer pouch of her purse and felt around until her fingers touched the handle of the folded knife. Still where she could get to it easily.

They climbed the first flight of stairs and walked down another hallway, where she stopped at the apartment marked *187*.

Matthew waited behind her as she knocked.

A woman opened the door after only a few seconds.

Yeah. They were ready for her.

"Welcome. Please come in." The brown-haired woman with a pale complexion opened the door wide and beckoned them in as if they were long-lost relatives.

Ashley entered, and Matthew followed her like a puppy. "Are you Chrissie's mother?"

The woman nodded, her gaze flitting to the floor.

Ashley quickly assessed the apartment. She could see the kitchen and living room from the entryway—all surprisingly neat, nicely decorated, and kept up. Or cleaned for her visit. She brought her attention back to the mother.

"Mrs. Childers, you know why I'm here. There's been a report that's of concern to us. Can you tell me anything about the possibility of abuse to Chrissie?" She knew before the words left her mouth that this woman wouldn't tell her anything, but she had to go through the motions.

"Why no…I—" The woman put her hands on her cheeks. "It's so awful." She shook her head. "I mean that anybody would say that."

Was that really all she meant? A shadow of real horror, or at least real fear, lurked in the woman's brown eyes.

Special Target

"Hi, there." A short, wiry man emerged from a hallway that must lead to the bedrooms. His smile stretched out the sides of his face. "I'm Chrissie's father, Kyle." He stuck out his hand for Ashley to shake.

No wonder the woman was nervous. Ashley took his hand and grimaced inwardly at the snake-like feel. Despite his attempt to instill confidence with a Cheshire grin, his eyes were hard and shifty, his grip slithery, and he smelled like she was standing in a cologne factory after a spill.

Ashley had dealt with the smoothest guys in luxury mansions who usually turned out to be the worst creeps of all. No way was she getting fooled by a smalltime operator trying to play her.

"The kid an orphan?" Mr. Smell-Good nodded to Matthew.

"He's in our care right now."

The man laughed, too loudly. "Isn't that great? It's awesome the way you people will help anybody like that."

Ashley squelched the urge to respond in a decidedly unprofessional manner and pressed her lips together instead. "I'd like to see Chrissie."

"Oh, sure, sure." The Cheshire grin aimed at the wife, who scurried off to get the girl.

She returned in a few seconds that felt like ten minutes. Chrissie, a pretty girl with wispy blond hair, clung to her mother's hand for dear life. Or was the mother holding on to her daughter? Hard to tell. The girl looked only at the ground on her way to them.

"Have you noticed any behavior changes in Chrissie lately?" Ashley watched the girl. "Is she especially shy, or does she become fearful easily?"

"No, no." The man kept up that ridiculous smile. "She's always been very happy and confident. She laughs a lot."

Was he kidding?

The girl stared at something past the adults, unresponsive.

"She doesn't seem very confident or happy right now, Mr. Childers."

"Oh, she's just shy."

Right. If only the girl would be an exception and actually have the courage to tell the truth herself.

What was she staring at?

Ashley followed the direction of the girl's gaze to... Matthew's face.

His beaming smile, the one Ashley had only seen from him once before, was directed at little Chrissie.

The girl tilted her head as she watched him.

"Chrissie, are you okay?" Ashley spoke gently, but Chrissie dropped her gaze to the floor again.

"Are you afraid of something?" Ashley crouched down in front of the girl, trying to meet her hidden gaze. "Sweetie, you can tell me the truth. Has anyone ever hurt you?" She lowered her voice to a whisper, her heart lodging in her throat. "I want to help you."

Chrissie leaned into her mother's side, her lips sealed.

Ashley barely held back a frustrated grunt as she stood. This was always so pointless. No child was going to say anything with the parents there if they were to blame. But this was how she was required to do it.

"Let's go." She made sure Matthew followed her to the door as she clenched her jaw until she thought it would break. "You'll be hearing from me again." She didn't look at the parents, letting them swallow her parting words in their own way. She hoped they took her statement as the threat it was.

Her gut said the father was involved, maybe the actual abuser. But she couldn't take her gut's evidence to court any more than the hearsay testimony of the grandparents about bruises and tearful stories the girl had told them.

Ashley struggled to hold in her frustration until they reached the car. She let Matthew get in on his own and went to the driver's side, pushing her hair back behind her ears to cool her face.

As she sank behind the wheel, she smacked it as hard as

she could. She bit the inside of her lips to hold back the scream that fought to escape.

She leaned her forehead against the hot vinyl of the wheel. *You will not cry. You will not cry.*

Something warm covered her hand that clutched the wheel.

She sat up.

Matthew's chubby hand gently rested on hers. She looked at him.

His small eyes and full lips sagged as he watched her.

Her heart squeezed. Did he understand?

No. He couldn't. No one could.

"Like him." His voice was thicker than usual as he said the two words, still staring at her.

Such a weird thing for Matthew to know how to say. Like who? The only *him* they'd just seen was a certifiable creep. Why did this boy always want her to like the worst guys? Maybe Matthew's dad had been a loser, too.

Ashley sniffed and pulled her hand out from under the boy's, swiping at her nose, although she'd held back the tears that wanted to come.

She glanced through the windows. No one better have seen that. The tough social worker being comforted by an orphaned Down syndrome kid who couldn't even put his shirt on right. She'd never be that desperate.

But that girl in the house probably was. Ashley tightened her jaw at the memory of little Chrissie. Ashley might have to drive away now, but she'd be back. She'd get the evidence they needed somehow. She'd talk to teachers, friends, neighbors. Anybody she had to, until she got that guy put away where he belonged.

Ashley turned the key. Wouldn't start, as usual. She tried again, her gaze drifting to the side mirror.

Wasn't that the same navy blue car she'd seen outside the office? Weird. No one was in it now. If Eddie were here, he'd have a good laugh over her trying to identify a car and would remind her how little she knew about them. He'd be right, for once. This car was probably a different brand than the other one. She wouldn't be able to tell. There had to be a million navy blue cars in this city.

Her own car's engine finally kicked in, and she pulled onto the street, reaching to scratch her neck as if that would make the crawling sensation go away.

chapter
six

Ashley pulled the curtains over her bedroom window, shutting out the night. She turned to Matthew, who watched her from the other side of the full-size bed.

He tilted his head, his eyes bright like he expected her to do something.

"You can wear those again." She pointed to Eddie's pajamas, which were neatly folded on the bed. Had Matthew folded them? Now it was her turn to look at him closely.

His blue eyes squinted more with a smile as he returned her gaze. If she didn't know better, she'd think there was more going on behind those eyes than she had assumed.

She shook her head. This is what came of spending all day with him and having to keep him yet another night. "Put those on and then brush your teeth. And take off your cap." She walked from the room. One day with the kid, and she was starting to lose her mind.

He would never be anything more than a boy with Down syndrome. He couldn't be anything more if he wanted to. And that was the sad truth.

Slipping her feet into flip-flops, she grabbed a flashlight and walked outside to get the mail. She checked LeBron's house as she went to the box.

Looked like he was inside, and the pounding bass from his subwoofer backed that up.

She pulled open the mailbox and shined the flashlight inside.

Another small stack of envelopes. Bills, no doubt.

She grabbed them and headed inside, trying not to think about the letter at the office earlier. At least she hadn't gotten one from him at her new house...yet. But if work was compromised, should she even go there again tomorrow and the next days?

She had to. She couldn't give up her job. Not because of him.

She went inside and set the flashlight on the entry table by the door. She flipped through the envelopes. Bill, bill, b—

A piece of paper, folded without an envelope, hid between two letters.

Her heart thumped as she slowly opened the paper. It wasn't his style. He'd have to mail it. Unless he was that close. Close enough to visit her mailbox in person.

Mismatched, cut-out letters glared up at her. *Dump the retard. Not wanted here.*

Her mouth went dry, but her heart rate calmed when it probably shouldn't have. At least it wasn't him. He couldn't know about Matthew.

But who would give her something like this? *Dump the retard?*

Eddie hadn't liked Matthew, but not entirely because of the Down syndrome. And he would never do anything like this. He might be lame sometimes, but he wasn't mean. She couldn't ever love anyone mean.

Rule out Eddie, and who was left? LeBron. He had access to her mailbox, and he'd called Matthew a retard just that morning. LeBron was definitely mean.

Matthew. Ashley's gut tensed. She hadn't heard anything from the boy for a long time. Too long.

"Matthew?" She hurried to the bedroom. Looked inside. Empty. The pajamas were gone.

"Matthew!" She spun away from the doorway and darted to the dark bathroom. She flicked the light switch.

He wasn't there.

Why had she left him alone so long? Her heart pounded against her ribs as she snatched up her flashlight and jogged outside. She paused to check the front of the house first.

She hadn't noticed when she got the mail how sticky the night was. Another heatwave moving in. The humidity seemed to muffle everything, weaving more secrets into the darkness. Would she even hear if anyone was following her?

She jerked her head in all directions, trying to watch behind and in front of her as she headed around the side of the house, her flip-flops making too much noise.

The beam of her flashlight created a weak yellow circle on the grass as she rounded the corner of the house. She swung it upward in case she was about to meet a person.

Movement caught her eye at the fence to the left.

She shined her flashlight on the man.

No. A boy. Matthew?

His foot slipped as he clumsily tried to push himself up over the fence that separated her little yard from LeBron's.

"Matthew!" Leftover adrenaline pushed the yell out sharper than she intended.

He dropped to his feet and ducked his head.

She walked up to him, taking some time to let her breathing slow to normal. Leave it to a kid to give her a heart attack. "What were you doing?" She tilted the flashlight down at his pajamas when she got close enough to see his face without it.

"Home."

Another new word. Didn't make any more sense than his other phrases. "That isn't your home. That's my neighbor's yard."

His lower lip pushed out. "Home." Was that a glimmer of moisture in his eyes? Like tears? Couldn't be. He didn't understand anything enough to cry about it, did he? Must have been a reflection in his eyes from the moonlight.

"I wish you could go home, but you can't." She met his slanted eyes. "I need you not to run off like that anymore, okay? It isn't safe." Did he understand? "You could get hurt. We don't want you to get hurt."

Was that a nod? Close enough.

"Okay. Let's go inside. It's been a long day."

As they walked to the house, he reached for her hand. She pulled hers away automatically. Like she had before. But this time, she had to look away from him, hurrying to the house. Almost like she felt guilty.

Ashley pushed the afghan down as she rolled over. Why couldn't she get comfortable?

Then she heard it.

Moaning.

She sat up and grabbed the broken table leg.

Another moan.

She got to her bare feet as quietly as she could, sure her heart pounded loudly enough to give her away. Clutching the table leg, she followed the direction of the sound.

The bedroom. Matthew. Was he being hurt? She picked up her pace and looked through the open doorway.

Matthew flailed back and forth in the bed, moaning. No one else was in the room.

He cried out. A nightmare.

Ashley leaned the table leg against the wall and went to the side of the bed. "Matthew."

He tossed from side to side.

"Matthew." She reached for him, but hesitated.

His face swung her way. His strange features knotted up, like he was in pain. He yelled, almost a scream.

She put her hands on his arm and shook.

He kept whining, whimpering.

She shook harder. "Matthew, wake up. It's okay. Wake up." She raised her voice with the harder pressure of her hands.

His arms went up, reaching for her neck.

She jerked back, then spotted his open eyes. He was awake?

He had her in a hug before she could pull away.

Moisture created cool spots on her neck. Was he crying?

"Ma...ma...ma..." The same sound, over and over again. Mama?

Tears pricked Ashley's eyes. She put one arm around him and gently rubbed his back, like she'd done for little Olivia.

Was it possible he understood about his parents? He hadn't even seemed sad except when she wouldn't hold his hand...and outside tonight when he had said, "Home." Could he feel sadness of that depth? Comprehend a loss that great?

"Ma...ma...ma..." His muffled voice caught on a sob.

"Shh. It's okay. You'll be okay." But he wouldn't. He had Down syndrome.

Ashley held him until he quieted. She got him to lie back down, comforting him as best she could until his eyes drifted shut.

She straightened and watched him sleep.

His features relaxed as if nothing had happened. Maybe he didn't understand his loss at all. Maybe he simply had a bad dream and thought Ashley was his mother.

How could she know? How could she help him when she didn't know what he needed, what he actually thought and felt?

She turned and walked from the room, picking up the broken table leg as she went. She returned to the couch, though there was no way she'd get to sleep again tonight. She sat on the afghan and lowered the table leg to the floor, propped against the cushion that held her.

This couldn't go on. She was getting too emotionally involved. She had to place him soon or she'd have too much at stake in his future. A hopeless future.

That scared her a lot more than the ominous letter that lay open on the coffee table, sneering up at her like a warning from within.

chapter
seven

"Sorry to keep you waiting, ma'am."

Ashley looked up as a man finally came into the room where she and Matthew had waited for a half hour.

"Detective Swoboda, Accident Investigations." The middle-aged guy sat in a chair on the opposite side of the table and gave her a tired smile. "I understand you're CPS."

She nodded.

"And you have questions about Matthew Haase. Is this the young man?" He turned his perceptive gaze on Matthew, who sat quietly trailing his finger over the speckled tabletop.

"Yes." Ashley leaned forward and rested her arms on the table. "The normal family history wasn't filled in much by your department. And I'm not finding anything at all for the names you put on the form. Do you have more information about his background or family? I'm trying to locate next of kin for custody."

"I wish I could help." Swoboda flipped open a file, probably Matthew's, on the table. He shook his head as he looked down at the information there. "We've tried, but we couldn't find anything beyond the home address and bank used."

"You have the address? That wasn't on the form. Where did they live?"

He glanced up at Ashley. "An apartment downtown."

That didn't come cheap. "What happened to their money? They didn't have any set aside for the boy?"

"No will was found at their apartment, and that's been placed on the market." He lifted his hand. "It probably wouldn't have helped anyway, since they only had one bank account and the couple closed it the day before their flight."

"Closed it." She watched him. "As in, took out all their money?"

Swoboda met her gaze. "Yes."

"Isn't that a little odd?"

"Could be."

Ashley folded her arms in front of her. "So you're checking it out."

"I really can't discuss that with you, Ms. Sorenson."

Of course. Never mind that she had a kid she couldn't place. She stood, gathering her purse. "I hope you'll at least keep me informed if you find family for the boy?"

"Absolutely. We want the same thing here, Ms. Sorenson."

Usually, she believed that. But this time, something didn't feel the same. Matthew needed a home. She needed him gone. And nobody seemed to care except the psycho who left the nasty note in her mailbox.

Her jaw still clenched by the time she reached the parking lot. She headed straight for the driver's side, leaving Matthew to handle getting in on his own. As she opened her door, her gaze swung across a navy blue car.

She looked again. Couldn't see the whole car, parked way down on the end of the row behind her, but that trunk and what she could glimpse of the roof were familiar. The same car as the day before. Wasn't it?

She got in her car and shut the door, her hand instinctively going to the broken lock. She moistened her dry lips. Why would the same car be at the police station when she was? Chicago was not a small area. The odds were...impossible.

Special Target

Was someone in it now? Watching her? She hadn't been able to see inside.

Matthew swung up his hands.

She jumped.

He swung them again, and again.

She took in a breath and let it out, trying to get her heart rate to calm down. He was just doing his repetitive motion again. Maybe he'd picked up on the tension in the police station or knew she was on edge now. Might be possible. Even dogs could do that.

She checked all the mirrors as she went through two tries before the car started. Who would be following her? The creep who sent the note? Or... Her pulse picked up speed.

He could have hired a private eye to tail her.

She pressed the gas pedal hard as she backed out of the stall. Her tires screeched as she slammed on the brakes, then turned the opposite direction of the navy blue car and pushed the accelerator, her eyes glued to the rearview mirror.

It didn't move.

She reminded herself to breathe as she reached the parking lot exit and pulled out onto the street. Still no sign of the blue car. Must not have been the same one.

But she couldn't relax her death grip on the wheel until they were a few blocks from the office. She glanced at the rearview mirror as she drove through an intersection, just in time to see the car behind her turn off.

A navy blue sedan took its place.

Her heart lurched.

She blinked hard and looked again. The car was gone.

"Still nothing."

Tina's words from that afternoon echoed in Ashley's head as she set Matthew's plate with instant potatoes, beans, and beef in front of him on her kitchen table.

"If you don't want to keep him, MHIC is the only option."

If she didn't want to keep him. Julie would have a thing or two to say about that when she got back if Ashley even considered it. But putting him in a mental institution still felt...wrong.

Ashley sat down at the table opposite the boy, her appetite nonexistent as she absently stared in his direction.

He bent his head down and folded his hands as he started mumbling.

Was he praying? Sure enough, his eyes were closed.

How incredibly ironic. If there was a God, He sure hadn't done Matthew any favors.

As soon as Matthew started eating, Ashley wished he was still praying. His slurping as he chewed with an open mouth echoed through the otherwise quiet house.

She sighed and took her untouched plate of food to the counter.

There was no point in avoiding it any longer. She had to get the mail. She'd only made the situation worse by delaying it this long. Now she'd have to go out in the dark.

She blew out a breath. What had gotten into her? She hadn't been sheepish in years. The letter at her office yesterday and the navy blue car that kept showing up hardly helped.

Matthew still had a long way to go before he'd be done with his meal. He should stay put this time if she left for a minute.

"I have to get the mail. You stay here until I get back."

He didn't look up from under his crooked cap as he sloshed potatoes, but hopefully he got the message.

Ashley grabbed her flashlight and walked to the window in the living room. She brushed aside the thin curtain just an inch and peered out.

Her shadowed yard appeared empty, and no car was on the street. Could be parked farther down, whoever drove it watching from a distance.

Special Target

She stepped back from the window and went to the door, then stopped, staring at it. A familiar taste reached her mouth. Fear.

No. She would not be a victim. She pulled open the door and marched to the mailbox, ignoring the darkness around her. She yanked open the box.

No letters. Just a piece of paper, folded like the one the day before.

She stared, then snatched it out, whipping it open like a yank on a painful bandage.

Mismatched letters met the beam of her flashlight. *Get rid of the retard. Or we will.*

Ashley crumpled the paper in her fist and slammed the box shut. She shot a glare at LeBron's house as she stalked up the driveway. Was it him? Who was the *we* in the letter?

No one should have any reason to care who lived with her. Were the people in this neighborhood really that prejudiced? Then again, none of them had interacted with Matthew. Only LeBron had even seen him, as far as she knew. Or was it the person in the blue car? Whoever it was had gone too far this time.

The ring of the phone blared as she shoved through the front door. Probably another telemarketer. Ashley didn't even know why she'd kept the landline that was there when she moved in.

She went to the handset on the kitchen wall. As she picked up the receiver, she glanced at the table. Matthew wasn't there.

"Got my letter?"

The harsh whisper grabbed Ashley's attention. "Who is this?"

"A friend. The kid belongs in an asylum."

"Not as much as you do."

The voice grew louder, but no less raspy. "Get rid of him. You'll be sorry if you don't."

"Listen, freak." She glared at the brown wall like it was the joker on the other end of the line. "I've been a social worker in this city for eight years. If you think you can scare me into dumping a foster child that easily, you really are insane." She slammed the receiver against the base.

Her fingers trembled as she pulled her hand away, the palm clammy with a cold sweat. "Matthew?"

No response.

Get rid of him. Or we will.

Had the creep gotten to Matthew already?

Ashley jogged to the bedroom.

Nothing.

The bathroom.

She flicked the light switch.

The shower curtain moved.

Her heart stopped. "Who's there?"

The curtain shifted again.

She froze.

The curtain slowly pulled back.

Slanted eyes stared at her. Matthew.

"Find! Find!" His shout bounced off the ceiling as he flung the curtain away and jumped up and down.

"Stop it!" She didn't try to keep her voice calm. She had all she could do to catch up on breathing. He'd scared the life out of her. "What are you doing?"

He stopped bouncing and looked at her. "Hide go see?"

Seriously? The kid was playing hide and seek at a time like this? "I told you to stay put and wait for me. I don't care if you were trying to hide or go home or whatever you were doing. You can't run away *or* hide anymore. Do you hear me?"

His lips drooped, and he pressed a flat hand against his chest. "Like him." His sad voice perfectly matched his expression.

Her stomach twisted. Now he thought she didn't like him. She blew out a breath. "It's okay, Matthew." She looked at his peculiar face. "I just can't do this anymore. I'm not what you need."

He lifted his head and aimed those blue eyes at her. "Like him."

Ashley sighed. He didn't get it. "You need to sleep. Go change into your pajamas and get to bed."

She watched to be sure he went to the bedroom, then headed for the couch. She shook out the afghan with extra force. Maybe an institution was the best place for him. He couldn't be left alone with his tendency to run off. He'd be safer where he couldn't get lost, with staff to watch him and care for all his needs.

She sat on the couch but hit something hard instead.

The broken table leg.

She pulled it out from behind the cushion and stared at it. Didn't need it for Matthew anymore, but at the rate she was getting nutty letters and phone calls, she'd still keep it close.

She set her would-be club on the floor next to the couch and lay down, letting her hand rest on the broken chunk of wood.

One more night. She'd find a new place for him tomorrow no matter what. Even if that meant the institution.

chapter
eight

Ashley had awakened in the morning to the crawling sensation creeping up the back of her neck. An hour later, the same feeling still plagued her as she drove Matthew to the Mental Health Institute of Chicago.

She checked the rearview mirror for about the tenth time. No navy blue car.

But a gray one had been driving behind her the last four times she'd looked. She was positive it was the same one. Two cars behind her on one drive wouldn't have identical black stripes on the hoods. Maybe it just happened to be going to the same area she was.

"You'll be sorry."

The raspy phone voice from the night before rang in her ears. The caller could be in that car behind her right now.

She was probably being paranoid. Then again, she hadn't made up that phone call or the notes.

But why would someone do that? Prejudice against people with Down's wasn't enough of a motive, was it?

She tried to relax her grip on the wheel and glanced at Matthew.

He sat quietly in the passenger seat, no weird hand motions as he watched out the side window.

She knew so little about him, about his parents. Did one of the many things she didn't know explain the threats? Had he done something to make someone hate him?

Didn't seem likely. All he did was spout feel-good sayings and pout a little.

She watched the road signs for her next turn. Maybe his parents had done something. "Matthew."

He didn't look at her.

"Matthew, do you remember your parents? What they were like or what they did?"

No response.

"Did people like your parents, Matthew?"

He turned his head to face her, a small smile curving his lips. "Like him."

Real helpful. Ashley's cell phone vibrated in the cup holder where she'd left it. She grabbed it with a sigh, checking the screen. Tina. "Hey, Tina."

"Hey, I know you're on your way to a meeting or something so I'll make it quick."

Ashley ignored the twinge of conscience at the reminder she hadn't told Tina where she was really going.

"I just heard from Javon that he's tied up at work so he can't make Navy Pier. You remember we were taking the twins? Anyway, even if my husband hadn't decided to work on a Saturday," her tone advertised her irritation, "I wanted to invite you and Matthew. I'm sure he'd love it."

You and Matthew. Like they were a family or something. "Tina, what are you thinking? I'm not keeping Matthew. We can't do things like that with him."

"Oh, don't be like that. I've never known you to give up on something so easily."

Ashley's fingers tightened around the wheel. Somehow, she still saw the sign for Elm Avenue in time to make the turn. "There's nothing to give up on."

The large MHIC building sprawled in front of her, its rigid architecture increasing her doubts.

"You're being fatalistic. I'll help you talk to Julie. This is a special case. She'll see that."

"Tina, stop." Ashley turned the car into the expansive parking lot. "I don't want to keep him. I'm taking him to MHIC."

Silence.

Ashley didn't say anything either as she found a stall and parked the car.

"I'd ask if you were joking, but I'm afraid I already know the answer." Tina's voice deepened to a grim tone Ashley had only heard her use when talking about their darkest cases. "I can't believe you're considering it. You know what life would be like for him. There's a reason we always place the kids in homes. At least a group home."

"But there aren't any openings. You said so yourself. Budget cuts, the recession, whatever." Ashley lifted a helpless hand in the air. "Thanks to the governor, there are only two state-run institutions to pick from now, too."

"You're blaming the system for something you could fix yourself. I've never known you to do that, Ash."

"I'm sorry to disappoint you, but I honestly don't know what else to do. He's too much for me to handle. I can't leave him alone for even a second without him running off. It isn't safe. I couldn't give him a happy life." She hated the sound of her voice, her list of facts. Like she was trying to talk herself into the decision she knew was right.

"But you care for him."

"No, I don't. No more than any other child we help. I care for them all, but not as my own."

"Sure."

Ashley pushed her hand through her hair. "Look, I have to go. I'll talk to you later."

"Ashley…"

She waited.

"Just don't do something you'll regret."

Special Target

An unexplained lump blocked Ashley's throat as she ended the call. She glanced at Matthew.

His lower lip protruded as he watched her with those funny blue eyes from beneath his crooked cap. He couldn't have understood.

She reached for the bill of his cap and straightened it. Pulling back, she unbuckled her seatbelt and opened the door. "Let's get this over with."

The electronic gate clanged when it slammed shut behind them.

Matthew jerked beside Ashley as they followed the male nurse who led them through the hallway. The boy wasn't the only one on edge because of the institution's tight security.

Locked doors, electronic gates. Felt more like a prison than a medical facility.

"This is the ward where the boy will stay." The nurse didn't look back as he walked ahead of them.

Noises came from behind some of the closed doors they passed. Ashley avoided looking through the small windows at the patients making the sounds.

Matthew started murmuring something unintelligible over and over again. He'd already been swinging his hands up and down since they'd entered the building.

A shriek came from somewhere past the nurse ahead of them.

Flailing arms and legs appeared as the shrieking turned to screams. A young boy, a teenager, struggled farther down the hallway as two orderlies restrained him.

"We should head back now." The nurse must have turned while Ashley stared at the patient. He smiled, forced.

"What's going on there?"

"I'm afraid I can't share the patient's medical information.

I do apologize for the commotion. Things aren't usually so chaotic."

Ashley turned to Matthew.

He walked one direction, then another, taking only a step or two in each. His features scrunched with fear, his wildly swinging hands shaking.

"Matthew, it's okay. They're just trying to help the boy. He's sick. No one's going to hurt you." The words stuck in her throat as she tried to get Matthew headed in the right direction to leave. Was that even true?

Ashley and the nurse guided Matthew back the way they had come, eventually reaching the lobby entrance. At least this room was more open and normal, not so confined and oppressive.

Matthew's breathing started to slow as Ashley took him to a soft armchair and had him sit down.

"It's okay," she repeated in her most soothing tone.

But he would be far from okay if she left him there. What had she been thinking? Tina was right. She must have been out of her mind to think he could stay at this place. He didn't belong there at all. He'd be shattered.

But he couldn't stay with her either. So what now? Back to the group home idea?

She stood next to Matthew's chair and kept repeating the best comfort she could manage as her mind explored the options. Maybe she could search more of the state for homes farther away. Or out of state if she had to.

"Excuse me."

Ashley turned to the side to see a bearded man in a white lab coat standing a couple feet away.

"Ms. Sorenson?"

"Yes."

He smiled and extended his hand. "I'm Doctor Crimson. I'm sorry. I intended to meet you when you arrived, but I got tied up with a patient." He had a confident handshake and a confident smile, clearly unaware he'd lost a prospective patient. Or maybe he knew, and he was going to try hard to change her mind.

"I understand you've toured the facility. I think Matthew will be very happy with us."

"Actually, I've changed my mind about leaving him here."

His smile didn't weaken a bit. "Oh, that would be a mistake. I'd like to talk to you about the many alternative treatment and care options we have for patients like Matthew who don't belong with the other more severely mentally ill patients."

"That sounds nice, but I wouldn't be able to talk about it now anyway. Matthew is too upset." She touched the boy's arm to get him to his feet.

His face wasn't so pale, and his hand swinging had stopped. But his features still bunched, and he didn't look at her at all.

"I really must insist you stay and reconsider." The doctor's voice dropped in pitch to a commanding tone.

She jerked to look at him.

He forced his smile back on, too late. "We all want what's best for Matthew, don't we?"

"I think I know what's best for Matthew." She narrowed her eyes at the man. "I'm the one who makes the decisions concerning him, and we won't be coming back here."

His smile left, revealing a scowl. "Don't do something you'll regret." His voice was almost threatening.

Was he for real? Hardly what she'd call a bedside manner.

"Miss?"

She turned to the voice.

Another man smiled at her, less of a smile and not so forced. At least he didn't look like a doctor in jeans and a brown sport coat over a dark T-shirt. But he seemed familiar somehow.

He tilted his head slightly. "Don't I know you?"

The very words that ran through her mind. She took in his light brown hair left shaggy on top, perceptive green eyes, and chiseled jawline. She'd remember that face, wouldn't she?

He snapped his fingers. "I've got it." He pointed at her. "The lady with the flat tire. A couple nights ago, right?"

She blinked at him. Her nighttime rescuer? He looked about the same size, with the same fit build. But it had been so dark.

His friendliness seemed unfazed by her hesitation. "Glad to see you must have made it home alright. I still have your old tire, if you want it." He winked. "You kind of drove off before I could put it in the trunk."

He seemed normal enough in the light of day, or, more accurately, the fluorescent lighting of the lobby. Maybe she'd been unfair to judge him so harshly that night. "Sorry about that. I was in a bit of a rush."

The doctor coughed pointedly behind her, probably trying to regain her attention.

The mysterious tire-changer ignored Crimson and shrugged. "You're smart to be cautious." His gaze drifted over her shoulder as his lips evened into a straight line. "You can never be too careful."

Was he looking at the doctor?

Ashley turned with a small step to the side so she could see both men, but the doctor was walking away without another word.

Strange. The doctor headed for the front door instead of the gated corridors.

The tingling feeling at the back of her neck returned. All of this was weird. What were the chances of bumping into the tire-changer guy at a mental institution? She glanced at him.

He already watched her.

"Strange we'd happen to meet each other here again." Her gut clenched, telling her something. "Why did you say you were here?"

His smile came back. Was that a twinkle in his green eyes? "Don't think I mentioned it. But I'm here to visit a friend."

He had a friend in a mental facility? Not too comforting.

"How about you? Were you visiting someone?"

"No, just—" She closed her mouth. No need to admit she was thinking of leaving Matthew there. "Just visiting."

The man turned his friendly gaze on Matthew. "Field trip, huh?" He put his hand on Matthew's shoulder and looked into his face like the boy was a completely normal teen. "Did you learn a lot?"

Matthew smiled broadly, the remaining traces of fear leaving his face.

There was something endearing about the smile the guy gave Matthew in return. Oh, honestly. Ashley had to stop herself from rolling her eyes at the direction of her thoughts. Picking up a guy at a mental institution who hung around bad neighborhoods at night was not her idea of a good start to a relationship. Besides, she might still change her mind about Eddie when he came back.

"We really have to get going." She tossed the guy a less-than-genuine smile as she touched Matthew's arm. "Let's go, Matthew."

She didn't look back to see the tire-changer guy's reaction as she ushered Matthew out of the unnerving building and into the hot sun that beat down on the blacktopped parking lot.

"Home." Matthew's sad expression was in place, along with some of the fear Ashley thought the tire guy had dissolved. "Home."

"You can't go home, Matthew." She had no clue where he could go.

Or did she? A smile found her lips. "I know something else that might cheer you up."

"He looks so happy."

Ashley looked at Matthew to see the evidence of Tina's observation. She was right.

His bright eyes bounced from sight to sight, taking in the bustle of Navy Pier, his mouth opening and closing with surprised gasps in between smiles. He pointed at the Ferris wheel and everything else that caught his attention, mumbling words no one could understand.

"Yeah." Ashley wiped away a drop of sweat before it fell in her eye. "What do you say we get out of the heat for a bit." She turned to glance back at the entrance to the pavilion.

"We just got outside."

And Ashley was already dying in the humidity, despite putting her hair up in a ponytail. The day was a scorcher, with only a slight breeze now and then from the lake.

"I thought the boys would really like the Ferris wheel." Tina gazed longingly at the famous five-story attraction.

Ashley looked from her friend to the little boys in the twin stroller. They contently licked the cotton candy that ended up more on their adorable brown cheeks than in their mouths. "You mean *you* love the Ferris wheel."

Tina crinkled her nose at Ashley as she pushed the stroller. "Getting stuck up there with two screaming kids is not my idea of fun."

"They're not screaming."

"Do you see how little they have left of that cotton candy?"

Tina bent to see beneath the stroller's hood. She straightened. "Okay. You're right."

"That looks more like the right speed for us." Ashley pointed to the carousel that slowly spun with colorful splendor near the Ferris wheel.

Tina let out an exaggerated sigh. "Yes. Someday they'll grow up, and I'll miss the sedate rides." She turned a teasing gaze to Ashley. "Or not."

Ashley laughed as they walked toward the carousel. "Enjoy it while you can, Mama."

"Hus." Matthew pointed at the carousel, leaning forward with what seemed to be excitement.

"Hus?" Ashley looked at Tina for help.

She shrugged. "Beats me. House maybe?"

As they got in line, the woman ahead of them pulled her two kids around in front of her, glancing quickly away from Matthew.

"Matthew." Ashley kept her voice quiet.

But he wouldn't stop pointing. He started waving like he'd seen an old friend, though his wave was directed only at the carousel.

More people stared from the next section of the line that curved back around in front of them.

"Matthew, stop." She put her hand on his arm and pulled it down. "Stop."

His lips dipped as he looked at her, the gleam in his eyes gone. At least he kept his arms lowered.

She straightened his cap bill and glanced away, only to collide with Tina's disapproving gaze.

"When did you become so easily embarrassed?" Leave it to Tina to say exactly what was on her mind, without so much as a sprinkle of sugar.

"I don't want him to make everyone uncomfortable." Ashley looked at the carousel.

"Everyone? Or just you?"

Apparently, Tina didn't notice how the mother in front of them kept scooting her children ahead, putting as much distance as she could between her normal kids and Matthew. Ashley couldn't really blame the woman. With the way he kept making noises that couldn't be called words and weird, excited gestures, Ashley wished she could get more distance herself.

By the time they reached the front of the line, she felt like everyone at Navy Pier must have spent time gawking at Matthew and her.

When the young employee finally let them through, Ashley

let out the breath she hadn't realized she'd been holding. At least she could get away from the stares as she followed Matthew.

He ran straight for an animal on the carousel. Keeping his hand on it, he turned to Ashley with a smile. "Hus!"

Horse. It was a horse. How was he ever going to make it in this world? He couldn't even speak clearly enough to be understood when he was talking about a silly painted horse on a carnival ride.

Ashley tried to push away the worries that rushed to her mind with the grim view of his future. She had enough on her plate trying to figure out what she was going to do with him tomorrow. She stepped up onto the carousel. "Are you going to ride it?"

He grunted and tried to climb the horse. He moved as clumsily as when he'd attempted to scale the fence at home.

She made a cup with her hands and bent over. "Put your foot here."

He stared down at her hands.

"Your shoe, Matthew. Put your tennis shoe right here in my hands."

He lifted his foot and rested it lightly on her hands.

"Now get on the horse, and I'll lift."

Somehow between his struggles and her effort pushing him up, Matthew ended up sitting on top of the horse, his mouth stretched into a smile that shrunk his eyes to little cracks.

Tina waved from where she held the twins, several animals in front of them. Was that a big frog she sat in?

"Unngh." Another noise from Matthew.

Ashley swung her gaze back to him in time to see him grip the pole and pull his slipping body back up. Looked like she'd spend the ride standing next to him to make sure he didn't fall off.

The carousel lurched with a loud machinery noise as music kicked in. The ride started to turn, slowly gaining speed.

Matthew seemed to find his balance a few minutes into the ride, luckily on a sedate gray horse that didn't move up and down like some of the others.

Ashley eventually let her gaze wander. She scanned the people that watched the moving carousel.

Mostly children and their parents. At least they shouldn't be able to notice anything odd about Matthew from this distance. He might even look normal from where they stood now.

A bearded face passed by. Dr. Crimson?

Ashley craned her head to see the man again, but she couldn't locate him. Why would the doctor be there? The very strange doctor who had walked out of MHIC after threatening her.

She was being silly. A beard didn't mean it was the same guy. This one even had sunglasses on. There was no way she could be sure.

Her heart didn't listen to her as it picked up speed. She tried to ignore her overreaction as the carousel reached the same location in its rotation, and she looked for the man. Still no sign of him.

She took a deep breath and let it out as the ride slowed. She had imagined it.

Honestly. She was so on edge lately. Something about having this kid around put her off-balance. Maybe he wasn't any better for her than she was for him.

The carousel stopped completely.

"Time to get off."

Matthew shifted on the horse and looked down like he wasn't sure how to dismount.

"Careful." She held her hand out behind him. As strong as she was for her size, she certainly wouldn't be able to lift him down.

"Need some help?" A male voice came from the other side of the painted horse, somewhere behind Matthew. Probably the carousel operator.

"Yes. He's having trouble getting down."

"I see that."

Wait a second. She knew that voice. She jerked her head around Matthew.

Dr. Crimson reached for Matthew's arm.

chapter
nine

Ashley's heart jumped into her throat as she grabbed Matthew around the waist and yanked him toward her. Maybe she was strong enough after all.

His feet hit the ground, and she steadied his thick body as she glared at the doctor. "What are you doing here?"

"You made the wrong call, Ashley."

How did he know her name?

"Matthew belongs with us." The dark eyes that stared at her over the horse were hard and cold.

What was he talking about? "You're not a doctor, are you?" She moved her hand to grip Matthew's arm, adrenaline shooting into her fingers.

He laughed and moved to the front of the horse.

She jumped off the carousel, pulling Matthew with her. He stumbled, but she didn't loosen her grip. "Run, Matthew! We have to run!"

She tugged on his arm as he got to his feet and started to run with her on the cement path that wrapped around the ride.

Why'd they have to put a fence around the whole thing?

She dragged Matthew along, his running awkward and

slow as she frantically looked for the exit gate. She spotted it and jogged through.

A few bystanders exclaimed and murmured as Ashley and Matthew pushed past them.

She didn't care anymore. She had no idea who that supposed doctor was, but she sure didn't like whatever it was he wanted.

She glanced back to see how close he was and smacked into something solid.

A man.

She lurched back, clutching Matthew's wrist.

"It's okay." The tire-changer guy? His steady green eyes looked down to meet her gaze. "Follow me."

She hesitated.

"You'd rather deal with him?" Tire-changer guy nodded behind her.

She looked to see the doctor pushing through people exiting the ride. She turned back to the guy who seemed like the safer call at the moment.

"Walk quickly. Don't run."

Ashley chafed under his authoritative command, but she followed him with Matthew.

The boy went along without even a pout, though the confused gaze he cast Ashley probably mirrored her own.

Was this a nightmare? She didn't even know what they were running from.

Tire-changer dude led them into the pavilion, where the air-conditioned chill slapped her in the face.

She checked behind them.

"Don't look back."

She turned forward, but Mr. Hero was already looking ahead, too. Why was she following this bossy guy to get away from another man she didn't even know?

"In here." Her supposed rescuer went to a dark door marked *Employees Only*. He opened it and waved at her like she was supposed to enter.

In his dreams. She looked back.

The bearded guy wasn't anywhere in sight.

"He's coming." The man sounded so confident.

"I don't see him."

"Trust me."

Right. If she had a penny for every time a guy had said—

He grabbed her arm with a vise-like grip and pulled her through the doorway before she could think.

She shoved him off, ready to kick and scream, but he had already let go.

"Shh." He put a finger to his lips as he turned away.

Matthew stood beside her, the door shut tight in front of them.

The noise of the air conditioner running and the blood rushing in Ashley's ears were the only sounds beyond muffled voices of people as they passed by.

The tire-changer listened at the door like he could hear something more. He didn't even look at Ashley. Was he seriously only trying to protect them from the psycho doctor?

Matthew started jerking his hands up and down.

Ashley put a gentle hand over his to calm the movement. "It's okay. We're okay."

Mr. Hero looked at her. "Should be clear now. If you're careful. You should go directly home."

She nodded, watching Matthew's bunched up features. She straightened the bill of his cap.

Poor kid was freaked out. Home would be best.

"Would you like me to drive you?"

Ashley turned her gaze on the man with renewed suspicion. The guy was far too mysterious to be trusted, even if he hadn't tried anything funny when he had the advantage...for a second time.

What was he even doing at Navy Pier? Following her? Seemed the only explanation. But he didn't act like a stalker.

She cleared her throat, avoiding his direct gaze. "We'll be fine. I need to find my friend first anyway."

"I'm sure she'll understand." His voice was firm, almost like it was lined with a threat that he wouldn't let her talk to Tina.

Maybe just getting away from this guy as soon as possible was the best call. "You're probably right." She forced a smile she hoped would convince him she was playing along as she looked pointedly at the door.

He took the hint and opened it, stepping through himself and scanning the crowd. He turned those green eyes her direction. "Go straight home. I'll follow you to be sure you get there okay."

He was announcing he was going to follow her? Her throat tightened.

He met her gaze. "Please let me do that." His annoyingly handsome face softened with a small smile. "If I'm going to rescue someone, I like to see the job through and make sure they're really safe."

What was she supposed to say to that? Something in his eyes made her want to trust him. She nodded, inwardly kicking herself for what was probably her stupidest move of the day. Next to taking Matthew to MHIC.

At least the walk to the car wasn't terribly far since Tina had splurged to pay for parking in one of Navy Pier's garages.

Mr. Hero stuck like glue all the way. His eyes seemed to watch everything as they walked through the concrete structure, an echo chamber for every smack of her flip-flops. For a random rescuer, the man sure was more practiced at this kind of thing than Ashley.

"This is mine." She went to the passenger door to unlock it for Matthew.

"Know it well."

She glanced at him, catching the twinkle in his eyes. Did he mean he'd been following her?

"Paint job looks better in the daytime."

Duh. The flat tire incident. At least this time she had plenty of reasons for her paranoia.

"I'll get my car and catch up with you."

"You really don't have to follow me home." And she wished he wouldn't.

"No problem. I want to."

Why? She slid into the car behind the wheel, trying not to think too hard about the answer as he walked off. There was no way he'd actually catch up or even find her car if she left right away. She started the car in three attempts and drove to the exit as quickly as she safely could.

Five minutes away from Navy Pier, her breathing reached its normal rate, and the tension in her chest started to ease. No sign of any kooks, behind or in front. "Looks like we're home free now."

Matthew sat next to her, surprisingly calm, looking out the window like they were taking a normal weekend drive.

As she slowed for the next stoplight, she glanced in the rearview mirror.

The navy blue car stopped behind her.

Her heart hit her ribs as she stared at reflection in the mirror. Was that the tire-changer guy? The chiseled jawline and slightly shaggy brown hair had become too familiar for her to mistake. It was him. And he drove the car she'd seen those other days.

She tried to remember to breathe as her fingers whitened, clenching the steering wheel. She couldn't go home with him following, could she? But if he'd followed her the other days, he probably already knew where she lived.

The thought made her stomach churn. She had to risk it. There was no other choice. She'd drive there and stop, but she'd take off again if he got out of his car.

She held her breath as she reached the house and reduced her speed for the driveway, gaze locked onto his car in the mirror.

He slowed, then pulled around her and waved as he drove on by.

She made herself relax her grip on the wheel, her fingers

trembling as she passed by the mailbox and pulled the car up to the side of the house.

She wouldn't check the mail at all today. If there was a note, she didn't want to know. She'd had enough for one day.

"Home?" Matthew looked at her with his eyebrows lifted. A look she hadn't seen before.

Was he asking? Or did he think her house was his home now? Neither option was good.

As she looked at his odd, round face, her questions returned. The crazy doctor had grabbed Matthew, not her. "Why was that man after you, Matthew?"

One corner of his mouth pulled up into a half-smile.

Why would someone want to kidnap an orphaned boy with Down syndrome? This one particular boy. What made him so special?

Ashley glanced at the empty hallway. "Matthew, time for breakfast." Her call died quickly in the silence of the house.

Strange. She'd never had to wake him before. He always came out to the kitchen before she did.

Maybe the excitement from yesterday had taken a toll. She'd slept late herself, enjoying the luxury of a day off from work.

She left the cereal bowls on the table and went to the bedroom. "Matthew, time to—"

The bed was empty, the covers twisted, no folded pajamas on top of them.

Not another game of hide and seek. She didn't have the patience for it in the morning.

"Matthew, come out now." She went to the bathroom as she called for him. At least it was Sunday. He'd be making her late for work any other day.

She stepped into the bathroom and pulled the shower curtain aside.

No Matthew.

He could have gone outside again, looking for the way home.

A caffeine-like kick sped her pulse. With Matthew around to scare her like this, maybe she didn't need her morning coffee.

She slipped her bare feet into flip-flops and went outside through the front door. Even the morning air was clammy with humidity.

"Matthew!" She thought better of her yell as soon as it left her mouth. What if LeBron was around, watching or listening? Nah, he wouldn't get up before noon on a Sunday.

Ashley walked around the house, her flip-flops smacking in the stillness. She checked along the fence.

Nothing.

She rustled the bushes, peered behind the rusted grill the previous house owners had left, crouched to look under the car.

Not so much as a footprint anywhere.

She swallowed, her throat dry. Squinting in the brightening sunlight, she walked back to the front of the house and scanned the empty yard.

"Matthew!"

Her stomach torqued. Where was he?

Maybe she'd missed him inside. She hurried back in, walking, then jogging through the empty rooms, checking under the bed and table, in closets...anywhere she could think of.

He was gone.

How could she have been so stupid? She shouldn't have slept in, shouldn't have left him alone. She grabbed her cell phone off the kitchen counter and selected Tina's number.

She smacked her palm against the wall as the phone rang. She knew she wasn't right for him. She'd told Tina that a thousand times. Why hadn't she taken him someplace where he would've been safe?

"Hello?"

"Tina. Matthew's gone."

The sleepy voice cleared to sharply alert. "What?"

"When I woke up this morning, he wasn't here."

"Did you look outside?"

"Of course I looked outside. I looked everywhere." Ashley stopped, forcing herself to take a breath. It wasn't Tina's fault. "He isn't here. I'm afraid he might have tried to go home, to his old home, wherever that was. He's tried before."

"Oh, Ashley. I'm so sorry."

A pain surged in her chest. It was a ridiculous thing for Tina to say. Matthew wasn't hers. They weren't family.

"Have you called the police?"

"No." She moistened her lips. "I was hoping I'd find him. He likes to hide."

"You better get them involved."

"Yeah. I will." First, she had to get the mail.

She ended the call and stalked outside, her footsteps firm and her jaw set as she went to the mailbox. She hadn't checked for another threatening letter yesterday. Maybe she should have.

She sucked in a breath and opened the box.

Two envelopes.

She pulled them out, separating them to see the folded paper. There wasn't one. Just the two letters in envelopes.

Ashley started for the house, not sure whether to be relieved or not. At least a note might have told her where Matthew was. But maybe no note meant he was fine, wandering around somewhere close by on his own, not taken by some prejudiced kook who hated him or by the crazy doctor.

Her gaze dropped to the envelopes as she neared the house. The top one was junk mail. The second...

She froze.

That handwriting. The same as the letter at the office.

Her stomach lurched. No. She couldn't do this now. She had to worry about Matthew, not herself.

Special Target

But she couldn't pull her gaze from that horrid scrawl. He'd found her home. She wasn't safe.

chapter
ten

Ashley's hopes dwindled by the second. She could see it in Detective Thompson's face as he sat on the other side of the table at the police station—he didn't believe a word she was saying. Or, at best, he had significant doubts.

"And this man you don't know continued to chase you away from the carousel?"

"Yes."

"And then the other man, also a stranger, helped you and the boy get away. Is that right?"

Ashley leaned forward. "We already went over this."

Thompson lowered the eyebrows that had been raised since she'd started telling her tale. "I just want to be sure I got it right. That really is quite a story. Quite a day you had."

Story. Like she'd made it up.

She sighed and leaned back in her chair. She couldn't really blame him. She had a hard time believing it herself. "Maybe it would help to talk to Detective Swoboda. He's the one who handled the plane crash that killed Matthew's parents."

"He's not in today, but he also isn't on the case anymore."

"So he didn't find out anything more about Matthew's parents or other relatives?"

"Well, I'm sure Homicide is looking into that now."

"Homicide?"

Thompson swiped at his nose and sniffed. "Sorry. Summer cold."

Ashley stared at the man. "You said Homicide."

"Yes, ma'am. I thought you knew. I'm sorry. Accident Investigations turned up evidence the crash may not have been an accident."

"Not an accident." She was being a parrot, but it was hard to believe. "You mean, murder?"

"Nothing's for certain yet." He held up his hand. "And I'd ask you not to spread that story around."

She met the man's gaze. "I don't care about rumors, Detective. I just want to find Matthew." Her imagination jumped ahead to frightening possibilities. If his parents were killed, was Matthew in even more trouble than she thought? What if that had something to do with the doctor who'd tried to take him?

"Because he has Down syndrome, we were able to get moving on his disappearance right away. We listed him as a missing endangered person as soon as you told us he was missing, and our men are still searching for him even as we speak. And, yes, we are canvasing the neighborhood of his parents' apartment." Thompson got to his feet. "In the meantime, I'd suggest you go to your home again and wait for him there. He'll likely return if he just wandered off for a bit."

"Sure. Thanks." She stood, absently hanging her purse over her shoulder. The detective could be right. Matthew might be at home, looking for her.

She bit her lip as she left the police station and went to her car, the night already dark. A whole day of searching, driving through neighborhoods, and visiting the police station one more time.

A whole day that Matthew was alone. Or with someone horrible. Or—

She closed her eyes against the thought, leaning against

her car door. Why had she kept him with her so long? She knew she couldn't take care of him. No one really could.

The moment she saw Matthew, she knew things could only end badly for him. His parents should have known that, too.

A bit of light flashed next to LeBron's house as Ashley turned the car into her driveway.

LeBron stood in the shadows by his side door, his just-lit cigarette sticking out of his mouth, the end glowing orange.

Only reason he'd be outside this time of night was to spy, signal somebody, or wait for a buyer.

Ashley braked and cut the engine in the driveway. She got out and slammed the car door, her exhausted fury finding a target.

The guy was bold, she'd give him that. Writing those crummy notes and then standing outside to watch her when she got home. He could be behind all of this. He could know where Matthew was. He could've taken Matthew himself.

She marched up to the fence that divided their properties, her eyes shooting sparks to light her way. "Where is he?"

He took a drag on the cigarette, watching her with his lazy gaze.

"Where is Matthew?"

He lowered the joint with a grin that made her skin crawl. "Lost the retard?"

"Did you take him?" What was she doing? Like he'd confess if he had. But she couldn't stop the flood of anger that poured out on the loser.

He laughed until a choking cough stopped him. "Why would I want a kid like that?"

"I don't want to know."

"Hey, I don't care. Come on in and check out the place. I got nothin' to hide."

"You wish." Her belly recoiled at the thought. "I'm not

stupid enough to do that, and I'm sure I couldn't stomach the sight. But if I find out you had anything to do with Matthew's disappearance, I swear you'll wish you'd never been born."

"I like my women feisty." He grinned, but Ashley thought she detected a glint of worry in his eyes.

She started to turn away, then paused. "By the way, your cute little notes aren't scaring anyone. But I bet the cops would love to see them. You're on parole, right?" She spun on her heel and headed for the house without gracing him with another glance.

She wanted it to be him. She hoped the notes were his. Hoped he was behind this. She could nail him to a wall. Chew him up and spit him out without breaking a sweat. She faced his kind—cruel, criminal, and sadistic—nearly every day.

But she had the terrifying feeling LeBron had nothing to do with Matthew vanishing. Maybe nothing to do with the threatening notes or the phone call.

She unlocked the side door and went inside the dark house.

Her hand reached to scratch the back of her neck. The itchy, crawling feeling didn't go away.

She stopped. "Matthew?"

The silence that answered her was deafening. But it felt like...someone was there.

She walked around the corner to the living room, fumbling for the outer pocket of her purse. For the knife.

A man stared at her.

Her heart stopped with her feet.

He sat on the couch, his face turned in her direction, cloaked in shadow. "Welcome home." He reached for the lamp by the couch and switched it on.

Tire guy?

"I don't think I ever introduced myself. Tiernan Hanks."

She moistened her lips. Should she say something or scream?

"And you're Ashley Sorenson. Sorry to surprise you like

this. I know you've had a long day." His tone was so polite, so normal. Like he was her best friend who'd decided to drop in.

She somehow found her voice as she slowly slid her hand under the flap of her purse's outer pocket. "You followed me?" If she could just get to her knife.

"Today? No. But I kept tabs on your movements."

Kept tabs on her movements? What kind of stalker talked like that?

"Why don't you sit down." More of an order than a question. He pointed his hand at the armchair next to the couch. Only a few feet away from him. "And I'd appreciate it if you took your hand out of that pocket."

She froze, her fingers touching the folded knife.

"The pocket of your purse there. This will go a lot easier if you don't try to use that on me."

He knew about the knife? Did he have a weapon of his own? Maybe a gun.

The crash may not have been an accident. Detective Thompson's words strengthened the fear choking her breath. What if this guy had something to do with the crash?

She slowly pulled her fingers out of the pocket. He might shoot her if she went for it.

"Really, you should have a seat."

She swallowed. "I'd rather stand."

He chuckled. "Don't blame you. You have bumpy cushions here." He swung something that looked like a club into the air.

She instinctively took a step back.

"Do you always keep table legs in your couch?" He turned his gaze to her, and his brow furrowed in the lamplight. "I'm sorry. I didn't mean to scare you so badly."

Really. Like breaking into her house and waiting for her in the dark would do anything but terrify her.

"I should have started with this." He set down the table leg as he stood and walked toward her, reaching inside his sport coat.

She stepped back again, glancing around for something she could grab to defend herself.

He paused, lifting his hand up, palm toward her. "It's okay. I was only going to show you this." He took out a flat oversized wallet and flipped it open.

In the dark, she could barely make out what looked like a badge and some sort of ID card. "Police?"

"FBI, actually." He sounded offended.

She reached to flick the light switch to turn on the overhead bulbs.

"I'd rather you not do that."

"Why?"

"Easier for people outside to see."

"Harder for me to see if your badge is real."

His teeth flashed in the dim light as he grinned. "Well, at least you're not scared anymore."

Her insides still balled in a knot that would take a lot longer to untangle, but her heart had stopped trying to break out of her ribcage. Even if he wasn't FBI like he claimed, she'd be safe if he tried to act like an agent. At least for the moment.

"Well, the badge isn't all that important." He closed the badge holder and put it back in his pocket. "The important thing is that we have Matthew."

Her heart jumped, but she tried to keep the reaction from her face. "'We,' as in the FBI?"

He nodded. "That's right."

"How did you get him?"

He didn't answer.

"Let me guess." Anger slipped into her voice. "You snuck in here last night and just took him out. That's what you did, isn't it?"

"Are you sure you won't sit down?"

"Positive." She hoped her icy tone said it all.

"We weren't going to bring you in on this. It would be safer for you and Matthew. But we didn't think you'd follow up on the boy so enthusiastically."

"What?" She plunked her fists on her hips. "I'm a social worker. You think I don't care when kids get kidnapped under my watch?"

"I thought Matthew's case would be different."

She stared at him, waiting for him to make sense.

"Given how you feel about people like him."

Her mouth fell open before she could think about closing it. How did he know that?

He turned around and sauntered back to the couch.

"Did you bug my office?"

He plopped on the couch and looked at her. "You wrote a paper on the subject in college. Very interesting. Totally wrong, but interesting."

"And I suppose you're an expert on child welfare as well as infringing on people's privacy?"

That grin would be almost cute if it wasn't so incredibly irritating. "We only monitored you to keep Matthew safe."

"So he's not under arrest, then."

He laughed at her sarcasm. "No."

"Am I?"

"No, ma'am."

"Good, then you won't mind taking me to Matthew so I can bring him home."

"I didn't say that."

"You won't let him go?"

"Not right now."

She stalked to the back of the armchair so she could pin him with a glare. "How do I know you're really FBI? This is all very far-fetched. What would the FBI want with a Down syndrome teen?"

The man's smile faded. "He's a special kid. But maybe you haven't figured that out yet."

Her blood heated at the cheap shot, even if it was partially true. "You don't seem to get this, but I'm a social worker. That means taking care of kids is my job. How am I supposed to know for sure that Matthew's safe or even alive, or if you're even the real FBI?" She gripped the top of the chair's back. "Since you're an expert, you should know Matthew needs special care. He's not like a normal sixteen-year-old."

The supposed agent leaned forward. "I agree. But didn't you yourself say you weren't qualified to give him the care he needs?"

She set her jaw, trying to ignore the pang in her chest that interrupted her anger for a second. "I don't even want to know how you knew that but get this through your head—I'm good at my job, and I'm very experienced with kids who need more help than the normal ones."

"Matthew's getting the help he needs. And he's safe."

She took a breath. Matthew was alone with strangers, frightened. Maybe hurt, if this guy was lying. "I'd like to see him." She kept her voice steady and firm.

"I'm afraid you can't."

She stepped around the chair, showing him she wasn't afraid to face him. "You don't have a choice. Matthew is legally in my custody and under my care. I have every legal right to take care of him. In fact, I'm required by law to do so." She tilted her head. "Are you prepared to take me on in court if I go public with this?"

"I was afraid you might say something like that." He stood.

She held her ground.

He looked at the jumbo watch on his wrist, then met her gaze. "I could say the FBI trumps your social worker status, but I'm going to give you a little leeway this time. Putting this out in public would only hurt Matthew right now, though you don't seem to understand that."

"Sure it wouldn't just hurt the FBI?" She crossed her arms over her T-shirt and tilted her chin as she looked up at the agent. "It's hard to believe you care about Matthew when you won't even let me see him."

Did his eyes twinkle as he looked down at her? At least she'd managed to wipe that smile from his face.

"Pack a bag."

She lowered her arms. "What for?"

"You want to see Matthew, don't you?"

"Yes, but I wasn't planning to sleep over."

"You won't be coming back here for a while."

"You're kidnapping me?"

"Do you want to see Matthew or not?" Impatience finally crept into his tone.

She clenched her teeth as her pulse kicked up. What would she be getting into if she went? But if she stayed, she wouldn't know what had happened to Matthew, and she'd be left alone with…those unopened letters, now coming to her house.

She nodded. "I'll be right back." She went to the bedroom to stuff what she could into her smallest suitcase.

A change of address wouldn't be a bad idea right now. If she was with the FBI, even he shouldn't be able to find her. And if they weren't FBI…she'd still be better off than if she had to face him.

chapter
eleven

"Put this on." The agent swung a black cloth toward Ashley.

A blindfold? She glanced at the dark surroundings as they drove on the city streets, strangely empty this time of night and glistening under the light rain. "What did you say your name was?"

"Tiernan. Tiernan Hanks."

"Strange name."

"Strange, huh? Most people call it unusual."

Ashley shrugged. "Same difference."

"'Unusual' sounds a lot nicer." He pushed the blindfold closer. "You need to put this on."

"Why?"

His eyes glimmered in the light from a passing streetlamp as he glanced at her. "I wouldn't even let you see Matthew if you hadn't been cleared with a thorough background check. Don't push your luck."

How thorough? She took the blindfold and wrapped it around her eyes, tying it behind her head as her gut twisted in its own knot. They couldn't have found everything. No one knew.

Leaving the blindfold loose enough that she could see her shirt when she looked straight down, she cleared her throat.

"Why are you holding Matthew? He can't have done anything wrong."

"I told you."

The car turned, and she had to grip the armrest on the door to keep from tilting to the right.

"It's for his protection."

She hadn't noticed how deep Tiernan's voice was until she'd put on the blindfold. "Isn't that what you FBI agents always say whenever you want to hold somebody hostage?"

"You watch too many crime shows."

Why did her lips want to pull into a smile? She pressed them together to stop the urge. There was nothing funny about this situation. And the agent beside her would love it if his charm worked.

The car turned again, making her tighten her hold on the door. "Would you slow down? It feels like we're in a race."

"It's the blindfold. Everything feels faster and unexpected."

How would he know? He didn't have to wear one. She'd roll her eyes, but there was no point when they were covered. "So why does he supposedly need protection?"

"You ask too many questions."

"Meaning, you're not going to answer."

"Meaning, we're here."

The car slowed, then stopped.

The knot at the back of her head tugged as fingers started to untie it.

Ashley jerked her head away. "I'll get it."

"Sorry."

She untied the blindfold and blinked as she lowered it. They were parked alongside a small house, about the size of hers. The neighborhood looked familiar. "Are we still in my neighborhood?"

He chuckled. "I'll never tell."

"Doesn't look like there was much point in moving Matthew here."

"When we get out of the car, you'll have to walk close to me and act comfortable in case someone's watching."

"Close to you?" She arched an eyebrow at him.

He met her gaze with a serious one. "No joke."

"Fine." What exactly did he mean by acting comfortable? Her muscles tensed as she got out.

"Wait there." His voice was quiet but commanding as he stood and walked around the car to her side. "Okay." He put a firm, unmoving hand on the middle of her back as they walked toward the house, whether to play the *comfortable* role or make sure she didn't get away, she wasn't sure.

They rounded the corner and stopped at the back door, where he knocked in an oddly rhythmic pattern. Probably some sort of coded sequence. Then he took out his cell phone from his pocket and dialed a number. He waited with the phone to his ear for a couple seconds, then lowered it.

Something clicked at the door, like a bolt lock being turned. It opened.

A man about a head taller than Tiernan moved the gun he held in his hand to somewhere behind his back as he welcomed them with a broad grin. "Hey, we were about to send the posse after you, mate. Have trouble gettin' the girl?"

Tiernan gave Ashley an apologetic look, though he was clearly fighting a smile. "You'll have to forgive Agent Jones. His Aussie humor is about as off-putting as his accent."

She brushed past the two men into the kitchen, not interested in the comradery of the kidnappers who'd snatched Matthew. They behaved more like FBI agents than criminals, but maybe they were trying to put her off guard by acting so relaxed. "Where's Matthew?"

"Jack?" Tiernan looked at Jones.

The big Aussie thumbed to the wall on the right.

Ashley felt them follow her as she passed an Hispanic-looking armed man sitting at a dining table and rounded the corner to a longer room with a TV and couch.

She stopped.

Matthew sat on the floor by a coffee table, fiddling with a deck of cards, his lips drawn and brow furrowed in concentration.

She stared at him.

He was okay. He wore his cap and clothes she hadn't seen before. They fit him better.

She moistened her lips. "Matthew."

He turned his head toward her, his cap bill crooked as usual. His lips stretched into that beaming smile that lit up every inch of his face.

A strange warmth spread through her as something pricked her eyes. Couldn't be tears. Though she would be entitled after a day like today. She glanced away from that smile, pretending to fish in her purse for something. "I'm glad you're okay."

When she looked up again, Matthew had stood and was walking to Tiernan, who met him halfway. Matthew hugged the taller, full-grown man, and Tiernan warmly returned the boy's embrace.

Tiernan looked at Ashley as Matthew let go and went back to his cards at the table. "Did you know your mouth hangs open when you're surprised? It's cute."

She pressed her lips together, hoping he didn't see the annoying flush that warmed her cheeks. "You didn't tell me Matthew knew you already."

"Only a few hours." Tiernan slid his hands into the back pockets of his jeans.

"But he hugs you." He hadn't even tried to hug her except with that nightmare. Thank goodness.

Tiernan shrugged. "I hugged him first."

"Why would you do that?" So much for the tough FBI image.

"He looked like he needed it." Tiernan tilted his head slightly as he watched Ashley.

He better not be about to say she looked like she needed a

hug. She turned away before she had to find out. The guy was either certifiable or playing some weird con game.

A petite woman with Asian features appeared from what looked like a hallway, wearing a gray fitted T-shirt and slim, black jeans with a holstered gun on her hip. She paused at the edge of the living room carpet and nodded at Tiernan past Ashley like she wasn't there. "Hanks."

"Nguyen." His voice had moved closer behind Ashley.

She faced him as the other woman turned away to the dining room.

"Are you satisfied about Matthew's condition?" Tiernan met Ashley's gaze. "You can see he's perfectly healthy and safe with us."

"You still haven't told me why he's being held here."

"That's need-to-know only."

She folded her arms in front of her. "If I'm being held hostage here against my will, that makes it need-to-know for me."

He lifted his eyebrows without a word, like he was waiting for a better reason than that to tell her anything.

A man's loud laugh came from the kitchen. Then a woman's. Were they laughing at her?

"Can you get Matthew to talk?" Tiernan's question brought her attention back to the stubborn agent.

"Sure. He talks to me."

Tiernan met her gaze with an intense stare. "We know he's non-verbal."

She transferred her hands to her hips. "Then I guess you don't know everything after all. Matthew does talk."

"Show me."

"Are you kidding?" Her voice rose with her irritation. "He isn't a puppet I can make speak on command whenever you want me to. He talks when *he* wants to, just like anybody else."

"Like him." Matthew's anxious tone matched the expression on his face as he looked at her from the table.

For once, his annoying phrase didn't bug her a bit, conveniently timed as it was. But she still wasn't about to like Tiernan just because Matthew wanted her to.

She moved her gaze to the agent and caught him watching her with an expression she couldn't quite read, like wheels were turning behind those green eyes.

"Maybe you can be helpful to us."

The knot in her stomach twisted. Being helpful didn't sound like a good thing in this context.

"I need you to tell me everything Matthew says to you. Even if it doesn't make sense, I want to know what it is."

"Why?"

Tiernan just stared at her.

She licked her lips. "Do I have a choice?"

"Sure." He nodded. "But only one is a pleasant option."

Could have been a threat, but the way he said it was so factual, so in control, it galled her more than frightened her.

She stalked around him without another word and marched over to the couch behind Matthew. She sat down by the boy, her mind sifting through ideas for how she could get out of the house, away from the supposed agents.

But could she leave Matthew behind, even if she could escape? The answer was obvious. She could never leave him alone with these nuts.

She set her purse on the cushion next to her and started digging in it for her smartphone. Tina was probably freaking out. Ashley could at least send a text to let her know they were okay.

She rummaged in her purse until she'd covered every inch of the interior, even taking out her wallet to make sure the phone wasn't hidden under it. No phone.

Tiernan. She looked up to yell at him, but he wasn't there. She pushed off the couch and stalked to the dining room.

The thief stopped laughing with his Aussie pal and glanced at her from where he sat at the table.

"Where's my phone?"

He didn't even look sheepish. Or guilty. "No one can know where we are. Since you aren't used to being so secretive, I thought it'd be simpler if I took care of your phone for a while. You'll get it back when this is all over."

Ashley's fury choked the words she wanted to shoot at him. It was official. She'd been kidnapped. She only hoped it was actually by the FBI and not people even worse.

Although, staring at Tiernan Hanks's maddeningly cheerful smile, she couldn't imagine a more irritating kidnapper.

"There are some things you can't make me do, Agent Hanks." Ashley raised her voice over the noise of the air mattress inflating as she held down the button on the attached controller.

"You should have your own room and a real bed."

"Matthew should have that." She tested the mattress with her foot and stopped the air flow. "This mattress will be an improvement from my couch, where I've been sleeping for Matthew's sake."

"Yeah, I noticed." Tiernan grinned, seeming to miss her point about how well she took care of Matthew. "Are there any springs left in that thing?"

"Cute." She grabbed her pajamas in one hand, toothbrush and toothpaste in the other, and left the room, walking through the dark hallway to the bathroom.

She reached the door she thought was for the bathroom and put her hand on the knob.

It swung open and someone nearly slammed into Ashley.

The woman agent.

"Sorry."

The place felt like a college dormitory with all these agents crawling around. There were only three left inside—this woman, Jack Jones, and Tiernan—but it seemed like they were everywhere Ashley turned. "What's your name again?" A little friendliness wouldn't hurt. Maybe being a woman would make this agent more sympathetic, even willing to help Ashley out.

"Special Agent Nguyen."

Ashley recalled the first name she'd heard Jack use in the dining room earlier. "Katherine, right?"

"Sure." She smiled briefly, but it looked forced.

"How long have you worked with Tiernan?"

"Not long." Her mouth curved again, but this time with a little more genuineness in her eyes. "I'm sure this is quite a shock for you, being here. Tiernan can be hardnosed at times, but he's a good agent. The best at what he does. That's why I came to work with him. You can trust him completely."

Katherine lost Ashley there. "I don't feel comfortable trusting people who won't tell me anything. If I knew more about why we're here...why he took Matthew. Can you fill me in a little?"

Katherine gave Ashley a knowing look that snuck under her skin. "Sorry. I can't tell you anything Hanks doesn't want you to know." She started to pass Ashley but paused. "Except don't swallow any of that tap water. It's disgusting."

Ashley glared at the agent's back as she sauntered away. So much for the sisterhood of women. Ashley was apparently going to have to wait this one out...or do something drastic.

Hours later, Ashley still swung back and forth on what she should do as she lay on the air mattress and stared at the darkened white ceiling, blinking away the dragging minutes she should have been sleeping.

Tiernan sat in the armchair, reading or sleeping. He was so quiet, she wasn't sure which.

Jones played solitaire at a little table near the front door, using a flashlight to see the cards. The agent queen was a pleasant distance away, supposedly watching Matthew in the bedroom.

Ashley's gaze went to Jones's gun under his arm. Three guards in the house, one or two outside. What was the big danger? Someone outside? Or were they there to keep Matthew and her inside?

If that was the aim, she'd have a much harder time escaping than she'd thought. If this went on much longer, she'd have to try anyway. She couldn't even sleep with guards all around, and Tiernan sitting right over her.

She let out a sigh as quietly as she could and closed her eyes. She'd never think of a solution if she didn't get some rest.

A shout pierced the silence.

chapter
twelve

Matthew?

Ashley scrambled to her feet, trying to untangle from the clinging sheet as Jones rushed for the hallway.

A hand gripped her arm. "Wait."

Tiernan's hold was hard, controlling.

She tried to yank free as Matthew shouted again.

Tiernan blocked her with a solid arm wrapped in front of her.

"Let me go!" Panic turned the words to a shriek as he closed around her.

"It's clear." Jones popped back into view. "Boy's having a nightmare."

Tiernan let her go.

She fled his hold and ran to Matthew, brushing wet tear streaks off her cheeks as soon as she passed Jones and was alone in the hall. She turned into the bedroom without giving herself time to think.

Matthew thrashed in the bed, just like at home.

She kneeled on the edge of the mattress as she gently gripped his arms and shook him. "Matthew. Matthew, wake up. It's okay. I'm here."

He reached for her like before.

She scooted to lean against the headboard as she held him in her arms and murmured comforting stock phrases she wasn't sure were true. Were they okay here? Was he safe?

"Does he often have nightmares?" A deep voice made her jump inwardly.

Tiernan stood at the end of the bed and watched them, his brow furrowed...with concern? Not likely. He probably thought she was comforting Matthew just to make it look like she cared.

She nodded.

"Home...home." Matthew muttered the word over and over again into her shoulder.

"What did he say?"

"Home." Ashley met Tiernan's gaze.

"Does he say that a lot?"

"Enough. It might help to take him to his parents' old place. The address the police had is an apartment downtown."

"I don't think so." Tiernan turned away and left the room before Ashley could get in another word.

She calmed Matthew as quickly as she could and got him to lie back down.

When she finally walked out of the bedroom, Jones stood outside the doorway. She gave him her glare. "Where's Tiernan?"

"Living room."

The bossy agent sat in the armchair again, reading a small book he held in his hand like nothing had happened.

She marched over to him and stopped, glaring down at him for a change. "Something tells me you know more about Matthew's parents than I do. Maybe more than the police, too."

He looked up at her, a provoking twinkle of amusement in his eyes.

"Well, do you?"

"Sorry. That's confidential."

"Confidential." She pointed toward the bedroom. "There's

a hurting boy in there who wants to go home. Is that even the place downtown or somewhere else?"

"Can't say."

"Then can we at least *take* Matthew to his home, if you know where it is?"

Tiernan sighed. "I'd like to, but at this point it's too dangerous."

"And I'm just supposed to believe that."

His nod didn't reassure her a bit.

"And why is it so dangerous?" She held up a hand. "Don't tell me. Need-to-know, right?"

"You have to trust me, Ashley."

She looked into those steady green eyes that locked onto her gaze. She'd never trusted a man in her life. "Why would I do that?"

"Because you want what's best for Matthew. And yourself. I'm here to keep you safe." His eyes seemed to look deeper, like he was trying to see inside her.

She turned away from his probing intrusion and crouched by the air mattress. She smoothed out the sheet that had tangled around her, trying to hold her prisoner. A dull throb in her arm brought the incident with Tiernan rushing back, when his fierce hold had cast her into the realm of her nightmares.

Nobody grabbed her like that. Nobody controlled her. Never again.

Her gut told her Tiernan was there for much more than keeping them safe. What, she didn't know. But she wouldn't stick around long enough to find out.

"Ashley."

Something clutched at her shoulder.

She jerked away with a gasp.

"Sorry." Tiernan looked down at her, his face right above hers.

Her heart pounded hard against her ribs.

He straightened. He was only standing there, not kneeling over her on the mattress as she'd thought in her sleep-induced fog. "We need to go. Now."

The room was still dark. She couldn't have slept more than a few minutes. "What time is it?"

"You don't want to know. You just need to grab your suitcase and follow me outside."

She pushed herself to a sitting position. "Where's Matthew?"

"He's coming, too. Hurry." He gestured with his hand that she should get up. "I've got your things packed." He packed them himself? Not that she'd really pulled anything out besides her toiletry bag. "Ashley." His voice was sharper than normal. Was it worry or just bossiness?

She slowly got to her feet and glanced toward the hallway.

Matthew appeared wearing his tilted baseball cap and carrying a duffel bag over his shoulder. He waved a thick hand at her with a smile. He was certainly wide awake.

Why did they have to leave so early in the morning? Or night...whichever it was.

After prodding Ashley to put on her flip-flops, Tiernan ushered them all—Matthew and company of agents—to the back door.

All this cloak and dagger stuff was ridiculous. Just what was this Tiernan guy up to?

Matthew, Katherine, and Jones disappeared out the door first. Then Tiernan stepped out and glanced back at Ashley. She stopped in the doorway.

The sky was still dark. What were they doing leaving when the sun wasn't even up?

"Ashley. We need to leave." He put his hand on her arm.

She pulled away. "You already bruised me once tonight." She rubbed her arm, though his hold had been much gentler this time.

"I'm sorry." His voice softened, almost like he meant it,

but she couldn't see his face well enough to tell in the dark. "I didn't mean to hurt you. I won't touch you again if you'll just keep moving. It's not safe to stay here."

She shuffled out the doorway and followed him as they crunched through dry, overgrown weeds that scratched her bare feet. The cooler air seeped into her nostrils, waking her up enough to think.

The FBI didn't behave like this. These agents acted more like criminals on the run, hiding from the cops. Had she been wrong to risk staying with them? What if they were taking her and Matthew somewhere less safe, somewhere they could get away with anything?

She shook her head. Her sleepy brain was far too imaginative for her own good. But in case her thoughts were on the right track, she picked up her pace to catch Matthew. The boy stumbled just in time to provide her with an excuse to take his arm.

They reached a narrow gate in the back fence, and Ashley let Matthew go through, following right behind him.

A black car waited on the empty street, cloaked in shadows.

She grabbed Matthew's arm and stopped. No way were they getting into that car without some answers.

"Now what?" Tiernan stepped around Ashley and faced her, irritation thickening his loud whisper.

"Where are you taking us?"

"Will you get in the car, please?"

She shook her head. "This is ridiculous. You tricked me into staying at a strange house, and now you're moving us in the middle of the night. If you're really FBI, you shouldn't have to hide what you're doing."

"Keep it down," Katherine hissed. Even from the distance of the car where Katherine stood, Ashley couldn't miss the woman's glare. "This is no time for a girly meltdown."

Heat rushed to Ashley's face, but not from embarrassment. Who did the woman think she was, playing cop in her petite black FBI jacket? Ashley could take on the pint-sized chick anytime and win. "This is called being smart and thinking independently. Something you're apparently not paid to do." Ashley gave her a smirk.

"Keep your voice down."

Ashley glared at Tiernan. "I don't work for you. You can't tell me what to do."

"Fine." His own voice rose past a whisper. "I've shown you my badge—"

"In the dark."

His eyes flashed. "I'll show it to you in the brightest light I can find if we ever get out of here. What else can I do to prove we're FBI?"

"Start acting like what you're doing is legal, for one. I don't look forward to either of our bodies being dredged from the river in the morning."

"Man, you do watch too much TV."

"Good education."

"Did it teach you that you don't have a choice right now?"

"Oh, I have a choice." She met his commanding stare. "I can make you sorry you even thought about kidnapping me."

A laugh came from the car. Katherine.

Ashley glared at her. "If any of you think it'd be easy to take me where I don't want to go, you have another thing coming."

"I have no doubt about that." Tiernan crossed his arms over his chest. "You're turning this into one of the most irritating cases I've ever had."

"Great show," the Aussie leaned across the roof of the car, keeping his voice low, "but we've got to leave. As in, now."

Tiernan looked at Ashley. "I don't want to force you to go. I want to do this as peacefully as possible. I'm not going to hurt you or Matthew."

"Unless I make you. Is that what you mean?"

"I need you to trust me, Ashley. I have Matthew's best interests at heart." He met her gaze, his green eyes soft and sincere. "This is all for good reasons, and you'll see that eventually."

She could almost believe him, but she wouldn't budge. She wasn't going to risk Matthew's life on a deadly con. "Tell me where we're going, or we won't get in."

Tiernan leaned startlingly close, his breath tickling her ear before she could pull back. "We're taking Matthew home."

Ashley fought the urge to tug at the scratchy blindfold as the car slowed to a stop.

"You can take it off now." Tiernan was an order machine. He had talked almost the whole way there, apparently commanding others over a phone.

The knot wouldn't come undone, so Ashley slipped the blindfold over her head, and her gaze met Tiernan's grin.

He watched her from the other side of Matthew in the backseat where they'd been stuffed. "Perimeter's clear. We're a go for the house." Tiernan seemed to be listening through his Bluetooth-like earpiece and talking to Katherine in the front seat, but he kept watching Ashley with that amused smile.

What was he looking at?

"Nice hair." Katherine tossed Ashley a smirk as she shoved open her door and got out.

Ashley touched her hair, which was a puffy mess around the top of her head where she had yanked off the blindfold. She'd like to tell Miss Perfect that she had much more important things to worry about in her life than a bad hair day, but the obnoxious agent was nowhere in sight when Ashley opened her door.

Bright sunlight blinded Ashley's eyes as she stood. Sunrise. A very beautiful sunrise, as it turned out when her pupils finally adjusted enough for her to see. She moved her gaze from the sun to the house—make that *mansion*—that loomed over her.

"Home!" Matthew jogged to the house in his clumsy way.

"Matthew!"

"It's okay. Let him go." Tiernan came to stand at Ashley's side as he nodded to Jones. "Jack."

The agent followed Matthew at a quick, long-legged pace, keeping his head moving in all directions, like he was watching for something.

"This can't be Matthew's home." She shook her head at the massive, beautiful mansion. Wasn't the biggest she'd seen, but it ranked right up there. "There must be a mistake. The address the police had was for a normal apartment, not a luxury penthouse."

"Like you said, I should know more about Matthew's history than you." Tiernan looked at her. "You were right."

Was that a smile tugging the corner of his mouth? At least he attempted to hide his amusement this time. "We should go inside." He extended his arm toward the house.

"I thought you said you couldn't take him home because it wasn't safe."

"Changed my mind."

"Why?"

He let the smile loose. "You helped me see the light."

Cute.

"Now would you go inside?"

"Oh, sure. Whatever you say, Agent Hanks." She sashayed with exaggerated cooperation up the stone stairs to the oversized front door.

The interior met her expectations exactly. Tiled floors, grand staircase, high ceilings, and a glamourous chandelier or two.

Her gut twisted as uneasiness tightened her throat. The place was too familiar. Too much like...

She physically jerked, stepping in the other direction to yank her mind off the track it was on.

"Whoa." Two hands touched her arms as she bumped into something firm.

She shrank back from Tiernan's chest with a gasp, her pulse rapid.

His gaze locked on her face as he raised his hands into the air, palms out. "Sorry. Are you okay?"

She nodded, trying to catch her breath and find her voice before he really wondered. He couldn't start to suspect. "Just a new place and all this...excitement."

"Yeah." His green eyes softened, the color lightening a little. "Sorry you have to face all this. It's tough."

"You do it just fine." Hopefully the small talk would take his mind off her odd behavior while she got ahold of herself.

"Sure. I was trained for it."

She barely heard his response as she herded her thoughts, forcing them to stay in the present. This was all new. The house was different. Everything was new and different. Nothing here had anything to do with the past her stupid brain had jumped to.

She tried for a curious expression as she glanced around the foyer and walked ahead to where the walls gave way to a huge living room with floor-to-ceiling windows. "So Matthew will stay here now? With you?"

Tiernan followed her to the edge of the living room carpeting. "For now. He wanted to come, so it was best to bring him. I can't say how long we'll be able to stay."

Probably best for the FBI more than Matthew. What was Tiernan really up to? Why would they bring Matthew to his home so suddenly after Tiernan had just told her they wouldn't?

She walked into the living room, pretending to look at the furniture and the wall art while her mind scrambled to put together the pieces of this mystery.

Tiernan wanted her to report whatever Matthew said to her. Was he hoping the boy would say or do something different while he was home? She glanced at the agent.

"Does Matthew know something you're trying to get out of him?"

If the agent was startled, he hid it well behind a little smile. "You sure are the suspicious type, aren't you?"

She stopped walking around the room and faced him. "I'm suspicious of the way you always try to distract me from my questions. It won't work."

A twinkle danced in his eyes. "I forgot you were raised by a lawyer."

A physical pain jolted through her body. She blinked rapidly and spun on her heel before he could see her face, probably a dead giveaway. "Not hardly." What else did he know about her? And her past? She crossed her arms in front of her, hiding her trembling hands under her biceps. "I should see what Matthew's doing." Her voice sounded almost normal. Good. She could do this.

"There's an agent with him."

"Pardon me if that isn't very comforting." She turned back to Tiernan, using a glare to cover any trace of the internal battle she'd just gone through.

"Eyes on Mockingbird." Tiernan waited for an answer from his little earpiece while Ashley rolled her eyes.

They had code names now?

Tiernan nodded at no one, then glanced at Ashley. "Upstairs." He started to head back to the staircase they had passed on their way in.

"I know where it is."

He stopped. "Suit yourself."

She passed him and headed up the staircase that curved along the wall. Maybe a moment alone would help her get her head on straight. She was here for Matthew. It was his home. Nothing like anywhere else.

She reached the landing, really a balcony hallway with doors along one side and a railing on the other that was open to the entryway beneath.

"Ashley?"

She hiked the shoulder strap of her bag higher as she silently inched past Veronica's room. One sound, and she'd wish she were dead.

"Looking for Matthew?"

The man's voice startled Ashley from the memory that pushed in on her like four walls about to crush her between them.

"In here."

She blinked at Jones, who peered at her through an open doorway at the end of the balcony. She picked up her pace, trying desperately to calm her breathing and appear normal as she reached the room without seeing anything else. She couldn't stay here. It was too much the same.

Matthew turned to her when she entered. He smiled.

She stared at the smile as a strange warmth filled her chest.

"Home." Matthew pointed an elegant red pen he held in his hand at a framed picture on the low dresser he stood by.

Ashley stepped closer.

A younger Matthew sat in front of a smiling couple. The woman had her arms around Matthew and the man wrapped his arms around her.

Hold on. Ashley knew that woman. And the man.

"Jones." She gave the agent a firm stare. "I want to talk to Tiernan."

"Your wish is my command." Tiernan walked in with a smirk to match his mock bow.

She should've known he would follow her. She pointed at the photo. "Their name isn't Haase. It's Borden. They're major financial backers to the politicians in this state."

His smile dropped. "Were." He gestured with a wave toward his chest that she should come in his direction. "Would you step out into the hall, please?"

"Fine." She brushed past him and crossed her arms when she reached the hallway. Maybe now she'd finally get some answers. "Is Matthew really their son?"

Tiernan took more steps away from the door so she would follow. He turned to face her. "Yes."

"Is that why you've been doing all this cloak and dagger stuff? Does someone want to kidnap Matthew to get his parents' money?"

"I can't answer that."

"Okay. Then maybe you can tell me why in the world you would leave Matthew alone." Her voice trembled as she pointed at the room where the boy waited. "To be put in foster care as if he had no money and no connections, when you knew the whole time who he was?" The FBI couldn't be that cruel.

"We were never far away."

The hospital. The Hispanic guy who watched her outside the hospital when she took Matthew. She should've recognized him when she saw him at the FBI house last night. An agent.

Anger boiled in her belly. They knew she thought Matthew had no home and no family, and they'd left him that way.

She glared up at Tiernan. "Were you far away when he had nightmares at night, moaning and crying?"

Tiernan met her accusation with a calm gaze. "We couldn't have prevented that regardless. His parents are still gone, Ashley."

She took a step to the side, facing the railing as she sucked in a deep breath. They still shouldn't have left him alone, with no one.

"We didn't want to draw the wrong kind of attention to Matthew. It would have put him in danger if certain parties knew who he was."

She turned back to Tiernan. "That plan sure turned out well, didn't it?"

"It worked for a while."

"Before I started getting the threatening notes, you mean?"

"You weren't in danger then. They were only trying to scare you."

"Who was?"

He shook his head. "Nice try."

She pursed her lips. "So that's it, then. You take Matthew now, and my work with him is done." She tried to ignore the odd sinking feeling in her chest. "Is that the idea?"

"Not exactly."

Her gaze went to his eyes.

"You're not free to leave yet."

"What do you mean I'm not free?" She planted her hands on her hips.

"Just what I said. You have to stay a little longer."

Choosing on her own to stay for Matthew would be one thing, but no way would she let some power-hungry FBI agent hold her against her will. "Look, I get that you're used to giving orders, but I'm not one of your agents. Nobody runs my life but me. I have a job to get back to."

Tina. Ashley had forgotten about her in all this chaos. "I'm sure my coworker is wondering where I am even as we speak. We always meet Monday mornings at work."

"Tina?"

Of course. They knew all about Ashley's job, too.

"That's been taken care of."

She didn't like the sound of that. "What exactly did you do?"

"Need—"

"To-know." Ashley glared at him as she finished his sentence. "Yeah. So are you going to explain why I can't go? Am I in danger, too? Oh, wait—I bet I don't need to know that either."

The corner of his lips twitched like he wanted to smile, but he kept a straight face. "No, you're not in danger that I know of. But you might endanger Matthew if someone were to see you leave the house. You'd reveal where he is."

"I'm smarter than I look."

Tiernan's gaze roamed over her face for an uncomfortable

moment. His eyes twinkled. "I'm not sure how to safely comment on that. I think I'll plead the fifth."

"I guess you have more rights left than I do." She spun away and stalked to the staircase without looking back. How dare he try to keep her there, always commanding and telling her what to do and when to do it. She hadn't let anyone run her life since she was fifteen. She wasn't about to become anybody's doormat now.

She paused at the bottom of the staircase, squeezing the top of the round banister with her hand. Matthew didn't need her anymore. He was happy and safe. She'd done her job. Or it was done for her. Either way, she only had to worry about herself now.

Getting out of here, safe and sound, would be her next order of business.

Tiernan underestimated her, thinking she'd endanger Matthew by leaving. She'd obviously have to make sure no one saw her leave if she had to sneak out under the noses of FBI agents.

She had taken on worse odds and survived.

Her gaze went unbidden to the spacious, opulent foyer. A shudder tripped through her. It wasn't exactly the same. But her brain and memories didn't care.

She couldn't face a night there, couldn't possibly sleep. She would get out tonight.

chapter
thirteen

"Everything okay?"

Ashley shot Tiernan a glance as she went up the stairs, the agent following behind her. Did he know? He'd been watching her funny since the sun started to go down.

"Oh, sure. I love being held hostage."

He grinned. "Protective custody."

"Why are you following me? I'd like to tuck him in alone."

"Hey, I'm just on my way to bed."

She twisted to see him as she reached the top of the staircase. "You're going to bed?"

"Agents need sleep, too. Though I know we do seem almost superhuman."

She couldn't believe she actually wanted to smile at his teasing. She stifled the grin and shot him a sideways glance as he stopped at the first doorway.

"So you don't think everything's a secret, I'll tell you that we're sleeping in shifts. I get first shift tonight."

"Oh, that helps a lot. Thank you for telling me." She flashed a smile as fake as the enthusiasm infused in her voice.

"Don't stay up too late." He pointed at her from the doorway, his eyebrows arched.

"Yes, Mother." She headed toward the bedroom at the end of the hallway.

Perfect. With Tiernan sleeping, she'd have a much better shot at getting out of here. No one else seemed to watch her as closely as he did.

She stepped into the room Matthew had chosen for his nighttime sleep. Judging from the dark blue and red color scheme, twin bed, and drum set in the corner, she guessed the room had been his. Though she couldn't picture him playing the drums. Maybe they'd been his dad's.

Matthew was too busy staring at the pages of a book to look up from where he lay on the bed, tucked under the top sheet. He wasn't trying to read, was he?

"Hey, Matthew. Time to tuck you in." She made the announcement loudly enough so that any agent who might be listening would believe her story that she tucked him in every night.

She had to see him one last time. Not that she felt sad or guilty for leaving him. She just had to make sure he was okay before she left.

She sat on the edge of the bed, and the movement finally caught Matthew's attention.

His blue eyes squinched up as he smiled at her.

"I'm here to tuck you in. Do you know what that means?"

He set down the same expensive pen he'd held earlier that day and clasped his hands together with a smack.

Ashley jumped at the sound. What was he doing?

He closed his eyes and bent his head. He opened an eye. "Pway."

That'd be the day. "You go ahead."

He closed his eyes again, apparently unfazed as he muttered unintelligible words for what felt like five minutes.

When he finally stopped and opened his eyes, Ashley had figured out what to do next. She could read him a story. "What book do you have there?"

He picked up the pen that looked like it cost about a

hundred wasteful bucks and nodded as if that answered her question.

"May I see it?" She reached for the book. The outside layer on the cover was torn and faded, making the title, if there had been one, unreadable. She opened the book to the middle.

Colorful illustrations decorated the pages, along with words printed at the bottoms of each frame that showcased a picture.

"What you meant for evil, God meant for good," Joseph said.

A Bible with pictures? Ashley slammed the book shut and shoved it away from her on the bed.

"Wead."

She could pretend she thought he meant to pluck out nasty plants from the garden. "No. I don't want to read it."

"Wead." His voice grew louder, and he tapped the book with his fingers.

"No. We're not going to read it. I can read you something else."

He grabbed the book and opened it. He pointed at the pictures and made noises like he was trying to read the words himself.

Ashley watched his features alternately scrunch up and relax, then twist in funny ways as his inflection changed far more than the actual sounds he formed.

A smile lifted her lips before she knew it was coming. He was almost cute.

"End." He looked up and smiled. He stuck out his hand like she was supposed to take it. She looked at the chubby hand she'd refused so many times. She was about to leave him—it was the least she could do. She put her hand in his, surprised by the warmth of his soft skin.

He closed his eyes again and muttered more almost-words. He'd tricked her into praying.

She'd once held another hand as its owner prayed, also in a bed. Veronica's face filled Ashley's vision, the dry lips shaping soundless words as she begged for forgiveness she didn't deserve.

Ashley waited for the bitter taste to come, but her gaze found Matthew.

His features had taken on a glow, like he was happier than she'd ever seen him as he kept his eyes closed and talked in a language only he could understand.

She had to be imagining things. But warmth seeped through her as she watched him. Maybe from the heat of his hand.

He finished talking and opened his eyes to give her that special, extra big smile.

Her heart squeezed.

She had to leave now. Before she got attached.

"Goodnight, Matthew." She leaned toward him for a brief moment and dropped her voice to a whisper. "Goodbye."

She pulled her hand from his and stood, walking from the room as quickly as she could. Good thing she was leaving tonight. He was getting to her. She only hoped her escape wasn't already too late.

Ashley fought off memories as she slowly lifted the screen from the crank-out bathroom window. The water from the shower ran in the background, like it had fifteen years ago when she'd made another escape.

Fear surged through her body as her mind went back to that night. She set the screen on the floor and leaned it against the wall with trembling fingers.

She squeezed her eyes shut, willing her thoughts to stay in the present. This wasn't the same. Not at all.

She took in a breath. Let it out.

For one thing, she had FBI agents to worry about this time. They should be so focused on keeping people out that they wouldn't think of watching for her escape. She hoped.

She cautiously leaned out the window. The lower roof jutted out a couple feet under the window before sloping downward onto another portion of roof. Shouldn't be impossible to manage.

She stretched out farther, peering into the dark night.

Cloudy skies blocked the moonlight. Good for not being seen, but it meant she couldn't spot the agents out there either. Jack and Katherine were still inside the house somewhere, and Ashley had seen two agents outside earlier. But there could be more. And she had no clue where they were stationed.

She'd just have to risk it. Leaning back in, she grabbed her overnight bag. Why hadn't she brought a duffel bag instead? The mini suitcase would be a hassle to take down the roof without clunking.

She stared at the suitcase for a second. Wasn't worth it. She'd leave it. Too bad the overnight bag hadn't held much clothing darker than blue jeans and a blue T-shirt. She'd at least had the sense to pack tennis shoes and her long-sleeved black zippered sweatshirt. She wore it zipped up tight for the dark coverage, though she'd probably get too hot.

She lifted her purse. How was she going to climb down the roof with the bag slung over her shoulder? She'd have to leave the purse, too. Digging her driver's license and credit card from her wallet as quickly as she could, she stuffed them in her pocket and returned to the window.

She climbed over the ledge and crouched on the rooftop, surveying the ground below beyond the house. The somewhat cool air kept her from sweating just yet.

Something moved near a tree on the left side of the driveway. An agent? Maybe the backyard would be the safer route. Trouble was, Ashley didn't know how many acres this estate had or where the back way led.

She knew where the Bordens lived, or at least the neighborhood. Tiernan probably didn't realize she'd figured out the house's location as soon as she saw the picture of Matthew's parents. All she had to do was reach the street at the front of the house, and she'd be home free.

Freer than Matthew.

Hiding on a rooftop in the middle of the night was hardly the right time and place for a bout of conscience. She'd never been the right person to care for him anyway. And now he didn't need her at all.

She halted her pointless thoughts and started to work her way down the roof.

The slant of the first part was steeper than she'd thought, but the slope was short, and she managed a somewhat controlled slide down to the last, flat portion.

She couldn't see or hear anyone under her. But should she go down the back of the house instead? No. If they were watching for someone dangerous, the back would be the most likely point of entry. The agents would focus there. Hopefully.

Ashley took a deep breath and walked over the more gradual descent of the roof. She moved as quietly as she could, but every tiny tap or scratch of her feet on the tiles seemed to echo like cymbals in the night air.

Her shoe touched the edge of the roof. She paused, listening.

Hushed voices floated to her from her right. Two agents talking?

She silently lowered herself to her hands and knees and crawled along the perimeter of the roof, away from the voices.

The knobby roof tiles pressed painfully into her knees as she reached what she thought was a safe distance. She listened.

Nothing.

No time like the present. She slowly turned and swung her legs off the roof, clutching the roof edge with squeezing fingers as her body dangled. At least she didn't have to hang from a flimsy gutter on this part of the roof.

She glanced down, her grip failing fast. The distance to the ground was greater than she'd expected, but she didn't have a choice. She let go and dropped, falling forward to her knees on a stone path.

She winced at the noise she made as much as from the pain in her knees and scraped hand. Pushing to her feet as quickly as she could, she squeezed back against the stone wall of the house and held her breath.

No rushing footsteps or shouts.

Had no one heard her?

Either that, or they were waiting for her to come out.

She was committed now. She had to go for it or surrender.

She snuck away from the wall, trying to keep her steps silent as she crossed the stone path that ran along the front of the house. She got to the grass as soon as she could and crouched down on the far side of a line of bushes.

Still no sounds from the house. But she couldn't shake the feeling she was being watched.

Thanks to the Bordens' apparent love of plants and landscaping, Ashley had a hidden path as she worked her way through the portion of the yard where she hadn't seen movement from the roof.

She stayed away from the driveway, moving along bushes and dashing from tree to tree, bracing to find an agent behind a trunk or see one pop out, gun drawn.

The manicured lawn, like a smooth cushion beneath her feet, kept her footsteps as hushed as the air around her.

She couldn't believe it when she reached the black chain-link perimeter fence without being stopped. But she couldn't relax yet.

The fence was tall, but not too tall to climb. She was about to start when a thought stopped her.

What if it was electrified?

She unzipped her sweatshirt and pulled it off, glad to let the cool air hit her sweating skin. Glancing around first, she took a step back and threw the sweatshirt against the top of the fence.

No flashes or surges as the sweatshirt plopped back down on the grass.

Maybe Tiernan was right. She did watch too much TV. She shook off her sweatshirt and tied it around her waist.

Finding the best handhold she could in the links of the fence, she started to climb. She should probably check to see if the noise of her climbing had attracted attention, but she had all she could do to hold her body weight against the fence and trudge upward.

She gasped for air as she reached the top and swung her leg over the fence so she could sit uncomfortably at the top and catch her breath. She seriously needed to start working out. This was way too hard.

She slid down the other side of the fence, rather than climbing, and landed on the sidewalk.

Sure enough. Looked like Oak Street. Empty and dark at this time of night, she still recognized the landscaping along the street and the width of it. Now she only had to go two streets over to the bus stop and wait for a ride.

She glanced over her shoulder at the Borden property as she walked away. That was easy.

She tried to ignore the niggling voice in her head that wanted to add, *Too easy.*

Some of the tension finally drained from Ashley's muscles as she neared her house, her legs starting to drag after her walk several blocks from the bus stop. Long night. Getting back to real life would be a pleasant change. FBI safe houses and kidnappings belonged in movies, not reality.

She passed the last bush before her yard and turned to cut across her decidedly unmanicured lawn to the front door.

Something moved. In the shadows next to her more normal neighbor's fence.

Ashley peered into the darkness.

Nothing.

She must still be too on edge. She was home. No one watched her here.

A crawling sensation traveled up her neck anyway, defying her inner reminders.

Great. Thanks to Tiernan and his buddies, she was paranoid now. She hadn't worried about being outside in the dark before all this started.

She picked up her pace to the house, trying to shake off her silly suspicions. She let out a breath as she neared the front door.

A light flashed in the living room window.

What was that? She froze.

Someone grabbed her from behind.

chapter
fourteen

Ashley tried to scream, but a strong hand covered her mouth as someone dragged her around the side of the house.

The man pressed her against the brick wall. Bile surged up her throat as memories of horror flooded her mind, blinding her to anything but raw fear.

Don't give up. Fight. She tried to breathe, tried to push away the feelings, the images that made her want to scream more or throw up everything she'd had to eat that day.

"Ashley."

Was someone saying her name?

"Ashley."

It was a whisper.

She brought her gaze to the face she didn't want to see, the face of her nightmares.

Green eyes watched her beneath a furrowed brow. Tiernan?

The pulse pounding in her ears calmed enough for her to hear what he whispered.

"Ashley, it's me. Tiernan. I'm sorry I scared you."

Apologizing for scaring her again. Had to be Tiernan.

He slowly took his hand off her mouth, but still gripped her arm. "Are you okay?"

Irritation pumped renewed energy into her veins. "Sure. I'm used to being dragged around and thrown into walls."

"Shh." He put a finger to his lips like she was a child. "And I didn't throw you."

"Do you mind?" She adopted his whisper but glared down at his hand on her bare arm.

"I'll let you go, but only if you promise not to move. And don't make any noise."

"What? You don't want to send up fireworks to announce your success?" Her voice dripped with sarcasm.

His eyebrows dipped, question in his gaze.

"Pretty fast work, finding me already."

"Nobody would be impressed by that." The corner of his lips tugged. "But you can't move because there are men inside that you don't want to meet."

"What?"

"Shh. Will you do as I say if I let you go?"

"I won't do anything you say if you keep manhandling me like some runaway kid."

"Fine." He dropped his hand, leaving her skin cold where he had touched her.

"How do you know there are men in my house?"

"Follow me. But quietly." He led the way to the front of the house, moving noiselessly. How did he know her place so well in the dark? Even she didn't remember exactly how far that bush stuck out at the corner, but he guided her around it perfectly.

They reached the edge of the window, and he waved at her to crouch down. He pointed to the bottom corner of the frame, watching as she moved close to peer inside.

Beams of light, like flashlights, swung around. Then she saw them. Two men...no, three...all wearing ski masks. One yanked cushions out of her couch while another kicked over the coffee table. The rest of the place that she could see was already ransacked, her afghan shredded and discarded on the floor.

She pulled back, her pulse racing again. "What are they looking for?"

"Not here." His whisper was barely audible as he turned to sneak around to the side of the house again.

By the time they reached the side wall, room to breathe had restored her fighting spirit. They couldn't just trash her place and get away with it. "Who are those people? Can't you stop them? You're FBI."

Tiernan's stance was relaxed, but his gaze kept moving, checking in all directions. "In the first place, there's four of them, all armed, and only one of me."

"I only saw three."

He raised an eyebrow.

"So call for backup."

"It's not as simple as on TV. We have bigger fish to fry than these punks. Arresting them would just slow our efforts to get the top man behind much more serious crimes."

"Personally, I think trashing my place is pretty serious." She glared at him with her hands on her hips. "If you're not going to do anything about it, I will."

"Not on my watch." There was no amusement in the stare he held on her. "You've caused enough trouble as it is."

"*I've* caused the trouble?"

His eyes glinted. "Keep your voice down."

"You're the one who kidnapped me and now you're hiding like a coward while my house gets trashed. Some FBI agent."

"I forgot. You always know exactly what the right thing is for everybody all the time." His voice took on a layer of steel she hadn't heard from him before. "Well, I have news for you. Running away is not the right thing. Not from the safe house today and not when you were fifteen."

She blinked at him as a jolt shot through her chest. How? How could he know about that?

"I'm going to give you a piece of advice that will save your life."

She barely heard him as her heart rammed into her ribcage. What else did he know?

"You need to follow me to the car and get in. Then I'll take you back to the safe house, where you'll stay until it's safe for you to leave." He touched her elbow.

She instinctively jerked away.

He watched her for a second, then must have made up his mind she wasn't going to run. Or he'd seen the shock she tried to hide.

"Stay close." He noiselessly led the way to a black car parked at the curb a couple houses down the street.

Ashley sat in the passenger seat in the front while he settled behind the wheel. At least five minutes of driving passed before she found her voice, or the courage to use it. But she had to find out. "How did you know?"

"You don't have to whisper anymore."

Maybe she did. She swallowed. "How did you know about...when I was fifteen?"

He swung the car into a turn onto another street lit with lamps. "I told you the FBI is very thorough."

Just how thorough? She stared out the window at the houses they passed, tiny hutches compared to the Bordens' mansion. She clenched her teeth. "You have no business talking about it. The only wrong thing about it was not running a whole lot sooner."

He was quiet for a minute, leaving her to regret having said anything. She'd only make him suspicious and too curious. Maybe he didn't know everything about it.

"I'm sorry."

She jerked her gaze to his profile. "You should be sorry about what's happening to all my things and my house."

He glanced at her face like he wasn't hearing her. "Are you hurt?" Another try at distracting her.

"No."

"There's a scratch on your cheek."

Her hand went to the mark, and she winced at the sting

when her fingers touched a small cut. "Oh, that. Somebody dragged me around the house." She gave him a phony smile.

He didn't smile back. His eyebrows pulled together. "You could have been hurt a lot worse."

"Sure, thanks to you. I can think of only one reason four masked men would want to tear up my house, and it's spelled F-B-I."

He stared at the road, his lips lowering into a frown. "They weren't after you."

"And I'm supposed to believe that, why?" She shifted in the seat to face him better. "It's well past time I knew everything. If I'm going to get killed, I'd like to know what I'm dying for. For starters, I want to know who those men—"

"You're in no position to make demands." His voice came out sharp as he shot a glare in her direction. "You've proven you can't be trusted."

"I—"

"If you do as you're told, I can keep you safe. You just need to stay with me and not run off again."

"For how long? A year?"

He let out a long breath, and his tone was calmer when he spoke. "Until we find some answers."

"I want some answers right now. I know those men were looking for something." She watched him for any sign, a twitch, anything to indicate she'd hit close to the truth. "Since my only connection to whatever is going on is Matthew, I'm assuming all this has something to do with him."

Tiernan didn't even blink.

"Were they trying to find him?"

No response.

"Or maybe they were hoping to find him through a clue I might have left at the house?"

Still nothing, other than angling the wheel for another turn. But he didn't say no. Did that mean she was right? If they were looking for Matthew, then...

"Do they want to kill him?" The concern that accompanied

her thoughts must have leaked into her voice, since Tiernan finally looked at her.

"No." His voice was soft, gentle. He looked at the road. "Not yet."

She cleared her throat. "Then they want the same thing you do. They want to get some sort of information out of him."

"We have to get it first." His deeper tone matched his tightened grip on the wheel. "If you want to end this and get out of danger, you have to find out what Matthew knows about something his parents hid before they died."

Finally, a tiny bit of information. "Were they criminals?"

"I can't answer that." He glanced at her. "But I need you to tell me everything Matthew has said to you and everything he says in the future."

Same old story. She glared out the side window. "Yeah. Got that the first time."

"Has he said anything about someone named Mike?"

Who was Mike? She kept the question to herself. "No."

"Okay. Tell me if he does. And you can get more specific with him. Ask him about something his parents might have hidden. We're hoping he knows."

She turned her head to look at Tiernan.

His chiseled jaw clenched. Did he care about every case this much?

"It would help if I knew what I was looking for."

He shook his head. "Believe me, it's better for you if you don't. You only need to do what I'm asking you to, and we all might get out of this alive."

Alive? She swallowed. "If our lives depend on a boy with Down syndrome, we're in bad shape. He barely knows how to dress himself let alone information about hidden secrets." She felt Tiernan's glance in the silence.

"You might be surprised." A hint of the man's usual smile started to curve his lips. "Sometimes I think Matthew knows more than any of us."

An opinion that belonged on an inspirational poster along with Matthew's favorite sayings. But if Ashley's life really depended on the kid, she'd better hope the FBI agent was somehow, impossibly, right.

The sun rose on the horizon when they pulled up to the Bordens' mansion, almost the same time as the morning before. The drive there never should have taken two hours, but Tiernan had insisted on including several detours to make sure they didn't bring a tail to the house.

Ashley headed directly for the mansion before Tiernan could order her to go inside.

The foyer stood empty and quiet as she entered. Was anyone awake yet?

"Someone wants to see you."

She glanced behind her as Tiernan nodded at something toward the ceiling. She turned back to follow his gaze.

Matthew stood at the railing of the balcony above them, his red cap askew. He waved wildly with that special smile on his funny face.

A laugh burst through Ashley's lips before she knew it was coming.

The feel of Tiernan's gaze sobered her up quickly. Wouldn't do her any good if he thought she'd become too attached to the boy.

Katherine appeared next to Matthew and said something to him. She went to the stairs, and Matthew followed her down.

He beamed his smile at Ashley when he reached the bottom. He held the picture Bible under one arm and stuck his other hand out like he wanted her to take it.

"No." Ashley shook her head.

He hopped a few steps in front of her and beckoned with the hand instead.

"We were about to watch his home movies." Katherine's tone was colder than usual. "He probably wants you to come along."

"Okay." Ashley fell in step alongside Katherine as they followed Matthew's skipping path through parts of the house Ashley hadn't seen before. This was hardly the innocent, fun activity Matthew thought it was. "Home movies with a purpose, huh?"

Katherine gave her a glance as they kept walking. Was that surprise in her dark eyes?

"Tiernan told me everything."

"I doubt it." Her superior smirk returned. "Pretty stupid what you did, leaving like that. You're lucky you didn't get killed."

So that's how it was. Ashley faked a sweet smile. "I was told I wasn't in danger."

A few feet ahead of them, Matthew stopped at a closed door and reached to open it.

"Hold it." Katherine barked the order. "Just wait a second." She somewhat gently pulled Matthew away from the door and opened it herself, peering through the opening like a killer waited on the other side.

"Okay. It's clear." She went inside herself and headed down the flight of stairs Ashley could see as she got closer to the doorway.

Katherine took her job way too seriously. Some people were like that. Their work gave them a sense of importance they wouldn't have otherwise. The agent just had to check the stairs even though the whole house had been cleared before Matthew even got there.

Ashley shook her head as she followed the boy down the stairs.

When she reached the bottom, she stopped. This basement was no ordinary basement. She moved her gaze across the expansive room accessorized with a pool table, two arcade games, and a bar.

"Theater's this way." Katherine followed Matthew, who started to jog and disappeared around the corner of the curved bar.

Theater? Ashley couldn't believe her eyes when she stepped through the doorway Matthew had taken.

Katherine wasn't exaggerating. Theater-style seats were lined up in rows that started high at the back and sloped downward toward the front of the room where a huge movie screen took up the whole wall. A real movie theater in a house? The Bordens had everything.

Matthew shouted some sort of exclamation as he bounced up and down in a seat in the middle row.

Everything except a normal, healthy child.

Ashley started down the steps toward him.

"Somebody's excited."

She startled inwardly at the man's voice.

Agent Jones grinned as he stuck his head out from a doorway near the front movie-screen wall. He nodded to Matthew.

Ashley shrugged. "Must like movies."

"I should have them running in a minute. Just trying to figure out what all this equipment is for." He vanished for a second, then looked out again. "I was sorry to hear about your place." He gave her a sympathetic frown. "At least you weren't home when they hit. You could've been hurt."

Amazing. The first kind words she'd ever gotten from an FBI agent. "Thanks." She glanced up to the back of the room, but there was no sign of Katherine. That was a relief. If the woman had disliked Ashley before, she was downright hostile now. Probably chafing over Ashley's escape right under their noses.

Ashley enjoyed a smug smile as she sat down two chairs away from Matthew.

A movie popped onto the giant screen.

"Got it!" Jones stepped into the theater to look at his workmanship.

The Bordens—younger than Ashley had ever seen them in pictures—appeared to be talking to the camera without sound.

"Can you hear it?" Jones glanced in Ashley's direction.

"No." Tiernan's voice suddenly answered from a couple feet away, but Ashley stopped herself from jumping this time.

Jones waved and disappeared through the doorway, apparently to adjust the volume.

Tiernan smiled at Ashley as he sank into the seat next to her. "I love home movies, don't you?"

The question seemed rhetorical, which was a good thing since his proximity left her too distracted to answer. Was he trying to make her uncomfortable?

The lights dimmed, and Ashley vaguely registered Jones walking away from a dimmer switch and sitting in the front row.

The smell of aftershave and something else drifted to her. Cologne? Heat traveled up her neck to her face. Could he smell her? She probably stank. She hadn't taken a shower for two days, thanks to him dragging her all over the place. She fingered her oily hair.

"Mama!" Matthew shouted unnecessarily loudly, but at least he broke through Ashley's distraction and got her to concentrate on the movie.

The house the Bordens were at looked like the same one Ashley sat in now. Mrs. Borden, looking about fifteen years older than most parents of a newborn, held a baby as the camera jerkily zoomed in on her face. She smiled, but it was a tired try at happiness that didn't reach her eyes, red and puffy as if from crying.

The camera dropped to film the baby.

No mistaking those slanted eyes, odd nose, and funny mouth.

"This is Matthew." The man's voice came from behind the camera.

"Da." Matthew made the observation quietly this time.

Ashley glanced at the teenager beside her as he stared at the screen.

His mouth hung open. He wasn't smiling, but he wasn't crying either. Didn't even look sad. Maybe he didn't understand the loss after all.

The man in the video, Mr. Borden apparently, spoke again. "This is Matthew's first day at home. The doctor told us before he was born that he was going to be...special. And now we see what he meant, right honey?"

Disgust crawled up Ashley's throat. They had known and still let it happen.

The camera swung up to the mother, who nodded like she was supposed to, but she couldn't stop a sniff and the slight tremble of her lips as she smiled.

The image cut and a new one took its place.

"Happy birthday to you..."

Two adult voices behind the camera sang the classic birthday song to a toddler-sized Matthew, who whacked a spoon against the highchair tray.

"Matthew, look up here," a cheerful woman's voice called.

He kept hitting the spoon on the wood without looking up.

She came into view. Mrs. Borden. She laughed as she approached Matthew and gently grasped his hand with the spoon. "Somebody's hungry for cake." The smile she tossed at the camera looked far more real than her others from before.

Ashley's frown deepened as she watched the videos strung together. No other kids at any of the birthday parties as Matthew grew older. Not even more family members. Always just the three of them.

They had filmed Matthew's first day at school and then his first day at home school, likely because he couldn't learn what the real school tried to teach him. They filmed his attempts at pottery, painting, numbers, shapes. He couldn't get any of it, even as he grew older and bigger.

"Great folks, huh?" Tiernan's quiet question squirted like a shot of fuel on the fire growing inside Ashley's mind.

"Are you kidding me?" She turned her glare on him.

Whoa, his face was closer than she'd realized.

She darted her gaze to the screen again, not letting his attractive features defuse her outrage. "What they did to him was cruel. How could they have him when they knew he would suffer and never be happy? The boy in that video will never be independent, self-sufficient, never be able to love or think like everyone else. He makes everyone uncomfortable wherever he goes—"

"Wait a second. Are you saying they should have killed him as a baby?"

"I'm saying they should've aborted the fetus. It would have been the most loving thing they could have done."

Tiernan's voice rose along with hers. "You can't watch these videos and tell me his parents didn't love him."

She crossed her arms in front of her. "Not enough. Real love isn't selfish. If they really loved him, they wouldn't have brought him into the world to suffer for his whole life."

He shook his head like he was in disbelief. "And that's all you got out of watching these videos?"

She went ahead and met his gaze, trying to hold on to her fighting spirit with his green irises so close to hers. "What were we supposed to get out of it? Secrets for the FBI?"

He didn't so much as blink at her challenge as he stared into her eyes.

"Hide!"

Ashley turned to see what had excited Matthew this time, taking in a breath she hadn't realized she needed so badly.

An image of a boat flashed on the screen, then changed to a shot of Mrs. Borden and Matthew on the moving vessel, the boy giggling as water sprayed his face and his mother wrapped her arm around his shoulders, laughing.

"He said 'hide.'" The irritation had left Tiernan's voice, which he lowered to a conspiratorial whisper. He leaned disconcertingly close to Ashley's ear. "Do you think he might be—"

"Hide go see?" This time, Matthew turned to smile at Ashley and Tiernan, his eyelids drawing up with his eyebrows in question.

"Nope." She glanced at Tiernan as she stood. She wasn't about to risk a repeat of whatever had just happened between them. "He got bored. So much for the trip down memory lane."

Tiernan didn't stand. He just looked up at her, his long legs blocking her escape route. "Maybe the photo albums would be more effective."

"You seriously think he's going to recognize a hiding spot from pictures?"

"Sure. Why not?"

The man seemed to think Matthew was like any other sixteen-year-old.

"Want to look at pictures, Matthew?" Tiernan tilted his head back to see the boy past Ashley.

The lights brightened to full strength again, thanks to Jones at the switch.

"Hide go see."

Ashley glanced down at Tiernan. "I don't think you're going to get him to do anything else."

"That's okay. Hide and seek might prove useful, too."

"Were you born this optimistic, or did someone teach you to be so annoying?"

"I've been told it's charming." He winked at her.

She refused to give him a reaction, fighting the smile that tugged at her lips. "You've been lied to."

"Ouch." He stood, mercifully turning away and heading out of the row to the middle aisle. "Just for that, Matthew and I will hide, and you get to find us."

So he could jump out and scare her? No, thank you. "I thought it wouldn't be safe for Matthew to hide alone."

Tiernan paused in the aisle and looked at her. "I'm going with him. We'll hide in the same spot together."

"Why can't I hide with him?"

"Now who's being annoying? Matthew can't get past you, by the way." Tiernan pointed past her shoulders.

The boy stood inches behind her, his features squeezing together like he'd been trying to puzzle out an escape route.

Too bad the lights weren't still low enough to hide the flush that heated her cheeks. She straightened the bill of Matthew's cap as an excuse to be standing there and turned to walk out of the row and up the stairs of the aisle.

When they stepped outside the theater, she looked at Matthew. "Do you want me to hide with you?"

He pointed a chubby finger at her. "Find."

Sure. Now he suddenly knew how to communicate.

Tiernan chuckled. "Looks like it's unanimous."

"Fine."

The agent probably only wanted to go with Matthew so he'd be there if the boy revealed some hiding place the FBI hadn't found.

She heaved a sigh and covered her eyes with her hands. "Ten, nine, ei—"

"Whoa, wait. That's not fair." The laughter in Tiernan's voice threatened to bring a smile to her face that would ruin her resigned expression.

She turned away to hide her reaction and kept counting down from ten.

"Start over. From one hundred this time."

"One hundred?" She kept her hands on her face.

"It's a big house!" Tiernan shouted the words from farther away. He must be getting Matthew to move quickly.

Wonderful. She had hoped they were only going to hide in the basement. A game of hide and seek in a house this size could take all day.

"Ninety-nine…ninety-eight…ninety-seven…" Never thought she'd be playing this game at thirty. Made her feel more like a twelve-year-old playing with friends. The reminder of childhood sent her mind in an unsafe direction.

She opened her eyes to keep from seeing any of the memories that threatened to push in.

Darkness surrounded her.

"Hello?" Her call went unanswered. "I'm still down here." Had Tiernan turned off the lights without thinking?

She forgot what number she was supposed to be at in her count as she peered into the darkness, trying to make out something of the furniture in the room. Anything would do. Couldn't the Bordens have put windows in their basement if they were so rich?

She couldn't stand there all day. Tiernan would probably think she was still trying to find them even if she was missing for an hour.

Extending her hands out in front of her, she slowly walked forward, bracing herself to hit something.

A noise came from behind.

She jerked toward it. "Hello?" Sounded like it came from the far end of the room. "Is someone there?"

She widened her eyes as she looked in that direction, but it didn't help. Tucking her hair behind her ears, she listened.

Nothing.

Must have imagined the noise. She started forward again, rubbing her moist palm on the back of her neck where her skin tingled.

If she was headed in the right direction, the staircase shouldn't be more than ten feet away now. Or twenty?

She slammed her toe into something hard. She swore and lowered her hands to feel what she had hit. A chair? She must have stubbed her foot on the leg of it. Pain surged through her toe as she continued on.

A sound reached her ears. Like a pool ball rolling across the table right next to her.

She was not alone.

chapter
fifteen

Ashley's blood ran cold as she froze, waiting to be grabbed by whoever was there. Or would they just stab her and hide her body in the basement? Were they after Matthew and she happened to be in the wrong place at the wrong time?

She should get ready to defend herself, but she couldn't find any weapon in the dark.

A minute passed. Or was it only half that?

Time seemed to crawl at a snail's pace as she waited.

Nothing happened.

Maybe something had distracted the attacker. Maybe she had a chance.

She rushed forward to where she thought the stairs should be, not stopping even when her sore toe hit another object. She waved her hands in front of her.

Her fingers grazed something. The end of a wall. She felt around to the other side of it.

The railing.

She stumbled up onto the stairs.

A narrow strip of light peeked through under the door at the top. Her gaze locked on it as she climbed.

She reached the door and grasped the knob with clammy fingers. She shoved open the door and stumbled into the light with a gulping breath like it was oxygen and she'd been drowning.

She could turn on the light with the switch at the top of the stairs and find out who was down there, but it'd be smarter to get an armed agent to check it out. That's what they were paid for.

She glanced down the hallway in one direction and the other way toward the back staircase that led upstairs. Where was everyone?

She closed the door to the basement and checked the knob. No lock.

Putting as much distance as she could between herself and the basement seemed like a good idea. She had to find Tiernan and Matthew. And not for some silly game.

They probably wouldn't have gone up another staircase since that wasn't Matthew's favorite thing to do.

She took the hallway, following the path back the way Katherine had led them when they'd gone to the basement. She stopped to check behind curtains and couches, under tables and chairs, but couldn't find a soul. Was everyone hiding? Not funny.

She finally reached the front entryway and spotted Katherine in the sitting room across the foyer. Never thought she'd be glad to see that particular agent.

Ashley passed the front door and stopped at the room where Katherine sat in a wingback chair, reading a book.

"There's someone in the basement."

Katherine looked up with a decidedly uninterested gaze.

"I mean, an intruder. The lights went off, and I heard noises."

"Okay." Katherine's dark eyes watched Ashley closely, like she was trying to gauge if the subject was lying. Apparently making a judgment call, she set her book down and stood. "I'll check it out. Might've just been a blown fuse."

Ashley nodded, trying not to show her surprise that

Katherine would act on what she said. "Have you seen Matthew or Tiernan?"

Katherine passed Ashley on her way out of the room. "They went upstairs a few minutes ago." The agent didn't look back as she confidently headed for the basement.

Ashley hurried to the staircase in the foyer and jogged up the steps. She scanned the empty balcony when she reached the top. Where would Matthew hide up here? His bedroom seemed the best guess. She glanced in the other rooms as she passed them, just in case.

When she reached his bedroom, she flicked on the light.

No one was there. At least, not that she could see right away. But if they'd come up here, they had to be somewhere.

She stepped inside and crouched on the floor to check under the bed. Then she tried under the dresser and in the small walk-in closet.

Nothing.

Maybe the heavy curtains that hung on either side of the window would be a good bet. She started toward them.

Someone giggled.

Matthew? It certainly didn't sound ominous, like whoever had followed her in the basement.

An odd noise came from the same direction, like someone trying to say an unrecognizable word.

"Shh." Had to be Tiernan shushing Matthew.

But where were they?

"Find!" Matthew's exclamation seemed to come from behind the bookcase against one wall.

"I think he wants you to find us." Amusement was audible in Tiernan's voice, muffled though it was. "Pull out the red book."

Ashley went to the bookcase and scanned the shelves.

"Second shelf down on the right."

She grabbed the top of the hardcover book and pulled, but instead of coming off the shelf, it only tilted, anchored at the bottom.

Something clicked, and the shelves slowly slid to the left, revealing a metal door in the wall.

Unbelievable. They seriously had a secret room? "Now what?"

"Hang on." No more sound came from the room for a few seconds. Then the door slid open.

"Woo!" Matthew lunged for Ashley, reaching his arms out.

"No." She stepped back, keeping him at a distance with her hands. "No hugs."

"Come here, big guy." Tiernan grabbed Matthew around the shoulders and pulled him into a sideways hug.

Matthew laughed as he leaned into the man.

"So it worked."

Tiernan raised his eyebrows at Ashley.

"He led you to a hidden room." She glanced at the padded chairs, rug, and shelves with canned goods on them. "Did you find what you were looking for in here?"

Tiernan shook his head. "We'd already found this spot. It's a safe room his parents had built. They must have taught him to hide in here so they could tell him to play hide and seek if there was ever any danger." He gave the bill of Matthew's cap a little tug, leaving it crooked again. "But Matthew did just what I hoped. He found a special hiding place. Maybe if we play again, he'll show me a new place we haven't found."

She reached to straighten the cap. "I don't think that's a good idea right now."

Tiernan followed her movements with his gaze as he smiled. "Aw, come on. I'll let you hide with him if you want."

"No, I mean because there's someone in the basement. Or there was."

His mouth firmed in a straight line. "I assume you mean someone who wasn't supposed to be there?"

She nodded. "Right after you left, I opened my eyes, and the basement was completely dark. I could barely find my way to the stairs, but I'm sure I heard someone down there with me."

He lightly touched her forearm as he looked deeply into her eyes. "You're not hurt?"

She swallowed. "No."

"Okay." He nodded grimly and took his feather-weight fingers away from her arm. "Did you tell anyone about this?" He pulled a radio earpiece out of his pocket and slipped it over his ear.

"Katherine. She went to look."

"Chicago to Cities." He waited.

"Do you think we should—"

He held up a finger as he put his other hand on the earpiece, apparently listening. "Copy that. 10-4." He looked at Ashley. "She said it's clear down there. Nothing changed except two chairs. One was moved and the other knocked over."

Heat rushed to Ashley's cheeks. "I probably did that. It was dark."

"Are you positive you heard someone down there?"

Did he doubt her now, too? No, the eyes that watched her were steady and concerned, not judgmental. She sighed. "I thought so. I'm sure I heard something, but I suppose it could have been a stack of something falling over or maybe the air conditioning kicking in." Though that wouldn't explain the pool ball.

He nodded, his gaze still not leaving her face. "They do have a loud unit down there. I'll have the team do another sweep inside and outside, just in case."

At least he took her seriously. Still, she started to feel like she was under interrogation. She could have been wrong.

She swung her gaze to Matthew.

He still held his Bible in one hand. With his other hand, he fiddled with the top of the red pen Ashley hadn't noticed he carried in his pants' pocket.

"Why does he keep those things with him all the time?"

Tiernan glanced in the direction of her gaze. He smiled. "I

guess they're important to him. And, yes, we did check them thoroughly for anything hidden."

She nodded, though she hadn't actually thought of that possibility yet.

"Matthew, how about we look at some photo albums now?"

The boy smiled at Tiernan like whatever he wanted was perfect.

Great. Tiernan already thought too much of his own opinions without the hero worship.

The over-confident agent had Ashley and Matthew sit on the couch in the sitting room that joined Matthew's room to his parents'. Tiernan picked up a couple hefty photo albums from the top of a table along the wall and went back to the couch, plopping down on the other side of Matthew.

He opened an album on Matthew's lap, and Ashley got another look at the boy's childhood with his parents. Judging from appearances, Mrs. Borden had to have been in her mid-forties when she had Matthew. She should have known better.

Ashley glanced around Matthew to see Tiernan's reaction to the pictures.

His gaze was fixed across the room, on the doorway to the hall, and he had put his earpiece back on. He must have felt her gaze, because he glanced at her and smiled, then looked down at the album.

A flutter stirred up the contents of her stomach. Was he worried about the visitor in the basement?

She tried to focus on the photos, watching for any clues to whatever it was they were looking for as Matthew turned the pages. She'd be all for finding out Matthew's secret if it meant getting out of here. Any more of this kind of stress and she'd be a wreck.

Tiernan glanced at the door again.

Ashley couldn't take it. "Do you think we aren't safe here anymore?"

He met her gaze for a moment. "If it wasn't safe, we wouldn't still be here."

She frowned. Would he lie to her?

His lips curved in a small smile. "Trust me."

The man who kidnapped her and wouldn't tell her why, who had more secrets than a girls' slumber party? She looked at those green eyes. "I will when you trust me."

He looked away.

Was she still dreaming? Ashley had to wonder when she was immersed in an idyllic morning of sleeping in, taking a leisurely hot shower, and being greeted by Matthew's bright smile on the indoor balcony of an almost-mansion.

The feeling stayed with her for the whole first part of the day. She had an early lunch with Matthew—fast-food burgers Jones had brought—and listened to his attempt at playing the drums. Pretty awful, but she had to hold back a laugh at the way he bounced his head to some rhythm only he could hear, his lips puckered with concentration.

No sign of Tiernan today. Ashley stopped herself twice from asking the other agents where he was. He might think she cared if he heard she'd asked.

The chaotic booming of the drums started to grate on Ashley's nerves. What was she still doing here, anyway? It's not like she'd landed in some fairytale and could stay forever. Neither could Matthew. Not if Tiernan's story about the danger to the teen was true.

Ashley tucked her hair behind one ear and looked around Matthew's bedroom. Where would she hide something important if she were the Bordens? Not in Matthew's room, that was for sure. He might find it and lose or wreck it somehow.

But she shouldn't waste time trying to think of the logical place. The FBI likely would have thought of all such hiding spots. What they couldn't have done much of was pump

Special Target

Matthew. Maybe the direct approach would yield some results.

"Matthew." She walked over to the drums, repeating his name. When he didn't respond, she touched his shoulder.

He stopped pounding the drums and looked up at her from under a crooked bill.

She straightened the cap. "I have a question for you." She moistened her lips, searching for the right wording he might understand. "Where do you keep your most special things?"

He stared at her, his blue eyes blank.

"Like..." Her gaze fell on the shiny red pen that stuck out of his pocket. "Like your pen. Where do you hide your pen, Matthew? When you don't want anyone to find it."

He pulled the pen out of his pocket and stared at it.

"What if you wanted to keep your pen safe? Where would you put it? Where does the pen go?"

He smiled and stood, heading for the door with a purposeful, but awkward, stride. Had he understood her?

Her pulse sped up as she trailed his progression across the indoor balcony, down the stairs and to the left. He seemed to be following the same route Katherine had taken yesterday.

Not the basement again. Ashley really didn't want to return there.

Matthew looked back at her from the hallway and grunted, swinging his hand like he wanted her to move faster. Did he know he was about to show her something important?

She picked up her pace and reached him as he turned and went through a doorway off the hall.

A formal, almost elegant office met Ashley's gaze. Sunlight streamed into the room through two large windows, highlighting two wooden desks placed at angles facing each other, suggesting the users wanted visibility of each other rather than privacy.

"Was this your parents' office?"

Matthew paid no attention as he rushed to one of the desks. His forehead wrinkled with concentration as he bent over the surface and placed his red pen in a standing holder. The holder was a matching color, like it belonged with the pen. He straightened and stuck his hand out toward the desk with a smile. "Mine."

"The desk is yours?" That couldn't be right.

He grabbed the pen and held it up. "Mine."

"Okay, Matthew." All that excitement, and she'd only been able to establish that the pen was his. Wonderful.

Maybe it wasn't all a loss. She could check out the office while she was there. Maybe even the brilliant FBI could have missed something.

So which parent had the desk with the red pen? The same picture of Matthew and his family that she'd seen upstairs perched next to the pen holder. Either parent could have had that, but most likely the mother.

She pulled out the middle desk drawer.

Empty.

She tried one of the side drawers, then the other one. All empty. Had the FBI cleaned them out?

In a child pornography case she'd been involved in, investigators had found incriminating photos caught at the back of a drawer the perpetrator had hastily cleaned out. It was possible.

Ashley opened the middle drawer again and bent slightly as she reached her hand in. She squeezed her fingers through the small gap above the back of the drawer.

Bingo.

Her fingers brushed a bit of something. Paper? She twisted her fingers, wincing as they scraped the rough wood. She finally grasped the paper and tugged it out.

The piece of paper looked like it had been torn off a bigger sheet. Part of a website address lined the bottom of the scrap. Maybe it was from an online article someone had printed?

Above the web address was the end of another line of print: *Abelli stated the rumors were...*

The air whooshed from Ashley's lungs like she'd been

kicked in the stomach. She started to sway. She gripped the edge of the desk.

It could be anyone. Didn't have to be him. Abelli was a common enough name. In Italy.

She couldn't feel her fingers squeezing the desk. She'd pass out if she didn't breathe.

Footsteps approaching in the hallway jolted her out of her sinking spiral.

She took in air, trying to get her breathing back to normal as she stuffed the paper into the front pocket of her jeans.

Jones appeared in the doorway.

She could have sighed with relief. Tiernan would have seen she was acting strangely. With Jones, she had a chance to cover with a smile.

The agent's gaze moved to the open desk drawer in front of her, then to her face. "I'm afraid we've checked the obvious places already." His grin made a joke of the comment.

"I know. Matthew was just showing me where he keeps his pen."

"What's he doing now?"

Ashley turned to Matthew, who scribbled with the pen on the brown desk pad. "Matthew!" She stared at the red ink streaked all over the pad. "You don't draw on desks." She stuck out her hand, palm up. "Give me the pen before you get into more trouble."

"Mine." He jerked the pen against his chest with a deep frown.

She blinked at him. He'd never disobeyed her before.

"Technically, Matthew does own the place, so he can really do whatever he wants to the stuff."

"That's ridiculous. We all know he's not capable of owning a house." She narrowed her eyes at Matthew. "And he should use paper." She went to the printer on the stand against a wall and pulled out white paper from the tray.

She took it to the desk and slapped it down. "Draw on that. Not the desk."

A smile replaced the frown as Matthew sat on the swivel chair and started to scribble on the paper.

"Maybe you should ask him to draw his hiding spot."

She arched her eyebrow at Jones. "Have you seen his drawing?"

He shrugged.

"I suppose it's worth a shot." She looked down at the unrecognizable lines on the boy's page. "Matthew, can you draw your favorite hiding spot? Where do you hide your favorite things when you want to keep them safe?"

Matthew looked up at her. "Hide?"

She tucked her hair behind her ear on one side. "No, not hide and go seek. Where do you hide...this pen?" She tapped the red pen in his hand.

Matthew ducked his head again, scratching more lines across the page.

She sighed. "Okay. Let's try this. Matthew, Jack is going to take your pen." She infused her voice with enough excitement to hopefully draw Matthew's attention. "You better hide it somewhere quick so Jack won't get the pen."

Jack winked at Ashley and stepped forward, reaching his hand out as if taking the pen in slow motion.

Matthew shot to his feet, the chair scooting backward on its wheels behind him. He clutched the pen in his hand and started to pace back and forth along the wall by the desk.

Oops. "It's okay, Matthew. Calm down." How was she supposed to know the little charade would upset him? But maybe this would finally get the results they needed so desperately. She had to get out of here...and keep Matthew safe, of course. "Just hide the pen quickly, Matthew, and it will be safe. Jack won't be able to take it if you hide it."

Matthew's lips pushed out as he looked at Jack, then at the pen, then back to Jack. The boy stepped forward and held the pen across the desk, toward Jack.

What was he doing?

Special Target

"Like him." Matthew looked down, still holding out the pen as a deep frown tugged his lips.

Ashley sighed to cover the squeezing of her heart. So much for that idea.

"Thanks, mate, but I don't want your pen."

Matthew continued to point the pen toward Jack.

The agent glanced helplessly at Ashley. "Really, I don't want your pen." Jack waved his hands, palms out in front of his chest.

Matthew still didn't move.

She shook her head. "He doesn't get it. You'll have to take it."

Jack took the pen out of Matthew's hand, then quickly gave it back.

The boy's eyes scrunched with his big smile. He clutched the pen and hugged it to his chest. "Mine."

"Why does he like that pen so much?" She didn't realize she'd spoken the question out loud until Jack answered.

"I reckon it was his mum's. That's her desk there with the red pen holder."

Did Matthew really know that? Did he remember? Maybe he simply liked a shiny, red pen.

One thing was sure, she'd never get out of here depending on Matthew's knowledge of anything.

Shouts came from outside the windows. A blur of a man ran past. Tiernan?

"Hold it." Jack pressed a hand to his earpiece. "There's been a perimeter breach." He pointed at Ashley as he moved to the door. "Stay with the boy."

Matthew pressed his hands over his ears. The yelling hadn't been loud from this distance, but it was apparently enough to stress him.

She stepped closer and gently touched his arm. "It's okay. We'll be fine." Her racing heart made a liar of her calm tone. Should she hide him somewhere? What if someone got in the house and found them?

A noise at the door made her start.

Katherine.

"Come with me." The agent adjusted her radio earpiece as she disappeared out of the doorway.

Ashley kept a light hold on Matthew's arm and followed Katherine.

Matthew suddenly tried to pull away from Ashley, starting to whine.

What was wrong with him?

He reached back toward the office as Ashley tried to keep following Katherine. "Mine, mine."

Katherine glanced back. "What's the problem? We need to move now."

Ashley struggled to keep her hold on the strong boy. "He must have dropped his pen." She scanned his pockets. No sign of the pen.

Katherine shook her head. "There's no time to look for it." She closed the gap to Matthew and grabbed his other side. "Matthew. Follow us now. I'll take care of you. We have to hide."

"Hide go see?" He finally turned the right direction.

Katherine nodded as she pulled him forward. "That's right. We're hiding together."

"What's happening?" Ashley hurried to match Katherine's brisk pace, trying to keep Matthew in step at the same time.

"We don't know for sure yet." Katherine let go of Matthew and moved ahead of them.

Exasperation mixed with Ashley's fear. "We might be about to get killed. Is that really need-to-know?"

Katherine stopped at a door and opened it.

Wait. Wasn't that the door to the basement? The last place Ashley would feel safe, especially with Katherine as her protection.

The agent met Ashley's gaze as she held the door. "I honestly don't know what's happening. There's been a breach. That's all I know." The understanding that filled her dark eyes made her seem almost human. "You're going to have to trust me. I'm here to keep you and Matthew safe."

Familiar line. Did the FBI teach that to all their agents?

"Now, follow me." Katherine's tone was as hard as ever. She took out her gun as she led the way down the stairs.

Ashley had Matthew go first, then followed, putting herself at the rear.

"Close the door." Katherine glanced up the stairs from the bottom.

Ashley went back up to shut the door, then met Matthew and Katherine at the base.

The agent scanned the room with her gaze, still holding the gun, now down at her side. She started walking toward the theater like the other day. But the circumstances weren't nearly so relaxed.

Katherine turned on the lights with a switch inside the theater room, then pointed to the rows of seats. "Take Matthew, and both of you lay down on the floor between two of those middle rows."

Ashley nodded and guided the boy to where Katherine had said. "Hide right here, okay? Lay down like this, so no one will see you."

Matthew chose a good moment to go back to his obedient self, stretching out between the rows without hesitation.

Ashley glanced toward the top of the room to check for Katherine.

The agent raised her gun higher and pressed her back against the wall by the closed door. She glanced in Ashley's direction. "Keep Matthew down and quiet no matter what. Especially if you hear shooting."

She turned off the lights.

chapter
sixteen

Ashley strained to hear past the sound of Matthew's breathing and the rapid beating of her heart. How long had they waited in the dark? Seemed at least thirty minutes, but maybe it was only ten. Hard to tell when each minute felt like an eternity.

"Find." Matthew's loud voice punctured the silence like a needle in a balloon.

"Shh." She touched the top of his head, glad she had lain with her head by his so she could talk to him or hold him down, if necessary. "We don't want them to find us yet."

"Quiet," Katherine hissed from her position next to the door.

Ashley had only whispered. She was about to sit up and send the agent a glare, but a noise stopped her.

Was someone outside the theater? Sounded like footsteps.

Ashley pressed her hand against the side of Matthew's head, willing him to keep quieter than the pounding in her ears.

She held her breath as the footsteps stopped by the door.

Katherine better know how to use that gun.

"Cities?" A man's voice. Tiernan? "You in there?"

"Code in." Katherine's voice was hard and steady, as if she hadn't been scared at all.

"Windy city."

"You got it."

Ashley quietly pushed up to a sitting position as the lights came on. She peered over the seats.

Tiernan walked in and spotted her. He waved with a smile like he'd just shown up for a barbecue. "It's all clear. You can come out now."

"Find." Matthew kept his face against the floor.

Ashley glanced at Tiernan, her stomach still in knots. "He wants you to find him."

"Ah." Tiernan headed down the stairs that divided the rows of seats. "Now where could Matthew be? He's such a good hider." Tiernan's voice carried the smile that crossed his face as he proceeded past the first rows, pretending to check each. He looked like he enjoyed the game almost as much as Matthew.

"Could he be...here? Nope." Tiernan slowed his walk as he reached their row. "What about...here. There he is. I found you!"

Matthew giggled as he scrambled to his feet and started jumping up and down, probably because Ashley unintentionally blocked his way to Tiernan for a hug.

She shook her head as she walked out of the aisle, clearing Matthew's path to run to Tiernan for the traditional embrace. "At least someone had fun."

Tiernan patted Matthew on the back as he ended the hug. "Sorry about the scare." He turned his green eyes on Ashley. "Nothing too alarming, other than Katherine's radio apparently not working."

"What?" Katherine watched them from the high part of the room.

"Didn't you hear the all clear?"

She shook her head and took the earpiece off to examine it.

"So the house is still safe?" Ashley tried to read Tiernan's expression. He was too good at appearing happy-go-lucky when the situation was far from it. "I thought there was a perimeter breach or whatever you call it."

He kept his smile on, but it might not have quite reached his eyes. "We've got everything contained now."

Which meant it hadn't been before. The biggest knot in her gut twisted some more. "That doesn't really help. I'm not going to stay here any longer like a sitting duck. If somebody's trying to get us, they just got way too close." She glanced at Matthew. "And this isn't good for Matthew either. He got so scared when he heard you all running and shouting outside."

Tiernan let his smile fade. "I'm sorry about that, but I had to take every precaution to protect you."

"To protect Matthew, you mean."

"Both of you. Like it or not, you're both under my protection now."

That might be a comfort if she didn't feel like a hostage. "Doesn't make me feel too safe when somebody got through your security."

A glint flashed in his eyes. "It was only a smoke bomb thrown over the fence onto the grounds."

"Someone tried to attack us?"

"They were either trying to get in while we were distracted, or they wanted to see how many agents we have and what our response would be. We responded well, so whoever was out there should be impressed." Tiernan turned and headed back up the stairs.

"So that's it? We just sit here and wait to find out if they're coming back?"

He turned to face her from the top step. "No. We're going to move out early in the morning now that Matthew's location has been discovered."

It was something at least. "Let's go, Matthew." Ashley straightened his wildly askew cap.

He whimpered and clutched his right ear with his hand.

"What's wrong?" She moved in closer to get a look. "Let me see." She gently pulled his hand off his ear.

The skin of his ear was pink where it must have pressed against the floor.

"Did he hurt himself?" Tiernan's voice came from right next to her as he bent in to see.

"Looks like he just had his ear on the floor too long. While we were hiding." She threw Tiernan a sidelong glance.

"If a bad guy had shown up, you'd be thanking me right now." His good humor had apparently returned, bringing along a lopsided grin. He sobered when he looked at Matthew.

The boy's lips pushed out in his sad frown.

"What would you like to do now, champ? Something fun?" Tiernan tugged the bill of Matthew's cap, angling it again.

Ashley sent him a perturbed glare. No wonder Matthew's cap was always crooked. She straightened it again. "How about you draw some more?" Too late, Ashley stopped herself. The red pen should still be in the office, but she better locate it herself before getting his hopes up.

Matthew didn't seem to notice she'd said a word anyway.

"I know. How about your blocks?"

His gaze came up. "Bogs."

"They're in your room." Tiernan nodded to Katherine. "Would you take him up to find his blocks?"

"I can go with him."

Tiernan turned those green eyes on Ashley. "I'd like you to stay for a second. I need to talk to you."

Just when her heart rate had finally slowed, his words kicked it back up again. But his agenda would have to wait. She had a question of her own.

As soon as Matthew and Katherine left, Tiernan opened his mouth to speak, but Ashley launched her question first. "How did you know about his blocks?"

Tiernan's eyebrows drew together. "We searched the house before bringing Matthew here."

"That doesn't explain how you knew he liked to play with blocks."

His mouth twitched. "Maybe I made a deduction."

Was he enjoying her irritation again? Argh. The man made her want to scream sometimes. Once again, he probably thought he'd succeeded in getting her off the scent. Of what, she didn't know. But he had far too many secrets for her peace of mind. She brushed past him and marched up the rest of the stairs.

"Hey, you didn't wait for *my* question." He quickly caught up as she stalked to the door.

"Shoot."

"Never say that to an FBI agent."

She sent him a glare and went through the doorway, quickly turning the corner around the bar counter to head upstairs.

"What did you find out from Matthew today?"

She didn't look at Tiernan as he reached her side again. "Just that he loves his mother's red pen."

"If you cooperate, it'd be easier on all of us." At least the amusement had left his voice.

She shrugged when she reached the bottom of the staircase that led to the ground floor. "I'm telling the truth. That's all I got." More than he was willing to share with her. She tried to dig some more as she climbed the stairs. "So why would you be willing to leave here when whatever his parents hid is most likely in the house?"

"It could be elsewhere."

Another evasive answer.

"But either way I can't risk Matthew's life by staying when his location's been made."

Ashley reached the hallway at the top of the stairs and turned to Tiernan.

He glanced at her as he took the stairs two at a time. Maybe even the FBI had their limits. Though Tiernan certainly wasn't in any big rush to leave, despite the danger.

"So why don't we go now?"

He reached the top and met her gaze. "Too risky when there's a known threat. The bomb throwers may have wanted to flush us out." He closed the door to the basement. "I'd only try it if it were absolutely necessary." He looked at her. "Did Matthew really not say anything else all day?"

She tucked her hair behind her ear. "Just 'mine' and 'like him.'"

"Like him? Who'd he say that to?"

"I'm never quite sure." She pushed her fingers into the back pockets of her jeans. "He usually says it to me when he wants me to like someone. I think this time he might have been saying it to me, or maybe to Jack. He said it when he was giving his pen to Jack."

"He gave the pen to Jack?"

Why did Tiernan seem so surprised? Like he again knew something she didn't.

"Yes, but—"

A scream shot through the house.

Her heart stopped.

"Second floor." Tiernan spoke into his radio, then pointed at Ashley. "Stay put." He took off running toward the front entry, probably to the staircase that led upstairs.

To Matthew's bedroom.

She took off after Tiernan, her frantic heart threatening to break through her ribs.

Matthew couldn't be having a nightmare this time.

The house blurred as she ran through the rooms to reach the foyer. She gripped the banister to stop herself from sliding past the staircase.

She lunged up the steps, leaping two at a time, not bothering to look ahead to see what danger awaited her. She had to get to Matthew.

She panted for air at the top of the stairs, but no breath would come as she looked across the balcony.

Matthew stood outside his room, Katherine holding him against the wall with one arm, gun gripped in her other hand.

Ashley slowed to a trot as she crossed the balcony behind Tiernan.

Katherine nodded to the doorway when Tiernan reached her.

"How many?" His voice was deeper than Ashley had ever heard it.

"Didn't see anyone. Just the present they left."

Ashley stopped behind Tiernan, apparently not as quietly as she thought, since she earned a sharp glance.

"Stay here." His gaze pinned hers for a second before he turned away and pulled his gun from the back of his waistband. He approached the open doorway and spun into the room, disappearing from view.

Ashley tried to remember to breathe as they waited.

"Clear."

Katherine relaxed her stance at Tiernan's call and holstered her gun.

Ashley stepped into the room, her hands shaking from the adrenaline rush. She scanned the space, taking in the bookcase that still protected the secret room, the bed—

Red, shiny pieces were spread in a small circle on the white sheet of the bed. Matthew's pen?

What were the streaks of red beneath the shattered pieces? Was that—

A huge, grotesque smiley face was drawn on the sheet in red ink.

A shudder rippled up Ashley's spine.

Tiernan still gripped his gun as he brushed past her and headed for the door. "We're getting out of here. Now."

chapter
seventeen

Ashley froze when her fingers touched the scrap of paper. Her regular habit, checking her pockets before she changed out of her clothes. Saved time on laundry day.

The shower water ran in the background as she pulled the paper from her jeans' pocket. Taking a shower tonight in case they were forced to move to yet another safe house in the morning seemed like a good idea. Now she wasn't so sure.

She set the paper on the edge of the sink and tried to ignore it as she stepped into the bathtub-shower combo. The water was a pitiful drip compared to the luscious rainforest spray at the mansion. And she didn't want to know what those spots were on the bottom of the well-used tub.

It was no use. Even the smell of the farmhouse hidden miles out in the country somewhere wasn't enough to keep her mind off that paper.

Might be nothing. Might be a different Abelli, or completely unconnected with Matthew and this strange mystery she was caught up in.

But those four hours of sleep she'd snagged in the windowless van that went on seemingly endless detours to reach this house were going to be the only rest she'd get unless she found the whole article that mentioned that awful name.

If only she had her smartphone, she could do a simple Internet search and probably find the web address for the article in no time. But Tiernan would never give the device back to her.

Unless she could come up with a good story. She could say she had to contact Tina about a foster child—a life and death situation.

No. He'd know she couldn't have learned any vital information about such a case while she'd been with him.

Her mind cycled through idea after idea as she showered. None would work.

She turned off the water and grabbed a green towel from the bar on the wall.

Then it hit her. The truth. She could show him what she'd found and say she was curious. She wouldn't have to say why, but just that she wanted to follow it up in case the article was some kind of lead related to Matthew's parents.

She toweled her hair more vigorously than necessary, keeping up with the speed of her thoughts. Could she trust him with the information? With that name? If she could convince him her only interest was because of Matthew, she could probably risk telling him. He did seem to care about getting the boy out of this mess.

She changed back into her other pair of jeans and a lavender T-shirt, her nerves unsettling her stomach as she planned what she would say to Tiernan. She grabbed the paper and stuffed it in her pocket. Once she gathered her things and put them in the little bedroom they had let her have across from Matthew's, she made her way toward the living room.

"I knew that house was too big to keep secured."

Ashley paused in the hallway at the sound of Katherine's voice.

She sounded angrier than normal. "We never should have kept him there."

"We do things differently in Chicago than the Twin Cities." Tiernan's answer was just as irritated. "It wasn't your place to say where we keep Matthew, then or now. You've been warned before, Agent Nguyen. You'll have to adjust to your new location and position."

Ashley wasn't about to walk into the tense silence that followed. And listening unnoticed was proving to be enlightening already. Apparently, Katherine hadn't wanted to work with Tiernan as she'd claimed.

"You going to say it, mate, or shall I?" Jack interrupted the stand-off. "The problem wasn't the house, it was Grayson's men finding us."

Grayson? A familiar name...but from where?

"Agreed." Tiernan's voice returned to his normal, calmer tone. "They shouldn't have found us so quickly."

"They probably found out from Ashley."

What? Leave it to Katherine to accuse Ashley behind her back.

"I don't trust her. She could have gotten word to Grayson's people when she left the Bordens' place. Maybe that's *why* she left."

"I don't think it was Ashley."

Warmth sparked in her chest at Tiernan's statement. Probably from the sheer shock of his support.

"I believe she truly cares about Matthew."

"I hope you're not losing your objectivity, Hanks." Katherine again. "She was going to dump him at an asylum."

Ashley swallowed back a feeling that seemed awfully close to guilt. She hadn't done anything wrong. Any other social worker would have put him in an institution the first night.

"Or at least she pretended she was going to leave him there."

"Meaning?" At least Tiernan had the decency to sound skeptical about whatever Katherine was implying.

"She doesn't seem like your average social worker."

"I agree."

Ashley's heart skipped a beat without her say so. What did he mean by that?

"Funny." Katherine didn't sound amused. "I'm saying there's something suspicious about her, something I don't trust."

"I don't know about that." Jack interjected another opinion, his Aussie accent making him sound friendlier than the others. "She seems pretty normal to me."

Thank you. Ashley wasn't too surprised Jack would defend her. He seemed like a nice enough guy.

"Blood is thicker than water." Katherine's remark stabbed Ashley's gut, but she didn't even know why. How could the contempt-laced statement possibly reference her? Unless—

"We won't go there." Tiernan interrupted the sudden rush of her pulse in her ears at the possibility she didn't want to consider. "It doesn't matter what she seems like to us or if we can trust her. We have to keep her here and safe. That's all."

"I don't like it."

I don't like being around you either. Ashley barely held back the retort she wanted to throw at Katherine.

"The sooner we can use her and get rid of her, the better."

Use her? Ashley's stomach clenched at Katherine's statement.

"I was hoping we wouldn't have to." Tiernan didn't set Katherine straight? Didn't deny what she'd said? "But Dillon wants us to switch to plan B."

"You mean we're giving up on the kid leading us to the gold?"

"Not entirely. But we're running out of time." Tiernan's tone turned grim as he answered Katherine. "Just hope Grayson doesn't come to the same conclusion, or there won't be much smoke in the next bomb."

Ashley's dinner churned in her belly. But from which part of this conversation?

"If Ashley will play along, we can beat Grayson before he can find us again."

She'd heard enough. She turned on her heel and walked away from Tiernan's disturbing comment as quietly as she could despite wanting to stomp down the hallway. She reached her room in seconds and shut the door behind her. Blood boiled in her veins.

How dare they? How dare they say they couldn't trust her? The bunch of liars. They lied for a living. And Tiernan was the worst of them all, sniveling and conniving to get her to the point where she was about to trust him. How dare he dissect her with his agent pals? And lie to her from the beginning.

She'd known he was hiding something. Turned out to be worse than she thought. What did Katherine mean, they were going to *use* her?

Ashley would like to see them try. Nobody was going to use her ever again. Not while she had breath left in her body.

She barely stopped herself from kicking the dresser, the only furniture besides the bed in her room. Too much noise might bring those FBI creeps breathing down her neck.

She was smarter than they thought. She could figure out on her own that the people after Matthew, this Grayson and his men, had to have found their location somehow. Not through her, so there had to be a leak in the FBI. Maybe one of the agents in this very house who were accusing her right now. Maybe even Tiernan.

If that was true...Matthew. She couldn't leave him alone with an enemy under the same roof.

She went to her door again and quietly opened it. She peeked out into the hallway.

No one was there, their voices still drifting from the living room.

She carefully crossed the hall and snuck through Matthew's open doorway.

He didn't look up from where he sat on the twin bed, playing with the blocks they'd brought from his house.

The blocks Tiernan had made sure to bring himself. The man was such a contradictory mix of alpha male and thoughtful gentleness. He was infuriating. And apparently up to no good. What did he mean, she'd have to *play along*?

Tiernan's sinister words made him seem more capable of being the one who'd betray Matthew than she would have thought.

Matthew's little stack of blocks fell onto the floppy mattress, but he reached to build them up again.

Would a guy who went out of his way to bring Matthew's blocks also want to hurt him? A guy who hugged a boy with Down syndrome as easily as if the kid were his own son?

Yes. She inwardly chastised herself for her inexplicable desire to think positively of Tiernan despite everything she'd just heard that confirmed her original suspicions. She knew better than anyone that appearances could often deceive.

Whoever was the mole, Matthew wasn't safe in this safe house. Neither was she. She had to get them out. Both of them this time, which would be a whole lot harder.

She took a few steps to reach the uncovered window.

Dark tree limbs crossed in front of the glass, one branch brushing the windowpane with a light scratch. Darkness cloaked the yard below where old, abandoned tractor parts leaned against the shed in the shadows as if to remind Ashley of how alone and isolated she was. They'd taken so many turns and detours on the way there that she wasn't even sure where they were.

Might be harder for the bad guys to find them way out there, but what if the bad guys were already in the house, armed with guns and FBI badges?

"Not thinking of running away again, are you?"

She started and spun toward the masculine voice in the room.

Tiernan stood inside the doorway, his muscular forearms folded across his black T-shirt. He was smiling.

Had he been joking?

His smile dropped in the split second it must have taken him to see the truth on her face before she managed to hide it.

"Didn't work too well last time." She tried for a pitiful chuckle. A lame attempt to cover the truth he'd probably figured out.

He sighed and walked to the bed. He fiddled with the blocks as minutes slowly ticked by without another word.

She waited for him to do something, say something, her nerves on edge as she formed ten stories in her head to hide what she was planning.

But he didn't speak or even look at her. He just stood on the other side of the bed, smiling at Matthew now and then when the boy's unidentifiable structure toppled on its impossible foundation.

"I know you're nobody's fool." Those green eyes finally lifted, disarming her with their intensity. "You're right. They shouldn't have found us. At least not so quickly."

He stared into her eyes, not letting her glance away. "But believe me, it'd be a hundred times worse if you tried to make it on your own. Those men you saw, the ones who ransacked your place and the one who tried to grab Matthew at Navy Pier...They still want him. If you go out there alone, you'd be walking right into their hands."

She crossed her arms over her T-shirt, hoping she looked more unfazed than she felt. "I've survived a lot more than you know. I'll make it just fine."

"Maybe. But what about Matthew?"

"I protect kids for a living, and I'm good at it."

Tiernan shook his head. "Not this time. This is a whole different ball game, and you don't know the rules."

"It would help if I knew the players. Who wants Matthew so badly? Are they even that bad or do they just want to talk to him and let him go?"

His eyes glinted. "I can't believe you'd even consider the idea that they're good."

"Well, why not? All I have is your word for it, and you

won't tell me who they actually are." She forced out a breath in an attempt to release her heightening tension. All the agents would hear if she didn't keep her volume down.

"I'm sorry, Ashley." He walked around the bed, heading toward her.

She stepped back.

He stopped, watching her. "Okay. I can't tell you who wants Matthew, but I can tell you they're dangerous and mean him harm." He rested tanned hands on his trim hips. "Sure, they only want to talk to him right now, but after that..." He lifted a helpless hand in the air, then brought it back to rub his forehead like he had a headache. "I know it's frustrating being left in the dark, but it really is best this way, for you and Matthew."

Sure it was. According to the man who intended to *use* her.

"One thing I can tell you is this." He met her gaze. "I guarantee that if you stay with me, I will keep you and Matthew safe." His jaw was set, his eyes gravely serious, even sincere. "I promise. You just need to trust me."

Trust him. Is that what he had meant about getting her to *play along*? She pressed her lips together to keep from throwing the words back at him. He'd only make up some excuse for what she'd heard or refuse to say anything at all. If she pretended to play along, on the other hand, she might be able to earn enough breathing space to get out of here.

She nodded, then turned back to the window, an escape plan starting to form in her mind. Despite his convincing performance, she couldn't trust Tiernan any more than Katherine, Jack, or the other agents crawling around the place.

Ashley could only trust herself, and she was the only person Matthew had to depend on. She'd get him out of here and somewhere she could keep him safe until she could figure out what was really going on.

She fingered the scrap of paper in her front pocket. It was a lead. She'd track the article down and find out something that way.

But first things first—lull the agents into thinking she wasn't going to try a thing, and then make her getaway. Tonight.

"Couldn't sleep?" Ashley walked into the kitchen as casually as she could, wearing the oversized T-shirt and cotton shorts that qualified as her pajamas.

Tiernan looked up from the chair someone had put in a corner. He held the same slim book she'd seen him reading at the first safe house. "I'm not paid to sleep." He smiled, but his eyes looked tired, and his shoulders sloped. "What's your excuse?"

She shrugged. "Never was great at adjusting to a new bed."

He chuckled. "And now you've had three in four days."

She gave him a small smile in response. He didn't seem to suspect she was scoping out the house. Jack was at the back door, Katherine at the front, and Tiernan at the door to the garage. Every exit covered. "Milk sometimes helps. Do we have any?"

"Sure." He stood and set the book on the small table on his way to the refrigerator. He pulled out a carton of milk. "Anything for our guests." He winked at her as he set the carton on the table.

Thank goodness he spun away with a flourish to grab a glass from the cabinet. The heat that shot to her cheeks might be gone by the time he turned back. When had that wink become anything other than galling? She seriously needed sleep and a normal life again.

"Your milk, madam." He'd apparently poured the milk while she was lamenting her emotional idiosyncrasies, and he held the glass out to her.

Their fingers touched as she took the glass, despite her attempt to avoid that very thing. "So what book are you reading?" Anything to get his eyes off her. The escape she was plotting must have her nerves more frazzled than she thought.

"What? Oh." He took a step away to grab the book and held it up. "The Bible."

She coughed, choking on the milk she'd just tried to swallow. As she set down the glass and covered her mouth for more coughs, she glanced at the book. Sure enough, *Holy Bible* was printed across the leather cover in gold letters.

"Are you okay?" His voice held concern, but the corners of his lips twitched at the same time. "Need some water?"

"I'm fine," she croaked. She coughed again and took a careful sip of milk. The smooth liquid slid down her throat, soothing the irritation.

"I should have waited until you were done drinking. Didn't know it would be that much of a shock." His green eyes twinkled.

She watched him, then shrugged. "To each their own. But I never would have guessed you'd be the religious type."

"I'm not exactly. Not the way you mean it. More the Christian type."

She raised an eyebrow. Sounded like more of his evasiveness.

He smiled. "I mean, I have a relationship with Jesus Christ. He saved me from my sins and freed me to live for Him. It's not a set of meaningless rituals."

"So you mean you really believe that stuff? The Bible and all that?"

"Absolutely."

"Then you must have lived a pretty perfect life. With what I've seen, I can guarantee you there's no God. Or if there is, He's unbelievably cruel."

Tiernan's brow furrowed. "I can understand why you might think that. I've seen a lot of hard stuff and bad people in my line of work, too. But the God I believe in," he lifted the book again, "the God of the Bible, is so much bigger than any of that. He can and will use even the worst stuff that happens for good in the end."

The worst stuff? For good? Tiernan had no idea what he was talking about. Unless he was purposefully lying again. "So Christians aren't supposed to lie, are they?"

"No." He set the Bible on the table. "Do you think I've lied to you?" The gaze he brought back to her face was clear, unreadable.

He was good. Very good. She'd believe he was telling her the whole truth if she hadn't heard otherwise with her own ears. He wanted to use her. For what, she didn't know. Which was exactly why she had to get out of here now.

Back to her plan. "I guess I should try to get some sleep." She faked a yawn. "Maybe I'm too worried about Matthew. I think I'll try sleeping on the floor in his room, if you don't mind."

"Not at all." Did that searching look mean he suspected something? Maybe he just wondered if she knew he was conning her.

"Thanks." She turned and started to leave the room.

"Oh, Ashley?"

She stopped. Had he figured out what she was up to?

"I almost forgot. I wanted to give you something."

Give her something? She faced him, half expecting to see one of those little New Testaments that overzealous evangelists had tried to shove at her on Michigan Avenue.

He held a small cylinder in his outstretched hand. "Pepper spray."

She looked from the mini can up to his face. Why would he want to arm her when he didn't even trust her?

"You don't carry one already, do you?"

"Sometimes." Not since she'd switched to a knife.

"Well, I'd like you to while all this is…going on. Just in case." He gave her a small smile like he was handing her a box of chocolates.

In case of what? Hardly the sort of thing to tell people

right before they went to bed. If she were actually going to bed. "Okay." She took the pepper spray from his hand, her fingers brushing his warm palm.

Did he honestly care about her safety? No. Not with what she'd heard him say only a few hours earlier. Maybe this was some sort of reverse psychology tactic.

"Goodnight." She spun away and gave him a wave over her shoulder without looking back. The sooner she escaped this guy, the better. She'd never met a man who operated like he did—a commanding control-freak with too many secrets one second and sweet enough to make her teeth ache the next. He was dangerous.

On her way through the dining room, Ashley's gaze crossed an ugly curtain drawn over the sliding glass door she'd seen earlier in the day. Wasn't that an enclosed porch? A porch that might offer a way out.

Glancing around to be sure no one was watching, she went to the curtain and pulled it back inch by inch, until she could peek through the edge of the glass door. Sure enough. The enclosed porch had a door to the outside. A pretty flimsy one, from the look of it.

The sliding glass door leading from the house to the porch was locked, and she had seen Jack wedge a board behind it earlier. Anyone trying to get in that way would have a challenge. Probably why no agent was posted by it.

Hard to get in, but easy to get out. She had her exit. Closer to the kitchen and Tiernan than she'd like, but she would make it work.

With more confidence in her step, Ashley returned to her room and double-checked to be sure she had her belongings packed and together in one spot. She slipped the pepper spray into the pouch pocket of her purse. A good companion for her knife. She slid her suitcase and shoes under the bed, grabbed the comforter off the mattress, and headed for Matthew's room.

She tiptoed over to the boy.

Special Target

He slept soundly, his face smooshed into his pillow. Could he breathe like that?

She pressed the pillowcase away from his nose and mouth, careful not to wake him. She'd let him get as much sleep as he could before their long night ahead.

She laid her comforter on the floor next to the bed on the side that was near the window, then went to look outside. She only had to get past two agents outside at this location. According to an irritated conversation Katherine and Jack had outside the bathroom while Ashley was brushing her teeth, they had fewer agents overall and only two at stationary posts outside. More would attract attention in this remote, but open, country.

Ashley hoped she'd guessed correctly about where those agents would be posted. Escaping through the porch door at the side of the house should help. They were probably super focused on this window to Matthew's bedroom. But they wouldn't care so much about the secure porch entrance, or, in her case, exit.

She moved away from the window and stretched out on the comforter. If she were smart, she'd sleep for the hour she had to wait for Tiernan to relax again. With any luck, he might fall asleep by the time she busted out. Smart or not, adrenaline pumped through her limbs, keeping her eyes wide open as she lay on the hard wooden floor.

Minutes ticked by on the old grandfather clock that stood against one wall in the bedroom. She started counting them.

Footsteps. In the hallway.

Someone coming to check on her?

She covered herself more completely with the upper half of the folded comforter and closed her eyes.

The person stopped in the open doorway. Tiernan?

Her eyelid wanted to open, but she kept it firmly closed, trying to even out her breathing as if she were sleeping.

Footsteps, this time going away from the room.

Ashley slowly opened one eye a crack.

The doorway was empty.

She let out a slow breath, her nerves tingling. Good thing she had brought in the blanket to fake sleeping. How often would he check? She better not wait an hour in case that was the time for patrol rounds again. An odd time would be better. Twenty-one minutes. Then she'd go.

She was more than ready when the last minute ticked by. No sound of an agent coming to check. It was now or never.

She got up and touched Matthew's shoulder. "Matthew, wake up." She kept her voice a whisper. Hopefully he'd be easier to wake when he wasn't having a nightmare. She shook him slightly. "Matthew."

He opened his eyes with a moan that sounded as loud as a gong.

"Shh." She glanced at the door. "Matthew, we have to leave now. Can you do that? I need you to be very, very quiet." She should have planned how to get him to cooperate, fresh from sleep. Her mind raced for an idea. "It's like hide and seek. Okay?"

His squinty eyes opened a tiny bit wider. "Hide go see?"

She nodded as she grabbed his elbows and guided him toward her to the edge of the bed. "Yes. We're playing right now. We have to hide. And be very quiet."

He followed her leading and put his feet on the floor with a smile. He apparently woke up faster than she usually did. His thick hand lifted his Bible from the nightstand. Of course, that would have to come along.

She handed him his Cubs baseball cap, which sat on top of his duffel bag. Ashley hadn't packed his belongings when they rushed out of the mansion, but hopefully the FBI had included everything he would need.

She barely stopped herself from snorting at the thought of trusting the FBI for anything as she pointed to his bag. "I need you to carry that. We're going to hide far away, so we need our bags with us."

He slid the cap on crookedly, as usual. The cap didn't

exactly match his long-sleeved Snoopy pajamas, but she couldn't risk having him change before they left. He picked up his bag and looked at her without saying a word. For once, she was glad he wasn't a chatterbox.

She tugged on her black hoodie and zipped it over her T-shirt. "Okay." Hopefully her whisper would keep him from using a loud voice if he did suddenly decide to speak up. "You need to wait here for a second. Okay? I'll be right back." She held up her hand as she backed to the door. "Stay." She turned at the doorway and paused, peeking into the hallway.

Clear in both directions.

She tiptoed across the hallway and gathered her belongings as quickly as she could, returning to Matthew's room.

Unbelievable. He was still there.

"Okay. Let's go. Remember, we're hiding. We don't want anyone to hear us, or we'll lose the game." She took a breath and stepped into the hall. She glanced back with her finger to her lips.

Matthew didn't see her. He was too busy watching his feet as he made an almost comical effort to walk silently. That would work.

She led the way to the porch door. The lights were off in the dining room, so no one outside should be able to see light if she pulled the curtains back far enough to get through. Hopefully.

Was that a sound? She jerked her head toward the kitchen. No light in there now. Wasn't Tiernan going to sit up all night to guard against intruders? Maybe he didn't want the light on when he did that. Probably made him more vulnerable, easily seen.

She held her breath as she carefully set down her suitcase and squatted to reach under the curtain. Her fingers touched the board wedged in the track behind the door. She tugged.

The board made a small noise as it pulled loose.

She straightened, glancing at the kitchen.

Nothing. Almost too quiet.

She made herself release her breath and take in another. She was committed now. No turning back.

She silently shifted the lock and slid the door open. At least it didn't squeak.

Matthew followed her through as quietly as a mouse. Until his bag rubbed against the door as he pulled it through.

Ashley couldn't get the door closed fast enough. At this rate, it'd be a miracle if they made it out without every single agent hearing them.

The darkness of the porch forced her eyes to adjust as she made her way to the outer door, hoping there wasn't any furniture to trip over on the way.

"Hide?"

She jumped at Matthew's voice behind her. "Shh." She put her finger to her lips, then tried to soften the harshness of her whisper. The last thing she needed was for him to pout right now. "We have to be very quiet, or they'll find us."

She turned to the door and undid the small latch that kept it locked. Pressing the handle forward, she slowly opened the door.

It scraped along the concrete step outside.

She stopped with a cringe. She took a breath and tried again more slowly. The noise wasn't quite as loud. Hopefully quiet enough.

She glanced around as she held the door open for Matthew.

Dark trees and bushes met her gaze. Their leaves and branches fluttered in the cool breeze. Any one of them could be hiding an agent. Or someone else.

She closed the door as slowly as she could stand, then nodded to Matthew. "Follow me." Hefting her overnight bag in one hand, she kept her other hand near the pocket of her purse and the weapons there. But would she use them on an FBI agent? A crooked one, she would.

She scanned the dark shadows as they made their way to the front of the house.

The outline of an object caught her eye just in time for her to grab Matthew's arm and pull him out of the way before he tripped.

She peered at the object. A rusty old rake, leaning against the wall of the house along with a tire and other useless items.

She paused at the corner of the house and held up a hand to make Matthew stop behind her. Peering around the chipped siding, she looked out into more crisscrossed shadows that shifted in the wind.

The sound of leaves blowing was almost ghostly. Who knew the country was so creepy at night? Give her the city any day.

A hand rested on her shoulder.

She gasped. Then sighed at her jumpiness. It was just Matthew. She turned to tell him not to touch her.

Tiernan's face was inches away.

chapter
eighteen

Ashley sucked in a quick breath.

"You're not going to scream, are you?" Tiernan's whisper didn't disguise the amusement in his question.

Her heart pounded against her ribs until she found her voice. "Should I?"

"Not unless you want them to find us."

She blinked at him.

"We don't have time for you to play dumb. The suitcase and duffel bag make it pretty obvious." He gently touched one finger to her chin like he couldn't resist. "Your mouth's hanging open again."

She shut it with a quick jerk away from his finger. Not in time to avoid the streak of heat that traveled from the spot he'd touched through the rest of her body.

"Are we going or not?"

Was this a dream? "You're...you're leaving, too?"

"Yep. If they didn't hear your noisy escape from the porch, that is." He moved in front of her and looked around the corner of the house. He turned to her again, his twinkling eyes too close to hers.

She took a step back and banged into Matthew. She spun to the boy. "Sorry. Are you okay?"

He just smiled at Tiernan, probably thrilled his hero had found them in his game of hide and seek.

"How about we get going before we have any more casualties?" Tiernan grinned as he pointed the way they had come. "We'll take the jeep over there."

She stared at him. "Why would you help us leave?" Did he think she was that stupid?

He tilted his head toward the front of the house, like he'd heard something. "Not here." His smile disappeared with the word as he snatched her suitcase out of her hand and gently grasped her elbow at the same time, guiding her toward the back of the house. "Matthew, follow me."

She pulled loose within a couple steps but kept walking, peering at the darkness around them as they moved toward something only Tiernan could see.

He led them behind certain bushes and trees, but not others. Like he knew exactly which ones would hide them. Like he'd planned every move.

This was insane. She was sneaking out with the very person she had wanted to escape. What if this was all a twisted trick or a joke? What if he wanted to get them alone because he was the one who'd sold out Matthew at the last location?

The thought made her blood run cold, chilling her more than the wind on her bare legs.

A white building came into view as they trudged through longer grass that brushed her ankles above her sneakers. The roof was tilted, like it would collapse if the wind were any stronger.

What did he plan to do with them in there? She moved her hand toward the pocket of her purse, which she luckily had on the shoulder away from him. But he'd given her the pepper spray himself. Would he expect her to try it on him?

"Hide go see?"

Tiernan put his hand on Matthew's shoulder with a smile.

"No, we won't have to hide in here. Just getting the jeep. Then we'll go for a ride. Would you like that?"

Awfully friendly for a guy who might be about to kidnap them. Or worse? She felt the flap of the pocket on her purse. He didn't know about the knife.

"I don't think I like that look on your face."

She shifted her hand to the purse strap, her pulse racing as she tried to give him a casual glance.

He watched her too closely, his gaze unreadable. "Don't do anything crazy. We're pretty far away from the others now, but they'll still hear you if you scream." He pointed at the big garage-like door they were only ten feet from. "The jeep is right inside this building. We'll be out of here in one minute."

He stopped in front of the door and crouched down to grab the handle just above the ground.

His back was to them. This was her chance.

She grabbed the knife from her purse and flipped it open as he lifted the door up.

"There. See?" He turned toward her with a smile. It dropped when he saw her knife, pointed at him.

"Matthew, come here." She waved her hand at the boy to get him to move toward her.

He just stood there, staring at her like she'd turned criminal. Not that he was even capable of understanding such things.

Her mind raced through jumbled thoughts as she forced herself to keep eye contact with Tiernan. She'd held her knife on men before. Her hand had never shaken then. Was it the look in those eyes? Almost like he was hurt.

He held up an all-too-steady hand. "Now wait a second. You don't want to use that. And you don't want me to take it from you."

So much for scaring him. His arrogance was unbelievable. Her turn to smile now. "You talk a good game for someone on the defense. I don't plan on letting you take the knife, no matter how good you think you are."

He started moving to the side.

"Stop right there." She took a step closer to him, her knife out.

"Okay." He stopped. "Look, Ashley, we don't have time for this. You want to get out of here with Matthew, right? The agents back there are going to notice we're gone in..." he pressed the backlight button on his watch, "two minutes. It's now or never."

"For us, maybe. Why would you help us?"

A note of exasperation broke through his patient tone. "I don't have time to explain. Will you just get in the jeep so we can get on the road? I'll tell you what you want to know then."

He looked behind her, whether to scare her or for a real threat, she didn't know. But he had a jeep and probably the only key to it. And he was right. They had to get out now. She lowered the knife. "Fine."

"Thank you." Exasperation laced the words as he ushered Matthew to the jeep and had him get in the back.

Ashley went around to the passenger side and shoved her suitcase on the seat next to Matthew before sliding into the front herself, purse with weapons at her side.

Tiernan hopped in behind the wheel and revved up the jeep, which sounded almost as rough as her car. No surprise, given how well-used the jeep appeared. Probably as old as the shack with the slanted roof.

But it ran well enough for Tiernan to drive over the long grass in a direction perpendicular to the way they had come.

Ashley gripped the armrest of her door as the jeep bounced over the rough terrain. She squinted to see where they were going but could only make out shadows of varying shades of darkness.

Wait a second. There wasn't any light in front of the jeep. "How can you see without headlights?" She spoke loudly to be heard over the noisy engine.

"We can't use them this close. We'll be fine. Trust me."

Right. She slipped her hand into the pocket of her purse and gripped the knife she'd folded. Could she really use that on Tiernan? She didn't want to answer that.

Her fingers wrapped around the pepper spray instead. She waited, the spray can sweaty in her palm by the time Tiernan ran the jeep up a big bump, and they landed on pavement.

He flicked on the headlights, illuminating the narrow road as he picked up speed. He tossed her a grin. "That wasn't so bad, was it?"

"I'm more worried about what comes next." She pointed the pepper spray at him, her finger ready to press down at the slightest threat. "Pull over."

"Not again." His eyebrows pushed together as his mouth tightened, not in a smile this time. "Would you put that down? I gave it to you, for Pete's sake."

"Your mistake, not mine. Don't make another one." She held the spray can steady. "Pull over now."

Matthew whined in the back seat. "Like him."

"Not now, Matthew." She didn't pull her gaze from Tiernan.

"I think I'll keep driving. You're not about to use that on me and cause an accident."

"Don't bet on it." She leveled her fiercest stare at him.

He glanced at her, then watched the road. "You wouldn't want to hurt Matthew."

He had a point, but she wasn't about to let the upper hand go so easily. "You better start doing some pretty fancy talking because you'll have to stop sometime, and I will spray you before you can go for any of your weapons."

The corner of his mouth twitched. "I was right. You are tough."

"Bet you say that to all the women you kidnap."

"Will you stop saying that? I didn't kidnap you."

"Maybe not before. Now it'll take more than your word to convince anyone."

He shoved a hand through the thick locks of hair on top of his head. "Whew. I hope not."

"Why did you help us get away, and where are you taking us?"

He glanced at her. "I wanted you to get away. You weren't going to make it on your own very well, were you?"

She tilted her chin. "We were doing fine."

He chuckled. "Sure you were."

His annoying amusement brought her attention back to notice what he'd said. "What do you mean you wanted us to get away? I was running away from you."

"From the FBI. I'm glad you thought of it. Really was the best way for me to get you and Matthew away from the other agents and somewhere safe."

"You think they're traitors?" Didn't seem likely he'd turn on his fellow agents that easily.

"Probably only one." His voice deepened. From anger?

Her arm that held the spray started to weaken. This would be so much easier if she could trust him. But what if he was conning her?

"Like him."

"Listen to the kid." Tiernan tried for a smile, but it was weaker than usual.

Ashley glanced at Matthew.

Even with the shadows that crossed his face, there was no missing the stress in those scrunched features.

She didn't mean to scare him. He'd been frightened enough. But she was his only protection right now. She turned her gaze back to Tiernan's profile. "Where are you taking us?"

"Another safe house."

"I've had enough of those."

"No one will think to look for you at this one."

She watched him until he glanced her way.

"Not for the time we'll be there. I promise."

Another promise. Probably wasn't worth the words he

used to say it. But what other choice did she have? Truth was, she still had no clue where they were, and her best chance of getting Matthew somewhere safe was sitting behind the wheel.

She moistened her lips as she slowly lowered the spray can to her lap. "You better be right."

Or what, she didn't know. She only knew that, for the moment, she had to trust him. At least until the sun came up.

Something tried to pull Ashley out of the deep darkness that had closed in around her. She wanted to stay there.

"Ashley. We're here."

A voice with no face. Just a sound that wouldn't stop.

"Ashley. Time to wake up."

She forced her heavy eyelids to open a crack. Light assaulted them, making her squeeze them closed again.

"Come on, Ashley. We have to get in there before anyone else is up to see us." A touch on her shoulder.

Heat tingled across her shoulder to her neck. Tiernan.

She opened her eyes and pulled away from his hand, pretending to reach for her purse on her other side. When had she fallen asleep? Quite a while ago, judging from the amount of morning sunlight already brightening the sky.

The sound of the door opening signaled Tiernan was getting out the driver's side, so she was free to look around more with squinted eyes.

A fairly tall brick building stood in front of the parked jeep. Looked like an apartment building of the upper middle-class kind. Behind the building, a manmade pond featured a fountain in the middle. She looked over her shoulder to see the rest of the parking lot, more apartment buildings bordering it, and a sign that read, *Hawkridge Condominiums*.

She knew where those were. This was Graterville, a wealthy Chicago suburb she'd visited several times for work.

"Hey." Tiernan poked his head through the open driver's door. "Ready to go in?"

No. But Matthew already stood behind Tiernan, duffel bag in his hand as he rocked onto his toes, then his heels. It was shelter, and Tiernan seemed to be on the up and up. He hadn't tried anything when she'd accidentally fallen asleep. Maybe he wasn't the agent trying to betray Matthew.

With a sigh, she pulled the purse strap over her shoulder and shoved her door open. She glanced in the back.

"Got your suitcase."

She nodded, looking at him to verify that he had. He gripped her suitcase by the handle and held two books under his other arm. She looked closer. Matthew's photo albums? Her sleep-fogged brain couldn't be sure.

Tiernan swung away and stepped onto the sidewalk.

She slowly trudged after Tiernan and Matthew as they followed the path toward the closest building. She really needed to wake up.

"Swim swim!" Matthew turned and tried to walk backward, smiling broadly at the pond behind them like it was his best friend.

"Yep." Tiernan's voice was much quieter than the boy's. "Can you turn around, buddy? Don't want you to trip."

Wide awake now, Ashley breathed again when the teen heeded Tiernan's direction and faced forward. One more teetering backward step, and she would've been cleaning his scrapes for the next half hour.

The air was already sticky as they followed the path that curved between two brick buildings. Another hot day ahead.

Tiernan stopped at the entrance to the building on their right. "No talking until we get inside the condo, okay?"

A musty smell greeted Ashley's nostrils as Tiernan let them in, and they headed up the carpeted staircase. Two flights up, he unlocked an apartment door.

He stepped inside and held the door open.

Ashley followed Matthew past Tiernan as the agent's gaze roamed the room.

Checking for intruders or witnesses? She surveyed the place herself as she walked down the three steps that led from the entry landing into an open dining room and living room. The kitchen, separated by a curved counter, was just beyond the dining table and bordered by a hallway that led to two doorways.

Her gaze skimmed the two bookcases along the dining room wall, landing on a framed photograph of Tiernan and a woman. Wait a second. "This is *your* apartment?"

He turned from locking the door, his shrug the picture of innocence. "Condo. Yeah."

"Just what are you planning for us here?" Nasty possibilities raced through her mind as her pulse matched their pace.

"Really?" He went down the steps and brushed past her with what looked very much like a smirk. He walked to the first door in the short hallway and peeked inside the room, then went to the last door and did the same.

Ashley stared at him as he started back in her direction.

He veered into the kitchen instead and rummaged through a drawer as though unaware she still waited.

But her heartbeat slowed as she watched his casual demeanor. Nobody would be that comfortable if they were about to do something dastardly, would they? And if he'd wanted to try something against her or Matthew, the jeep in the middle of nowhere at night would have been the place for it. She might have to face the concept of trusting him. A tiny bit.

He looked up, fiddling with...was that a phone in his hand? "Sorry. Just make yourselves at home."

Matthew apparently hadn't needed the invitation. He already sat in an overstuffed, oversized armchair, flipping through a magazine.

"I'm still wondering why we're here."

Tiernan walked around the counter into the dining room,

looking down at the blue smartphone in his hand. "It's the perfect spot. Nobody would think I'd be dumb enough to bring you to my own place."

"That's encouraging."

He glanced at her. "Should be. All we need to do is stay hidden until we nail the guy."

"You mean Grayson." That earned his full attention. She barely held back her smile at the surprise in his eyes. "You FBI agents aren't the only ones with information."

He watched her for a few silent moments, his gaze searching hers like he was trying to read something in her eyes. "You were listening."

She shrugged, hoping he wouldn't think from the flush in her cheeks that she'd heard more than Grayson's name. "Isn't that what you do all the time?"

A smile curved his lips. "I said I thought you'd make a good agent."

When had he said that? Before or after he'd said he wanted her to play along? If this was a new selling tactic, some way of getting her to cooperate with whatever he had in mind, he'd have to try something else. "Was that your big plan?" She raised an eyebrow. "Make me an agent, and I'll solve the case?"

"I'm serious. Though if you're not interested, I don't blame you. It can be dangerous work."

"Seems like social work is, too."

He breathed a laugh. "Yeah, I guess it does." He set the phone on the table in front of him and met her gaze. "I know you don't really like me. And I know you probably still don't trust me. But whether you trust me or not, I'm going to have to trust you. We're alone now, the three of us, and we'll have to work as a team if we're going to get Matthew out of this unharmed."

She swallowed. "What do you mean, we're alone? Doesn't the FBI know where we are?"

"Not exactly."

"You mean you've left, like...gone rogue?"

"Sort of." The corner of his mouth twitched. He thought this was funny? "It's complicated."

"I'm smarter than I look." She folded her arms in front of her.

"Okay. Dillon, my boss, knows what I'm doing but not where I am. No one else knows anything about it."

She lowered her arms. "So we'll have the FBI after us now, too?"

"It's a possibility."

Wonderful. With Tiernan along, she'd hoped to avoid that little complication. "What do we do now?"

"First, we get some sleep."

She was trying not to pay attention to how weary her limbs still felt. "And then?"

"Then, we'll find those documents."

"Documents? That's what they hid?"

He opened his mouth, then closed it. Must not have remembered she didn't know that much. His brow furrowed when he finally answered. "Maybe." His set jaw said she wouldn't get anything more.

"How are we going to find them?"

He pointed behind her.

She turned to look, seeing only Matthew, who leaned his head against the plush back of the armchair.

"I brought the photo albums from the house. I'll look at every picture with Matthew, and hopefully he'll give me some clue about one of the places or objects in the photos."

She watched Tiernan as he spoke.

There was no humor or joking glint in his eyes. Just an intensity that matched the firm set of his mouth. "He loves hiding, and his parents knew that. They would have banked on him noticing where they hid something important."

"So you really think he can find the documents?"

"I'm not ready to give up on him yet. If he can lead us to them, this whole thing will be over for him." His gaze drifted past her and softened, probably when it landed on Matthew.

Different tune than the one he'd sung to Katherine and Jack at the house. Was he trying to trick her again? There was one way to test him. "Who's Grayson?"

He shook his head as he picked up the phone again. "Sorry."

Need-to-know, no doubt. "Wasn't your phone black?"

He tossed her a glance. "I always keep a spare in case of emergencies."

"What happened to the old one?"

"Left at the farm."

"You're afraid it will be traced."

He looked up and gave her that wink. "You're catching on." He smiled. "You look like you're about to fall asleep standing up. You didn't get much sleep on the way here. Why don't we crash for a while? We'll do better when we're rested."

We? A shot of panic perked up her sleepy brain. "Where would I sleep?"

"You can take the bedroom."

His bedroom. "No, thanks."

"I'm too tired to argue." He set the phone on the table again and stalked to the couch along the wall, kitty-corner from Matthew. He plopped onto the cushions and stretched out. "I'm sleeping here. There's an air mattress in the closet for you or Matthew. Sleep wherever you want." He laid back and covered his eyes with his arm.

Matthew brought his legs up onto the large ottoman in front of the chair and sank down until he was low enough to fling his arm over his eyes and sleep just like Tiernan.

"Matthew." She narrowed her gaze at them both. "Do you want to sleep in the bed?"

No answer. Was he already asleep or just intent on imitating his hero?

Fine. With a frustrated grunt she hoped Tiernan heard, she

lifted her suitcase and marched to the first door off the hallway.

A double bed stuck out from the wall and took up most of the room. A small desk stood against the other wall under a Chicago White Sox poster. The guy was awfully neat for a bachelor. If he was single. The bed looked like it had been made by housekeeping at a hotel, the trash bin next to the desk stood empty, and there wasn't a single stack of paper or discarded laundry item anywhere. Did he really live here?

Her gaze returned to the bed. No way was she sleeping in his bed, even if he was supposedly staying in the living room. She located sliding closet doors in the wall and opened them, only to find the air mattress, of course.

A more intense version of Tiernan's scent wafted out and around her—a blend of a spice she couldn't place, aftershave, and that intangible smell of masculinity.

The closet was only half full. Mostly button-down shirts, blazers, and FBI-style suits.

A cinched-up blue bag covered something bulky that leaned against the wall in the corner. She hefted the weighty bag out of the closet and opened it. As she thought, it held the air mattress.

She unrolled the blue mattress and plugged it into a socket in the wall. As she held the button to pump the air, her gaze fell on the book that rested on Tiernan's nightstand. Another Bible. This one had something inscribed on the bottom corner of the cover. She couldn't make it out.

She dropped the pump controller and stepped closer to the nightstand.

A name. *Martha Hanks.*

Tiernan's wife? She'd never considered he might be married.

Nah. A wife wouldn't let a strange woman stay at her place with her husband, would she? She'd be an idiot if she did. Not that Ashley was interested.

She blew out a breath. Talk about an idiot. The fatigue must be messing with her brain.

Trying to make her mind a blank, she tested the mattress resistance with her hand before settling onto it. She stretched across the fuzzy mattress cover without looking for a sheet to put over it. She wasn't about to ask Tiernan, and she couldn't keep her eyes open much longer.

But she wasn't too tired to get up again and lock the bedroom door, testing the knob to make sure the lock held.

chapter
nineteen

A noise. Something pulling her from the darkness again.

She tried to push her eyes open but couldn't seem to do it. So tired.

The noise stopped.

She relaxed back into sleep.

Another sound.

Her eyes popped open. Was that Matthew? Had he cried out?

She dragged herself off the mattress as quickly as she could, given her drowsy state and the wobbly surface. She stumbled to the door and pulled on the handle. Didn't budge.

Where was she? Adrenaline rushed to wake her in the seconds it took for her to recognize the room. Tiernan's apartment.

And Matthew was alone with him in the living room.

She fumbled with the lock and yanked open the door, running the few feet to the corner of the living room.

Tiernan sat on the coffee table by the armchair as a soft, deep sound floated around him. Was he...singing?

She rubbed her eyes and looked again.

Tiernan still sat there, singing what sounded like a lullaby to Matthew. The agent covered the boy's hand with his larger, tanned one as Matthew laid back on the chair, sniffling, tear tracks on his face.

She had to be dreaming. But the warmth trailing through her body seemed very real. She watched without making a sound as Tiernan continued to sing. When he eventually stopped, Matthew's eyes had closed again.

Tiernan turned, his gaze meeting Ashley's. He smiled and quietly stood, making his way over to her.

She took a couple steps back to make room for him in the hallway.

He stopped two feet from her. "Another nightmare."

"What? Oh." Why had his singing, the scene of him comforting Matthew, had such a strange effect on her? A person would think she liked the guy. "Matthew, you mean."

His eyebrows dipped briefly. "Yes."

"Do you have children?"

That rare glint of surprise flashed momentarily in his eyes.

"The lullaby."

"Oh." He shook his head. "Never married."

As if that explained the absence of children. What era was he from? The stone age?

"You?"

The question stung like the unexpected prick of a needle. He sure knew how to hit the mark every time. She glanced away. "I thought you already knew everything about me."

"Only what's on paper. I'd like to know more."

She brought her gaze to his face. Big mistake.

Those green eyes plunged into hers like he was trying to see inside her.

She turned away, stepping into the kitchen for an excuse to do something so he wouldn't notice she needed the distance to breathe. "You? Or the FBI?"

"*I* want to know."

She risked another glance.

He looked right at her with alarming sincerity and meaning in his eyes. Just what was he pushing for?

He suddenly smiled, averting that intense gaze. "Hungry?"

"What?"

"We slept through breakfast. Want lunch?"

She moistened her lips. "Sure, I guess."

He thumbed over his shoulder toward the living room. "I'm betting hunger will win out over fatigue pretty soon for Matthew. I don't have much here since I didn't know when I'd be back. I'll have to run to the store. What does Matthew like?"

She shrugged. "He eats whatever I give him. Fast food would probably be fine."

Tiernan's mouth opened in shock, but his eyes twinkled. "Not at my place. I don't have guests often, and I am not going to pass up the chance to cook for you both."

A smile tried to crawl onto her face. She held it back. "Somehow I can't picture you as a cook."

"Ha. Just for that, I'll have to prove it to you. What do you prefer, filet mignon or poached salmon with salsa verde and asparagus?"

She blinked at him.

He waved a hand to dismiss the question. "Never mind. I'll make you my favorite. I guarantee you'll love it. And so will Matthew."

Her stomach churned. He liked gourmet food? She'd avoided gourmet cuisine for fifteen years. Still didn't have the stomach for it. "Must be nice to be so used to this kind of life. We're on the run, and you go grocery shopping to cook a fancy dinner."

"A boy's gotta eat."

"Talking about yourself or Matthew?"

He grinned. "Take your pick." He went to the table and tapped the phone. "I'll leave the cell for you since it's the only phone in the place."

Was he worried they'd need it?

"I like to prepare for all contingencies. You and Matthew

will be perfectly safe here. If I didn't think so, I wouldn't leave."

Her concern must have shown on her face.

"The store's just around the corner, so I'll only be gone a few minutes." He took a step toward the door, then turned back. "If the impossible were to happen, and you thought you were in danger, get Matthew out of here and take the phone. I can call you on that phone. Okay?"

She nodded.

He tilted his head. "But nothing's going to happen, so none of what I just said matters." He gave her a cute, almost self-conscious smile.

"Right." She hoped the snappy reply would cover the answering smile that tried to reach her face, threatening to reward him. She held it back until he left, and she locked the door behind him. Never thought an FBI agent could come so close to endearing. Maybe trusting him wouldn't be so painful.

Matthew's eyes were still closed as he made soft, sleepy noises from the armchair. He must be beat to sleep through all their talking.

She finally had time and room to think. But a certain agent's smile kept popping into her mind's eye. Why was he so different from the other agents? From everyone in law enforcement she'd ever met? From every man she'd ever met, period.

Maybe this was her chance to find out. She could easily search the apartment while he was gone.

She walked to the bookshelves and checked out the volumes. A mix of classics, contemporary legal thrillers, and... religious books? Her gaze moved from a thick volume of Bible commentaries to that picture she'd seen before.

The blonde beauty next to Tiernan looked thrilled to have her face so close to his as they smiled at the camera. Was she the *Martha* inscribed on the Bible cover?

But there was no trace of femininity in the apartment, so

she apparently wasn't live-in yet. Then again, Tiernan's funny crack about not having kids because he wasn't married suggested he wasn't that interested in the blonde.

She narrowed her eyes at the woman's image, taking in the high cheekbones, thin face, and big green eyes. She looked like the star cheerleader at Ashley's high school, the obnoxious girl who'd been popular when Ashley had been invisible.

She let out a huff as she spun away from the photo. How pathetic could she get? She wasn't here on a date. She was practically a hostage. If not to Tiernan, then at least to this lousy situation until she figured a way out. This was the first time she'd been left alone, and she'd better not blow the opportunity.

About time she found out what was really going on. Her fingers found the scrap of paper in her jeans' pocket. Somewhere between the fight for survival and exhaustion, she'd actually managed to forget about it.

She glanced at the printed words. *Abelli stated the rumors were...*

Couldn't be him. He couldn't have anything to do with Matthew, his parents, Tiernan. Her paranoia about him had to be the only reason she'd even suspect something so impossible. The world wasn't that small.

Still, since the paper had been in the Bordens' office, it could be a potential clue to solve Matthew's situation. She'd better see what she could find out. Alone, just in case. She went to Tiernan's phone on the table and pulled out one of the chairs to sit down.

The last part of the website address on the scrap included the words, *governor-investigated*. With any luck, that would be part of the article's title.

The smartphone wasn't protected with a security code, probably so she could use it in emergencies, like Tiernan had said. She found the search box and typed in "governor investigated." Not like that would be specific enough to find anything conclusive.

Special Target

Grayson. Governor Grayson? Staying as far away from politics as she could had its advantages, but in this case her lack of knowledge made her slow on the uptake. Hadn't she seen political ads on TV with Grayson running for governor?

She added *Grayson* and *Illinois* to the search terms, tapped the search function, and waited.

"Home?"

Ashley jumped at the voice from the living room. She let out a long breath and looked at Matthew.

He sat up in the chair, rubbing his eyes with a closed fist like a toddler.

Something in her chest squeezed. "No. We're not home." She lowered her voice as she looked at the phone. "But I hope to find you one soon."

A list of search results filled the screen. She scrolled down past the paid ad results. Her eyes locked on the next heading: *Gov. Grayson Investigated for Alleged Racketeering.*

"Egg?"

She dragged her gaze from the phone. Since when had Matthew wanted to eat an egg for breakfast? She'd only fed him cereal, and he'd never complained. The breakfast at the mansion must have spoiled him. Or maybe he used to eat eggs? "Tiernan's going to make us lunch. Fish, I think."

His lower lip started to push out as he ducked his chin.

Wonderful. "It'll be good. He promised." Whatever that was worth. She frowned at her inner critic. Tiernan had treated them well enough so far. It was possible that he really was the protector he claimed to be. At least for Matthew.

She sighed. "Why don't you look at one of your photo albums?" She pointed to the coffee table where Tiernan had stacked the two books.

Matthew's little eyebrows knitted together.

"The picture books. On the table."

Understanding seemed to dawn as his forehead smoothed and his gaze went to the books. He pulled one off the table and onto his lap. That should occupy him for a minute at least.

She looked down at the search results excerpt. Her attention latched onto a line under the heading she hadn't seen before.

Grayson's lawyer: "Trumped up" charges will never come to court.

Her breath stopped. Her pulse pounded in her ears. His lawyer. She forced her finger to press the link to the article.

She waited, trying to breathe while the phone took a year to load the article. She stared at the low bars at the top of the screen.

A noise—a thump—sounded somewhere close.

She jerked her head up. Had the sound come from outside the door?

She stared at the closed wooden door. Listened.

Nothing.

Had she imagined it? Tiernan couldn't be back already, could he? Could've just been someone who lived in one of the other condos passing by.

Her gaze yanked to the phone.

The full article finally appeared on the screen.

She scrolled down past the heading in large letters, her eyes skimming the words that followed.

Frank Abelli.

Bile surged up her throat at the sight of the name in the first paragraph. She forced down the disgusting taste and battled to see past the fog that started to mar her vision. She couldn't shut down. Not now.

Breathe. Breathe. She pulled air in and pushed it out, one breath at a time until the fog cleared.

Her hand shaking, she held the phone up to her face and read further.

Frank Abelli, Gov. Grayson's attorney, claims that the racketeering charges are unfounded, fabricated on rumors and "personal vendetta" rather than actual evidence. "Gov. Grayson's reputation," said Abelli, "will not be tarnished by such an obvious attempt to jeopardize his position in office. There is no evidence in this case because my client is innocent."

The voice that matched the quotes crept into her head, spreading through her body like shards of glass as she read the words.

She pushed on past the pain.

The rest of the article confirmed the claims. As of printing, there was no solid evidence against Grayson, and it seemed likely that the investigation would conclude shortly.

Abelli stated the rumors were erroneous and unfairly prejudicial.

She looked at the scrap of paper she'd set on the table. It was the same sentence from the fragment printed there. But why would Matthew's parents have an article about Grayson and…that name?

She scrolled back up to the top of the article, looking for a date.

Three years ago. Hadn't Grayson been reelected since then? If he was still around, Abelli could be with him.

The sooner we can use her and get rid of her, the better. Katherine's words blared in Ashley's ears like a warning siren.

They couldn't mean…Frank Abelli. The name lodged in her brain as her stomach lurched. She was going to be sick. She had to get away. Anywhere away from that name.

"Matthew." Her heart slammed against her rib cage as she launched out of the chair and hurried to the boy. "We're leaving. Now." Before Tiernan, that lying traitor, came back. She'd use the knife or pepper spray or both if she had to look at his smug face one more time.

Matthew whined as she pulled his arm.

Was she hurting him? She relaxed her hold. "Come on, Matthew."

He clutched the photo album with a deep frown.

So that's what his problem was. "You can take it along. I don't care." Her voice rose with her accelerating pulse. "But we're going right now. Get up and get your bag."

She sprinted away from him to the bedroom where she grabbed her suitcase and rushed back.

Matthew stood by the couch, wearing his crooked baseball cap as he tried to hold the two albums and his Bible in one arm while they slipped from his grasp.

"Oh, for—" Ashley grabbed one of the photo albums. "There. You carry those two and pick up your bag." She went to the door and unlocked it.

What if Tiernan was on the other side, about to come in? The thought made her heart jump into her throat.

She shook her head. She'd escaped from worse than this. *No fear.*

Matthew came up behind her with his duffel bag as she swung the door open and looked out.

The flight of stairs was empty.

She didn't remember to breathe until they were out of the building and walking away from the parking lot on the sidewalk along the street. Heat cloaked her like a sticky blanket as she dragged her overnight bag on its wheels behind her.

Her legs wanted to push faster and faster, but Matthew fell behind. She forced herself to wait for him to catch up.

She looked ahead to the street corner. Tiernan had said the store he was going to was just around the corner. But had he meant on foot or by car? There was only a gas station at this corner. Couldn't get gourmet ingredients there. Maybe he'd meant by car. In that case, he would drive back this way.

A chance she'd have to take. She knew where they were this time. She would get them out of here and far away from Tiernan.

Matthew lagged behind, his hands too full to try to hold her hand for once.

"Come on, Matthew. We're almost there." She repeated those words several times before they finished the trek another block down to the bus stop where they had to wait for the bus.

What if Tiernan drove past and spotted them? As casually

as she could, Ashley maneuvered herself and Matthew behind the two other people who stood by the street.

Her heart rate slowed a fraction when they got on the bus, and it started moving. She watched out the windows as they drove, scanning every vehicle as it approached, braced to see the jeep. Or would he have switched to a different car somehow?

How could she have thought for a second she could trust a man like him? Any man?

She was so stupid. As if she hadn't learned anything in her miserable thirty years of life. She pressed the side of her finger against her teeth until the skin hurt.

"If Ashley will play along..."

She'd heard him say it with her own ears. And she'd let her guard down anyway. He was the only man who could still manage to con her.

"Egg." Matthew pointed at a billboard on the side of a building.

The sign advertised the famous all-day breakfast food of a restaurant where Ashley had eaten once when she'd done a foster home check in the area. Best to get off the bus in short stops anyway. Tiernan would be more likely to think she'd take the first bus she saw and stay on as far as it went.

"Okay. We can eat while I figure things out."

She watched for the Riverwalk stop and pulled Matthew, along with his books and bag, off the bus.

By the time they sat in the crowded, air-conditioned café, Ashley was still far too nauseated to eat. But she was finally calm enough to think. Reviewing what a creep Tiernan was wouldn't get her or Matthew somewhere safe.

She still had Tiernan's phone with her. She could call Tina, maybe stay with her.

No. If Grayson's people were the ones who had found and trashed Ashley's house, they'd know about Tina, too. *Yikes.* Was Tina okay? Ashley hadn't thought about the danger to her before. Maybe Grayson would leave Tina alone since she hadn't done anything with Matthew.

The teenager in question slurped the runny yolk of his egg, the yellow liquid dripping down his chin. At least the normal clothes he'd changed into in the bathroom attracted less attention than his pajamas.

All this fuss over a kid who couldn't possibly know whatever big secret his parents had, despite what the bad guys—Tiernan included—thought. Poor Matthew. His parents were probably criminals working with Grayson. Maybe they'd double-crossed him and got knocked off for it. Matthew wouldn't have had a clue what kind of people they really were.

Maybe that was a good thing. In a way, life could've been easier for Ashley if she'd been unable to comprehend the awful things people did.

No. That wasn't true. She'd still feel their painful effects without being able to do anything about it. Being like Matthew would be far, far worse.

The cell phone rang in her purse.

She pulled it out and checked the caller ID.

No name. Just an unknown number. Probably Tiernan.

Would he think she'd left because of danger, like he'd said? Maybe he'd know she left because of him, possibly the most dangerous character in this whole mess.

She selected *Ignore* and stuffed the phone back into her purse. When she glanced up, a dark-haired waiter watched her from another aisle, across a partition.

He glanced away.

That was the same guy who'd looked at them funny when they'd come in, too. She had chalked it up to Matthew's Down syndrome and Snoopy pajamas at the time, but now...

The knots in her stomach twisted, reminding her why she hadn't touched the eggs and bacon on her plate. Talk about a crash diet.

She left just enough cash to cover the bill on the slip the waitress had laid on their table. Ashley might need the tip money herself before this was all over. Couldn't use a credit card. Too easy to trace if anyone was looking for them already. Tiernan most definitely was.

"Time to go. Wipe your chin." Ashley scanned the restaurant for that suspicious waiter while Matthew cleaned the yolk off his chin with a napkin.

No sign of the guy. At the moment.

She made herself take a calming breath as she reached across the table to straighten Matthew's cap. No one besides Tiernan could know they were out on their own yet. The guy had to be staring only because of Matthew's strangeness. Ah, for the days when she and Tina used to giggle about men eyeing them in public.

Matthew struggled to stack his Bible and photo albums in his arms.

"Here. Give them to me." She got out of the booth and unzipped her suitcase. Who cared if the customers thought she was crazy. At this point, she was starting to believe it herself. She held out her hand toward Matthew.

He looked at her, something like worry in his eyes.

"Give me the photo albums. I'll put them in here. We'll still have them."

He reluctantly handed her the heavy albums, and she stacked them on top of her already wrinkled clothes. She flipped the suitcase lid down and pressed with her knees on the top until she could zip it shut again. "Give me that one, too." She pointed at his Bible. "I can probably get it in the outside pocket."

He squeezed the Bible to his chest.

She rolled her eyes. "Oh, fine. But I'm not carrying it for you if you get tired." Not like he'd let her carry it anyway.

The heat felt pleasantly warm on her skin when they walked outside. For the first second. Then the humidity reminded her why she'd been so happy to reach air conditioning.

Matthew let out one of his excited grunts, pointing at the fountain across the street.

Ashley recognized its distinctive shape. The Dandelion fountain in the pavilion area of the Graterville Riverwalk. A real kid-pleaser.

She didn't stop Matthew as he jogged across the empty street, right up to the fountain. She followed more slowly, not eager to encourage the sweat that started to moisten her forehead and neck.

His duffel bag behind him on the brick, Matthew touched the spraying threads of water with his fingers, then jerked back with a giggle. He gave her that sunny smile, his features scrunched around it as he laughed.

She couldn't help the smile that pulled up her mouth. What a kid. On the run, and he was having the time of his life.

Then she looked at the fountain.

A memory barreled into her, knocking the air from her lungs like a kick in the gut.

He watched her, laughed at her over the arching streaks of water.

Veronica wore her plastic smile.

The water hit Ashley's small body, soaking her blue swimsuit. But not enough to wash away everything.

She gasped as she shook herself free from the memory's clutches.

Matthew still played in the water, next to a little girl wearing a pink swimsuit.

Ashley stumbled over to an empty bench. She sank onto the firm wood. She'd been here before as an adult. Hadn't remembered...Had she blocked out the memory along with all the others she tried so desperately to forget?

She blinked. She had to return to the here and now before the pain reclaimed her.

A teenager walked past.

Matthew?

She turned to look.

Sure enough, he headed up the path that led to the covered bridge and the other side of the river.

"Matthew!"

He either didn't hear or didn't want to.

They couldn't stay there any longer. Not now that she remembered.

She followed Matthew through the covered bridge and to the other side, trying not to look around in case she'd see something that was another trigger. Had to focus on something else.

Her plan. What were they going to do after she got Matthew away from here? Where would she take him? It wasn't like she could find him a home while they were on the run from a corrupt politician *and* the FBI.

The handle of her suitcase slipped from her grip thanks to her sweaty palm. She stepped back to grab it again with an irritated grunt. Those stupid albums made the bag so much heavier.

She paused. The albums. Tiernan said he thought Matthew could still lead them to the documents through the pictures of where he'd been with his family. Tiernan might have lied about everything else, but he did seem genuine about that part. And he had no reason to lie to her about that. It was his own idea that had nothing to do with her.

If he was right, Ashley would be very glad Matthew had insisted on bringing the albums along. Those clunky books might be their ticket out of this mess.

She didn't stop Matthew as he went down the steps next to the bridge. She was too busy thinking while she lugged her suitcase down behind him.

All they had to do was find a safe place to stay tonight while she had Matthew look through the photo albums. Then if he reacted to any location in the pictures or hinted about a hiding spot at one, she'd take him there tomorrow.

But where could they stay in the meantime? Tina's place was out and so was Ashley's. She'd need money to stay anywhere else, especially if they had to travel to more than one location. The kind of money she didn't carry on her or have in her bank account. Not her personal account anyway.

The thought of the other option made her already sickened stomach churn. She'd sworn she would never touch it.

Matthew giggled. He stood at the edge of the river, watching a couple ducks that dove under and popped back up.

She walked over to him and put her hand gently on his arm. "Don't stand so close."

He took one step back from the edge, still leaning toward the water like he wanted to dive in with the ducks. "Swim swim!" He started paddling his hands in front of him, then switched to swinging his arms over his head and pulling them back, like he was swimming on dry land.

A laugh escaped Ashley's lips.

He looked so cute and funny at the same time, his lips puckered together like a fish and his chubby arms tugging through the hot air. His gaze moved to her, and he smiled.

She laughed again, the tightness in her chest relaxing until she could breathe better than she had in days.

Then a man walked behind her. So close, she felt the air move.

She instinctively gripped the strap of her purse and Matthew's arm.

But the man passed on without looking back.

The tension returned, along with a quickened heartbeat. She hadn't seen him coming. He could have done anything. To either of them.

Matthew watched her like he was waiting for her to fix the world.

She was his only hope. She had to keep him safe and get him out of this mess.

Steeling her jaw, she picked up the suitcase and turned her back to the water, scanning for people watching or approaching.

Special Target

Memories be hanged. She'd do what she had to, and no one was going to stop her.

chapter
twenty

Ashley wasn't sure which she dreaded more—going to the bank or her house. She could only hope the thugs who had trashed her place hadn't taken her birth certificate...and that they were long gone.

She had pulled her hair up into a ponytail but sweat still gathered on her neck and forehead as she tried to keep up a good pace on the sidewalk, dragging her suitcase behind her.

The phone vibrated, shaking the fake leather of her purse against her side. She could turn the phone off, but knowing what Tiernan was doing for those seconds he called seemed like a good strategy.

Matthew shuffled at her side, his duffel bag sagging lower in his hand and banging against his jeans. The long walk from the commuter train to her house was apparently taking a toll on him in this heat. Poor kid's cheeks were flushed and sweat dripped from his nose, the humidity undaunted by the shade his cap provided him.

Ashley slowed as they neared her front yard. For once, she was there during the day. A rare thing except on weekends. Seemed the best call to go in daylight. If anyone was watching, maybe they wouldn't risk taking action.

The thought of an observer prompted her to stop and look

around before going inside. The place seemed quiet. More neighborhood noises echoed during the day than what she was used to on weeknights. Normal sounds, like lawn mowers and dogs barking.

No sign of LeBron outside his place. Unusual for a hot day like this. He spent so much time sitting outside in a lawn chair during heat waves that she figured his air conditioner didn't work. Shouldn't he be there now? Maybe he only did that on weekends.

She shrugged. She should be glad the creep was hidden away. But it felt more like watching a spider scurry into a vent right next to her bed. She could only wait for it to crawl back out...when she was unsuspecting and vulnerable.

Matthew walked past Ashley as she stood there. He headed straight up the driveway, like he knew the drill.

Maybe ignorance was sometimes bliss. Still, his boldness was a reminder she needed.

She was succumbing to fear again. She would not let it paralyze her anymore. Tightening her grip on the suitcase, she marched up the driveway and passed Matthew to reach the side door. With Grayson and that awful name she didn't even want to think, Ashley had much bigger fish to deal with than LeBron right now.

She jiggled the doorknob, but it didn't turn. Nice of the thugs to lock up when they'd left. She unlocked the door and opened it.

Matthew started to step through, but she put up her hand to stop him. "I'll go first. You follow me."

She cautiously stepped inside but refused to let fear drive her movements. She kept her breathing even and strong, making her pulse follow suit, steady and normal. As she neared the corner of the living room, she forced herself to step around it without hesitation.

She saw Tiernan on the couch, watching her as he had that night he'd scared her.

But he wasn't there. Only the memory.

The couch wasn't the same either. The cushions lay on the floor, torn or sliced down the middle, stuffing strewn across the carpeting. The overturned coffee table was missing a leg, making a pair on the floor with the broken table leg that had once been her weapon.

The kitchen was only a little better. The table still stood on its feet, but the chairs had been upset, one of them thrown into the living room. Cabinets and drawers hung open, silverware and plates tossed on the floor amid broken pieces.

Anger swelled in Ashley's chest as she surveyed her possessions, treated with such violence for no reason. Destruction like this wasn't necessary just to find information about Matthew. Not if Tiernan had told the truth about the housebreakers and what they wanted.

"God good." Matthew stared down at a broken plate at his feet.

His timing with those sayings would be funny if the situations weren't so frustrating. He obviously didn't have a clue what the words meant. Maybe there was a way to untrain him and get him to stop spouting them all the time. Especially at moments like this.

She blew out a sigh and headed for the bedroom. She'd wasted enough time wallowing. The birth certificate should still be where she'd hidden it. She would defy even those professional thugs, or whatever they were, to have found it.

As she stepped into the bedroom, she scanned the chaos there. Bedcovers stripped off the mattress, which lay at an angle across the bed and the floor. Her clothes tossed with Eddie's all over the floor. Her fish...

Ashley hurried to the dresser where the fish tank sat. The tank looked like it hadn't been touched, but her two fish lay at the top of the water, bellies up.

A lump ballooned in her throat as she stared at them. She blinked away the stinging moisture that came to her eyes. They were just fish.

Matthew stood next to her.

If he said *God good* again, she'd clobber him. She sniffed and went to the armoire, now conveniently empty thanks to her free cleaning service. She ran her fingers along the back of the armoire's floor, the chocolate-colored wood of the interior too dark for her to see the secret board.

Her finger dropped into a little hole where the chunk of wood was missing. Bingo. She raised the board and lifted out the recipe-sized box under it. She opened it quickly, not looking at any of the contents except what she needed—her birth certificate. She pulled out the folded certificate and shut the box, dropping it back in the hole and covering it with the board.

"She lives."

Her heart nearly crashed against her ribcage as she whirled to the man's voice.

Eddie. He glowered at her from the doorway, his massively thick eyebrows forming a black bar above his eyes.

She resisted putting her hand on her chest as her heartbeat slowed, and she breathed again. She wasn't about to give him the pleasure of knowing he'd scared her.

"Did you have to destroy the house and ruin all my things?" He gestured to the mess. "I would have come back to get them already if you had just returned my calls."

He seriously thought she was that immature? "I didn't get any calls." Thanks to Tiernan holding her phone hostage.

"I texted you, too. Many times. It's just like you to ignore reality when you're angry."

Had she really thought that accent was cute? How quickly things changed.

"But this," he waved a hand at the clothes, "this is crazy. You are insane."

"You seriously think I'd trash my own house over you?"

His square chin lifted. "There's no other reason."

She laughed without humor and stalked toward the door. "You think that if it makes you feel like more of a man." She brushed past him without a glance. "Let's go, Matthew."

"And you still keep the boy?" Eddie turned to face her at the door as Matthew moved close to her. "You will never keep your new boyfriend with him around. Men don't want women with children not their own."

Now Eddie thought she'd gotten rid of him for another man?

"And him." Eddie jerked his chin toward Matthew. "He is too ugly for anyone."

Ashley caught the full impact of Eddie's misdirected anger. There was no call for that. She took a step toward him, meeting his glare head-on. "Not as ugly as you."

She let the comeback and her double meaning sink in as she grabbed Matthew's arm and guided him through the door in front of her. "Leave your key when you get out of here." She didn't look back with the order as she rushed to get Matthew away from the man she'd been stupid enough to love.

Next stop, the bank. Another encounter with her past. This was going to be a very long day.

"Your son?"

Ashley blinked at the yellow-haired woman who watched Matthew from behind her rimless glasses. "No. I'm a social worker. He's in foster care." Or something resembling it.

The bank clerk smiled. "Oh, that's too bad he doesn't have his own family. Did they leave him because of his condition?"

"I really am in a hurry." Ashley tried for a polite expression. "Can we get this...completed?" She stopped herself just short of asking to get this over with, though that wording would have fit her feelings at the moment.

"Of course."

Ashley's stomach clenched as she sat in the chair across the desk from the middle-aged bank clerk who supposedly knew Veronica. From way back, the woman had told Ashley. More than Ashley had ever wanted to know.

"Let's see." The woman typed more things into her computer. She'd been doing that for ten minutes already.

Matthew sat quietly beside Ashley, waiting with more patience than she had. At least he wasn't swinging his hands up and down. The last thing she needed was to draw more attention. Thank goodness this was all under different names, or she wouldn't even be able to get the money without drawing Tiernan or Grayson's men.

"Here it is. Yes." The clerk nodded at the computer screen like it was talking to her. "I thought so." She turned her gaze to Ashley. "Your mother stipulated that her daughter would bring a birth certificate as verification of her identity in order to access the account. Do you have that document with you?"

Ashley handed the lady the certificate she'd clutched in her fingers since arriving.

The clerk pulled her glasses down to the tip of her nose as she examined the certificate. "Mm-hmm. Veronica Dona—"

"I know what it says." Ashley pressed her lips together. *Stay calm.* Or the woman might not give her the money. "Sorry. It's just...painful." Now that was the truth.

The lady's brow furrowed, and her mouth pulled down with deep concern. "Oh, I'm so sorry, dear. I know you must miss your mother terribly. Veronica Donavan was a special girl when I knew her, and she grew into a fine lady."

Ashley gathered all her effort to force a smile. *Fine lady*, meaning rich. She certainly had been that.

"There's a young lady at our church just like him."

"What?"

The woman nodded to Matthew. "She has the same condition. She's such a sweet young lady. Truly special."

A nice way of saying weird and different from everyone else. Ashley barely stopped herself from challenging the clerk. "So are we all set now? I can withdraw from the account?"

"One last thing."

Great.

"Your mother wrote you a letter she wanted you to read. I

took it out when you called ahead." She held out a sealed envelope.

Ashley's heart stopped. She stared at the envelope. "No." She swallowed and tore her gaze from the letter. "I really don't need to read that."

"I'm afraid you do." She gave Ashley an inappropriately sweet smile. "As a condition of your access to the account, she stipulated that you must first read this letter."

"Fine." She snatched the envelope and stuffed it in her purse.

The clerk watched her.

"I'll read it later."

"You're to read it in front of a witness." Her eyes filled with something that was probably supposed to be compassion. "Is the loss of your mother still that painful for you, dear? It's been what, ten years now?"

"*I'm sorry*," Veronica had said. Begging. Only to taunt Ashley now from the grave. If she was going to try and buy the forgiveness she didn't deserve, this was a crummy way to go about it.

"Do you need to answer that?" The clerk's meddling question alerted Ashley to the loud vibrating of the phone in her purse.

Tiernan. She should have turned it off. But it was a good reminder of the reason she came here to get the money she'd sworn she would never touch. It wasn't for her. She'd still keep that promise to her death.

She yanked the letter from her purse and tore open the envelope before she lost her courage. All she had to do was move her eyes over the page like she was reading it. She didn't have to absorb a single word.

Veronica's handwriting stabbed like a knife into her side.

Ashley lowered the paper to her lap to hide that her hands were shaking. She skimmed over the words, her resistance giving way only at the bottom of the page.

"*I pray someday you can forgive me.*"

Special Target

Prayer to what? The almighty bottle or the painkillers? Amazing she'd lived long enough to write this letter.

Ashley fought the powerful urge to crumple the paper and throw it across the room. Or better yet, to slowly tear it into a thousand little shreds. But she gritted her teeth and folded the paper neatly before slipping it into the envelope. She slid it across the desk.

"Oh, you can keep it."

Ashley shook her head. "I'd prefer it be here." She showed her teeth in what she hoped passed for a smile. "Where it will be safe." And far, far away.

"Well, I suppose we could put it in your mother's safe-deposit box."

Ashley nodded. "Please."

"All right." The clerk tapped more keys. "That's it. You now have full access to the account." She added one more paper to the folder in front of her. "This folder has all the account information, including the number to call if you have any questions or concerns. Your debit card is in there, and this account can also be accessed by ATM." She handed Ashley the folder and clasped her hands together on the desk. "Is there anything else I can help you with today?"

"Yes. I'd like to withdraw some before I leave. In cash."

"How much?"

She might as well clear the whole account and be done with it. Veronica was helpless with finances and lived on an allowance all her married days. There couldn't be that much in there. But carrying a lot of cash around right now wouldn't be smart either. "How much is in the account?"

"Oh, I'm sorry. I thought you knew. With the interest accrued these last twelve years, it's now over six hundred thousand dollars."

A shadow moved in her room. That horrific shadow she knew.

It moved closer.
She couldn't see him. Couldn't see his face.
But he drew closer, closer.
She tried to scream. Nothing came out. She strained, stretching her vocal cords.
She couldn't make a sound.

Ashley sat up, screaming.

She clutched the sheet that covered her, holding it over her head. She was crunched in a ball, her knees by her chin.

Someone touched her.

She jerked away, terror silencing her lungs.

"Azwee."

She held her breath.

"Azwee."

Matthew?

She slowly pulled the sheet down with trembling fingers, uncovering her eyes.

Matthew watched her in the shadowed dimness of the room. Had he been trying to say her name? He stretched out a chubby hand toward her head.

For some reason, she didn't pull back. She watched those slits of eyes as he rested his hand on the side of her tilted head. "God good."

His hand was heavy and warm on her hair.

Her eyelids drifted shut, darkness taking her to a sleep without shadows, without fear, where she saw only a boy, smiling…happy.

It was all Tiernan's fault. Ashley shouldn't have had to spend such an awful night at the hotel, to face a nightmare like that after all these years.

She ground her teeth together as she watched the Chicago traffic out the window of the taxi, glaring at the people on sidewalks like they were that jerk FBI agent.

If Tiernan hadn't dragged her into this situation and lied to her about the real reason he wanted her help with Matthew, she wouldn't be fighting long-buried memories. She'd be comfortable in her undamaged home right now, or at the office chatting with Tina. Or out saving some child from a fate worse than death.

She hadn't even been able to enjoy the five-star downtown Chicago hotel she could now afford, where the staff was paid enough to act like Matthew and his staying in a two-room suite with Ashley was normal. At least she didn't have to worry anymore about how to fund the exploratory trips to follow Matthew's clues.

The plan to follow his hints about places in the photo albums seemed far-fetched, but she had Matthew look at some pictures after breakfast anyway, her expectations low.

Excitement had lit his face when he saw photos of a shipyard and a boat with the name, *Mary*, on the bow. Looked like the same vessel as the one in the home video they'd watched with Tiernan. Matthew had pointed at the pictures, repeating "Hide" over and over again. Maybe there had been something more than coincidence when he'd said the same thing at the mansion with the video.

Ashley looked at the boy as he stared out his window of the cab, holding the Bible against his chest.

He alternately smiled and gaped at the objects and people they passed but appeared as uncomprehending as usual. Didn't look much like a nighttime angel.

The incident last night seemed so surreal, she wasn't even sure he had woken her up or been there at all. She could have dreamed it. Just like she was probably wishfully dreaming that he could know where his parents hid the documents that had gotten them killed.

She still didn't have any greater confidence in Matthew's competence as an evidence-finder by the time they reached the harbor. Hopefully, the right harbor.

From the pictures, the boat appeared to be docked at one

of the popular downtown harbors Ashley thought she recognized. But she could be about to make a very big fool of herself.

The taxi pulled up to the harbor building, and Ashley paid the driver—a silent man who'd tried to avoid looking at Matthew at all. She led the boy to the building, her tired arms finally free, for once not having to lug her suitcase around. If all the locations they'd have to visit were this close, they would be able to leave their luggage at the same downtown hotel the whole time. But the three outfits she had fit into her overnight bag would get repetitive, even with laundry service at the hotel. Maybe she'd squeeze in a little shopping before the day was done.

She caught herself as she opened the glass door to the building. What was she thinking?

She was not going to compromise. She would not use the money on herself. Only for food and lodging to stay with Matthew until this was over. Then she'd walk away from whatever money was left in the account and never look back.

Cool air from the AC brushed over her skin like a welcome breeze as she started toward the information desk.

"Matthew!"

The shout stopped Ashley in her tracks. She turned to see a tall, thin man headed right for them. She moved to stand partially in front of Matthew.

The boy smiled at the stranger as innocently as only he could.

As the guy got closer, Ashley could see a broad grin dividing his white mustache and beard. Would Grayson hire a friendly man in his seventies to kidnap Matthew? Didn't seem likely.

"Matthew, my boy." The black band on the man's sailor hat gleamed under the fluorescent lights as he shook his head and rested closed fists on his hips, still smiling at the teen. "Come 'ere." He slurred the words together as he threw out his arms, and Matthew stepped around Ashley in time to be grabbed in a back-slapping hug.

"And who is this lovely lady you brought with you today?"

She closed her mouth that had hung open as she watched the warm welcome. "Ashley Sorenson. Social worker."

Sailor man's smile dimmed. "Aye. I wondered where Matthew had gone. His parents?"

She shook her head, and a frown sagged the man's thin mouth. "Who are you?"

"Where are my manners? It isn't often we meet a lady like yourself at sea." He brightened again, teeth too perfect to be his own shining between his lips. "Keith Boxley. Harbor Master."

She raised her eyebrows.

"Unofficially, if you like."

"I see."

"I know...I *knew* the good lad's folks. Finer people you will never meet." He slapped Matthew on the back. "So, lad. Have you come to visit the *Mary* then? Come to take her out maybe?"

"Just visit." Ashley flashed a quick smile. At least she'd found the right place. And this guy could help her with step two. "Matthew couldn't remember where the boat was parked. Can you help us find it?"

"Aye, that I can. And I can also tell you we don't *park* boats, we dock 'em." His quivering lips appeared to be barely holding back a laugh. At her expense. He and his fake pirate accent were going to get on her nerves very quickly.

He wrapped his arm around Matthew's shoulders and turned him in the direction of another glass door that led outside.

Ashley followed behind, only partially listening as Keith chatted with Matthew nonstop about the book he carried, the sailing conditions of the day, and new boats at the harbor. Quite pointless since Matthew couldn't understand any of it. At least the man seemed to like the boy. Rare to find someone

Matthew didn't make uncomfortable. Keith behaved almost like Tiernan did with the teen.

Tiernan.

Ashley frowned as she followed Keith and Matthew through the door into the heat. The cell phone hadn't vibrated all day. Did that mean he'd given up?

Not a chance. Probably meant he was trying a different tactic. Or that he was closer to finding them than she thought?

Hiding in the most crowded area of Chicago seemed like a good idea. And he'd never suspect they could afford to stay at a five-star hotel downtown. No one should find them there.

Keith glanced back at her. "We'll have to get you some sailing shoes, missy."

She glared at the man, refusing to look down at her flip-flops, which slapped loudly on the wooden dock as they passed the first row of parked—*docked*—boats.

She'd never pretended to be a sailor. Matthew would have to pick a harbor and a boat for the hiding place.

A boat that looked too much like the one she was trying not to remember crossed her line of sight.

She glanced away. "Are we going to walk through the whole harbor?"

Keith paused and turned back to her. "Weak legs? We'll be there soon. She's at dock C, right over there."

Ashley stared down at the dock the rest of the walk, glancing up only in time to see Keith take a turn onto a narrower dock.

She followed the turn and kept her eyes on the boards instead of the boats, trying to ignore the familiar sound of lapping water.

"Here we are. Isn't she a beauty?"

Ashley looked up to see an average-sized boat, white and blue with *Mary* printed on the bow, just like in the photo. "Little small, isn't it?"

"Well, sure, there's bigger." He gently touched the side of the boat. "But she's steady and true."

Kind of like an old dog. Ashley was working on hiding her smirk when Matthew suddenly took off.

"Hide!" He didn't slow down to let out his yell as he raced for the steps that led onto the boat.

"Matthew!"

"It's all right." Keith waved to quiet her call. "The boy knows her well. His parents used to bring him to take her out nearly every other weekend during the summer when the weather was good. When they weren't at their cabin, that is."

"That's nice, but I'd still like to make sure he's okay." And see what he was doing. Finding documents, maybe? It was too much to wish for, but she did anyway. Could this all end today? The danger, the connection to her past, the running. All of it.

She followed Matthew's path to the boat and climbed on board. Or was it *aboard*? Whatever.

"I have some things to take care of, but I'll check on you two in a bit." The old sailor gave her a nod from the dock.

"Okay." She turned away from him to scan the boat. "Matthew?" She couldn't see him anywhere. A little doorway split the steering part of the boat down the center, but with the bright sun outside, everything past the doorway was dark.

She ducked to fit through the opening and stepped down into the lower part of the boat. The cabin. Seats lined two sides of the small space, which also held a mini kitchen with a stove and microwave.

"Matthew?" Her nerves started to tingle. How could he have disappeared? Had she missed him up top?

She turned around to go back up.

"Find."

Matthew. Don't tell her he was just playing hide and seek again. Disappointment sank from her chest and settled in her stomach. Was that all he had associated with the boat this entire time?

She sighed. "I can't find you. You'll have to show yourself." She waited.

No response.

Fine. "Come out, come out, wherever you are."

A giggle. Then one of the seats started to move. The cushion pushed up, revealing Matthew's smiling face.

"Is that all you hide here? Just yourself?"

He stood and stepped out of the compartment. "Ma...ma. Hide."

Her heart squeezed. Did he realize his mother wasn't there? Could he remember that?

His lips pushed out in either a pout or a frown. She wasn't sure.

"Come on. Let's go back to the hotel." And what? Try again with another picture? Or was this all a joke, and he'd never lead her to the documents?

As long as she was here, she might as well look around. Maybe the FBI hadn't searched the boat yet. "Before we go, you can play a little if you want. I have to look for something."

"Find?"

Sounded like a question instead of his usual statement. "Yes. I need to find papers." Or microfilm or a flash drive or anything. But telling him all that wouldn't help. "Can you help me look?"

He nodded, but just stood there.

She started with the cushions that she now knew housed storage compartments underneath. The one Matthew hadn't hid in was filled with life jackets and other boating junk. She worked her way through the little cabinets in the kitchen area, the bookshelf, and the very small bathroom.

Matthew followed her, pretending to search everywhere she just had.

But there was nothing to be found.

Maybe there'd be something up top. Boats had a million storage compartments.

"Let's go, Matthew."

Special Target

He looked up from peeking under the seat she'd just checked one last time and moved to follow her.

She climbed the steps, a cool breeze brushing her cheeks when she reached the deck. The lake was usually cooler than the rest of the city on days like this, but she hadn't noticed it earlier. Maybe being in the claustrophobic cabin made her more appreciative of any open air.

A few buckets stood on the deck, and there were more seats to check under. She walked over to the closest bucket and bent over it.

A pinging sound came from just beyond her.

What was that? She straightened. Had something hit the rail of the boat? She checked behind her to see if Matthew might have thrown something.

He stood at the top of the steps, his nose scrunched as he looked around. Had he heard the sound, too? He waved at someone.

She followed the direction of the wave, her gaze landing on the boat next to them.

And a man with a gun.

chapter
twenty-one

"Get down!" Ashley ran at Matthew and pushed him down the stairs into the cabin.

Splinters shot into the air behind her head as she dove after him.

Someone was shooting at them? Or just at her? Her brain slogged through shock to try to grasp what she had just seen.

A man wearing a fishing hat had crouched behind the rail of the boat behind them, a gun pointed at her. Like something out of a movie.

Had she imagined it?

She peered at the splintered wood on the wall along the steps. No, that was very real. She was no expert, but it looked like the kind of damage bullets did on TV.

Her breath came in pieces.

But Matthew was watching her, his lips pulled into a frown. Did he understand the danger? Or was he upset that she'd pushed him?

Either way, she had to keep him calm. If she could stay calm herself. She had to think.

Why would someone shoot at her? Did Grayson want to kidnap Matthew so badly that he was willing to kill Ashley to get her out of the way?

Her throat went dry with another thought. Maybe the shooter wasn't Grayson's at all. Maybe he was hired by someone else. Someone worse.

She shook her head. This wasn't helping. The man could be climbing down from his boat and coming at them right now. Did he know they were unarmed?

She couldn't take down a guy with a gun. He could easily kill her and snatch Matthew. If that's what he was after.

Tiernan. She hated the thought, but she needed his help. If he were close by, maybe tailing them, he could get them out of this. She grabbed the phone from her purse and pressed the button to illuminate the screen.

It stayed black.

Her oxygen thinned. That's why it hadn't vibrated today. The battery was dead.

A flurry of nasty names for herself rushed to her mind. How could she not think of the fact she didn't have a charger for it?

A thump on deck jerked her thoughts to a halt.

She looked at Matthew and pressed a finger against her lips. She pointed to the seat he had hid under earlier. "Hide." She more mouthed the word than whispered, but he seemed to understand.

He went to the seat and lifted the cushion, crunching into the narrow compartment underneath. She pushed the cushion down on top of him. Not a very good hiding spot, but hopefully it would be enough.

A creak of a board on the deck. Then footsteps.

Nearing the cabin.

Ashley's pulse pounded in her ears. She inched farther into the cabin. Maybe she could hide in the bathroom. But she'd be too far away from Matthew.

What if the man with the gun found him first? He could take Matthew or, if Abelli had hired him, maybe he'd shoot Matthew to keep him quiet.

She took a step back toward the sitting area.

Footsteps thudded toward the cabin entrance.

She froze.

Black tennis shoes stopped at the top of the stairs.

She was dead.

"Hello, down there. Permission to come aboard?"

Tiernan?

The lying trickster's deep voice sounded sweeter than anything she'd ever heard. "Hello? Oh, I get it. Matthew, are you hiding again?" Tiernan took the remaining steps casually, bringing his grin into view. "A game of hide and seek?"

She managed a nod, her throat so dry she probably couldn't get out a sound if she tried.

His hair was more tousled than usual and fell a little onto his forehead as he walked into the cabin and started to search for Matthew.

"Let's see, could he be on the stove? Or in the microwave?"

A giggle came from under the seat.

Tiernan winked at Ashley like they were at a playground on vacation. "Gets him every time." He whipped off the seat cushion. "There you are!"

Matthew popped out like a jack-in-the-box, jumping up and down until he landed in Tiernan's arms for a hug.

Ashley's breaths still came in uneven spurts around her erratic pulse, but Matthew acted like nothing had happened at all. If Tiernan hadn't come when he did...

Running from potential kidnappers was one thing. She was not prepared to handle guns. Even her knife wouldn't do her much good.

"The shooter is gone. For now." Tiernan's green eyes watched her as he stepped back from Matthew. "Are you all right?" The meaning in his gaze signaled he intended more than a polite nicety.

Could she trust him? She met his gaze. "We're alive."

His lips pressed into a firm line. "I'd like to keep it that way."

But at what cost? She'd bet all Veronica's money that she wouldn't like his answer.

"What were you thinking?" Tiernan's eyes flashed in the dimming light of early evening as he drove yet another car Ashley had never seen, taking them somewhere he wouldn't reveal. "If I'd thought for a second you were going to run again, I never would have left the condo. I thought I could trust you."

Nice delivery. A touch of childlike innocence blended with shocked hurt in the tone. He was good, all right. But she was through being played. "You were the one who was so sure we'd lost everyone when we left. How did they find us today if you lost them?"

He tossed her a glare. "If I can find you, they can find you." He turned his head back to the road. "You left Graterville *and* me, if you recall. I can't protect you if you don't follow my instructions. You would have been completely safe at my condo until I got back. No one even knew you were there." He tried a glance with less anger in it this time. "I thought you were going to trust me."

"Trust you?" Should she get out her pepper spray now or later? The jerk. "Is that the same as 'playing along'?"

His eyebrow went up. "What are you talking about?"

"I heard you telling the others you wanted me to play along. Pretty low, you telling me to trust you when all along you've been conning me."

"Conning you?" Both eyebrows reached for his hairline this time as he looked at her with confusion in his eyes.

"Oh, you're good. Is FBI training really like in the movies, where they teach you how to lie really well? Or does it just come naturally to you? Oh, I forgot. You're a Christian." Sarcasm dripped from her tone. "You never lie."

His grip on the steering wheel tightened as he stared at the road. "I never pretended I told you everything. I said I couldn't. There are some things you aren't supposed to know."

She shot daggers at his profile with her gaze. "Like Frank Abelli?" How she ever got the words out without them choking her, she'd never know. The fast-food sandwich churned in her stomach while she waited long minutes for Tiernan to speak or react.

"Let me guess." His voice was low, the set of his mouth grim. "You used that phone for more than an emergency call."

"What does...that man have to do with Matthew? With this...mess?"

Tiernan opened his mouth—

"And don't tell me 'nothing.' I know it's no accident that I'm here or that you got me to take Matthew. You can't sell that lie anymore."

"I don't know what you think you found out or who told—"

"Nobody told me anything. Believe it or not, I can think on my own."

"But you're not thinking clearly. Not if you ran away from me because of someone named Frank Abelli."

She snorted. "Don't tell me you're going to claim you don't know anything about him."

He checked the rearview mirror, then looked out the side window. Like he was buying time. He pressed his lips together. "No. But I can't talk about it either."

She gripped the handle of the passenger door. "You better talk about it, or I'll jump out of this car. I mean it. I don't care if it's moving."

"Are you crazy?"

She stared at him.

"It'd be a little hard to do with the doors locked."

"Don't push me." Her voice was as steely as her determination. She'd unlock it or break the window if she had to. No way was he sending her in blind to Abelli anymore.

"Would you calm down?" He sounded more irritated than concerned. Figured. "You'll wake Matthew."

She glanced into the dark back seat.

The boy's cap was nearly pushed off his head, which leaned against the back of the upholstered seat as he slept.

"He's fine."

"That's a miracle with your shouting."

"If you think manufacturing guilt is going to get me off your back, you'd better give up now." She kept her fingers on the door handle. "I'm not going to stay with you any longer unless I get some answers."

"You'll have to wait. I need to get Matthew somewhere safe without any tails before dealing with that." With her, he meant. "And I don't want him to hear what I have to tell you."

Nice try. "He wouldn't understand any of it."

"I can't believe it." He chuckled, but the sound didn't carry a jot of humor. "You've been with him all this time, and you still don't have a clue."

Another shot of irritation blazed through her chest. She knew Matthew better than Tiernan did. She was just more realistic than Tiernan or Matthew's parents had wanted to be.

Matthew wasn't some superstar child. He was a kid with Down syndrome. No chance at anything good.

She crossed her arms in front of her, setting her jaw. "I have more than a clue. That shooter was aiming at me today. I want to know if he was trying to kidnap Matthew or if he was part of that secret you don't think I need to know about. I only know one person who'd want me dead and the name's Abelli."

He didn't look at her. Just sighed. "If you stay in the car, I promise I'll tell you everything when we reach the next safe house."

"Can't wait." For his version of *everything* and the fulfillment of one of his unreliable promises? She'd have an eternal wait.

Matthew shouted behind her.

She jerked to see around the headrest.

He flailed his arms, moaning in the dark. Looked like his eyes were still shut.

"He's having a nightmare." She tried to reach for him, but he was too far away. "Stop the car."

"It's safer if we keep going."

She glared at Tiernan. "Stop. The. Car."

He slowed and pulled over to the shoulder.

She hopped out and yanked open the back door. Sliding in, she folded Matthew into her arms and started rocking. "Shh, Matthew. It's okay. It's just a bad dream. You're okay."

His moaning turned into a soft whimper.

"Shh. I'm here now." She murmured the words against the boy's hair. "You're safe." Tiernan wasn't the only one who told lies.

Ashley and Matthew followed Tiernan across yet another grassy piece of land in the black of night. At least this grass was trimmed short.

Tiernan checked behind them and every other direction as they walked. There was no missing the increase in his watchfulness. Maybe the upped stakes of a shooter put him on edge, too.

Though there was nothing at all nervous about the way he confidently guided them across the open land, headed for who knew where. Why she still followed him blindly like this was beyond her. Getting shot at did strange things to a person's judgment.

He had been right to tell her to change into her tennis shoes in the car. Flip-flops would have been as loud as a gunshot in this country stillness. She'd recognized most of his driving route until the end, when he'd taken some back roads she didn't know. But she was pretty sure they were around Portville somewhere.

Tiernan stopped at a chain-link fence. Looked like a gate with a lock. He fiddled with the lock a few seconds, then opened it. Did he have a key?

She didn't want to know. She brushed past him as he held the gate open.

Why a fence and gate in the middle of nowhere? Only open lawn continued as far as she could see, which wasn't far at all really. The clouds seemed to have blocked what little moonlight shone from the sky. "Don't you have a flashlight?"

"Do you want to get shot?" His whisper came from closer beside her than she thought.

Whatever happened to his old promises that he'd keep them safe? Maybe he really was going to stop conning her.

"This way." He lightly touched her elbow.

She jerked away. "I can follow you."

"Shh."

She could barely see his dim outline as he took hold of Matthew's arm and started forward again, still carrying her suitcase in his other hand and two bulky sacks on his back.

She started after them, half expecting to crash into something at any moment. Or feel a bullet rip into her flesh. Tiernan just had to bring that up.

Answers. He promised answers as soon as they got to wherever they were headed. If they made it there alive, she'd make sure he kept his promise this time.

The ground under her feet became firm, and she looked down to see pavement instead of grass.

When she raised her gaze, her surroundings had lightened a little. A cloud must have moved away from the moon.

An outline of unfamiliar, large structures loomed in front of her.

"Watch it." Tiernan pointed at her feet.

She stopped. Inches before she would have stepped into...a pool of water?

"Walk where I do. Nowhere else." He continued on,

leading them past tall, spindly poles that appeared to hold up giant tubes, high above their heads.

What kind of place was this? She couldn't make out anything clearly enough to tell in the dark shadows.

A figure stood on her right.

A gasp shot up her throat, and she slapped a hand over her mouth to silence it.

"That's the Croc Doc. He's friendly." Humor laced Tiernan's tone.

How dare he laugh at her at such a time? There was nothing funny about this place or the statue of a standing, cartoon-like crocodile that stared at her with its grinning mouth open. A relative of Tiernan's no doubt.

Was this an amusement park? That wouldn't explain the water they'd been walking along, but there was nothing creepier than an amusement park at night, and this place qualified.

Tiernan stopped again, this time by heavy-looking steel doors attached to a building. He unlocked one in short order and waved Matthew and Ashley inside while he held it open. He checked outside one last time before closing the door behind them.

It was pitch black.

Before Ashley's rising panic had a chance to reach her lungs, a light came on. Several lights—fluorescent bulbs that hung in columns from the ceiling. They flickered on dimly, like they were the energy-saving type that took a while to reach full strength. But they gave enough light for Ashley to see Tiernan's gaze swiftly scan the room.

Cement blocks formed the walls of what looked like an unfinished basement, but with a lot more equipment and machinery. Tanks climbed floor-to-ceiling in some corners, and large pipes stuck out nearly everywhere.

"This way."

A loud groaning noise suddenly started, nearly drowning out Tiernan's direction.

Sounded like it came from one of the tanks they passed as Tiernan took them to a tunnel lined with more cement walls. The passageway led to another room like the one they had entered at the beginning, but smaller. One more tunnel, then another room, this time a rectangular one with limited floor space between tanks and pipes.

Tiernan set Ashley's suitcase next to one of those tanks and dropped the two sacks on the floor.

"We'll stay here tonight."

She looked around at the prison-like accommodations. From a five-star hotel to this? "You're kidding."

"Afraid not."

"I thought you said safe house. This isn't even a house."

"Ah." He held his index finger up in the air. "But it is safe."

She raised an eyebrow. "I've heard that before."

"Stopping here, Matthew." Tiernan glanced past Ashley. "You can set down your stuff."

Poor Matthew sank to the hard floor as soon as he dropped his duffel bag.

"Hang on, buddy." Tiernan bent down to open one of the sacks and pulled out a rolled up…sleeping bag? Great. Now they had all the comforts of home. He spread the sleeping bag on the floor along a strip of blank wall and patted it. "This one's for you, buddy."

"Cam!" Matthew hefted himself to his feet and marched over to the sleeping bag with a smile.

Another word. "Did he mean camp?"

"Sounded like it." Tiernan started to get out the other sleeping bag.

Maybe Matthew used to camp at his family's cabin? She watched absently while Tiernan smoothed out the sleeping bag about a foot away from her.

Wait a second. "Why is there only one more sleeping bag?"

"Because the store I stopped at only had two."

"So where am I supposed to sleep?"

"Right here." He gave the sleeping bag a slap.

She glared at him. Wondered when he'd get to this.

He stood, and his gaze hit hers. "Oh, brother. I forgot how you think."

More like how every man thought.

"No, I do not mean with me. I told you I don't get paid to sleep. I'll sit up."

Maybe she could believe that. Most guys would have at least tried to talk her into it, even if only as a joke. She crossed her arms. "So where are we?"

He sat on the floor a couple feet away from the sleeping bag and leaned his back against the wall. "You mean you don't recognize Illinois' largest waterpark?"

"Not in the middle of the night. So this is behind the scenes?"

"More like under."

Her exhausted leg muscles began to make themselves known with a vengeance. She lowered herself to sit on the end of the sleeping bag that stuck out from the wall, farthest away from Tiernan. The sleeping bag was softer and warmer than she expected, cushioning her tired legs.

Matthew started to talk, mumbling unintelligible sounds. He stretched out inside the sleeping bag, holding his picture Bible in front of his face as he pretend-read in his gibberish language.

Another pump or something kicked in.

She started inwardly. Clenched her hands into fists.

"You okay?" Tiernan watched her.

Must not have hid the jump so well.

"You've been through a lot today." He smiled slightly. "Not every day you get shot at, right?"

Was he seriously joking about it? "Thanks to you, it might not be the last."

"You ran away."

"You got me into this."

He met her challenging gaze but didn't say a word.

"You said you'd tell me everything. The true everything, if you don't mind."

"I didn't lie to you." He glanced down as he rubbed his thumb on the concrete floor in front of him. "At least, I hope I didn't. In this business, it's easier to slip into than I'd like."

She didn't need the psychoanalysis. Probably another avoidance tactic.

He sighed and looked at her. "You were right, Matthew's parents weren't normal."

She nodded. "They were criminals, right? Working with Grayson until they double-crossed him?"

His lips curved into a half smile. "You've given this some thought. No, they weren't criminals. They were lawyers." He held up a hand. "No lawyer joke intended."

She wasn't laughing.

"They were heavily involved in the political world until they got fed up with the corruption they witnessed. But instead of getting out, they were recruited by the FBI to stay in that world as undercover sources. They were highly qualified, so they were rushed through the hiring process."

"And Grayson was one of the people they knew."

He leaned his head back against the wall and aimed his gaze at the ceiling. "They weren't sure who was behind it all at first. They brought what they suspected to the table, but they didn't have hard evidence at the time. Jane and Kevin had been trying to gather evidence for six years, and the FBI held off prosecuting the small fish they could've put away in an effort to find the big fish behind it all."

"Grayson. For racketeering?"

He pulled his head away from the wall to look at her. "Very good." Like it was some lighthearted guessing game.

"What did he actually do?"

"We suspect him of bribery, extortion, and transportation of stolen property, to name a few. Jane and Kevin figured out he was behind everything three years ago, but it's been a long wait trying to prove it."

Tiernan pushed himself to his feet and jammed his hands in the back pockets of his jeans. "In my last contact with Kevin, he said they'd found the piece of evidence they needed to finally put Grayson out of business for good." Tiernan stared at the wall or something across the narrow space. "They were supposed to pass the information to me two days later. The day they died."

"So they *were* killed."

His gaze darted to her, his eyes narrowed. "Who told you that?"

"The police started a homicide investigation."

"Oh." His shoulders relaxed.

"Though with everything that's been going on and the hidden documents, I think I could've figured it out on my own."

His mouth tugged at the corner. "I guess."

"So Grayson's added murder to his list of crimes."

Tiernan nodded. "We suspected he was already guilty of murder for hire before this. The challenge is always in proving it."

Ashley pulled her legs out from under her to sit more comfortably. "If the Bordens were going to give the information to you, wouldn't they have had the evidence with them on the plane that crashed?"

He faced her, folding his arms over his chest. "We scoured the wreckage and didn't find a thing. Jane and Kevin liked to do things their own way. I could easily believe they wouldn't have taken the evidence with them, especially if they suspected they were in greater danger than normal. They didn't trust anyone much. Not even the FBI."

Ashley could understand that. She stopped herself from voicing the opinion, which might shut Tiernan up. "But they still took Matthew on the plane with them?"

He took a few steps away from the wall and turned toward her again. "Yeah. They must not have thought anyone would try something on the plane. They hated being separated from Matthew, even for short meetings with me."

"If they didn't trust anyone, how did Matthew end up in foster care? Didn't they have a will or some means set up to provide for him?"

"Sure." As he spoke, he continued to pace back to the wall and out again. "They left him the house and their considerable assets. They left him nursing staff and a conservator."

"Ah. And that guy's holding onto the money, right?"

He winced. "Not exactly."

Realization dawned. She leaned forward. "You? You're the conservator?"

"We became close those six years I worked with them."

He'd claimed he hadn't known Matthew before. "But you never met Matthew?"

Tiernan shook his head. "They liked to keep him safe. Protected from all this." He circled his hand outward, like the underbelly of a waterpark qualified as standard FBI working conditions.

"Then they probably thought he'd be safer with you as the conservator."

He stopped walking to meet the accusing stare that matched her tone.

"You shouldn't have let Matthew go into foster care with strangers, whatever the reason."

"I told you before. It was necessary to protect him. I had to keep the wrong people from finding out who and where he was for as long as possible."

"The wrong people." Funny how often the wrong people masqueraded as the right people.

"And I knew you'd take good care of him."

Liar. "You knew I was..." she searched for a word that wouldn't make her gag, "associated with another person." She tilted her chin, daring him to deny it.

He didn't. "Frank Abelli came to the FBI shortly before Kevin and Jane were murdered. He said he had solid evidence that would convict Grayson and that he'd testify against Grayson for racketeering."

"Not for free." Ashley could only manage to get the three words out of her rapidly closing throat.

"No. He had two conditions."

She stared at the blue pipe behind Tiernan.

"One, he wanted immunity from prosecution for his crimes and, two…"

Her gaze homed in on a dark speck on the pipe.

"He will only do his talking to you."

Her eyes slid shut. She tried to breathe, the only way of keeping the contents of her stomach from rushing up her throat.

"We've suspected Abelli of being involved in some of Grayson's crimes, but we've never had solid evidence on him either." Tiernan's voice drifted to her, filtered through her rising panic. "We're sure he knows what he's talking about. We tried forcing him to tell us with threat of charges, but he's a slippery guy. He knows we can't get him on our own and that we want Grayson."

Her throat swelled. She couldn't breathe. Her pulse rapid-fired like she was going to have a heart attack. If that's what a heart attack felt like. Pondering the question kept her mind from dwelling on her lack of oxygen. On the swirling of the world around her even though she kept her eyes closed.

"Ashley." The word, the voice, intruded with a reality she couldn't face.

Breathe. Just breathe. Bits of air filtered through her nostrils. Cold, damp air that matched the clammy helplessness seeping into every fiber of her being.

"Ashley?" His voice was closer. He wouldn't touch her, would he?

No more fear. She was strong. She forced her eyes to open.

Tiernan stood above her, looking down. "Would you do it? You could end all of this in just one hour."

She moistened her lips. Swallowed. Then tried to speak. "No." The word came out surprisingly smooth.

"He said you wouldn't want to. Said you've been estranged for years."

Quite an understatement. Slippery was the right word for him.

"May I ask why you won't talk to him under these circumstances?"

"No." More of a croak this time as Abelli's image pressed in on her, trying to take over her mind.

"I thought you'd tell me it's need-to-know. I probably deserve it." Tiernan's attempt at humor fell into the darkness that surrounded her. Then Tiernan's face appeared in front of her. He squatted to meet her gaze, bringing her back to the present reality. "I didn't mean to joke. I can tell how much you're hurting inside right now." His eyes filled with compassion.

Did he really care?

"I don't know what happened between you two, but I'm sorry for it. And I'm sorry I need to ask you to talk to him. Believe me, I delayed this option as long as possible. If there were any other way, I wouldn't ask you now. But after today... I think we both know we're running out of time." He gently touched her hand that gripped her knee. "This is the only option left, and we have to take it."

She ripped her hand away and jumped to her feet. "Maybe it's *your* only option, but I have another one. It's called walking away and forgetting I ever met you." She started forward, but he stepped in front of her.

"Don't touch me." She shot out the words with the fury that burned through her veins.

His mouth formed a grim line. "I won't. If you listen."

"Like him."

Tiernan glanced over her shoulder. "It's fine, Matthew. We're just talking. We like each other."

Maybe the biggest lie he'd told yet.

Tiernan lowered his voice as he shifted his gaze back to her. "You don't seem to get it. You can't walk out there. You'd be dead by morning, if not sooner."

She steeled her jaw. "Why would Grayson care about me if I'm not keeping him from Matthew?"

"He'd assume you've been told everything, which, thanks to your insistence, you just were. You'd have to be killed."

She glared at him. "I would rather die by a bullet tonight than get within thirty miles of Frank Abelli."

Surprise flickered in his green eyes, probably because he saw she meant it. "I've heard of fathers and daughters not getting along before. But this is ridiculous."

"Don't!" The word exploded out of her, echoing in the underground prison. "Don't you ever call him my father. Ever." She turned away from Tiernan before she socked him in the jaw.

"What happened?" His voice sounded almost pained, like he was the one who had been hurt.

She swiveled, took a swift step around him, and made it past. Or he let her go. She didn't care. She stalked farther away.

"Those bullets today may have been aimed at you. But the next ones will be for Matthew."

She paused. What was he saying?

"Grayson doesn't want to just kidnap Matthew anymore. He wants to kill him. Don't you see that?"

The words hit their mark.

She faced Tiernan. "That doesn't make sense." Her gaze went to Matthew, now much farther away, tucked in his sleeping bag. He had set his Bible down, maybe to sleep. Why would anyone want to kill him? He couldn't hurt anyone. "You said they wanted what he knows...about the evi—"

"My bosses gave up on thinking Matthew can help find the evidence. Grayson apparently came to the same conclusion."

She shifted her gaze to Tiernan. "Then why kill him?"

"Because as long as he's alive, there's always a chance he

could reveal something someday. Grayson can't risk that. He has too much at stake." Tiernan took a few steps toward Ashley.

The urge to run rose from her belly to her chest.

He stopped. "If you walk out that door, you're taking away Matthew's chance to have a safe and happy life. You're his only hope now."

She narrowed her eyes. How dare he? "Look at him." She tilted her head toward Matthew. "That boy will never have a happy life, a normal life. And it's not my fault. His parents made that decision when they had him."

"Oh, Ashley." Something glimmered in Tiernan's eyes. Couldn't be tears. "How could you spend so much time with Matthew and still not have seen him at all?"

She looked away from the sadness in Tiernan's gaze. She'd had enough. She started to leave.

"Wait. You may not care for Matthew like I do, but I'm begging you. Please don't let him spend his life like this." The decidedly uncharacteristic pleading in Tiernan's tone brought her gaze back. "I'm good at what I do, but I'm afraid of making a mistake this time. Matthew could get killed." He put his hands together. "Please don't let that happen."

No smug grin. No twinkle in the eyes. Just raw concern—almost like fear. Or love? Did he really care for Matthew that much?

She swallowed. The confidence Tiernan usually exuded was gone. He was seriously worried. Seriously in need of her help.

Matthew was quiet now, apparently sleeping. But what happened when he had his next nightmare? He'd have no one to comfort him if she wasn't there. Or what if the nightmare became a reality? If he were kidnapped...or killed? Because she wouldn't have one simple conversation with Abelli.

She looked the reality in the face for the first time—Matthew taking a bullet because of her cowardice. She couldn't live with herself if she knew she could've prevented it.

She pressed her lips together. Took a breath. Moistened her lips.

Her wandering gaze reached Tiernan's face, touching his pleading eyes for half a second. "Just once." The words came out as a broken whisper.

Tiernan's brow furrowed like he hadn't heard.

She cleared her throat. "I'll do it one time."

His tense features relaxed into a smile.

"But not alone."

His smile disappeared as he watched her. He nodded. "Whatever you want."

"Promise." Her voice faded as she found a dark smudge on the gray wall and locked her gaze on it.

"Promise what?"

"You'll be there."

He was silent a second. "I'll be there." He took a step closer. "Ashley…"

She sensed, rather than saw, his hand reach to touch her arm.

But he pulled back. "Thank you." He walked to the wall and sat on the floor again.

This one time, she almost wished he'd tried to comfort her. Anything to hold back the terror that grew inside her with every painful breath.

chapter
twenty-two

Ashley awoke to a nauseated stomach, her insides tied in knots in the middle of a swirling mess.

The worst kind of fear coated her mouth—a dry, acrid flavor she hadn't tasted since she was fifteen years old.

She had to meet him today.

She lay in the sleeping bag longer, though there was no chance she would sleep. She'd only drifted off after many fitful hours last night, but her body didn't have much need for sleep in survival mode. She stared at the pipe-lined ceiling above her, the pump sounds that had scared her last night like comforting white noise now.

Tiernan had set up the meeting quickly. She was no fool. He'd probably had it set up in advance. She should be furious that he knew she'd give in, suspicious that he'd played her again. But she would need him today too much to be angry.

Whether or not Tiernan had meant what he said about caring for Matthew, the fact remained that Ashley had seen and heard real bullets yesterday. She couldn't be responsible for them hitting Matthew next time.

"Thanks for doing this." Tiernan's face appeared in her line of sight as he stood next to her sleeping bag. "I knew you would want to save Matthew."

She shoved herself up to a sitting position. Now who was going to save her?

"We need to get out of here for a while now. The rest of the day, probably."

She gently cleared her throat. Swallowed, staring at the shiny satin of the sleeping bag's surface. "I thought the meeting was here."

"At the waterpark, yes. But up top. We can't be found down here during the day."

She slowly got to her feet on the soft sleeping bag.

"We'll hang out at the park until the meeting. Maybe enjoy some rides, if you'd like. I brought swim trunks for Matthew. They have a great kids' area here that he'll love. And maybe the wave pool."

She heard him talking, but the words didn't mean much to her. He sounded so normal. Like this was any average day of running for their lives and confronting her nightmares.

"Azwee." Matthew walked up to her and waved with the free hand that didn't hold his Bible. He already wore bright green swim trunks, a Crock Doc T-shirt, and sandals. Tiernan thought of everything.

At least he hadn't tried to buy her a swimsuit. Another atypical guy move. She stepped into her flip-flops and watched the agent quickly roll up her sleeping bag and shove it into the cloth bag it came in.

He glanced at her as he set the bag next to Matthew's, already rolled up and bagged. "I'm going to stash these in the car with your luggage, once you're done with it." He nodded to her overnight bag standing up against the wall. He checked his watch. "We should still have thirty minutes before the first employee shows up, so now's the time to do what you need to."

She went to the suitcase and pulled out the extended handle to wheel it behind her.

"Can you find your way out okay?"

She gave him a backward wave over her shoulder for her answer.

"Come back in ten. That will give me time to take the stuff out and get back."

Was he afraid she wouldn't come back at all? She could just keep walking through this tunnel to the outside and not stop until she got far away, somewhere truly safe, away from...him. There had to be somewhere he wouldn't find her.

"Swim, swim."

She jerked to see Matthew walk up alongside her.

He smiled under his crooked baseball cap. "Swim, swim."

Tiernan must have told him about the waterpark. Did he tell Matthew to follow her, too?

No irritation took the place of her nausea as she reached to straighten the bill of Matthew's cap. Maybe his smile could light the way out of here.

Matthew squealed as water from a huge bucket at least thirty feet in the air dumped onto him and other gleefully screaming kids.

Their screams only reminded Ashley of the tension in her chest that begged for such a release. Waiting for three hours, first hiding underground and then watching Matthew have the time of his life getting wet, had only put Ashley's nerves more on edge.

Just a few more minutes now. He was supposed to show up here, at the Kids' Carnival section of the waterpark. Ironic choice.

She scanned the crowds of parents and children.

A deep laugh suddenly came from beside her.

Tiernan. She'd almost forgotten he was there.

"Can you believe that?" He pointed at Matthew.

The boy jumped and kicked in the foot of water, giggling when he got splashed.

The other children kept their distance, sometimes staring at Matthew. One man pulled his girl to another section of the play area. Ashley couldn't save Matthew from that. Couldn't prevent—

"There he is."

Her heart stopped.

"Try not to act like anything's unusual." Tiernan had to be kidding. "He's over on that path to your right."

She started to turn her head that direction. Her stomach lurched. "I can't do it."

"Sure you can. Do it for Matthew. It'll be okay."

She shook her head, the only part of her she could move. "You don't know what you're asking."

Tiernan stepped in front of her, staring into her face like he'd just noticed something was wrong.

She tried to focus on the creases that lined his tanned forehead or the concern in his green eyes. Anything to keep the terror from pulling her into a black hole she'd never crawl out of.

"I'll be here the whole time. I won't leave your side."

"Promise me." Her throat was so dry. So empty. She couldn't swallow.

"I promise."

She turned.

Frank Abelli watched her from the path, a slim gray business suit in a crowd of swimwear. Black hair, sunken eyes under prominent brow line.

Those awful, awful eyes.

No memories came, just every feeling of the past. Horror, repulsion, fear, helplessness rushed at her in a dark wave that crushed her.

She ran. Water splashed her feet, then her feet hit dry land and she kept running, pushing her legs to carry her through a blur she couldn't see. She slammed into something. A person?

She shoved away and ran until the churning of her

stomach pushed up her throat and she had to stop, doubling over a railing to throw up on grass.

She stumbled away from the rail, wandering on trembling legs until she was behind some building somewhere.

"Ashley." A hand touched her shoulder.

She screamed, jerking away.

"It's me. Tiernan."

She finally saw his face as she started to tremble. Her fingers, hands, arms. She shook everywhere. She pressed against the wall and sank down to the ground, covering her face with trembling hands. Her cheeks were soaked with tears she didn't know she'd been crying.

"Azwee." That sweet voice reached for her in the darkness.

She tried to breathe. Wanted to lower her hands. But she couldn't.

Matthew sat down beside her. She knew it was him without looking. He smelled of chlorine and sunshine.

His arms came around her and gently hugged, damp and warm.

She pressed her face into his soft shoulder and sobbed.

chapter
twenty-three

Ashley twisted the strap of her purse in her hands. Cold from the concrete floor leaked through her jeans as she sat in the dim corner of the waterpark's underground world.

Matthew stood next to her, *reading* his Bible in a voice that was probably too loud to go undetected if anyone came near.

He tilted the book toward her, pointing at a picture as he said something she couldn't understand. He kept doing that and looking at her as he told the unintelligible stories, almost like he was trying to read to her. He'd never done that before.

Could he be trying to distract her from the pain? Did he understand things like that? He had hugged her when she was coming apart. And he'd touched her hand that day after the spot check on the little girl, Chrissie. But he always tried to hold her hand. Maybe it wasn't for her at all, but something that made *him* feel good. That's probably all he could understand.

At least his reading took her mind off things, like the numbness that had invaded her body when the trembling finally subsided. And she forgot for a minute to wonder what Tiernan was doing and what he would say when he came back to them.

He'd left her and Matthew in the tunnels without an

explanation, not even to say where he was going. He'd just told them to stay hidden and disappeared. Surprising he'd leave her alone after she had run again. Probably thought she was too weak to run anymore after that spectacle. He was right.

Her aching head felt as heavy as a bowling ball, and her eyelids tried to push shut. As if sleep would make any of this go away.

A noise came from the corridor.

She should be scared, but she didn't have any energy left for fear.

Tiernan came into view, his eyebrows pushed together and his mouth a firm line. Even the way he stalked toward them signaled anger. "We need to leave." His tone was grim. "Now."

She stiffened when he bent over her.

He grabbed her purse and lifted it away. "Matthew, can you carry this for Ashley?"

Matthew smiled and puffed up his chest, like he was proud to have the job. He took the purse and held it in the arm without the Bible.

"Can you get up?" Tiernan's hand waited in front of her.

She obviously still wasn't thinking clearly, because she put her hand in his and let him help her to her feet.

He let go as soon as she stood and stepped back, though he watched her closely. Did he think she was going to fall over or was that a mistrustful glare?

"Try not to make any noise." He included Matthew in his glance as he turned and started back toward the corridor.

Matthew eagerly trotted after him, leaving Ashley to follow at a slower pace, her legs like stiff lead under her.

Tiernan checked behind often, in the building and outside where they emerged at the rear of the park and took a long walk across open land. Must be the way they had arrived... Was it just last night? Seemed like a year ago.

When they were what felt like miles away from the waterpark, they reached the familiar chain-link fence. Tiernan unlocked the gate again and let Matthew through.

Ashley's numb legs stumbled as she brushed past him.

Tiernan caught her by the arm. "Can you make it okay?"

She nodded. She'd made it through much worse. She could survive this. Standing straighter, she hauled in a breath and started to walk with more strength. She caught up with Matthew and stayed beside him as Tiernan passed them to lead the way.

Tiernan didn't sound mad when he spoke to her. But it was only a matter of time. He probably wanted to wait until they reached the car to light into her, lecturing her on how she had failed and let Matthew down. Maybe he'd call her out for being a weepy coward. A weakling. He'd be right.

She wasn't a kid anymore. The name couldn't hurt her. *Frank* couldn't hurt her. But the memories that he brought back could.

By the time they reached the car, Ashley's legs threatened to collapse under her. But some of her senses were returning. She noticed the sweat that dripped into her eyes and made her tank top stick to her back. Birds sang to each other in some distant tree.

Tiernan opened the door for Matthew, and Ashley followed him onto the back seat. She looked away before she'd have to see if Tiernan disapproved.

He closed the door without a word and walked around to the driver's side.

The thick heat in the car felt oddly comforting. Like a blanket wrapped tightly around her. She leaned her weary body against the seat's back and closed her eyes.

When she opened them, the car was cool, the sky black outside the tinted windows as Tiernan drove them somewhere.

She didn't move for a bit. Just watched Matthew as he slept, his mouth hanging open slightly.

She turned her head to see the road through the windshield past the headrest of the front seat.

The headlights illuminated wet pavement lined by dark trees on both sides. The windshield wipers flicked back and forth to swipe drops off the glass.

"Are you all right?"

She shifted her gaze to Tiernan's eyes in the rearview mirror.

He watched her, but she couldn't see enough of his face to read his expression.

"Y—" Her dry throat caught the word before it could get out. She swallowed, trying to wet her lips without any luck.

He held up a bottle of water and extended it back to her.

She took it and drank, the cool liquid running down her throat in a soothing stream. She screwed the cap back on the bottle and made herself meet his reflected gaze. "I'm sorry."

"I don't think you're the one who needs to apologize." He glanced away. "I had no idea." His voice grew thick as he paused between his words like they were difficult to say. "I shouldn't...I wouldn't have asked you to do that if I'd known." He looked at her in the mirror again. "I am so sorry."

Unbelievable. No lecture? No anger? She swallowed a lump that replaced the dryness in her throat. She would have known how to handle those reactions better. "What about Matthew?"

Tiernan's hands shifted forward on the steering wheel, like he was gripping tighter. "We'll find another way."

Instead of using her? This couldn't be the same Tiernan who had plotted to bring her into this mess, who'd deceived and manipulated to get her where he wanted. She couldn't have misjudged him that much, could she?

"Are you hungry?"

She blinked at him. Wasn't he at least going to grill her about Frank? His FBI agent's curiosity must be killing him. Unless he'd already figured it out somehow. The nausea that had dissipated started to swirl in her stomach again. She couldn't stand it if he knew everything. She'd almost rather face Frank again. Almost.

She looked out the darkened window. Trees still lined the road, thick like a forest. "Where are we?"

"Wisconsin."

"Wisconsin?"

"Up north."

"You think we'll lose Grayson in another state?"

He watched the road instead of looking at her. "The distance should help."

Did he mean help her or Matthew? "We won't end this by running." If only she could grab the words back, but they'd already come out.

He glanced at her in the mirror, likely aware of the irony in her statement. "We're not running. We're going to a place I hope might be the key."

"You mean where the documents are hidden?"

"Possibly. I'm hoping Matthew will tell us."

So they were back to hoping the boy who couldn't say his own name would save them all.

Matthew started to snore somewhat quietly, apparently undisturbed by their voices. He must have taken off his baseball cap before he slept, like he usually did. It lay on the seat beside him, and a clump of the brown hair he had freed fell onto his forehead.

Ashley gently brushed the hair back into place. What would happen to him if he couldn't lead Tiernan to the evidence and Grayson's men found him? What would happen if he found the documents, Grayson was put away, and life for everyone but Matthew went back to normal? The answers to both questions were far from comforting.

Why, oh why did his parents put him here? Ashley's heart ached as she watched his sleeping face, his lips quivering as he breathed in and out. They could have prevented the suffering of this sweet kid.

Tiernan slowed the car and turned onto a darker road that took them into the forest. He glanced in the mirrors.

"Are we being followed?"

He'd better not say that info was need-to-know. "We were. Closer to Chicago. Abelli must have brought a tail."

"On purpose?"

"Better not." Tiernan's tone was as dark as the trees that surrounded them as he turned again. This time the road became unpaved dirt and gravel.

The car bounced over a rough patch, and Matthew lifted his head. At least a nightmare hadn't woken him this time. He looked around, his eyes widening like he didn't know where he was.

"It's okay. We're in the car with Tiernan." She glanced at the man behind the wheel. "He'll probably have to use the bathroom." And so did she.

"We stopped two hours ago, and he used the bathroom then."

"You stopped? I didn't notice."

"You were really out. But we're almost there now. Just a few more minutes."

Almost where? The forest around them kept getting thicker with no signs of civilization.

The road curved and gaps started to appear in the trees on one side. Moonlight shone through the spaces, reflecting off…water?

They neared a little dark building. The area around it had fewer trees, opening up the view of water along the dim and rainy horizon. Was that a lake?

"Swim swim!" Matthew started bouncing on the seat as he strained to see past Tiernan.

"Is this the cabin?"

Tiernan pulled up next to the small building built out of logs and stone—or at least made to look like it was. "Yep. Did you see the pictures in the album?"

"Yes. The harbor master mentioned Matthew's parents took him here during the summer."

"Yeah. They loved it up here." A hint of wistfulness colored his tone.

"You've been here before, haven't you?"

"Just once. After the…" His voice drifted off as he looked through the windshield. He stopped the wiper blades, letting the rain block the view.

He really had cared for them. Didn't that go against the FBI handbook? "So you already searched it."

"There are countless places to hide things in these woods and by the water." He turned to look at her. "There's still hope."

She wouldn't mind seeing the full version of the smile that only slightly tugged at the corner of his lips. Or even that obnoxious grin. Been a long time without either one.

"Swim swim!"

Tiernan swung his gaze to bouncing Matthew and chuckled.

Her heart lifted at the sound for some strange reason. Of course at this point, any hint of happiness from anyone would be welcome.

"Hang on, buddy. We'll get you to the water tomorrow."

Too bad Matthew couldn't actually swim when he loved water so much.

Ashley's muscles were back to working order as she slid out of the car to help Tiernan gather the luggage from the trunk. Without the humidity that had plagued Chicago the last week, the night air was as cool as the raindrops. Going north sure made a difference.

"Umbrella?" Tiernan stuck out a large, black umbrella toward her.

Raindrops hit her nose while she stared at it. "Are you prepared for everything?"

"Not quite everything." An undefined glint in his eyes

when he met her gaze made her look away. Did he mean Frank or...something else?

She popped the umbrella open and held it over her head, her bare arms getting cold. She reached for her suitcase as Tiernan set it on the ground.

He glanced at her. "I'll get it."

She shook her head and grasped the handle.

Matthew, wearing his crooked cap again, joined them at the back of the car.

"Here." She extended the umbrella to Matthew. "Hold this for me and walk with me, okay? Can you hold it over both our heads?"

He nodded and took the umbrella while she straightened his cap.

"Okay." She hefted her suitcase and matched his slow pace as they started for the cabin. His umbrella skills were about what she'd expected, and one side of her body was splattered with rain by the time they reached the door. The Bible he held in his other arm was probably perfectly dry.

"Get inside." When had Tiernan come up behind them? He pushed a key into her palm, his warm fingers causing a curious skip in her pulse.

No, she must have been reacting to the way he peered into the darkness away from the cabin.

"Now. Hurry."

She caught the edge to his voice she had missed before and opened the outer screen door. The darkness made her fumble to get the key in the lock. Her pulse pounded in her ears as she finally inserted the key and turned, pulling Matthew through the inside door as soon as it opened.

Tiernan closed the door behind them, shutting himself out in the rain.

She held her breath. What had he seen or heard out there? Shouldn't he have come in? He'd be exposed outside. In danger.

She jumped when lights came on.

Matthew stood next to a light switch. She didn't even know he could work those.

She turned to look at the place. An open floor plan included couches on a large rug in front of a fireplace, a small kitchen with a table, and a loft above. Two doors opened off the main area, leading to dark rooms she couldn't identify.

What if someone was hiding in one of them? No. They would've already come out shooting, wouldn't they? Cheerful thought.

Where was Tiernan?

Her gaze drifted past the couches to the wall, lined with a row of windows. Way too many windows. Dark outside, and the lights on inside. They could be seen.

She rushed to the switch and flicked off the lights.

A thump hit the door.

chapter
twenty-four

Ashley swung around to stare at the wooden door, the only thing that prevented whoever was out there from getting to them.

"Ashley, it's Tiernan. Open up."

Her breath released with a whoosh, and she hurried to open the door.

Tiernan stepped inside with the rest of the luggage and closed the door behind him, locking it.

"Kind of dark in here." He flicked the light switch and turned to her with a sheepish grin, pushing his hand through his wet hair, which left the dark locks standing up every which way.

She smiled. She couldn't help it. He looked adorable.

His eyes twinkled as he scanned her face. "Do you know you've never smiled at me before?"

She pressed her lips together, squishing the smile. "I didn't think we should have the lights on with someone out there."

He nodded. "You were right. But turns out it was just a bear."

Should she be relieved? "*Just* a bear?"

He flashed his grin again. "A little black one. Nothing to worry about." He looked at the windows. "But I don't much like those either." He glanced at her. "I'll hang some sheets and blankets. Won't cover all the light but should make us harder to hit…er…see."

Terrific. Cheerful Tiernan was back. She should be more careful what she wished for.

"How about you get Matthew settled in the loft while I cover the windows?"

She glanced at the boy in time to catch his yawn.

"You look ready for bed, champ." Tiernan tugged the bill of Matthew's cap, slanting it again.

Irritation chafed Ashley's raw nerves. "What is with the cap?"

Tiernan glanced at her like he was surprised at her sharp tone. He shrugged. "Don't blame me it's the Cubs. His dad gave it to him. I'm a White Sox fan myself."

She rolled her eyes. "I mean, why do you have to make it crooked all the time?"

His eyebrows lifted. "Why do you have to straighten it?"

Matthew yawned again.

She blew out a loud sigh. "Never mind." The kid looked like he was about to fall over, and *she* cared about taking care of him more than winning the argument.

Matthew was so droopy as she got him to the loft that she didn't stop him when he got into the bed, sliding under a quilt with his swim trunks and T-shirt still on.

"Goodnight, Matthew." She turned to go down the steep staircase.

"Wead?"

She looked back.

He patted the Bible that lay on his chest.

She sighed and went to the bed. A wooden chair stood beside it, as if it were there just for that purpose. Had his mother read to him there?

She took the Bible and sat in the chair. "What do you want me to read?"

"Jom."

Special Target

What was that? "Show me." She gave him the Bible, and he opened it about halfway, then turned some pages until he apparently reached what he wanted. She would've thought he'd be happy to have her read anything.

He said something else unintelligible and handed her the book.

She looked at the colored drawings on the page. A blind man and someone who looked like the pictures she'd seen of Jesus at church as a kid.

She sighed. Here went nothing. "One day, Jesus saw a man who had been born blind. His disciples asked him, 'Teacher, who sinned, this man or his parents, since he was born blind?' 'Neither of them made the man blind,' Jesus answered. Then he told them, 'This man was born blind for the glory of God, that the works of God might be shown in him.'"

She stopped and reread the words silently to make sure she had it right. Was it really saying God had made the man be born handicapped on purpose? She would've thought a Bible for children would want to tell kids that God was all love and happiness. That'd be the only way to sell these stories to anyone.

Matthew grunted, watching her with those slanted eyes.

She hurried to finish the lame story. "Then Jesus spit on the dirt to make mud and put the mud on the man's eyes. He told the man to wash in a pool. The man did what Jesus said, and when he came back, he could see. Jesus had healed him." From something God had supposedly done to him in the first place? Nice. "The end."

"Wead."

She shook her head and closed the book, giving it to Matthew. "You need sleep. I can tell because you forgot to take your cap off." She lifted the cap from his head and set it on the nightstand next to the bed. "Sweet dreams, kiddo."

He smiled at her, then ducked his head, his hands folding together in front of him. Praying again. To the God Who probably didn't exist and definitely didn't care about the suffering boy with Down syndrome.

She headed down the stairs, going slowly on the steep and narrow planks.

"What do you think?" Tiernan swept his arm to encompass the sheets and blankets he'd hung over every window, securing them at the top with silver duct tape.

"Well, if the FBI thing doesn't work out for you, I don't think interior design should be your next option."

"She jokes!" He put his palm over his heart like he was going to swoon. "I'm a goner."

She almost smiled, but the glint in his eyes behind the amusement held her in check. There couldn't be any truth in the act. Someone like him would never even look twice at her. She wasn't his type. And he wasn't hers. "Martha wouldn't be too happy about that."

"Martha?" He blinked, tilting his head slightly.

"Your girlfriend, or whoever she is."

No sign of recognition.

Probably trying to hide it. "You're not going to lie about her, are you? I saw the picture at your condo. The blonde."

"Oh." A smile slowly came back as he watched her, his gaze turning disconcertingly warm. "That's my sister."

His sister. She gulped as heat traveled to her cheeks. Now he'd think she was interested.

"And Martha is my mother. I'm guessing you saw the Bible she gave me?"

Ashley stared at a brown sheet that hung over the windows as her face burned. She had to change the subject fast. "So where do I sleep?"

"Ah." He walked to one of the darkened doorways and reached inside the room, mercifully building in distance that might prevent him from seeing her blush.

The ceiling light beyond the door came on, illuminating a bedroom with a king-sized bed.

"I tossed for it and lost."

She gathered her faculties enough to raise an eyebrow at him.

"And I will sleep out here, a very long way away on the sofa. That okay?" Amusement twinkled in his eyes, but it didn't irritate her as much as usual. At least if he was that chipper, they must be pretty well out of danger...for the moment.

"It'll do."

"Excellent. Bathroom's there," he pointed to the other open door, "with a washer and dryer so you'll be able to wash your clothes tomorrow."

"Great." She went to her suitcase, which still stood near the door.

"Not to change the subject, but you're a good reader."

She pulled the suitcase toward the bathroom as he stepped away, moving closer to the couch. "You were listening?"

"Hard not to. But it's one of my favorite Bible stories anyway."

"Weird story to tell children."

"You think so?"

She shrugged and stopped outside the bathroom door. "Doesn't make God very likable the way it's written, saying He made the poor man blind from birth."

"Oh, I see. You think somebody made it up."

"You don't?"

He shook his head. "No way. It really happened like it says. It's history. That's why it isn't written to please people or make God seem different than He is. He did make the man blind...for a purpose."

"But if you believe that, then you'd have to believe God made Matthew the way he is."

Tiernan nodded.

"You do believe that?"

"One hundred percent. God made every one of us."

"But how can you believe in a God who would do something like that to an innocent baby?"

Tiernan gestured to the couch behind him. "You want to sit down?"

"No." Had she made him squirm with that question?

He plopped down on the couch himself and propped his foot against the coffee table. "Well, for one thing, God is still real whether I believe in Him or not. But I also don't think of Matthew as a mistake like you seem to."

That was putting it a little harshly.

"I know God made that boy for a very special purpose." Conviction shone in Tiernan's steady gaze.

"And what is that? To suffer humiliation, loneliness, the inability to think..." she ticked off the list on her fingers, "oh, and then die young?"

"I don't know his whole story yet, but it's a lot better than what you can see."

Cop-out. He didn't have an answer. "Sure. I'm going to get ready for bed." She turned to the bathroom and lifted her suitcase through the doorway.

"Ashley."

"What?" She didn't try to soften her tone as she glanced back.

"What if God made Matthew for you?"

Her chest tightened as she stared at Tiernan. "Then I'd say your God's crueler than I thought." She shut the door and turned to the sink. She twisted the knob on the faucet, her fingers trembling as she reached for the bar of soap on the back corner of the sink. *Breathe.* She shoved her hands under the cold water, trying to think only about her breaths...in, out, in, out...

She was right, Tiernan was wrong. Matthew was evidence of that. She wasn't guilty of anything.

The door to her room swung open, casting light onto her bed.

A dark outline stood in the doorway.

He moved, entering the room. His black shadow came toward her bed, closer, closer—

"Ashley." His hands touched her.

She screamed, thrashing, trying to pull away from that horrible touch.

"Ashley, you'll hurt yourself." The grip tightened. "It's Tiernan. It's just Tiernan. You're okay."

The voice started to break through her shrieks. She stopped, opening her eyes.

Tiernan looked down at her, his brow furrowed, eyes filled with something she knew very well. Pain.

He let go of her arms.

She pushed herself up against the headboard, pulling in ragged breaths. She shoved her hair away from the sides of her face where it stuck like her clammy nightshirt. "What..." She swallowed, her mouth pasty and dry as she scanned the unfamiliar room. The cabin. Matthew's parents' cabin. "What happened?"

"You must have had a nightmare."

"Did I wake you?"

"You were screaming." He watched her like he was afraid she might start again.

"Sor—"

He stopped her by covering her hand with his on the sheet. "Don't. I'm the one who's sorry. It's my fault you had the nightmare."

"No." She met his hurting gaze. "It is not your fault." The blame belonged to someone who was the polar opposite of the gentle soul she was starting to believe really hid beneath Tiernan's FBI agent exterior.

His gaze dropped to their hands on the bed.

She hadn't noticed how much larger his hand was than hers, how perfectly he covered her fingers in protective warmth.

He pulled his hand away, clearing his throat as he stood. He glanced at the door, then back at her. "Can I get you anything? Glass of water maybe?" He didn't seem to want to meet her eyes anymore.

She shook her head as she slid her hand under the sheet, trying to ignore how cold it felt now.

He quickly went to the door, like he couldn't leave fast enough.

"Tiernan?"

He glanced back, halfway through the doorway.

"Thank you."

He nodded and left without a word, closing the door gently behind him.

Had she made him mad? Maybe he wished he hadn't touched her hand. Probably afraid she'd get the wrong idea.

No chance of that after tonight. Men didn't run from the room when they were attracted to a woman. Not that she wanted him to make a move. Far from it.

She scooted down and gave her pillow a good punch before burying her face in it. If she could just get through the night, maybe Matthew would save the day tomorrow and she could go home, staying as far away from anything resembling a man for the rest of her days.

chapter
twenty-five

A scent teased Ashley's nostrils, luring her from a dreamless sleep.

She slowly opened her eyes and sniffed the air. Eggs?

She sat up and stretched. Must be imagining things.

She scanned the room she hadn't been alert enough to study last night. A framed painting hung on one log wall—a little boy hanging his feet over a dock by a lake, holding a fishing pole in his hand. Words were printed underneath the image.

Her bare feet landed on the cool wooden floor, and she walked to the painting.

"Follow me, and I will make you fishers of men." Matthew 4:19

Figured. More Bible stuff.

The smell of sausage mixed with the aroma of eggs as Ashley grabbed her jeans and pulled them on under her thigh-length nightshirt.

She cracked her door open and peered through.

Tiernan cheerfully chatted with Matthew in the kitchen where, sure enough, it looked like the FBI agent was cooking. He flipped something on the stove as he laughed.

Grabbing her toiletry bag and a clean tank top from her

suitcase, Ashley snuck to the bathroom where she took a superfast shower and made herself somewhat presentable. Though with breakfast waiting, she didn't have time to dry her hair. Why she suddenly cared, she didn't want to figure out.

Her lips tugged up at the culinary vision of the two guys in the kitchen as she approached. "Hi."

They turned away from the stove to face her, Matthew wearing an apron tied around his waist and Tiernan holding up a spatula. Their smiles warmed her to her bare toes.

"'Morning." Tiernan pointed to the plate on the bar counter without losing his big smile. "Have a seat. Breakfast is ready."

She sat on the high stool as Tiernan brought a sizzling frying pan over and dished out sausage links, bacon strips, and eggs. Her eyes widened at the feast. "When did you get all this?"

"When we stopped yesterday."

Always prepared.

"Eat while it's hot. You too, Matthew." He had Matthew sit next to Ashley at the counter, heaping his plate higher. "I didn't know what you like for breakfast. But we'll have waffles and pancakes tomorrow, if you prefer that."

She savored a perfectly buttery bite of egg before letting it slip down her throat. "This is perfect. You weren't kidding about being able to cook."

He looked at her with an impressively somber frown. "I never kid about food." The frown melted into a smile that did funny things to her heartbeat. "Speaking of food, how about fish for lunch?"

"Where are you going to get fish?"

He pointed at the lake that could be seen through the windows he must have uncovered before she awoke.

She raised an eyebrow. "You fish?"

"Thought I was too much of a city boy, huh?"

She shrugged, taking a bite of bacon to hide the smile that wanted to come.

"Matthew loves to fish, don't you, Matthew?"

"Swim swim!"

Tiernan laughed, a sound as warm as the sunlight pouring in the windows. "He must get wet when he fishes, because when I told him what we were doing today, he insisted on wearing his swim trunks. *And* he left his baseball cap in the loft."

Tiernan looked ready for vacation fun himself, dressed in shorts and a T-shirt that showed off sculpted muscles.

"Should I search the house while you guys fish?"

"Can if you want to, but like I said, we already went over the house. I'm thinking outside somewhere is the best bet."

She nodded. "Then I'll scout around out there." It helped to remind herself of the goal, the only reason they were there.

She kept reminding herself as they finished breakfast, Tiernan eventually sitting beside her to eat, making Matthew giggle throughout the meal, and getting Ashley to smile once or twice.

But the idyllic feel of the day didn't dissipate when they moved outside. Ashley chuckled to herself as she stood on land and watched Matthew and Tiernan at the end of the dock, trying to teach each other how to fish. This was apparently one area in which Matthew wouldn't take instruction. Instead of getting upset with the rebel, Tiernan laughed and sent Ashley a few winks when he tried to give Matthew tips.

Sunlight reflected off the lake, making the surface sparkle in some spots and gleam like glass in others. A cool breeze offset the heat from the sun, bringing the temperature to somewhere around an ideal mid-seventies, judging from Ashley's comfort level.

She turned to walk along the abruptly sloped shoreline. The place was like a little hideaway. A bit of heaven in the middle of a storm. Too easy to forget that storm while they were there. But to forget could be deadly.

They were there to find the evidence. A hiding spot. She glanced down to watch her footing on rocks that mixed with grass and mud under her flip-flops. She looked up, trying to see as far as she could down the shoreline. There was nothing noticeable. No boxes or odd places that stuck out. But the hiding spot wouldn't be obvious.

If she were to hide something out here, the safest place would probably be among the trees somewhere. As in, take ten steps to the stump, five to the rock, and so on. But then wouldn't the Bordens have left a list of clues or a treasure map somewhere Tiernan would find it?

"Matthew!" Tiernan's shout reached Ashley's ears.

She spun around.

Tiernan leaned off the end of the dock, looking at the water.

Where was Matthew?

Splashes squirted up at Tiernan as Ashley sprinted back to the dock.

Had Matthew fallen in the lake? Why didn't Tiernan jump in after him?

Adrenaline surged through Ashley's limbs as she reached the dock, ready to launch off of it if she had to.

But Tiernan's laugh stopped her. He glanced at her as she came up behind him. "He's fine." Surprise lifted his tone along with his eyebrows. "He's a good swimmer."

She found Matthew in the water, already about ten feet away. Sure enough, he was swimming, no awkward kicking or flailing. His thick arms stroked smoothly through the water.

"I thought he was just talking about water when he said, 'swim swim,' all the time."

"Yeah." Tiernan smiled like a proud papa as he watched the boy. "I don't know why I assumed he couldn't swim. Kevin and Jane never mentioned it to me." He shifted his smile to Ashley. "Want to join him?"

A hot flush crawled up her face. "I don't have a swimsuit with me."

He watched her. Did he see the blush? "You can swim, right?"

She tilted her chin. It wasn't a failing. "No."

"Really?"

She glared at him.

"Sorry. I guess I thought you'd have to…You know, to help kids and all that."

"I don't usually have to pull them out of the water."

He met her sarcasm with a grin. "You never know when you'll need to. Maybe I could teach you."

Her cheeks burned like they were on fire. "Don't you think we should be finding the documents?" She put her hands on her hips. "I'd really rather not spend the rest of my life here, if you don't mind." She spun on her heel and tromped back toward the cabin, refusing to acknowledge that her declaration may not have been entirely true.

Why was she going to the cabin? Nothing was hidden in there. She veered off into the trees past the cabin instead, her flip-flops bending over sticks and other bumps on the uneven terrain. Hardly practical footwear for a hike, but she had to do something to get her mind off the idyllic scene at the lake.

Tiernan always knew how to play tricks with her head. Did he want her to like him for some reason? Did it serve some purpose for his FBI assignment?

But he had been so unexpectedly kind about her reaction to Frank, so understanding. And he had even said they'd find another way so she wouldn't have to face Frank. That didn't seem like an FBI agent bent on using her anymore. Still, it wasn't possible he could actually like her.

She let her hand slide along a rough tree trunk as she walked around it, watching her step over an exposed root.

Tiernan was probably just trying to be nice since he'd seen her have an emotional breakdown. Made her quite a sympathetic character in his eyes, no doubt.

She pressed her lips together at the revelation. At least that explained his softer behavior.

And the warm fuzzies she got over the family-like scenes today made even less sense when she dosed herself with the Matthew reality check. A kid with Down syndrome was never part of her ideal family dreams. Wouldn't be for anyone.

"You're doing the right thing." Veronica's pale, dying face blocked Ashley's vision, those scrawny fingers squeezing her hand.

Pain shot through Ashley's toe as she stubbed it on something.

The culprit, a rock, stood uninjured and unmoved in front of its victim.

She pressed her teeth into her lip as she waited for the pain to subside. She should thank that rock. It had burst the inexplicable lump growing in her throat and banished the memory at the same time.

As the surge dulled to more of a numb soreness, she glanced around. She really should have been paying more attention. None of the trees around her looked familiar. Not like any would, since she'd never been to these woods before. *Smart, Ashley. Real smart.*

How long had she been walking? She checked her wristwatch. *11:16.* Why hadn't she looked at the time when she'd started out? She couldn't have gone very far, even at her angry speed-walking pace. Better head back before she got really lost. She turned to what she hoped was the direction she'd come from. Or was it slightly more to the right?

The trees were too thick to see the water or find the shoreline. Too bad Veronica hadn't listened to Ashley when she'd begged to join the girl scouts. Not sophisticated enough for Veronica's daughter.

Ashley shook her head. Childhood memories were the last thing she needed to keep her company right now. Taking a deep breath, she picked a direction and marched forward.

When her legs started to tire, she checked her watch again. *11:30.* She should have reached the cabin by now if she were going the right direction. What if she was walking around in circles? That happened to people in forests.

At least she had plenty of light this early in the day. She didn't want to think about what would happen if she were still lost come nightfall.

She stopped and looked around. There had to be some way to figure out the direction of the lake at least. Climb a tree?

Something that didn't look quite like a tree caught her eye. A building?

She walked toward it. Yes. A little shed-like building. Tiny, like it would only hold two people standing up. Looked as if it had been thrown together with mismatched boards by someone who didn't care much about appearances or warmth.

A shed, even a tiny one like this, wouldn't be too far away from a cabin or something, would it? Maybe she hadn't wandered as far from the Bordens' cabin as she'd thought. Or did the shed belong with a different place?

Or…it could be a hiding spot even the FBI hadn't found.

Goose bumps popped out on Ashley's arms as she hurried to the shed. Could this be the break they'd been hoping for?

A voice stopped her.

"No." A woman. "I…" Sounded like she was in the shed, but the voice grew too soft to hear.

Ashley slowly snuck closer, tightening her toes against her flip-flops to keep them from snapping as she neared the back wooden wall.

"With all due respect, I disagree. Hanks gave that up when he ran out."

She was talking about Tiernan? Ashley held her breath as she peered through one of many small cracks between the boards.

Someone walked past the crack, black clothes the only thing she could see.

"I think you need to count him out of the plan."

Wait a minute. Katherine? Ashley would know that cryptic, always sarcastic tone anywhere. Her heart thumped against her ribcage. What was Katherine doing here?

"Hanks was supposed to earn her trust with our help, not go into business for himself."

Go into business for himself? What was she talking about?

"For all we know at this point, she may have served her purpose, and he could've already terminated her and the boy."

Ashley sucked in a breath. She clapped her hand over her mouth and froze. But her mind raced to comprehend Katherine's words. *Terminate* could only mean one thing. Was Tiernan part of the leak he pretended to distrust?

Her stomach lurched. She should have known. The worst criminals were the smoothest operators, the undetectable liars. He must have been working for Grayson along with Katherine until he decided to go into business for himself. No wonder she sounded so put-out. She'd probably lost a big cut of a payoff when he left her behind.

Was that Grayson himself on the phone with her? No, he wouldn't risk it. A guy who could hide criminal activities while holding a prominent government position for so long would build in a hundred layers of protection.

Hold it. Katherine hadn't said anything for a while.

Ashley's pulse raced in her ears. Should she run? But to where? There was no one to go to. No help to be found.

She slipped out of her flip-flops and picked them up, slowly tiptoeing away from the building on her bare feet. She watched the ground in front of her as she tried to avoid the more painful sticks and rocks.

"Well, who do we have here?"

She jerked up her head at the sound of the man's voice.

Jack Jones stood five feet in front of her with a grin on his face. "I do believe it's Miss Ashley Sorenson." He shook his finger like he'd caught his favorite niece with her hand in the cookie jar. "You, young lady, have caused us a considerable amount of trouble."

She gulped. Was he on Grayson's side, too?

"I thought I heard someone out here."

Ashley spun to face Katherine, who walked toward them from the shed. She smiled—a decidedly unfriendly expression—as she scanned Ashley up and down. "Looks like we've hit the jackpot."

Three FBI agents gone bad versus Ashley and a boy with Down syndrome. Ashley didn't like the odds.

chapter
twenty-six

"You shouldn't have been so predictable, Hanks."

Ashley glanced at Tiernan to catch his reaction to the smug little smile Katherine gave him from her seat at the table.

He stopped pacing and looked at the agent with a dark expression very close to a glare.

If Ashley didn't know better, she'd feel bad for Tiernan. Katherine sure was savoring every moment of her superiority.

She flicked her index finger across the table at Jack. "Jones here figured you wouldn't give up on the boy finding the evidence. All we had to do—"

"Was check the likely places the Bordens used to go to." Tiernan crossed his arms over his chest, his eyes glinting. "I did actually think of that."

Katherine raised an eyebrow. "But you still came here."

"And the harbor in Chicago. You didn't happen to stop there, did you? Maybe do a little hunting?" Yep, Katherine had definitely gotten under Tiernan's skin. Ashley had never heard him use sarcasm before.

Division in their ranks could be good. If they were fighting against each other, Ashley and Matthew might have a chance to escape. Or was this a show for her benefit? After all, if Tiernan was with Grayson, he'd be just as glad about the shooting at the harbor as Katherine. Unless the shooter had missed on purpose and was only there to scare her into trusting Tiernan? If that was the mission, it had been accomplished without a hitch.

Her thoughts tied in knots almost as unpleasant as those in her gut. What a horrible feeling—realizing she might be a puppet but unable to cut the strings because she didn't know who held them.

"Well, I hate to burst your bubble, *Agent* Nguyen." Tiernan lowered his arms and walked to the empty chair at the table. "But Dillon knows what I'm doing. I had his full approval to take Matthew on my own."

And take Ashley. He was smart enough not to call her attention to that fact.

"I knew it." Jones smiled like he'd regained his best friend. He glanced across the table at Katherine. "I told you he wouldn't go rogue." He pointed to Tiernan. "This man is like the FBI personified. I'm telling you."

Ashley feared he was right. Was there anyone she could trust in the FBI? Jack didn't seem to know anything about Katherine's phone conversation or Tiernan's real motives. Could they be fooling Jack along with Ashley? Or maybe he was part of the con on her.

Ugh. She was so confused she didn't know which end was up. She forced herself to breathe, quietly, trying to calm her nerves before she got sick.

At least Matthew was safe at the moment. He contentedly ate his fish at the bar counter in the kitchen, red cap on his head and his Bible by his plate, seemingly unaware that anything was wrong. He had been the only one happy to see Katherine and Jack, giving them a warm welcome and showing them the fish he—probably Tiernan, in reality—had caught. He was the only hungry one, too, judging from the others' barely touched plates.

"I just talked to Dillon." Katherine met Tiernan's stare.

"He didn't say anything about giving you special permission to go off on your own."

"That was the whole point." Tiernan didn't blink as he rested his hands on the back of the empty chair. "Not to tell any of you."

"Ouch. Thanks, mate."

Tiernan's gaze softened slightly as he glanced at Jack. "Sorry. But you're both smart enough agents to know there's a leak in our group. I didn't want to risk letting that leak go unplugged until Matthew got hurt."

"So you think one of us is a mole?" Katherine didn't appear at all pleased with Tiernan's explanation. "Funny. I thought it was you."

Tiernan smiled, one of Katherine's humorless versions, as he met her challenging stare. "That *is* funny."

Were they for real? Or was this all a big drama to fool her even more?

It wasn't working. She couldn't figure out which agent to trust, so her only option at this point was to trust none. Back where she started.

"You realize I'll have to call Dillon again and ask him about what you claim."

Tiernan nodded to Katherine. "I wouldn't have it any other way." He pulled the chair out and sat in it, some of his defensive demeanor melting away with the change in posture. "In the meantime, what's the news from down south?"

Katherine and Jack exchanged a look, then Katherine pointed a meaningful gaze at Ashley.

"It's okay." Tiernan gave Ashley a slight smile. "She knows everything now."

"Does she?" Katherine raised an eyebrow at Tiernan, as if to add, *That wasn't very smart.*

Jack leaned forward, pushing his plate to the side so he could rest his long arms on the table. "Our sources tell us Grayson's plans for Matthew have changed. Grayson may have put a contract out on him now."

"I assume from your comment about a shooting at the harbor, this isn't news to you?" Katherine watched Tiernan and Ashley.

Tiernan tapped a finger on the table, his mouth in a firm line. "Unfortunately, no."

"There's also one more bit of news." She paused, glancing from Ashley to Tiernan. "You say she knows *everything*?"

Ashley shot the woman a glare. "I'm sitting right here. Yes, I know about—"

"Ashley." Tiernan held out his hand toward her, signaling she should stop.

Katherine smiled, a cattish curve of the lips. "Oops. You almost gave away all the secrets."

Ashley looked at Tiernan. "You mean they don't know?"

He shook his head.

"We know you were brought in to work Tiernan's source, but we don't know his source's identity." Jack grinned. "Bet it feels good knowing more than us, ay?" The twinkle in his eyes said he didn't resent her for it.

"Not all of us, Jones." Katherine smirked like the cat that got the cream.

"You know?" Jack raised his bushy eyebrows.

"I have my sources, too."

"Aw, and you didn't share with me?" Jack glanced at Tiernan. "That's not very nice now, is it, Gale?"

"Not very nice that she knows at all, I'd say." Tiernan's eyes darkened.

Katherine actually looked directly at Ashley. "So you've talked to him?"

Ashley shifted her gaze to Matthew, trying not to let her mind go where Katherine wanted it to.

The boy drew circles on his plate with the fork, the tines scraping the surface.

"Him." Jack happily lapped up the tidbit. "That narrows the field a bit. Did he give you the goods on Grayson?"

The question was probably meant for Ashley, but she

wasn't inclined to face their stares and interrogation on this subject. She stared at the sheets Tiernan had rehung over the windows instead.

"I see you didn't." Katherine's irritating tone pulled Ashley's gaze back to her. "I'm surprised Tiernan couldn't persuade you. He seems very good at that."

"That's enough." Tiernan's snap made Ashley start. Had Katherine hit too close to the truth?

The agent arched a slim eyebrow at Tiernan like a disapproving schoolmarm. "Well, perhaps I can persuade you with this news I just heard. Regarding your mysterious source."

"Hold it, Katherine." Tiernan looked at Jack. "Sorry, pal. Procedure."

"No problem." Jack got to his feet. "I'll just take my mate here for a walk down by the lake." He went to Matthew and clapped him on the shoulder.

Tiernan gave Jack a relieved smile. "Thanks. I'll join you in a few minutes."

"Come on, Matthew. Let's go for a walk."

Matthew slid off the stool and picked up his Bible, his blue-eyed gaze going to Ashley. "Hide go see?"

"Not now." The knots in her stomach pushed up into her chest while she waited to hear Katherine's ominous information. If it really had to do with Frank, Ashley would probably be better off not hearing it at all.

"Coming, Matthew?" Jack's question brought her attention back to Matthew, who just stood there facing her, cap askew and his lower lip pushed out.

His familiar pouting expression relaxed some of the knots. Even Matthew was learning how to get his way.

Ashley held back the smile that tugged at her mouth. "Okay. You go hide with Jack, and I'll come find you in a bit."

A broad smile was her reward, stretching across Matthew's face as he clutched his Bible to his chest and beat Jack to the door.

"Oh, Jack."

Special Target

The tall agent glanced back at Tiernan from the open door. "Watch him by the water. He likes to jump in."

"Roger." Jack winked. "Don't have too much fun without me."

Tiernan waved, then turned to Katherine when Jack closed the door. "So what's the big news?"

"Just so we're clear, I know your source is Frank Abelli." Katherine kept her voice low, holding a steady gaze on Tiernan, then switching to Ashley. "And I know he's your father."

Ashley narrowed her eyes, clenching her jaw to keep from responding. *Just get to the information.*

"The word is, he had to get the FBI to trick you into talking to him." Katherine watched Ashley. "Not exactly Daddy's little girl, are you?"

Hot anger flushing her cheeks, Ashley opened her mouth to respond—

"Would you get to the point?" Tiernan's sharp scold took care of the irritating agent instead.

"Well, didn't you wonder why he wants to see you now after all these years?"

How did Katherine know how long it had been? Maybe she was guessing. "No."

Katherine paused with her mouth open. Surprise? That'd be too much to hope for.

Ashley shrugged like she was completely detached from the topic. "He's been trying ever since I left."

Katherine shifted in the chair. "That may be, but he has a more particular reason now." She paused, probably for dramatic effect. "He's dying."

Ashley waited for a reaction to come, some kind of feeling inside. Nothing.

"Dying?" Tiernan responded for her.

"He has kidney disease. He's too far along for a transplant, if they manage to find a match, which they haven't been able to for five years. My intel says he won't last more than a few months."

Ashley vaguely registered Katherine watching her.

"I guess he must have something to make up to you, huh?"

There it came. A sensation moved through her body, opening up her lungs, freeing her of the nervous knots, energizing her limbs. Relief. Like she'd never felt before.

"Ashley?" Tiernan's brow furrowed as he looked at her. "Are you okay?"

She nodded, trying her best to fight back a smile that would invite too many questions. He'd be out of her life. Forever.

"I imagine this will change your mind about talking to him now." Katherine was so smug. And so wrong.

"No." Half of a laugh escaped Ashley's mouth with the word, earning raised eyebrows from both agents.

"You're not serious?"

Ashley got her frown back by meeting Katherine's judgmental stare. Like the agent was in any position to condemn Ashley. She had no clue. "Dead serious."

"What did he do to you?"

Ashley clung to her rising anger to keep from seeing the memories Katherine's question threatened to bring up. "That," she glared at the agent, "is need-to-know."

Tiernan's twitching mouth signaled he held back a grin as Katherine shoved her chair out.

She got to her feet. "Whatever. I have to say, that's pretty sick, not even caring when your own father's about to die."

Ashley looked up at Katherine's accusing glare. "You have no idea what sick is. And you sure got the wrong person."

Katherine crossed her arms. "That's what every convicted felon says."

"Katherine." Tiernan's voice rose with exasperation. "We're on the same side here."

"Sure, Hanks. Whatever you say." Katherine stormed out of the cabin, slamming the door behind her.

Tiernan let out a long sigh.

Tension squeezed Ashley's chest. Is this where he'd turn

on her and demand answers? Or would he try to charm her into trusting him again? She'd beat him to it. "No, I don't want to talk about it."

He held up his hands as he met her gaze. "I wasn't going to ask."

Right.

His eyes softened to a lighter green color as he watched her.

"Katherine was wrong, you know." Ashley moistened her lips. Why was she even saying anything? "About not caring. I do care. I'm glad."

Those eyes filled with pain, like when he'd woken her from her nightmare. "I know."

She looked down at the wooden tabletop, running her finger along the grain. "Do you believe God made evil people, too? Men like Grayson?" *And Frank.*

"Yes."

"Why?" She searched Tiernan's face like the answer was there in his features. "Why would He make someone so awful? Why would He even let him be born?"

Tiernan didn't so much as glance away. "For the same reason He made Matthew. You. Me." His voice was soft but filled with conviction. "For His purpose." Tiernan leaned across the angle of the table and covered her hand with his. He waited until she met his gaze. "And that purpose is good."

Bile welled up in her throat as Tiernan's face blurred before her eyes. Good? That was the sickest thing she'd ever heard.

She yanked her hand back and stumbled away from the table.

"Ashley."

She ignored him, finding her way to the door through a blur of anger and tears. She yanked it open and stepped out into the fresh air.

"Matthew!" Jack's call carried on the breeze from the lake.

Ashley wiped the wet streaks off her cheeks. Ridiculous.

She didn't cry anymore. This mess had her going to pieces. Would it never end?

"Matthew!" Jack again.

Wait. Why would he call for Matthew if they were together? Ashley's heart rate picked up speed as she walked in the direction of the dock. There was probably no need to get excited. Or had there been a note of alarm in Jack's voice?

She walked faster, looking ahead to the shoreline and the dock.

No one was there.

"Was that Jack?" Tiernan jogged to Ashley's side.

She nodded.

Jack ran out of the bunch of trees to the left of the dock. He sprinted their way. "He's gone."

"What?" Tiernan's voice was as sharp as the pain that surged in Ashley's chest.

"I don't know what happened." Jack lifted a hand and let it slap down against his leg. "We were looking at a fish in the water along the edge down there," he pointed in the direction of the shoreline, "and when I looked up, he was gone."

Tiernan looked at Ashley. "He used to do this with you, right?"

She nodded, her heart lodged in her throat. But out here, he could get lost in two minutes. And in five…lost enough that they might not find him.

"Do what?" Jack glanced back and forth between them.

She swallowed. "Wander off when I wasn't looking."

"Where would he go?" Tiernan watched her.

He could be anywhere already. If he kept walking, he could get turned around like she had. What if he tried to swim farther down the shore, alone? He could tire out, get pulled under—

"Ashley." Tiernan's firm tone called her out of her spiraling thoughts. "He'll be okay. We will find him. I need you to tell me where he used to go when he wandered off from you."

"Home." The word came out a hoarse whisper.

"What?"

She took a breath. "Home. I'd find him trying to go home. That made sense before, but now..." She swung her hand toward the cabin. "Isn't this already like home for him?"

He had acted like it was. He was happier, more relaxed. At least she thought so. She hadn't really stopped to think about it until now. Wasn't he happy there?

"What's going on?"

Wonderful. Katherine. Just what Ashley needed right now.

"Matthew's missing. Jack thinks he wandered off."

Thinks? Ashley looked at Tiernan, trying to read what he meant by that, but she only saw determination in his set jaw.

"How long ago?" At least Katherine wasn't smirking now.

Jack checked his wristwatch. "Six or seven minutes."

"Okay. He couldn't have gone far." Tiernan pointed in the direction of the cabin and the trees beyond it. "Katherine and Jack, you two search that direction. Split up to cover more ground." He nodded to the portion of trees Jack had emerged from. "Ashley and I will head that way." He glanced at his watch. "Meet at the cabin in thirty."

Tiernan stalked to the trees at a fast clip, but the adrenaline hitting Ashley's veins enabled her to keep up.

"What did you mean?"

He glanced at her as they speed-walked through the trees. "When?"

She almost didn't want to ask. "That Jack *thought* Matthew wandered off." Her heart rate climbed as she waited for Tiernan's answer.

His gaze kept moving, scanning ahead and around them as they progressed. "Nothing gets past you, does it?"

She pressed her lips together. "Like your attempt at stalling right now?"

He sighed. "I didn't mean to worry you more than you already are."

She stopped walking and faced him. "Tiernan, what is it?"

He paused, turning halfway toward her. "I don't know for

sure. We just..." He looked away, his gaze moving all around them instead of toward her. "We can't be sure he wandered off."

"You mean he—" The words caught in her throat.

Tiernan nodded, finally meeting her eyes. "It's possible he was taken."

"But Jack was right there with him."

"And Jack's a good agent." He shrugged. "You're probably right. It would've been a pretty stupid move to take Matthew with an agent so close to him."

Or a very bold move.

"Forget it. It's far more likely he wandered off. We know he does that. But we better keep moving, or we won't catch up with him." Tiernan started forward again.

Matthew had to have wandered off. Grayson didn't even want to kidnap him anymore, did he? He wanted him ki—

Ashley stopped the jolly thought right there. She jogged a few paces to catch Tiernan. "Why aren't we splitting up like Jack and Katherine?"

"A couple reasons." Tiernan went back to scanning the woods and avoiding her gaze.

Wasn't going to tell her, apparently. "Are you afraid I'll run away again?"

He turned those green eyes on her. "I don't know. Would you?"

Her turn to look away. Had he figured out she distrusted him again? Until she knew for sure what Katherine meant about him going into business for himself, she had to stay suspicious.

"If you want the truth..."

That would be a nice change.

"The reason we're not splitting up is because you aren't carrying one of these." He lifted his right hand, which had been hidden from her sight at his side facing away from her.

The hand that held a gun.

chapter
twenty-seven

Ashley winced with every step. She'd worn these flip-flops nearly every day all summer, but on this uneven terrain, they rubbed her feet in all the wrong places, creating blisters that burned as she tried to keep going. Her throat was nearly as raw from shouting Matthew's name.

The woods grew shadowed as the sun fell in the sky, seeming to mimic the plunging of her heart.

Still no sign of Matthew.

Katherine and Jack reported the same lack of success every time they met at the cabin or called each other by phone.

Tiernan had insisted they head back to the cabin now to regroup for the night. He claimed a search in the dark would be more dangerous than helpful to anyone. But Ashley had caught him watching her enough times to suspect he might think she couldn't take more searching.

She would change shoes at the cabin and be ready for all-night walking. No way could she sleep knowing Matthew was out there alone somewhere. Or not alone.

She shuddered.

At least Tiernan had put the gun away behind his waistband, hidden by his T-shirt. Every glimpse of it was a reminder she didn't need of Matthew's danger.

"Let's stop by the dock." Tiernan veered in the direction of the lake as they emerged from the trees within view of the cabin. He probably wanted to check for clues while there was still light.

The sun hung just above the water in the distance, an orange orb with wide streaks of pink tinging the sky around it. Any other time, the sight would be stunning. Now, she could only observe it as a random detail, irrelevant to the deadness creeping through her insides.

She stopped when Tiernan did by the start of the dock.

He looked down as he stepped onto the planks and walked the length of the dock.

Matthew had been right there. Had he stood where her sore feet now touched the ground?

His determined face, those pursed lips as he had fished his own way, filled her vision. Had it only been that morning?

Where was he now? He could be huddled somewhere, cold, as the darkness came. Grayson's men could be holding him at gunpoint. Or...worse.

She shook her head, trying to stop the direction of her thoughts. She saved kids on a daily basis. She shouldn't have to stand around helplessly while they got hurt.

Taking a deep breath, Ashley lifted her shoulders and started to search the shoreline next to the dock. She'd find him and rescue him, just like she had dozens of other children.

The rocks and grass close to the water transitioned into light colored mud. A footprint marked the ground a couple inches from the point where the dock met the land. Matthew's? She crouched down to look for more prints, peering under the dock where the water lapped over rocks and...a book?

She reached to pull the book out of the inch of water it sat in.

Matthew's Bible.

"Tiernan!"

He jogged to her side. "What is it?"

"Look." She held up the dripping Bible, the red color of the front cover smeared thanks to the water.

Tiernan's jaw tensed as he stared at the book.

Her chest tightened as she voiced the truth they both knew. "He wouldn't have left this behind. Not by choice."

Tiernan jerked a quick nod. "Get your things together. We've lost too much time already." He sprinted for the cabin, and Ashley attempted to jog after him on her blistered feet.

The cabin had become a whirlwind of precise but fast-paced activity by the time Ashley stepped inside. Katherine and Jack were already there, rapidly tidying the place up.

Jack cleaned up the uneaten food, washing and putting away the dishes faster than Ashley thought possible.

Katherine took down the sheets from the windows and stalked through the cabin, checking all the rooms. What she was looking for, Ashley had no clue. Evidence left behind? But weren't they the good guys?

Their actions reminded Ashley of her suspicions about Katherine and the others. Being united for the hours they looked for Matthew had lulled Ashley into the idea that they were all on the same side. But now the memory of Katherine's phone conversation returned.

"Hanks was supposed to earn her trust with our help."

Was this part of that plan, too? Or maybe Katherine had really cut Tiernan out, like she had said in that phone call. But what was the plan? Matthew's disappearance?

Ashley only needed to zip up her suitcase and bring it out of the bedroom to be ready. She clutched Matthew's still-damp Bible while she waited by the door, narrowing her eyes as she watched Katherine and Tiernan.

They stood in the loft talking in hushed tones. Did they know where Matthew was? What had happened to him?

And what about Jack? He had come out here with Katherine, and he had been nearby during her secret phone conversation in that shed. That probably meant he knew about this plan, too. But if all three of these agents were crooked, then why hadn't they just killed Ashley already?

She swallowed. Comforting thought.

"You okay?"

Ashley jumped at the voice behind her. She turned her head to look.

Jack.

At least there was no chance he could have guessed her thoughts without seeing her face. She hoped.

He moved to stand by her side. "I'm sorry about all this."

She glanced up at him.

"I was so *stupid*." He looked down at her with brown eyes full of remorse. He shook his head. "I'll never forgive myself."

She nodded, looking at Tiernan as he came down from the loft with Matthew's bag.

"This has to be hard for you. I know how much you care about him."

The statement jerked Ashley's gaze up to Jack. "No more than all the kids I help."

He blinked. "Oh. I thought—"

"I care about all the kids I help in my work, but we can't get attached to them. The job's tough enough as it is."

"Ready?" Tiernan stopped in front of her, Matthew's bag slung over his shoulder. Had he heard what she said?

She inwardly shook off the question. Why should she care if he had? It was the truth. She picked up her suitcase.

"We'll be in contact." Tiernan nodded to Jack and led the way out the door.

The sky had grown nearly dark, the remaining light rapidly giving way to blackness and cold air that shocked her bare arms.

Tiernan grabbed her suitcase from her hand before she could protest and quickly loaded it with Matthew's duffel bag into the trunk of the car.

"I know how much you care about him."

Jack's words echoed in Ashley's ears as she slid into the

passenger seat. It couldn't be true. She didn't care if her chest hurt like someone had ripped something out and left a gaping hole. She couldn't be wrong about Matthew. It would mean she had been wrong about...She couldn't. It would be unthinkable.

She pitied him, but that was all. Pitied him because his parents had subjected him to a life of suffering. They were the ones who had been wrong.

"Here."

Ashley blinked out of her internal battle.

Tiernan held her black hoodie out to her with one hand as he pulled the car onto the dirt road.

She hadn't even noticed when he got in and started the car. She took the hoodie and slipped her cold arms into the soft cotton. Where had he found her hoodie? He must have taken it from her suitcase when he loaded it in the car. And he knew she was cold.

She looked at his profile as he drove.

His jawline was firm, his eyes intense even from the side. So serious. And yet, she'd never known a man who would do what he just did. He didn't even seem to be waiting for a *thank you* or brownie points. Could a guy like that really be sadistic enough to want to kill Matthew?

The thought brought Ashley's mind back to where it should be. "You said they wanted to kill Matthew now. But there was no..." Body. She couldn't say it.

Tiernan glanced at her, then the road. "If they saw a chance to grab him without needing to kill him, Grayson would probably still prefer that. Getting rid of the evidence Matthew might know about *and* Matthew himself would be a win-win."

"You think that's what he did?"

Tiernan nodded.

"How much time do you think we have to find Matthew before...?" Another thing she couldn't say. When had she become such a wimp?

His hands clenched on the wheel. "Not much."

"Do you still think God has a good purpose in this? Making Matthew so vulnerable, a victim to a man like Grayson?"

A muscle flexed in his jaw. "Yes."

Maybe that helped at a time like this. But she wasn't going to believe it just because she wanted to. And it sure didn't help to believe God purposefully made people like Grayson or Frank.

She pressed her hand against the textured cover of Matthew's Bible, which lay closed on her lap. She hadn't noticed before how the hard cover was wrapped in cloth slightly rough to the touch. Too bad about the red color fading on top. Matthew probably wouldn't like that.

She bit her lip to hold back the tears that sprang to her eyes.

He never wanted to leave this book. The loss of it alone would probably make him cry.

"If you want to read it, there's a flashlight in the glove compartment there."

Ashley just sat there for another minute. She couldn't. It was Matthew's. She'd hear his voice, making those unintelligible reading noises as he ran his chubby finger across the pages.

She closed her eyes. This couldn't be happening. He couldn't be gone. "What are we going to do, Tiernan?" The words came out as a whisper.

He cleared his throat. Was that a glimmer of moisture in his eyes? "I have a source. If Grayson has Matthew, my source will know."

What source? Not— "Do you mean Frank?"

Tiernan didn't meet her gaze. "He's our fastest and best shot right now at getting to Matthew before something happens."

Something. The ominous word hung like a threat in the air. She swallowed. "But he won't tell you anything."

"I'll find a way to make him tell." The cocky boast of the

FBI agent. Only he wasn't that cocky. He was just hoping. An empty hope.

Ashley gripped the armrest on the door. Her stomach churned. She had to do it. "I'll talk to him."

Tiernan's gaze jerked to her face. "No, you won't."

The sharp command nearly knocked the breath out of her. "Isn't that what you wanted me to do all along?"

"No. Well, maybe at first."

"Maybe?" Was he trying to con her again?

"Okay. Yes." He took a deep breath and let it out. "I'm sorry. Deception is a way of life in this business. I try to be honest, but too often I find myself skirting around the truth to find the truth." He shook his head. "Yes. I did want you to talk to your...to Abelli. But that was before I saw what it did to you."

Ashley braced herself. Was he going to question her now? Want to know why she reacted like that?

"I promised myself I wouldn't ask what he did. But what I've guessed is enough to make me sick." His voice tightened. "I want to put that guy away and keep you as far from him as possible."

She stared at him. Was he serious? Had to be a con.

But his eyes when he looked at her were dark and fierce. Then they softened as his gaze moved over her face. "Your mouth's hanging open again."

She shut it.

"Is it so hard to believe someone would care? Or just me?"

"No one ever did." Her voice was so weak, he probably wouldn't hear her.

"Not even your mother?"

Ashley turned her head away and stared at the black night outside the window. "She didn't believe me." Or refused to. Until it was too late.

"I'm so sorry, Ashley."

Her cheeks started to burn. Would she never outlive the shame? "No, you're not. You think there was a good purpose for it, right?" She gave him a sarcastic smile. "I'll tell that to the next victim of a monster like him."

"I never said it was easy to understand."

"Try impossible." She made no attempt to soften the bitterness in her words.

"Why don't you tell that victim that God can be their strength and ever present help in trouble? That He's there in that awful stuff with them, ready to love and comfort them if they just turn into His arms."

Ever present help. Then why hadn't she felt it? She glared out at the trees they passed. "Why don't you leave the counseling to professionals and do your own job? Just set up the meeting so we can get this over with."

"You're still going to meet him?"

"God seems a little busy at the moment, so I guess I'm going to have to be Matthew's help. That okay with you?" She embraced her rising anger for all she was worth. Anything to keep from seeing that cloud of terror closing in on her again.

She would do it this time. For Matthew.

chapter
twenty-eight

The girl scrunched into a ball under the sheet as the shadow approached the bed.

Closer, closer.

The girl tried to scream.

No sound came out of her mouth.

The shadow moved over the girl, falling on her trembling body. The warning of the monster coming behind it.

The girl couldn't open her eyes to look.

But Ashley wasn't the girl this time. No.

The shadow and the monster behind it.

It was...her.

Ashley sucked in a breath as her eyes opened. She panted, gasping for air as her pulse raced.

What happened? Where was she?

She sat up on the mattress of a bed.

Shadows crossed a Chicago White Sox poster that hung on the wall across the room.

Tiernan's condo.

Her heart rate started to slow as she remembered. She'd fallen asleep in the car and was too tired to fight about not taking the bedroom when they'd arrived in the middle of the night.

Tiernan had slept on the couch in the living room, and Matthew—

Her chest squeezed so hard it sucked the air out of her.

Matthew was gone.

Would Grayson keep him alive one night? *Please, let them keep him alive.*

Who was she asking? Not God, the one who'd turned a deaf ear when she was a little girl and had pleaded time after time that Daddy wouldn't—

Stop. It wouldn't do any good. She was only reacting to the weird dream, the situation with Matthew.

Her gaze fell on the Bible on the nightstand next to the lamp. Tiernan had taken his mother's away before Ashley went to bed, and she had set Matthew's Bible there instead.

If she believed like Tiernan and Matthew, she'd have someone to ask for help right now.

"God can be their strength and ever present help in trouble."

Tiernan was so sure God was the answer to everything. But would God help someone like Matthew? Someone only half human? A mistake?

He had never helped her. Why would He help Matthew?

She reached for the switch on the lamp and turned it on, blinking as her eyes adjusted to the light. She hefted the Bible and laid it on the sheet covering her legs.

"Wead."

A smile curved her lips even as the memory of Matthew's cute voice brought moisture to her eyes. "Sure, Matthew." A salty tear touched her lip, meeting the soft words that spilled from her mouth. "What do you want me to read?"

She opened the book, and her gaze fell on elegant handwriting inside the cover.

To Matthew, our precious son—

Always remember, you are fearfully and wonderfully made in the image of God. We love you, and He loves you more.

Love,

Mom and Dad

Wonderfully made. With a staggering disability. Did they really believe that?

She turned the pages until she reached the first story.

Animals being created, the Garden of Eden, Adam and Eve.

Handwritten words in red ink next to one of the picture boxes caught Ashley's eye. She looked more closely.

Like Him.

The words were printed, rather than in cursive like the note at the front of the book. But had one of Matthew's parents written them?

"*Like him.*" Was this where Matthew had gotten his favorite phrase? Could be significant. Tiernan must have seen this, but maybe he wouldn't have thought anything of it.

She swung her legs out from under the sheet, her bare feet pressing into the plush carpeting. She pulled on a pair of jeans under her nightshirt and quietly left the bedroom.

She tiptoed to the living room, not sure she should wake Tiernan if he was sleeping.

Moonlight illuminated the thin curtains across the balcony doors, making the room lighter than the hallway.

Tiernan sat on the couch, reading a book. Martha's Bible from the look of it.

She didn't think she made a sound, but he looked at her without surprise anyway.

"Hey." The tender way he said the word sent a shiver up her spine.

Nonsense. She was just cold. The air conditioning had been running too much all night.

She held up Matthew's Bible and walked to the couch. "I need to show you something." She opened the book to the page with the writing and handed it to Tiernan as she stopped in front of him. "Did you see that before?"

He turned on the lamp next to the couch and peered at the writing. "Oh, yeah. Kevin's writing. I think he must have put it there to help explain it to Matthew."

"Explain what?"

"This passage." Tiernan tapped the printed text under the nearest picture box. "So God created man in His own image," Tiernan read, "in the image of God He created him; male and female He created them."

"So?"

"So, the *Him* in Kevin's 'like Him' is capitalized here. This verse tells us that every human being is created in the image of God. We're all *like* God in that sense, so we all have intrinsic value, no matter how twisted we become with sin." Tiernan gave Ashley a pointed look. "Even a boy with Down syndrome."

Ashley fought to keep her mind from following the direction of that idea. She wouldn't go there. He was wrong. It was just a story. Better never to live at all than live in suffering. She knew that better than anyone.

And she knew how to take down Tiernan's know-it-all attitude, too. "Funny you didn't seem to know before what Matthew meant."

"What do you mean?" His eyebrows lifted innocently.

"You said I should listen to him when he told me to like you that night we argued in the car. Only he didn't."

"Well, in a way he did. He wanted you not to get angry with me and to treat me with love because I'm a human being, created in the image of God." The man had an answer for everything. "Kevin told me they were working on teaching Matthew that so he would know he was special and so he would always treat others with kindness and respect. He had more of a temper before he started to understand the concept."

"Wonderful." Her frown undergirded her sarcasm. "So it's not a code?"

Tiernan grinned. "Code for 'like me.'"

"Funny." She wasn't smiling. "Now that I interrupted my sleep to bring you this useless information, I'll go back to bed." She turned to leave.

"Oh, Ashley."

She looked back.

"Abelli responded. He'll meet you early tomorrow morning." Tiernan's lips pressed into a firm line. "I'd like to go with you."

She nodded, trying to ignore the pressure that squeezed her ribs together as she headed for the hallway.

"Ashley."

What now?

"Thanks."

She raised her eyebrows.

"For trying to find a clue to the evidence. I wish this one had been a clue." He glanced down at the page. "I just…"

She waited for him to finish, but he bent over the Bible like the pictures had come alive. Or become a clue?

She walked back to him. "What is it?"

"Do you have any paper?"

"What?"

"Never mind." He popped to his feet and brushed past her. He went to the dining room and reached over the counter that divided it from the kitchen.

Like a magician, his hand came out holding a tablet and pen. "I need to make sure I'm right about this." He scribbled on the tablet as she moved closer, her heart thumping against her ribs.

"Did you find something?"

He stopped scribbling and looked at the paper, a smile tilting his lips. "You did."

"I did?"

"Look." He handed her the tablet.

He'd written *Like Him* at the top of the paper and underneath, he'd put *Mike Hil*.

What did that mean? Then she saw it. They were the same letters, transposed. "Who's Mike Hil?"

Tiernan looked like he couldn't stop smiling if she paid him. "I don't know, but the last time I talked to Kevin, he said they were going to introduce me to their friend, Mike."

"You didn't tell me that." Did she really think he'd started telling her everything now? But it meant that he still didn't trust her. Or maybe that she couldn't trust him. After all, why wouldn't he have wanted her to know if he was only trying to find the hidden evidence?

"Sorry. In this business, you get used to being careful with information. Makes it hard to share all the secrets even when you find someone you can trust." He met her gaze, looking into her eyes, for effect no doubt.

Nicely played, but wasn't it a Bible saying that actions spoke louder than words? Wherever it was from, it was a good one. "I know the feeling." She started back up the hallway.

"Ashley, don't be mad." He followed her until she stopped in the doorway to the bedroom. "Now you won't have to meet Abelli."

Her breath caught. "What?"

"We didn't know about the Mike Hil name before. I'd bet my life that this is an alias they came up with to hide the evidence. We'll search for a safe-deposit box or files with that name." A spark lit his eyes. "We'll find the evidence on Grayson and put him where he belongs."

"And how long will that take?"

The spark faded. "We'll get word to Grayson. If he knows we have the evidence, he won't..."

She shook her head. "You can't sell me that one."

Tiernan rubbed his hand over his chin as he looked away.

"He'll still have to get rid of Matthew, won't he? Tell me the truth."

Tiernan brought an anguished gaze to her face. And nodded.

"I'll meet him." She stepped into the bedroom and shut the door behind her.

Going to the bed, she started to set her watch alarm for the morning.

Who was she kidding? She wouldn't even close her eyes.

chapter
twenty-nine

"We agreed last night that I'd go with you."

Ashley avoided Tiernan's gaze as he drove them to the hospital. Traffic delays and constant worries about Matthew were about to send her already shaky nerves right off the edge of a cliff. Reaching her destination might be the straw on the camel's back. "I only agreed that you wanted to."

"Now who's being deceptive?"

"I need to do this on my own."

He surged past a car. "You forget. I've seen you around this guy."

Nice. He would throw that in her face.

"I'm not going to let you go through that again."

"You can't prevent it by being there."

His jawline clenched. "Maybe not, but at least you won't go through it alone."

She sighed and looked out the window.

The towering hospital loomed a short distance ahead.

If she went to pieces again, she was not going to have witnesses this time. Just the idea of having Tiernan in the same room, possibly figuring out the gory details of the history between her and Frank, was humiliating enough to give her courage to face the terror on her own. That's how she'd always faced it in the past anyway. Alone.

Tiernan swung the car into the parking lot and drove to the drop-off entrance. "I'll meet you in the lobby."

"No."

He stopped the car in front of the doors. "It's not your call, Ashley."

She met his gaze with her equally firm one. "Yes, it is. The truth is, you'll only make it harder for me."

His lips tugged into a deeper frown.

"I have to do this for Matthew, and I have to do it alone."

His eyes narrowed, then relaxed as he sighed. "I'll wait for you out here. But if I don't see you in ten minutes, I'm coming up."

"I'll be fine. I have pepper spray, remember?" She patted the outer pouch pocket of her purse.

"Funny." He didn't smile.

She slung her purse strap over her shoulder.

"Ten minutes."

She met his serious gaze. Was he honestly worried about her? Or just afraid she would mess up the mission?

She nodded and pushed open the car door, standing on legs that felt like they'd collapse beneath her any second. She forced a confident stride out of them. One sign of the wreck she was inside, and Tiernan would never let her go alone.

Strange feeling, someone trying to protect her like that. Why did he care? Maybe it was part of his creed. The value of human life and all that.

That was hardly the train of thought she needed to follow going into a hospital. The memories of that day had never bothered her at hospitals before, but she had a bad feeling this time might be different.

Sure enough, the visitor in the elevator reminded her of the lady who'd asked so many annoying questions that day. The nurse behind the desk on the fourteenth floor had a sharply pointed nose very like the nose of the nurse who had—

"Frank Abelli?" The nurse's repetition of the name Ashley had given her was like a shot of reality in the jugular. And it was not just a prick, as they liked to say in these places.

"Uh...yes."

"Are you family?"

The bile that had been climbing from Ashley's stomach reached her throat. She tried to keep a normal expression as she swallowed the repulsive taste. "Yes."

"Room fourteen ten."

Ashley left the desk and walked down the hall. Matthew. She was doing this for Matthew. He was probably more scared than she was right now. If he was still...

One mountain at a time. She stopped outside the door marked *1410*. It was partially closed, but she didn't knock. Just silently pushed it open enough to look inside.

She felt him before she could see him. Like the shadow that crawled to her in her dreams, in her memories.

She should have let Tiernan come. Anything to keep her from having to face the monster alone.

"Ash?"

That voice, calling her that name.

She started to retch. She put her hand on her stomach. No. She had to keep it together. She had to do this for Matthew. He was alone and helpless. In part, thanks to this man. She could stop him from hurting another innocent victim.

She reached in the outer pouch of her purse with a shaking hand. The knife and pepper spray were still there. She wrapped her fingers around the knife as she took a breath and forced herself to put one foot in front of the other to step into the room. She pulled the closed pocketknife from her purse as she finally dragged her gaze to the man in the bed.

The black hair was streaked with white now. The face wrinkled, pale, like life was being sucked from him by the tube that ran from his chest to a machine near the bed. Dialysis probably.

"Things aren't as bad as they look. I'm only here for a check-up." He smiled, making her insides churn. "I come in every so often. Otherwise, I usually do this at home."

Memories she had worked so hard to erase pressed in on her from all sides. Terror, pain, filth. She squeezed the knife. She would not run. Would not run.

"Aren't you going to say anything?" His question ignited her raw emotions into a blaze of fury.

She glared at him with all the hatred blazing through her heart. "I'd rather kill you."

His eyes widened.

Was he honestly surprised? What did he expect? Maybe he was scared she'd really do it.

She should. Give the world one less monster. Her thumb rubbed the smooth surface of her pocketknife. He didn't deserve to live, to keep using up oxygen that others should have.

The noise of the dialysis machine pulled her gaze to it. She didn't have to kill him. His kidneys would do the job for her.

"I know..." His voice was raspy. "I know I did ter—" He moistened his lips with a disgustingly pale tongue. He looked away. "I'm sorry." He lifted a hand to touch his hair. The fingers trembled. "I'm so sorry." His chin wrinkled, quivering. Was he starting to cry? "Please. Please...forgive me." He choked on a sob as he turned watery eyes to look at her.

She stared at hm, her fears receding as she finally saw what he had become. He was the weak one now. The tables had turned.

"I...couldn't help it." He blubbered through the words. "I was sick."

He couldn't help it. The apology, the plea for mercy, then the excuses. The pattern was the same as Veronica's. The same pathetic attempt to get off scot-free when they saw the end coming near. But he still couldn't say it was his fault. No, he had to blame it on sickness. Just like Veronica had blamed ignorance and her husband.

"Please. I could die soon. Say you forgive me."

Her pulse steady, her breathing normal, she walked to the side of the bed without an ounce of fear left. He was done for. She had beaten him. She had survived.

"You want me to say something?" She looked down at his weakened body. "You are disgusting. You're the sorriest excuse for a human being I have ever known. You deserve to die. I just wish you'd done it a lot sooner."

Those dark eyes glinted with what she would have thought was hurt, if he were actually capable of such a normal human emotion. "Ashie, isn't there anything I can do? I just want to make it up to you somehow, while I still can."

She narrowed her eyes. Perfect. "Where's the boy?"

"What?"

"You said you'd tell the FBI everything if I met with you. I'm here. Now I want to know where Matthew Borden is."

His shifty eyes moved to the empty doorway.

Always protecting himself.

"I know a certain person wanted to find the boy, but that's all I know."

"He was taken from us by a lake in Wisconsin yesterday afternoon. Your 'certain person,' *Grayson*, must have him." Or had already done something to him. A knot twisted in her stomach. This was taking too long.

"I don't know anything about that."

"Are you going to keep covering yourself or actually do what you said?"

His sunken eyes watched her much too closely. "You care about the boy that much?"

Her jaw clenched as she turned her back to him. What was he getting at? "Just find him."

"I only told Hanks I'd give evidence on Grayson for the other racketeering charges. This is something different. I can't afford the chance I'd be tied to something like—"

"Like what?" She spun to face him. "Like child endangerment? Hurting an innocent kid? Is *that* what you're suddenly afraid of after all these years?" She gripped the guardrail of the bed with all her strength, wishing it was his neck. "What if I told the FBI what you did to me? What would happen to your precious reputation then?"

He shook his head. "You don't have any evidence. They would never believe you."

The statement stabbed through her attack. He was right. That had always been the problem and the result.

He sighed, closing his eyes. "I'm sorry." He opened them again to look at her. "I didn't mean to do that—fall into defending myself. Too many years as a defense attorney."

And as other, much worse things. She stalked to the window and glared out at the bright, sunlit sky.

"I want to prove to you that I am truly sorry. I'll find out. I'll find the boy for you."

For her. Like he was doing her some tremendous favor that would fix everything. She ground her teeth together. She'd have to play along to find Matthew. Every second that ticked by could make them too late. Her chest squeezed at the thought. "Hurry."

She waited, standing by the window as he called the nurse, and she detached him from the dialysis machine.

He stood, slipping on a suit jacket over his dress shirt. The old familiar work outfit, his height when he straightened—he looked more like his younger self. His horrible self.

She shuddered as he picked up his cell phone.

"I have to make some calls in private. Would you wait out in the hall?"

She nodded. Anything to get away from him as the taste of fear returned.

She stepped out into the hallway, the distance like fresh air to suffocating lungs. Standing or not, he was still dying. And she was still stronger than him now. He couldn't hurt her.

"Ashley."

She jumped, her nerves raw.

"Hey." Tiernan's voice softened to match the concern in his gaze as she turned to face him. "Are you okay?"

She bit the inside of her lip to hold back tears that suddenly pricked at her eyes. *Get it together.* She couldn't help Matthew if she went to pieces. She took a breath. "He's making phone calls to find out where Matthew is. At least that's what he said he's doing."

"Good." Tiernan gently touched her arm. "You did it. You can wait in the car now if you want. I can handle it from here."

She shook her head. "I don't think he'll give you any information. I had to push him to get this much. I'll probably have to push again."

"Let me push instead."

"You don't have the ammo I do."

His gaze hardened. "Is it enough to take him to court?"

She wished. The crime certainly was, but not the evidence. "You better go. He won't tell me anything with you here. He's too afraid of incriminating himself."

"I won't leave you alone. You're not okay. I can see it."

No, he couldn't. He didn't know anything about her. "Maybe not, but I can handle this. I have to get Matthew back."

"*We* have to get him back."

She glanced toward Frank's room. "Would you just go? We can't afford to risk losing this lead. It's our only chance to get to him fast enough." She looked into Tiernan's eyes. "Isn't it?"

He met her gaze. "Five minutes."

"I'll meet you at the car."

He turned and headed in the direction of the elevators.

She watched as he got into one and the doors closed. She was alone again.

"I think I might know where he is."

Ashley hid her start this time. *Show no weakness.* She slowly turned.

Frank stood uncomfortably close as he looked down at her.

She forced her features not to move, her voice not to wobble. "Is he all right?"

"I think so."

She could feel Frank's breath. Her skin crawled. "Where is he?" She took a slow step back.

"I can't say. Not until I know for sure."

She crossed her arms over her chest. He was covering himself again. Always Frank first, above all else. "We don't have time for that."

He glanced at the nurse who walked by and lowered his voice even more, nearly to a whisper. "I'm going to G—" Another look around. "To the place I think your friend might be."

"I'll go with you."

He reached for her arm.

She jerked back, a jolt of panic shooting through her body to her toes.

He dropped his hand, blinking at her. "I'm sorry. I—"

"Save it."

"I was just going to say that you can't go with me. It could be dangerous. It would be for you."

She snorted. "Since when is that a concern of yours?"

His black eyebrows dipped with that stern expression that flashed more memories before her eyes. "I may not have been perfect, but I'm still your father."

She nearly gagged. "If you ever say that to me again, I will do something you'll seriously regret." She took a step toward him, glaring into his face. "If you think for one second I'm going to trust you to find Matthew and leave you to tip off your cronies or run and hide instead, you're as crazy as you are pathetic."

His eyes widened slightly, despite his attempts to hide it behind his lawyer facade.

She'd won.

He nodded. "All right. But you'll have to play along and do as I say."

Her throat constricted. Not in a million years. "We'll see."

"If anything happened to you, I'd—"

"The worst that could happen to me already did." She glared at him, letting the meaning sink in. "We're wasting time. Take me to Grayson's place, and maybe I'll think about trying not to hate you for the rest of my life."

That couldn't be pain in his near-black eyes. He couldn't feel pain, only inflict it.

His walk as they went to the elevator put her at ease. He was slow and weak, like a shell of the strong giant he'd seemed to her as a child.

She could go with him and not have to worry what he might try to do.

But what about Tiernan? The thought nearly stopped her in her tracks. He was probably on his way to find her now. "Where are you parked?"

"The parking garage."

So they would leave by a different exit.

"I should get Tiernan."

"Hanks? He brought you, I suppose."

The elevator doors opened, and they stepped inside. Frank pressed the button for the parking garage sub-level. "He can't come. I can possibly get you in as my daughter, but they know him."

"Then I at least need to tell him where we're going."

Frank looked at her. "You want that boy alive?"

She nodded.

"Then we do it without Hanks."

Did he mean because of the leak in the FBI? Or was he saying Tiernan specifically couldn't be trusted? Didn't really matter at this point.

Either way, she was headed into the villain's lair with the monster of her nightmares as her escort.

chapter
thirty

"Where did you go when you left us?"

Ashley gripped the wheel tighter as she kept her gaze locked on the tollway. Driving Frank's car herself seemed like the safer call, but maybe he was too free to ask questions just sitting in the passenger seat. "The streets."

Out the corner of her eye, she saw him shake his head. "You were only fifteen. You didn't have to live like that."

Was he serious? "The streets were a cake walk compared to what I'd been through at home."

"Your mother was worried sick when you left, you know." He continued as if he hadn't heard her at all, scratching his chin. "She couldn't last long after that."

Disbelief and her rising blood pressure nearly choked her. A couple seconds passed before she could force words out of her constricted throat. "Don't you dare. Don't you dare think you can put that on me. She drank herself to death because she was a loser like you. And if she wasn't before she met you, I'm betting it only took a couple months for her to get there."

Ashley shot Frank a glare. "Or was it when you started with me? Is that when she hit the booze? How about the truth for once?"

"This exit." He pointed at the sign for the next tollway exit.

An easy out. Ashley tried to calm her impassioned breathing as she angled the car onto the exit and turned right when Frank pointed again. She couldn't let him get to her. He wanted to mess with her mind. She didn't have to let him. She was here for one thing—to rescue Matthew. Then she'd never have to think about this monster again.

"At least you came to see her before she died." He looked at Ashley. "Your mother."

Like Ashley didn't know who he was talking about. But how did he know she'd visited Veronica? "She told you."

"Of course she told me. She was my wife."

A match made in...heaven? Tiernan would say God made them and probably that He intentionally had them be Ashley's parents. How could that be good?

Tiernan. The thought prompted Ashley to check the rearview mirror. No car following that she could tell. Good. Her sinking heart seemed to deny the thought, but if Tiernan showed up, he could jeopardize Matthew's life. If Matthew was still alive. She had to believe he was. Or all this would be for nothing. And she might end up dead herself.

"How much farther is it?"

Frank scratched his neck. "About five minutes." He opened the glove compartment and fished out a paper bag. He kept paper bags in there? He held the bag open in front of his mouth.

"Are you going to be sick?" The nausea in her own stomach from being near Frank worsened as he retched a couple times and threw up into the bag. She waited until he'd set the bag on the floor to glance at him.

His face was the color of a Chicago blizzard as he closed his eyes and leaned back against the headrest.

"Car sick?"

"Stage five CKD." He didn't open his eyes. "This is what death-in-progress looks like."

Death-in-progress. A perfect description of what he'd always looked like to her.

"Here it is."

With his dramatic display of illness, she'd missed the start of the huge mansions that signaled they'd entered a neighborhood that made the Bordens' look middle class. Most of the properties boasted gates and fences at their edges that blocked all but glimpses of the wealth hidden behind them.

She turned where he indicated and pulled up to a wrought-iron gate. A security guard in a little one-person guardhouse examined her from behind a window. Her pulse sped up. Did he know who she was?

"She's with me." Frank leaned down so the guard could see him through the driver's window.

"Oh. Mr. Abelli. Mr. Lincoln's expecting you." A buzz sounded, and the electronic gate opened.

Ashley let out a breath as she slowly drove the car through and followed the long driveway that curved into a crescent shape at the front of the house. "Mr. Lincoln? I thought you said this was Grayson's place."

"Stop here. They'll park the car."

A guy she assumed must be the valet jogged around to her side of the car and smiled politely as he opened her door. How absurd. Like she was going to a concert instead of a kidnapping.

"Lincoln is Grayson's right-hand man." Frank moved closer to her as they walked up the grand steps that led to a pillared entrance. "Grayson almost never gets directly involved himself. Especially in something like this."

She pulled away to the side, her stomach contorting at his proximity. "So he's done this kind of thing before?" She wouldn't be a bit surprised if Frank had helped. What else he might have done made her wish she'd grabbed one of those brown bags for herself. She'd never thought of it before. What if she hadn't been the only one? What if he'd hurt someone else after she left?

Her legs weakened under her, but they were at the door. She had to stay strong.

Matthew. She focused on his face, pictured his smile.

The door opened and a real-life butler in a dark suit stood there. He nodded at Frank like he knew him well.

"My daughter, Ashley Abelli."

She started inwardly at the name. She hadn't been an Abelli for twelve years. But she didn't need the name she'd legally chosen for herself to be sullied by him saying it anyway.

The butler let her through without so much as a blink. So far, so good.

He led them slowly through a marble entryway, another high-ceilinged room that seemed to exist just for show, and finally to a study or office of some sort.

A black-haired man in his forties stood up from a leather armchair when they entered, smoothing his gray suit jacket. He approached Frank with his hand out, a pseudo-friendly smile cracking his closely trimmed beard. "Frank." He transferred his dark gaze to Ashley. "You didn't mention bringing a guest."

Were beards a Grayson requirement? That doctor who'd tried to snatch Matthew had one, too.

"My daughter. Ashley, I'd like you to meet Paul Lincoln. Lincoln, Ashley Abelli."

Lincoln forced a smile that didn't get anywhere close to his eyes. "Charmed."

"I didn't think anyone said that anymore." She wasn't sure where the smart-alecky comment came from but could be the way the guy swept his gaze over her from head to toe. She shouldn't really blame him. In her tank top, jeans, and sneakers on her blistered feet, she was definitely the odd one out in this place.

"What's she doing here?" Lincoln kept his eyes on Ashley.

"Grayson said I was welcome to bring a guest along."

Along where? Just to the house? Ashley fought to keep the alarm from her expression. What hadn't Frank told her?

"I see. A complication has come up that might make that impossible."

"Complication?" Frank donned his very practiced look of ignorance.

Lincoln tilted his head toward the doorway and walked out, obviously expecting to be followed.

Frank glanced at Ashley. "Stay here." He followed Lincoln from the room.

Ashley pretended to study the many books on the shelves that lined the walls while her heart thumped against her ribs so hard she was afraid it might be heard. The complication had to be Matthew. That meant they hadn't hurt him, didn't it? Her pounding heart skipped a beat with hope. She had to get out of here. Had to find where they had him.

She started for the doorway, then stopped herself. She was unarmed and alone. Couldn't even trust Frank. He'd give her up in a split second if it was him or her. If only she could have brought Tiernan or told him where they would be.

No time for *if only's*. She had to think and figure something out. This house was so big, maybe she could manage to sneak around and find Matthew without being spotted. She turned to the door again, just in time to see Frank return, alone.

He looked straight into her gaze and gave her a tiny nod.

"Well?"

"I'm afraid you might not be able to go on the yacht with me this time, Ashley. I'm so sorry."

She blinked at him. "What are you talking about? What about—"

"Do you remember when you were a little girl…"

Her throat tightened. He wouldn't. Not now.

"And I used to read you that law book?" He pointed to the very top of a shelf, back in the corner. "And you hated it because you couldn't understand it. I always guessed that must be why you didn't become a lawyer." He gave her an uncharacteristically wide grin that appeared to stretch unused muscles. "See?" He pointed again.

She followed the direction of his finger this time and her gaze fell on a camera wedged in the corner just below the ceiling. They were being watched.

"Oh. Yes. I remember." She turned to face Frank and took what she hoped looked like a natural step to the side so she could have her back to the camera. "So I can't go on the yacht?" She mouthed, *Matthew*.

"No. I'm so sorry, sweetie. I think I might still go. Since I'm here."

She met his pointed gaze. Did he mean he was going to stay and look for Matthew alone? No way was she going to trust him to save Matthew. "That wouldn't be fair. We came to do it together. Though, I suppose..." Another plan started to form in her mind. She could search for Matthew uninterrupted if everyone left the house. She shrugged. "That's fine, I guess, if you want to go. I'll wait for you here at the house."

His bushy eyebrows pulled together. "It would be quite a few hours. I understand there's some sort of complication that needs to be taken care of on the yacht."

Her heart plummeted to her toes. Matthew. Taken care of? Did that mean what she feared?

She clenched her jaw. Then she had to get to Matthew now, here. "I need to use the ladies' room before I leave. Where is it?"

He stared at her.

She glared back, daring him to stop her.

He licked his lips. "It's a big house. It might be easier if I go along and show you."

"I'm a big girl, Daddy." She somehow managed to make herself put her hand on his shoulder with a simpering smile as her nausea threatened to overflow. "I can go to the restroom by myself."

"Of course." He turned away from the camera to point at the door. "Go out here and take a left, go back to the foyer, then go up the staircase on the right and the restroom is the third door on the right when you reach the top." He glanced at her out the corner of his eyes and lowered his voice to a barely perceptible whisper. "Don't. Too dangerous."

"That doesn't sound too difficult." She kept her own voice loud and cheery. "Wait for me here, and I'll be back before you know it." With Matthew in tow.

"Ashie."

She paused in the doorway and looked back, ready to clobber him for the stupid nickname.

But the look in his eyes stopped her. If she didn't know better, she'd say Frank was worried. "Don't take the wrong staircase by mistake. You could get lost."

Was that a hint or a threat? She smiled for the camera. "I'll be careful." She swept out of the room and scanned the path ahead.

No sign of Lincoln or anyone else, but there could be more cameras.

She tried to check without being obvious as she walked. Hopefully, whoever watched the cameras would think she was interested in the houses of the grossly rich and infamous.

"Don't take the wrong staircase." Had Frank meant that she *should* take the wrong staircase? Maybe it would lead to Matthew.

She reached the foyer again and paused on the slippery marble.

A camera was attached to the wall between the two staircases that flanked the oval room. It pointed at the front door. Could she be seen from the side of the room where she had entered? Probably. The camera was likely set to cover most of the room.

The staircase against the far wall must be the one Frank had said to take for the restroom. But the one closest to her would get there, too, since they both connected with the same balcony level above. Why had he said to take the farthest one?

She had stood still too long if anyone was watching.

Breathe. Act normal.

She casually walked across the room, glancing around without moving her head as she headed for the staircase. When she neared the steps, she saw it—another staircase beneath the one that led upstairs.

Hidden from view if she'd been at the front of the room, this staircase went down instead of up.

Her breath caught. Was Matthew down there? She quickly veered in that direction before she could hesitate. If she walked confidently enough, she would be less likely to draw attention to her movements. At least that was the way it worked in movies.

Her pulse picked up speed as she went to the staircase under the grander one. She paused at the top. Darkness shrouded her destination below. What if she walked into some kind of trap?

The thought hadn't occurred to her until that moment. Frank was far from trustworthy. He could have lured her there with his repentant act on purpose. Maybe he had even steered her wrong about Matthew. Maybe he wasn't alive.

Or maybe Matthew was at the bottom of the stairs, alone and terrified in the dark.

Trap or not, she would find him.

She started down the stairs, trying to keep her steps as quiet as possible. A creaking stair foiled her efforts.

She stopped, listened. Had anyone heard her?

Nothing.

She took another step, one stair away from the bottom, and peered into the darkness. That old creeping sensation slithered up the back of her neck. Someone was there.

A sound, muffled.

She jerked in the direction of the noise. A moan?

"Mmm-hmphh."

"Matthew?" Her whisper sounded as loud as a trumpet to her ears.

"Mmm-hmphh." Louder this time, as if responding to her.

She left the imagined safety of the bottom step and felt with her hands along the wall on her right side. Her fingers finally touched a light switch, and she flicked it on.

Fixtures lit up in the ceiling, revealing a carpeted room with a large, flat-panel TV mounted on one wall and couches arranged in front of it.

No Matthew.

She tried to remember to breathe as she scanned the room. Should she keep going?

A doorway-sized opening ahead appeared to lead to another carpeted space, but she couldn't see it well from the stairs. She cautiously moved forward, glancing around for hidden attackers as she reached in the pocket of her purse for a weapon.

A couple dolls lay on the floor near a couch. For Grayson's children? He had two young daughters. Hadn't thought about them since this mess began. Were they at the house now? She swallowed. Daughters of a secretly criminal father. Had he done to them what Frank did to her?

"Mmm-hmph."

The moan jerked her attention back to the open doorway only a few feet in front of her. Were the girls tied up in there? Or was it one of Grayson's men, trying to draw her into a room?

Didn't matter. She had to take the chance for Matthew.

She gripped the pepper spray can, and softly walked to the opening. She paused just outside, shifting to the right so she could peer into the room in one direction without being seen herself.

A computer monitor and keyboard sat on a desk in the corner with an office chair in front of it.

A thump. From the part of the room she couldn't see.

She took a breath and a big step, pepper spray aimed. "Nobody move!" The bluff bought her a second, but only long enough to see Matthew, struggling to escape from the duct tape that wrapped around his wrists and covered his mouth.

Special Target

"Matthew!" She stuffed the pepper spray in her purse as she rushed to the corner where he sat, tied up on the floor and left alone like an animal.

His slitted eyes beneath his red cap were wider than she'd ever seen them as he thrashed.

Pain seared through her chest. "It's okay, sweetie. It's okay. I'll get you out."

He swung his hands, whether to get them free or in his nervous habit, she wasn't sure.

She tried to grab hold of his taped wrists. "Hold still so I can get this off." She grabbed her pocketknife from her purse.

He kept jerking and trying to pull his hands apart. "Matthew." She looked at him directly in his blue eyes. "I'm here."

Panic stared back at her.

She'd have to try something else. "God is here, Matthew."

The boy paused.

"He'll protect you...right? Jesus loves you." She reached in the recesses of her mind to grab the line from the song she'd learned in church as a child.

Matthew nodded, whimpering.

Her heart squeezed at the sound. She reached for the tape over his mouth first instead. "Now this might hurt. I'm going to pull the tape off, but you have to be very, very quiet, okay?"

He watched her, hopefully understanding.

She slowly tugged, the sticky tape stretching his skin as she pulled it off as gently as she could. The red skin in its wake told her it wasn't painless. Her blood started to boil, running hot through her veins. Who would do such a thing to a boy like Matthew? He was helpless, harmless. Anyone could see that.

Matthew rubbed his bound hands over his mouth, then looked at Ashley. Here would come the pout, very justifiable in this case.

But he smiled instead—that beautiful smile he saved just for her.

"Oh, Matthew." Moisture blurred her vision, and she looked away, opening her pocketknife. "Hold still." She sniffed as she blinked, trying to see the tape more clearly past the tears, one of which escaped down her cheek.

"There's really no point in doing that." A man's voice, right behind her.

chapter
thirty-one

Her heart stopped as she jerked toward the voice.

The doctor from the mental institution, or whoever he really was, stood behind Ashley, watching her with a smug set of his lips and a gun in his hand. No lab coat this time, just suit pants and a white shirt, sleeves rolled up to his elbows. "We'd just have to put new tape on him again."

His mouth opened in feigned surprise. "Are you crying? Aww. This is a touching scene." He grinned.

Creep. She wouldn't give him the satisfaction of wiping away the tear. She put her hand over Matthew's still-bound ones, staying crouched next to him. "I suppose it's useless to tell you to let us go."

"Smart girl."

Anger flared her nostrils. "I'm nobody's girl. And for your information, the FBI knows where I am, and they'll show up in a few minutes when they don't hear from me."

"And that's why they sent you in alone, I suppose?" He wasn't buying it.

Anything else she could try? "Matthew doesn't know anything."

The guy snorted. "Yeah. I've seen him."

"I mean, he doesn't know anything about the evidence his parents hid."

The man's grin fell. "But I guess you do."

Oops. She'd thought they were assuming that already. "I only know that much. That his parents supposedly hid something they had on Grayson. That's all I know." She checked on Matthew out the corner of her eye.

His face paled as he stared at the man with the gun.

She gave his hands a gentle squeeze, looking at the fake doctor. "And I'm very good at keeping my mouth shut."

"Huh. I bet you are." He took a step closer.

She tried to keep herself from instinctively leaning back.

"You really Frank's kid?"

Yes or no? Which answer would be safest? Frank could be in on this for all she knew.

"The boss is gonna love that." He apparently took her silence as a *yes*. "Put down your knife and kick it over here."

She did as he said, closing the blade first to avoid giving him any ideas.

The knife only made it halfway to him, thanks to the carpeting, and he left it on the floor.

"What are you going to do to us?" The question nearly lodged in her throat. The words of a victim. The one thing she had promised never to be again.

"If you're lucky, you'll get to go on the little cruise we had planned for your friend here."

The yacht. "And then?"

"Then you won't be able to ask any more questions. Now shut up and turn around." He grabbed a roll of duct tape from the desk by the computer, keeping his gun pointed at her the whole time.

If he taped her up, she wouldn't be able to comfort Matthew. And she couldn't free him. "Do you have to do that? I'm not going anywhere as long as you have him."

That snorting laugh again. "Yeah, right. Nobody would risk their life for a retard like him."

She hoped her anger showed in the glare she gave him as he came closer. He was the one with the warped brain. "I did, didn't I?"

He tossed her the roll of tape, and she caught it. "You and the FBI want him for the same reason we do, lady."

The FBI would have already found the Bordens' evidence, or Tiernan likely had with their clue by now. Ashley bit the inside of her lip to keep from spitting that information out. It wouldn't help add value to their lives right now.

"Start wrapping that tape around one wrist."

She pulled the end of the tape off the roll and stuck it to her wrist.

"That's it. Now I'll finish it. Stand up." He stopped right in front of her, making her skin crawl like he was Frank. Probably cut from the same filthy cloth. "Hold your wrists together."

He was only going to tape her wrists. That meant he wasn't supposed to shoot them. At least not yet. Might give her some room to work with. She pressed her wrists together in front of her, shaping her hands into fists as he grabbed the tape roller.

He started to wind the tape around her wrists with the hand not holding the gun.

Before he'd made one circle around her wrists, she launched her arm forward in a jab to his face.

He fell back a step as she yanked the tape off her other wrist. He took his hand off his jaw just in time to meet her kick to his stomach.

He doubled over, wheezing like the wind got knocked out of him.

"Let's go." She grabbed Matthew's arm and pulled him to his feet. She moved forward, but Matthew stumbled.

She looked at his feet. How could she forget they were taped?

The doctor started to straighten. "You're not going anywhere."

She took two quick steps to the desk.

"I still have the gun."

She grabbed the computer monitor and whirled around, launching it at the guy as hard as she could.

The screen smashed into his hand that held the gun, knocking the weapon to the floor as the screen glass shattered around it.

The doctor let out a strangled yell and gripped his wrist, staring wide-eyed at the bloody spots all over his hand.

Ashley dove for the gun, ignoring the sting when bits of glass punctured her fingers from the shards around the weapon as she picked it up. She grabbed her pocketknife a foot away and backed up to Matthew.

The doctor still moaned over his wounded hand.

She risked lowering the gun for a second as she opened her pocketknife. She cut through the tape around Matthew's feet more quickly than she'd hoped.

"You won't get away." The doctor's pale face contorted as he grimaced through his beard, cradling his arm like it was a baby.

"You said that before." She pushed her hair away from her face with her arm as she snapped the knife closed and shoved it in her jeans' pocket. Then she guided Matthew to the doorway she had come through, keeping the gun trained on the bleeding would-be doctor. "Don't try to follow us. I will use this."

The doctor spewed out a stream of nasty names for her as she backed through the opening after Matthew and spun toward the boy, hurrying him to the stairs with her hand on his back.

"Wait." She stopped him at the staircase. "I'll go first." She stepped around him to lead the way up. Would anyone else be coming down? She hadn't noticed any cameras downstairs, so no one would know the doctor dude had failed. Not yet.

She reached the top of the stairs and quietly stepped onto the marble floor in the corner under the upward staircase. She gently held Matthew's arm, keeping him close by her side. She peered around the upper staircase. All they had to do was make it to the front door. The path was clear.

She looked at Matthew, pressing her finger to her lips, and motioned with her hand that they should start to walk. They slowly moved along the staircase, every muscle in her body screaming at her to run. Maybe that would be smarter. The camera would see them in two more steps.

"Ashley."

She froze.

The owner of the hoarse whisper stepped around the banister of the upstairs staircase. Frank. He looked at the gun she pointed at him. "What have you done?"

"Did you send that guy after me? Is this a set up?" She was wasting time. But she had to know. Her hand holding the gun shook.

"No." His eyes widened just the right amount to appear authentic. But no one lied better than him.

"How do I know that's true?"

"I'll help you get out of here."

She glanced across the foyer. "All I have to do is make it to that door."

"Even if you do, there are more of them outside. You need me."

Never.

"Let me help you."

A noise at the bottom of the stairs reached her ears. The doctor guy?

Her pulse jumped. "Help Matthew."

Frank nodded and led the way across the oval room.

"I'm surprised at you, Frank." Lincoln stepped out from a doorway near the front door and blocked their exit, a gun in his hand. "Grayson will be, too."

She waited for it—the simpering, the lies, the excuses that would hang her and get Frank out of trouble. But Frank just stood there. He turned his head to glance at Ashley. Was that genuine fear in his eyes? Couldn't be.

"I have a gun, too." Ashley glared at Lincoln, aiming the weapon at him. "And I'm not putting it down until we're out of here."

Lincoln laughed. "Charming daughter you have here, Frank. I don't know why, but I'm guessing if I simply point the gun this way," he swung it slightly to aim at Matthew, "you'll do whatever I want."

Why hadn't she kept Matthew behind her? "You wouldn't shoot him here. If you were going to do that, you would have done it already." She met Lincoln's gaze with a challenging stare.

"That may have worked on Bradley."

Must be the doctor character.

"But I have the authority to dispatch anyone I please. I do prefer to get you all on the yacht first, but you'll find I can be very flexible." He added a convincingly carefree shrug. "Which will it be? Now or later?"

Great options. Either way, she wasn't about to watch Matthew get shot. She lowered her gun.

"Set it on the floor and slide it to me." He shot Frank a glare. "If you so much as make a twitch to grab it, I'll shoot your daughter."

Like Frank would care. She bent to put the gun on the floor and gave it a shove. The gun stopped a foot from Lincoln. He smiled as he picked it up, keeping his weapon pointed at Matthew. "Wonderful. Well, this shouldn't be too difficult."

His grin broadened as he looked past Ashley. "Wow. Somebody got worked over."

Bradley limped toward them, the white sleeve above his injured hand splattered with drops of blood. Faker.

She hadn't even hit him in the leg at all.

"What did she do, Bradley? Use her karate on you?" Lincoln laughed as Bradley passed her, glaring with a deep scowl.

He stopped by Lincoln's side and turned to face the captives. "Let me take care of her."

Lincoln gave Bradley's shoulder a condescending pat. "All in good time. Grayson called. Departure time has been moved up. We're to meet him at the yacht."

Ashley looked at Frank. Did he know what they were talking about?

He wouldn't meet her gaze, staring at the floor instead while he scratched his neck. Some help.

"And then what happens to us?"

Lincoln glanced at Ashley. "You don't want to know."

That bad. Wonderful.

"Now turn around and go back down to the basement where you played hero."

Her pulse raced. Had they changed their minds about the yacht idea? "I thought we were leaving." If she were taken somewhere, she'd have time and opportunities to escape. The basement meant something very different.

"We are. Frank, your girl talks too much."

Bradley laughed like Lincoln was the greatest comedian since Bob Hope and gave Frank a shove in the shoulder from behind.

"Easy, Bradley. We don't know what Grayson wants done with Frank yet."

Ashley looked for a chance to attack these losers on the way downstairs, but two men, each with a gun, was a challenge.

Lincoln was smart enough to keep a gun constantly covering Matthew as they went down the steps, through the TV room, the office, and to a door she would have thought led to a closet.

Lincoln told Frank to open it.

Frank stepped to the door, tossing Ashley an apologetic glance from under a furrowed brow. What was he sorry for now? Making this kidnapping so easy? So much for his promise to help.

Bradley pushed them through the doorway into a garage the size of an airplane hangar.

A choice of six luxury cars stood parked in a row, gleaming like they got polished every day.

"That one." Lincoln pointed them to the gangster black SUV, of course, complete with darkened windows.

As they walked toward it, guns held at their backs, something touched Ashley's hand.

Matthew.

She let him take her hand. Warmth traveled from his soft skin into her heart.

Whatever Grayson's cronies had planned, she would get Matthew out. She would save him. She had to.

chapter
thirty-two

They were going to kill them for sure. Grayson's men didn't wear masks, and they didn't blindfold Ashley or Frank on the drive to the Chicago harbor. Bad sign.

The knots that had tangled together in Ashley's stomach during the trip there started to push up into her chest when the SUV stopped. She squeezed Matthew's hand.

He sat on the seat next to her, his lower lip protruding slightly as his barely-there eyebrows tilted downward. He'd probably be doing his jerky arm motions if she hadn't kept holding his hand.

She reached to straighten the bill of his cap.

The door next to him opened, flooding the interior with sunlight.

Bradley waved his gun at them. "Get out. Slowly."

Matthew slid off the seat, obedient as usual. But he held onto Ashley's hand, making her have to scoot out quickly to follow him.

She blinked at the bright sky as she stepped out of the SUV, into the afternoon heat.

"Now, you're going to act very normal or the boy gets it." Lincoln opened his suit jacket just enough to show Ashley the gun he held under it with one hand. He glanced at Bradley, who still had his gun out in the open. "Hide your weapon, will you? No one is going to do anything. Right, Frank?" Lincoln stared pointedly at Frank. "I know you don't care about the boy, but you do care what we do to your daughter."

Or not.

Frank nodded. Still clammed up like he'd been the whole ride there. His deepening frown and lowered eyebrows created a brooding expression that was taking over his pale face.

Grim thoughts didn't do them any good if he didn't take action. Where was that slippery tongue of his when she could actually use it?

He braced his hand against the side of the SUV like he needed the support.

Great. She wasn't going to get any help from him.

"He'll walk with me." Lincoln pulled Matthew's arm to take him away from Ashley.

"No." She clung to Matthew's hand, her breath catching.

Matthew whimpered as Lincoln continued to pull on his other arm.

"Let him go." Lincoln shifted the hand inside his coat.

She let go.

The jerk put Matthew on his far side away from Ashley and gave the boy a glare. "Shut up."

Matthew's whine softened, but he didn't stop. He kept looking past Lincoln at Ashley.

"It's okay." She tried to give him a smile.

"Move, people. That way." Lincoln nodded in the direction of the dock that ran along the shore.

A huge yacht waited in the water next to the dock. Ashley had to stop her jaw from dropping. Now she understood the term super yacht. The bronze-colored boat looked too long to fit in the regular stalls along the other docks and appeared to have four levels stacked on top of each other. Grayson had sure done well for himself.

"Swim, swim!"

She jumped at Matthew's excited exclamation.

He bounced up and down by Lincoln's side, then tried to cross in front of the glorified gunman.

Lincoln jerked him back. "Calm down and shut up."

"We're not swimming today, Matthew." She had to get him quieter before Lincoln lost his temper. "We'll go on that boat instead. See?" She pointed to the yacht.

Matthew stared at the boat, slack-jawed.

As they got closer, Ashley saw that the back end of the ship had a large staircase that started on a wide, lowered platform and climbed to the first level of the ship where couches and chaise lounge chairs beckoned passengers into the lap of luxury.

Only she had the feeling that luxury wasn't where she and Matthew were headed. She paused on the dock by the boat, glancing around.

Wasn't this the moment when Tiernan was supposed to show up? He would come and save the day, like he had with that shooter, the thugs who ransacked her house, and when she had tried to run away from the farmhouse with Matthew.

"Stop stalling and get on. We have your kid on board already." Lincoln looked at her from the platform at the base of the stairs where he stood with Matthew.

She stepped onto the platform. "He's not my kid."

Frank shot her a look she couldn't read as he followed her onto the boat. If he was trying to send her a signal, he'd have to do better than that.

She climbed the short staircase, keeping an eye on Matthew and Lincoln until they all reached the top. The boat's first level spread out before her, featuring the outdoor seating area and, behind that through open glass doors, an indoor lounge with more couches, tables, and chairs.

She turned around, scanning the other boats in the harbor, the blue water, and the parking lot from where they'd come. No Tiernan. Of course he wouldn't be there. How could he know where she was? She'd run out on him again. Maybe for the last time.

"Follow me." The urgency in Lincoln's voice made her turn toward him, but her gaze caught movement in the parking lot.

A black limousine pulled to a halt and the doors opened. Grayson?

"You heard him." Bradley punched something hard into her back. The gun.

"Doesn't Grayson want to see us?"

"Move." He pushed her shoulder with his hand.

"Ashley, do as they say."

She tossed a glare at Frank. Coward. She didn't need his input unless he was going to be helpful. She followed Lincoln, who kept his hand around Matthew's arm as he led the way past one of two curved staircases.

He stopped by a closed door, opened it, and shoved Matthew through.

Ashley lurched toward Lincoln, but Bradley grabbed her arm. "You don't have to be rough with him." She redirected her fury at Bradley as she tried to shake off his hold. "And get your hands off me."

His grip tightened as he pushed her through the same doorway.

Onto a staircase. She caught hold of the railing just in time to keep herself from falling.

Bradley finally let go of her arm as they went down the stairs to a lower level.

They turned into a narrow hallway and passed by several closed doors.

"I bet this boat has amazing staterooms. Is that where we're going?" She directed her question at the back of Lincoln's head as he pulled Matthew along in front of her. "Or does Grayson not want riffraff like us mingling with the guests?" The show of tough nonchalance worked to calm her rapid pulse, but the knots in her gut only tightened. Were they really going to kill them?

Lincoln glanced back at her, and she quickly put on a smirk.

"These are the crew quarters. And the only people you're going to mingle with will be us."

Matthew whimpered.

"Will you let go of his arm?" Concern lifted her voice as she called to Lincoln. "You're hurting him."

Bradley snickered behind her. "Won't matter in a couple hours anyway."

A couple hours. Is that how long they had before…? Ashley moistened her lips.

"Leave it alone, Ashley." More stellar advice from Frank.

"It matters now." She glanced at Bradley behind her. "Or are you both that sadistic?"

Lincoln chuckled as he took his hand off Matthew's arm and lifted it in the air to show her. "Anything to make our guests comfortable." The glint in his eyes lit a spark of fear in Ashley's belly.

Bradley went over-the-top in his effort to convince everyone he was a bad guy, but Lincoln was honestly starting to scare her. It was there in his eyes—that look she knew far too well. He was looking forward to whatever lay ahead. He needed it.

Her gaze went to Frank as Lincoln halted them by a closed door at the end of the hall. Frank's eyes used to hold that same awful glint. Now they just looked…empty.

He leaned against the wall while Lincoln opened the door. Was he really that weak? His face was even whiter than before, and beads of sweat dotted his forehead.

"This is where you'll be staying with us." An amused smile cracked through Lincoln's beard as he gestured to the doorway, apparently wanting Ashley to enter first. She was careful not to touch him as she stepped past and into the very noisy room.

Of course. The engine room or some such thing.

There was barely enough space to turn around on the narrow, four-way path that formed a cross pattern between tanks, pumps, pipes, and other machinery. Rubbery, bright blue material lined the paths, almost sticking to her shoes with too much traction.

Matthew trotted in after her, probably pushed.

"Tie this around his wrists." Lincoln tossed Ashley a plastic cord.

"No way. This would hurt him."

Lincoln pointed the gun at Matthew. "At this point, you're all dead. It really doesn't matter how or when I do it."

Not likely or he would have killed them already. But she wasn't about to risk Matthew's life calling the bluff. She met the boy's worried gaze. "It's okay. I have to put this around your wrists because that man wants me to. Can you hold real still for me?"

A lump grew in her throat as he watched her, his pale eyebrows lowering with confusion. But he nodded and let her lift his hands to the right height in front of him. "I'm sorry," she whispered. Moisture stung her eyes as she wrapped the cord around his wrists and cinched it.

"Tighter."

She shot Lincoln a glare. "It's tight enough."

"You." He pointed at her. "Step over here." He directed his finger down to the floor in front of him.

She glanced around. There had to be some sort of weapon in there. Some way to stop this maniac from getting his way.

"Now." He shook the gun slightly, as if to remind her it was aimed at Matthew.

"Ashley, please just cooperate." Frank looked at her, his face the color of the white tubes and tanks next to him.

"So they can kill us more easily?"

Lincoln laughed and walked toward her, pushing past Matthew.

She backed up, ready to fight him off with every bit of strength in her body.

"Don't flatter yourself. I just want to put this on you." He lifted another plastic cord in the hand without a gun. He met her gaze with that glint in his eyes.

She watched him for a moment, then put her wrists together for him to tie.

"Bradley, cover her." He put the gun in his waistband behind his back and stepped closer to her.

She ignored the shudder that moved through her as his fingers brushed her skin along with the plastic cord. She looked down at her hands to keep his attention there, then launched her fist at his face.

His hand stopped her blow midway. He clamped his fingers over her fist, squeezing hard as his gaze turned stony. "I'm not so easy to disarm, Miss Abelli."

Anger ran through her veins, despite the frantic racing of her heart. "Don't call me that." She refused to look away. She would not be a victim.

"Not too happy with daddy, are you? Did he hurt the little princess?" The sheer enjoyment glittering in his eyes as he smiled made her recoil, but he didn't let go of her fist. His fingers clamped harder.

She stifled a wince, refusing to give him the satisfaction. "Lincoln."

What was Frank planning to do now? Apologize for her?

"Let her go. She is my daughter and Grayson won't be happy about the way you're treating her."

Lincoln turned his gaze on Frank, then released Ashley's hand.

She covered her aching fingers with her good hand, fighting to keep the pain off her face. He would have to crush the hand already cut by the computer screen glass.

He grabbed her wrists and looped the cord around them, cinching it tight enough to bring tears to her eyes. His lips curved as he gave her one last unnerving stare.

He sent Frank the same kind of look as he brushed past him. "Grayson won't be happy with *you*, old man. Better worry about that." He went to the door, leaving Bradley to back out with his gun pointed at the captives.

The floor suddenly moved under Ashley's feet. She took a

step forward to keep her balance, and Matthew teetered to one side.

Bradley grinned. "We're underway. Don't worry, folks. It'll all be over soon." He spun around to follow his leader out.

The door slammed shut and clicked. Locked no doubt.

Matthew swayed again, bumping into a pipe.

"Spread your feet apart like this, Matthew." Ashley demonstrated a wide stance.

He imitated her, his forehead wrinkling with concentration.

"That was nicely done." Frank's sarcastic tone undercut the words. "Lincoln isn't someone to play with." He sent a scolding gaze her way, like he was still her father, keeping her in line in public and torturing her in private.

She ground her teeth together. If they hadn't tied her hands, she'd probably kill him. "I see your silver tongue couldn't get you out of that." She directed a pointed glance at the plastic cord that bound his wrists behind his back. Bradley must have tied him while Lincoln enjoyed his show of power with her.

"Maybe not, but I will get you out of here yet. At least I'll try my best."

She raised an eyebrow. "How do you plan to do that?"

"Grayson will want to talk to me. When he does, I'll try to make him believe you know nothing about the boy or Grayson himself."

"How is that going to help Matthew get away?"

Frank glanced at Matthew. "It doesn't."

"Are you crazy?" A rhetorical question. "I'm not going anywhere without him. Why do you think I went to find him at the house?"

"I thought he was your son."

She stared at him, then realized her mouth had dropped open. She closed it. "What are you talking about?"

"Why else would you risk your life, and mine, for him?" He met her gaze with an accusing stare.

"How could you think he's my..." she glanced at Matthew, for some inexplicable reason lowering her voice, "...son?"

Frank looked away. "Your mother told me."

"Told you what?"

"That you'd gotten yourself pregnant. When you saw her...before she...passed."

Ashley narrowed her eyes, her heart starting to thump against her ribs as it beat faster. She never should have told Veronica, even if she had guessed it on her own. "So what?"

He faced her again. "I knew you'd get yourself into trouble running off like that."

She took a step toward him, then changed her mind. She didn't want to be any closer to the creep than she had to be. "You are pathetic." Didn't matter what he said. He was the monster here.

"Your mother said you were going to have an abortion." He kept talking like he hadn't heard her, his gaze finding Matthew. "Because the baby was like him."

She swallowed past the lump that lodged in her throat, but tilted her chin in a show of cockiness she hoped Frank would buy. "I did. No child should be brought into the world just to suffer."

"When I heard you were risking your life for him, I thought he must be yours. That you gave him up for adoption instead, and the Bordens took him."

She glanced at a tank about a foot from Frank. "That's impossible. Mine was a ..." Girl.

An image flashed in front of her eyes. A little girl with brown hair like hers, a funny nose and slanted eyes, just like Matthew's.

Pain stabbed through Ashley's chest, as real as if Lincoln had stabbed her with her own knife.

She grabbed the closest thing to her for support. A pipe. Heat seared her palm, and she jerked away. She stared at her hand, barely feeling the bite from the burns on top of her cuts, so intense was the sting behind her ribs. She'd never pictured...Never felt anything since that day at the clinic.

"If he isn't yours, then why did you run off at the house to look for him?" Frank's whiny voice was almost a welcome distraction as it broke through the searing pain. "Do you realize what you've done to us?"

She stomped across the path to stand directly in front of Frank. "That boy is worth more than a thousand monsters like you." She glared at his pale, sickly face. "It's lucky for you they tied me up or I'd rid this world of you once and for all."

"Like him?" Matthew's small voice was barely loud enough to be heard above the noise of the machines in the room.

But she did hear it. The words sank into her heart as she turned away from Frank to look at the sweet boy. "No, Matthew. He's not what you think. He's worthless."

Matthew shook his head, his lower lip protruding. "Like him."

"We all have intrinsic value, no matter how twisted we become with sin."

Great. She could hear Tiernan's voice in her head now. Was this what happened when a person faced imminent death?

"Well, this is a cozy picture."

Ashley jerked her gaze to see the owner of the male voice. Jack?

Hope leaped in her heart as he walked into the room.

"The whole family together." His jolly grin and familiar Aussie accent soothed her tattered nerves like a balm.

They were free.

chapter
thirty-three

"Is Tiernan with you?" Ashley peered behind Jack at the door he had left open.

"No, but he is." Jack jerked his thumb toward the door where Bradley entered, holding his gun.

She looked at Jack. "I don't understand."

"No, I imagine not." Jack looked like he might burst out laughing at any moment.

"He's the mole." Frank swayed on his feet as he watched Jack.

The mole? In the FBI?

Jack sobered as he returned Frank's stare. "That's the pot calling the kettle black. You can go now, mate. You're wanted on deck." He glanced at Bradley, who reached for Frank's arm. "Be ready to catch him. Doesn't look like he's gonna last."

Bradley nodded as he pulled Frank out of the room.

Ashley swallowed, trying to moisten her dry throat as she comprehended the scene unfolding before her eyes. This couldn't be happening. Jack was there to save them. He had to be.

She waited as the door shut behind Bradley. Now Jack would drop the act and untie them.

"I just wanted to give you the good news."

She knew it.

"Tiernan found the evidence that the Bordens had against Grayson."

"Wonderful." Ashley smiled as relief began to loosen the knots in her stomach. "Where was it?"

"A bank vault under an assumed name. And," he pointed at Matthew with a wink, "it was found thanks to you, I hear." His gaze shifted to Ashley. "And you." He tilted his head. "Grayson's not too happy about it, of course." His grin started to fade. "And now I have to take a little unplanned trip myself." Something dark replaced the amusement in his eyes.

She must be imagining things. She tried to smile. "Want to untie us now?"

"Why would I want to do that?" There was no trace of a smile on his usually laughing mouth. No teasing twinkle in the eyes.

Her pulse started to double-time. No. It couldn't be.

"You're the one to blame for all this. I could stay and keep working at the FBI if it wasn't for you and your interference with this kid." He swung a dismissive hand toward Matthew. "You made me have to give myself away. No one even knew there was a leak until you came along and threatened to get the secret out of the boy."

He wasn't there to help them escape. He was the leak. Her brain fought the grim facts that stared her in the face. Nausea churned in her belly. "I can't believe it." Had she said that out loud?

Jack grinned at her. "I know. Katherine seems like the more likely traitor, doesn't she? All prickly and cold. She took the focus off me beautifully. Until you came, and I had to force things."

"It was Tiernan's idea, not mine." Maybe if Ashley could get on Jack's good side, he'd consider helping them out.

"Oh, I know. Tiernan, my old mate. Always thinking of everything and everybody." Jack swept his gaze around the room. "Guess he didn't plan on this for you, though, ay?"

Special Target

Or maybe Tiernan had saved them anyway. "If he found the evidence, then Grayson has no reason to hold us anymore. He's caught even without Matthew now."

Jack sneered at her. "Grayson's no more caught than I am. This trip just got a lot longer for all of us. Except you two."

"Make that three." Bradley shoved Frank through the open door.

Frank stumbled and fell to his knees on the blue mat. A dark bruise colored his cheek under his eye, probably from a punch or two.

Didn't look good for their hopes of getting off this boat. Ashley stared at him until he lifted his gaze.

He shook his head. "We're dead weight now. He's jumping the country. He has to get rid of us."

"Well put, Frank." Jack patted the older man's shoulder as he stepped over him on the way to the door. He glanced back at Ashley. "I bet you really wish the Bordens had followed your advice now, ay?"

What was he getting at?

"That bit you told Tiernan about the boy. You're right, they shouldn't have let him be born. Downright cruel. And awfully inconvenient."

She pulled her wrists, straining at the cord so she could wipe that grin off the traitor's face.

"What I don't get is why you ended up here for somebody like him." Jack shook his head, glancing at Matthew. "I mean look at him. Only half a person. He's not worth it." Jack turned to the door. "Feel free to have a seat like Frank." He paused in the doorway and looked back. "You won't have long to wait now. Cheers." He waved, then shut the door.

"What did he mean?"

Frank dragged his gaze up to meet Ashley's. "They're going to dump us in the middle of Lake Michigan."

Panic rose in her throat, or maybe the swirling nausea was pushing its way out. She couldn't swim.

Idiot. None of them would survive out there. That was the

point. She took in a shaky breath. There were worse ways to die...much worse.

Matthew walked on wobbly legs to Frank and sank to the floor beside the fading man.

She blinked at the sight. Like a lamb sitting next to a wolf.

Matthew had no idea what kind of person Frank was. He didn't understand, just like so many other things that made him vulnerable to harm. He needed her to protect him. And she was not going to fail.

If only she hadn't left her purse behind at the house. She'd have her pepper spray and her—

She could've rolled her eyes at her own stupidity. The knife was still in her pocket. No one had thought to search her once they took the gun.

She angled her tied hands so she could tuck her fingers into her front pocket and pull out the knife. She opened the blade, swallowing back the gross taste that reached the back of her throat. She couldn't afford to get seasick.

Now, how to cut the cord with her hands tied? "Matthew." She walked over to him, adrenaline starting to energize her body. "Hold out your hands."

She crouched down in front of him, ignoring another surge of nausea as she tucked the knife blade under the plastic cord around his wrists. "Hold still." She pulled and sawed, the tiny blade taking some time to make progress on the thick cord. What felt like an eternity later, the cord snapped.

Matthew smiled and waved his freed hands. "God good!"

She couldn't help the answering smile that pulled up her lips. At least he'd picked an appropriate moment to say that this time.

"You're not going to give him the knife, are you?" Frank's doubtful question made her pause as she was about to do just that. She hated to even look like she was listening to Frank, but she didn't particularly want her hands cut up more from Matthew's clumsy knife skills either.

"Fine. Turn around."

Frank sat up on his knees and shifted, wincing as he turned his back and his tied hands to her.

She started sawing at the cord with her knife. "What did they do to you?"

He was silent a moment as she cut. "Nothing more than I deserve."

She clenched her jaw as the knife split the cord. Truest words he'd ever said.

"Now me." She didn't look at him when he took the knife.

His fingers pressed into her skin as he gripped her wrist.

Her stomach lurched. "Don't touch me." The words shot out with the force of the hate and terror behind them.

He let go quickly, as if he was surprised.

"Just cut the cord." She kept her eyes averted. Seeing him so close in front of her might push her over the edge. She couldn't afford that right now.

The tie fell off, and she pulled her wrists apart, rubbing the sore, red lines across them. She held out her hand, and Frank dropped the knife into her palm.

She stood, scanning the room as she swallowed back more queasiness.

"Even if we could manage to get through the door, we'd never make it off the boat." More Abelli pessimism. "And we're already on the lake."

She glanced at Frank, who had sagged back down, legs folded under him. "Why don't you try to be helpful? If we can find a weapon in here, we can be ready to defend ourselves when we get out."

"We're not—"

"Shh." Ashley pointed to the door as the knob twisted.

Someone was coming in.

She sat down on the floor next to Matthew. "Pretend your hands are still tied."

He met her whisper with a blank stare.

"Shh. Don't say anything."

The door slowly opened a crack, then a few inches, then—

Tiernan?

"Gain!" Matthew sprang to his feet before Ashley could stop him.

Tiernan caught Matthew in a hug while Ashley's heart raced, whether from the sight of Tiernan or fear that Matthew's yell had been heard, she wasn't sure.

Tiernan's gaze found Ashley over Matthew's shoulder. "Are you all right?" Those green eyes were filled with concern, lines crossing his brow beneath his shaggy hair.

She nodded, not trusting her voice as her throat tightened. Aside from becoming an emotional wreck, she was just fine.

He let go of Matthew and looked the boy over. "And you're as handsome as ever." He smiled and angled the bill of Matthew's cap.

Didn't bother Ashley a bit this time. "Is it over?"

Tiernan's smile faded as he looked at her. "Not yet. But it will be. Katherine's on the yacht with me. We got a tip Grayson was preparing to leave the country. The department started watching the airports, but I figured his yacht would be his only hope of making it. I knew about the secret yacht purchase from Frank."

"So you've been here this whole time?"

"Yep. Holed up waiting to see if Grayson got on board. We didn't know you all were here until I spotted Jack heading down to this level." Tiernan's gaze dropped to Frank, still seated on the floor. "Is he all right?"

Ashley shrugged, crossing her arms in front of her. "He seems sick. And I think they worked him over."

Tiernan walked to Frank and crouched in front of him. He gently rested a hand on Frank's shoulder. "Sir, are you okay?"

Bile climbed up Ashley's throat. "What are you doing? He's a criminal, Tiernan. He's..."

Tiernan turned his soft green eyes on her. "Be merciful, even as your Father is merciful."

"What? Oh, a Bible quote, right?" She put her hands on her hips. "Well, we're not in church. We're in the real world where we're about to get killed. Do you have a plan to get us out of here?" Three minutes after seeing him, and Tiernan already had her exasperated.

He got to his feet. "There are a lot of men on this ship. We have to assume the crew members are part of Grayson's organization, as well as his gunmen."

"Meaning, we're still trapped?"

"No. I'm just making you aware there are some challenges."

"I could've told you that."

The corner of his mouth twitched as he watched her. He better not be about to smile. "Katherine's working her way to the helm to get to the radio."

"*That's* the plan?"

The smile appeared. "Man, I missed you, Ashley."

Her heart skipped a beat without asking her permission. She looked away. How could he not even be mad that she'd ditched him again at the hospital?

"Katherine will get through to the radio and call the coast guard. She might be prickly, but she's good."

Prickly. Someone else had just called her that. Ashley brought her gaze to Tiernan. "I'm sorry about Jack."

He nodded, his lips pressing into a firm line. "Me, too."

A click at the door.

Tiernan spun around, pushing Ashley behind him. "Hide."

chapter
thirty-four

"Hide go see?"

"Shh." Ashley grabbed Matthew and pulled him to the crossing path, the nausea she'd forgotten stirring in her stomach. "Get down."

The door swung open just as Matthew slowly kneeled.

"What have we here?" Lincoln stepped into the room, his gun already drawn.

Ashley peeked over a pipe to see Tiernan facing Lincoln with his own pistol.

"A hero? I love heroes." Lincoln's mouth twisted into his sadistic smile. "And here I thought Ashley might be lonely down here." His dark gaze immediately found her. "I see you."

A shiver ran up her spine at his creepy tone. She mentally shook it off. She didn't have to let him get to her. Tiernan stood between them with a gun.

"Find!" Matthew leaped to his feet with a big grin as Ashley reached for him. She missed. He jogged toward Tiernan, then passed him.

Ashley watched in horror as the actions seemed to unfold in slow motion.

Matthew was going for Lincoln.

"Matthew, no!" Tiernan grabbed Matthew, trying to hold him back with his free arm, but the boy pushed through.

Lincoln snatched Matthew and suddenly had his arm around the boy's neck, the gun pressed to his head.

Ashley's heart lodged in her throat. She couldn't breathe.

"Lincoln, don't do it." Tiernan's voice was eerily calm. "You don't want any bodies with bullet holes."

"You know my name." Lincoln smiled next to Matthew's frightened face. "I'm flattered."

"Let him go." Ashley stepped out from the crossing path.

"Tell your friend to put down his gun."

"Tiernan?" The fear on Matthew's face, his strangled features were killing her.

Tiernan lowered his gun.

"Excellent. Now give it to Frank there, and he'll hand it to me like a good boy. Won't you, Frank?"

Tiernan crouched in front of Frank, who still sat on the floor, now between Tiernan and Lincoln. Tiernan handed the gun to Frank with a barely perceptible nod.

"Now give it to me. Slowly."

Frank leaned backward, twisting toward Lincoln, and a *pop* blasted through the room.

The gun. It had gone off.

Lincoln screamed and dropped to one knee, grabbing his thigh as his trouser leg turned red.

Matthew stared at him a foot away. Matthew was free?

"Ashley, get Matthew." Tiernan barked the command as he lifted Frank to his feet and draped the man's arm across his shoulders.

She hurried past the men, grabbing Matthew without looking at Lincoln, who groaned at their feet. "We have to go, Matthew. Hurry." Tugging finally drew the boy's gaze away from Lincoln, but his mouth hung open in shock.

She pulled Matthew with her through the narrow hallway, glancing back to be sure Tiernan followed.

"Like him." Matthew's voice was tight. Was he crying?

"Matthew, honey, it's okay. He's a bad man. He was going to hurt you." She caught sight of a wet streak on his cheek. Her heart squeezed. "I'm not going to let anyone hurt you, okay?"

"Like him."

"Ashley."

She looked behind at Tiernan.

"Hold it here."

They were still about twenty feet from the stairs.

"They might have heard that shot." Tiernan checked the still-closed door to the engine room. "I don't think Lincoln's coming from behind anytime soon. I'll take the lead."

"But you have him." She looked at Frank, still dangling from Tiernan's shoulders.

"I can make it." Frank pulled his arm off the younger man and straightened, bracing a hand against the wall. He bent over again, and vomit escaped his mouth, splattering onto the floor.

Ashley's unsettled stomach churned at the sight. She tried to breathe evenly, swallowing back the bile that pushed up from her throat.

Tiernan touched Frank's shoulder. "Are you seasick?"

"It's more than that." She watched Frank as he stood taller again, his face ghostly. "You weren't supposed to leave the hospital, were you?" Now she knew why he had wanted to talk to the nurse alone when he checked out.

He tried for a weak smile. "Wasn't supposed to do a lot of things." He looked at Tiernan. "But I'll make it. Or you can leave me behind if you have to."

"We won't leave you behind. But we need to keep moving." Tiernan brushed past Ashley and Matthew.

"To where?"

"Katherine. She should be at the helm by now." He glanced at Ashley and Matthew. "If we meet anyone on the way, I want you both to run. Don't try to help me." He met Ashley's gaze. "Save Matthew, okay?"

She nodded, an ache squeezing her chest. Was he saying goodbye?

They slowly climbed the stairs, Tiernan signaling with his hand when they should stop or move forward.

She glanced back.

Frank paused, only on the second step. He clung to the railing like it was the only thing that prevented him from falling backward.

She couldn't risk leaving Matthew to help him. Frank would have to make it on his own. Just like she had all her life.

Tiernan's open palm told them to stop as he reached the door at the top of the stairs. He opened it without a sound, peering through a slit at first. He swung the door farther and darted through, pointing his gun right, then left.

He glanced at Ashley. Waved her forward.

"Hide go see?" Matthew's question burst like a balloon in her ear.

"Shh." She grabbed his arm and stuck her finger to her lips, checking with Tiernan.

He looked back and forth again. "Still clear. Let's move."

Ashley guided Matthew out the door.

A gust of wind nearly knocked her off her unsteady feet. A *boom* sounded overhead, and the floor beneath her shoes seemed to vibrate. Thunder?

Sure enough, the sky had turned a smoky gray as if evening had already come, and the water beyond the railing they crept along was dark and choppy. Waves reached high to smack against the side of the yacht.

No wonder her stomach felt like it was being run through a blender. Rain spattered her arm as the drops blew onto the boat. Or was the water from the waves? At least the noise of the wind and rain might have covered Matthew's shout.

A flash lit the sky as she followed Tiernan toward the back

of the yacht. She gripped Matthew's hand tightly, trying to stay steady on her feet as the boat tilted with the waves. Crazy the weather could change so fast.

Thunder rumbled again as they reached a curved wall that she recognized—the staircase that led to the next level up.

Tiernan stopped, raising his hand.

She paused behind him.

He took another step ahead and craned his neck, probably trying to see better. He glanced back at her and nodded. But then his eyes seemed to lock on something past her.

She turned to see Frank dragging himself along with his hand on the wall.

Tiernan waited until Frank caught up with them, then walked out farther, waving the others to follow.

She rounded the end of the staircase, taking in the open seating area with the couches. The pillows and chaise lounge chairs had been removed, leaving only the empty couch frames, like skeletons left out in the elements.

She shook off the morbid thought as she guided Matthew up onto the curved staircase. At least this weather should mean no one would be outside. Maybe they could hide somewhere out there and not be found.

Ashley reached the top of the stairs behind Tiernan, emerging next to...a pool? More like an extra-large Jacuzzi or something. A huge light illuminated it from below, shining through the clear blue water that was getting pummeled by rain. Who would need a pool on a yacht?

She started when someone touched her arm.

Tiernan. *Move*, he mouthed as he pointed to two tinted glass doors that faced them from the center of the boat. Were people in there, watching?

She pulled Matthew's hand and followed Tiernan as he jogged away from the doors to the side of another curved staircase.

He pressed his back against the outer wall of the stairs,

putting his arm out to direct Ashley and Matthew to stop next to him.

A line of windows began just beyond Tiernan's elbow. How could they get past those? What if they'd already been seen by someone behind those doors?

Her pulse thundered in her ears nearly as loud as the sky above.

Tiernan checked behind.

Was someone following them? She swung her head around.

No one was there. Not even Frank.

Tiernan looked at her. "We'll go back for him when we find Katherine." He kept his voice as low as could still be heard above the rain pounding the overhang that covered their heads.

She held back the response she'd like to voice. No need to go back. Frank deserved to die there.

"We need to get to the front of this deck. Katherine should be inside there."

Ashley wiped away the drops of water that sprayed her face. "The windows?"

"Have Matthew crawl if he can't crouch low enough."

"Matthew." She leaned in close to his ear so she didn't have to raise her voice as much. "We're playing hide and go seek with someone behind those windows." She pointed at the row of glass panels. "We have to duck down so they don't see us. Okay?"

He nodded. His tear tracks had been replaced by the blowing water that shimmered on his cheeks.

She wiped a big drop away from his eye and tugged on the brim of his cap, leaving it crooked. "Hold onto your hat." She turned her head, and her gaze collided with Tiernan's.

The corners of his eyes crinkled as he gave her a smile that warmed her to her toes, even with the cold rain hitting her bare arms. "Ready?"

"Ready." She squeezed Matthew's hand as Tiernan started

forward, crouching low under the windows. "Just like that, Matthew." She pointed at Tiernan and gently pulled the boy along as she squatted down and headed after Tiernan.

Matthew mimicked her position, staying close behind her as they moved along the wall under the windows.

She looked ahead at Tiernan.

Her foot caught on something, stopping her for a second.

Matthew tumbled into her from behind.

She reached for him, too late to stop the thud as he fell against the wall and the floor.

Thunder shook the yacht.

She breathed again. Maybe anyone inside would blame the noise on that. She glanced for help from Tiernan, but he was too far away, close to the end of the windows and probably the front of the enclosed area.

"Can you get up?" She softly held Matthew's arms to help him off the floor and up into a crouch. But he stood instead.

"No, Matthew. Get down." She grabbed his hand and pulled until he knelt. "You go in front of me." She kept her hand on his back as they crawled forward.

Tiernan looked back at them, watching as they made their way to him.

Felt like an eternity later when they finally caught up with him.

He touched Matthew's shoulder as he stayed crouched under a window. "Good job." Tiernan's gaze met Ashley's, his green eyes not as calm as she'd expected.

"What's wrong?" She kept her voice at a whisper, hoping he could read her lips to understand despite the wind noise.

"Too easy." He pointed to a door on his other side that had a glass window in the top half. "Katherine's in there. Wait here while I check it out."

Ashley nodded and kept her hand on Matthew so he would stay as Tiernan lifted up enough to see in the window.

He lowered and tossed Ashley a smile. "She gave me the

okay. Let's go." He stood to his full height and opened the door, stepping aside to let Ashley and Matthew enter first.

"Took you all long enough." Katherine stood behind a wheel and gave Ashley the first real smile she'd ever seen from the woman.

Three men laid on the floor around her. Were they out cold or something else?

"Kathr—" Tiernan's voice cut off.

Ashley whirled around to see him fall into the room. Or was he pushed?

Jack darted through the doorway and launched a kick at Tiernan on the floor.

Tiernan rolled and jumped to his feet.

More men poured in. Three, four.

Shots fired.

Matthew shrieked, covering his ears.

Katherine's aim brought a man down as two more ducked behind a control panel in the middle of the room and the other sprinted toward her. She fired again.

He fell.

"Ashley, get out of here!" Katherine dropped behind a counter.

Ashley gripped Matthew's arm, holding him close as her gaze swung to Tiernan.

His nose bloodied, he launched a kick and chop at Jack. Some kind of martial arts.

Jack responded with similar moves of his own.

One of the men hiding behind the panel watched Matthew. The man pointed his gun.

"No!" Ashley stepped in front of Matthew just as Katherine popped around the end of the counter and shot at the men in hiding. They moved back from her view, staying low.

"Ashley," Katherine sent her a hard stare, "get Matthew out of here now!"

Ashley headed for the door, pulling on Matthew's arm.

"Like him! Like him!" Matthew shouted the words over and over again as Ashley dragged him from the room. He kept facing the fighters, his features contorted as if he was in pain.

The rain blew hard against them outside. "It's okay. You have to come with me. It'll be okay." Her heart raced as she looked for an escape route, adrenaline surging through her limbs.

"No, not that way." A man's voice behind her.

chapter
thirty-five

Ashley turned, angling Matthew with her as she kept her grip on his hand.

Bradley held Frank by the arm. And pressed a gun to the pale man's head. "You should really come this way." A short wall formed the only barrier between the men and the raging water behind them.

She looked pointedly at his gun. "That won't do any good."

Bradley brought his eyebrows together for a second, then relaxed them. "Oh, you mean to get you to do what I say. I forgot. You don't care about this old guy." He swung the weapon to aim at Matthew instead.

Her and her big mouth.

"Funny for a daughter to hate her old man so much." He shrugged with a grin. "But I guess I never had much use for mine either."

Lightning whitened the sky behind Bradley.

He didn't even flinch. "Nasty weather we're having, isn't it?" Like he was making small talk while they were out for a stroll on deck together, with a gun just in case.

She tightened her hold on Matthew's hand as thunder rumbled all around. She glared at Bradley. "Aren't you going to ask us inside?"

"Can't do that. Not safe in there. You're supposed to be out here." He turned sideways with Frank and glanced at the water below, grinning. "Way out there."

She tensed as she followed his gaze. The water was choppier than her stomach and nearly black, thanks to the darkness of the sky. She squared her shoulders to hide her fear. "I'd like to see you try."

If she got all Bradley's attention aimed at her, Frank should be able to take his gun or at least shove him away, giving them time to escape.

Bradley's grin broadened as he stared at her, apparently needing a moment to hatch his plan of attack.

Now, Frank, now. She tried to signal him with her eyes, but he just sagged like he was dying right in front of her.

"You're on, lady." Bradley chuckled. "Gotta get rid of this weight to make it fair." He lowered the gun and suddenly grabbed Frank, throwing him over the wall.

Matthew shrieked as Ashley lunged for the gun in Bradley's hand. She hung on when he lifted the gun above her head, trying to shake her off while hard rain beat down on her face.

Then his laughter reached her ears, freezing her blood. "Your little buddy jumped."

She dropped her hold.

Matthew. Where was Matthew?

Panic gripped her chest as she looked down at the dark water. Nothing close. She searched farther away.

Movement in the choppy waves. A person. Frank? No, two people.

Her heart in her throat, she spotted a white life preserver ring attached to the wall. She tore it off the hook and grabbed the ledge.

A hand clamped her shoulder. "No life preservers."

She threw herself into Bradley with all the fear coiled in her body.

He fell back, dropping the gun.

She spun back to the water, gripping the life preserver as she pulled herself up onto the wall and jumped.

Her stomach leaped to her chest as she plummeted to the black water below.

She hit hard, breaking through the waves.

Water covered her face, got into her lungs.

She held her breath. Tried kicking, her fingers locked around the life preserver.

The ring seemed to be pulling her up.

Her face broke through the surface, and she gulped in air.

Water splashed into her mouth with the oxygen as waves pushed her up and down, smacking her face. Another dropped over her, pulling her under again.

She popped through the surface, turning her head, searching for Matthew. The yacht wasn't going fast. He had to be close.

The sky flashed, lighting the water for a split-second.

A head bobbed in the distance.

"Matthew!" It had to be him. She kicked, trying to swim toward him. Why hadn't she learned how to swim? "Matthew!" She paddled with one hand, hanging onto the life preserver with the other.

A huge wave crashed down, yanking her hand off the ring.

She struggled under the water, kicking as hard as she could.

No use. Her soaked jeans and sneakers pulled her deeper into the swirling depths.

She was going to die.

Something grabbed her from behind.

She started to fight it off.

But she was moving toward the surface. Her lungs gave out just as she reached the top. She coughed, choking as she inhaled water, then air.

The life preserver appeared under her hand.

She blinked through the water to see her rescuer.

Matthew's blue eyes stared back at her as he kept himself

afloat without the ring. He put his heavy hand on her head. "God good."

Then he was gone.

"Matthew!" Her sore lungs strangled the shout.

She waited, wrapping her arm around the life preserver ring as she strained to see through the increasing darkness.

Something red floated toward her. A wave buried it, then the red appeared again. Another wave shoved it about a foot away.

Matthew's cap.

She lunged for it, keeping her arm hooked around the ring as she kicked and pulled until she clutched the cap in her fingers. She gripped it like it was her life preserver.

It didn't mean he was gone. He hadn't been wearing it when she just saw him. It must have come off when he jumped.

Why? Why did he have to jump?

A head bobbed above the water between the waves about ten feet away.

"Matthew!" Her heart leaped against her ribcage as she tried to kick toward him.

He wasn't alone.

Another head floated in front of Matthew, clutched against the boy's chest as he swam sideways to Ashley.

Matthew grabbed the ring with his paddling arm and dragged the other person over to it.

The dark hair and pale face she thought she'd never see again. Frank.

Matthew draped Frank's arms over the small ring next to her, pulling it down into the water.

"No, Matthew. It's not strong enough."

Frank's eyes were closed, his skin the pallor of death. Was he even still alive? His arms started to slip off the ring.

Matthew grabbed the dangling limbs and hooked them over the life preserver again. He panted, his mouth open as he kept kicking and moving his arms back and forth to keep himself afloat.

"Matthew, you have to grab on. You're getting too tired." And she didn't know when they would be rescued. If ever.

Frank started to fall, his arms sliding off the ring.

Matthew lifted Frank's torso this time, trying to lay the man over the life preserver, pinning her arm in the process.

"Matthew, no. You're putting too much weight on it." She shoved Frank off her arm, and he sank into the water.

Matthew disappeared under the surface.

"Matthew!" Her yell timed with another bolt of lightning. Her breath stopped as she waited, moving wherever the waves pushed her. She scanned the water over and over again. "Matthew!" He had to be there. He would come back.

A head broke through the surface.

Black hair. Frank.

Matthew followed behind, gasping for air as he wrapped Frank's arms over the ring again.

"You have to let him go, Matthew. He's not worth it."

Matthew grabbed the cap out of her hand and dropped it in the water. What was he doing?

He took her emptied hand.

Yes, good. She could hang onto him.

But he put her hand on Frank's arm.

She pulled it off.

Matthew grabbed her hand again and put it back, holding it against Frank's clammy skin. "Azwee." He stared into her face. "Like him."

Her heart squeezed like someone was pressing it in a vise.

Matthew let go, swinging his arms back and forth in the water as he panted more heavily than before.

She stared at Frank and her hand on his arm.

He moaned, his pale eyelids twitching, then opening.

"Matthew, he's awake."

She turned to look at Matthew.

A flash of lightning illuminated the empty water.

Matthew?

"Matthew!" Her scream echoed with the booming thunder.

"Ashley!"

Tiernan. He swam to her, dragging a buoy of some sort.

"Matthew went under!" Sheer terror strangled her voice. "I can't see him!"

"Hang onto this."

Ashley grabbed the long buoy he shoved at her as he dove under a wave.

Frank murmured something she couldn't hear. He rolled his head, his arms still hanging over the ring.

She pulled her hand off his arm. If there was a God, now would be the time for Him to do some good. "Please." She stared at the choppy water as she whispered. "If You really made Matthew, if You really love him, please save him. Please."

The surface of the water broke.

Matthew?

No. Tiernan.

He gasped for air, grabbing onto the other side of the buoy. "I couldn't..." He shook his head, panting. "I couldn't find him. Too dark."

"No!" She let go of the buoy and tried to dive down, but something yanked her back.

"Ashley." Tiernan's voice was as firm as his grip on her arm. "You can't swim. I'm going to look again. Stay here." He dove under, popped up farther away, then swam across the surface with strokes that took him out of sight.

Colored lights flashed in the distance. Red. Blinking.

The lights came closer, attached to a boat. The coast guard?

A siren blared.

For only a second. Before it was drowned out by the screaming of her heart.

chapter
thirty-six

The doorbell rang a third time, the loud *ding-dong* easily making the short trip to Ashley where she sat on the couch, her head in her hands. She dug her fingers into her scalp, grinding her teeth as she waited for him to go away.

The door opened.

Tiernan shut it softly behind him, his gaze drifting from her to the overturned furniture.

"I didn't say you could come in." She muttered the words, letting her hair fall over her eye.

"You won't answer your phone."

As if that explained why he was breaking and entering again. Between constant calls from him and Tina, she'd had to turn off her phone for good.

"I thought you were going to clean this place up." He went to the toppled dining chair that didn't belong in this room and set it upright.

"I put the couch cushions back."

He glanced at the gutted cushions beneath the ruined afghan tossed beside her. "You're sleeping out here?"

"Why not?" She pulled the afghan onto her lap, looking down at its crocheted purple and white yarn, now cut and torn like her shredded heart. Even the thought of her bedroom made the ache worse. She couldn't look in there without seeing Matthew's folded pajamas or his smile as he'd looked up at her from the bed.

She felt Tiernan watch her as she stared at the afghan. She knew she looked like a disaster. Not that it mattered.

He plunked the chair down in front of her and sat on it. "Ashley." His deep voice reached for her through the pain squeezing her chest. "Don't do this. Matthew wouldn't want you to give up on living."

"You mean because he saved my life?" She lifted her head, looking at him through the hair that hung over one side of her face.

Those green eyes reflected back the blistering sorrow swallowing her soul. But there was something else in them. A glint of something better, something she couldn't feel.

"I couldn't save his." She whispered the words as she searched Tiernan's gaze.

"You didn't have to. God saved your life and Frank's. For a reason."

Her eyes narrowed. "And didn't save Matthew, right?" She leaned back to get away from him, a bitter taste reaching her mouth. "It's that easy for you." The second the words were out, she wanted to grab them back.

He got to his feet and stalked a few paces away, his back turned. "Not a day goes by that I don't weep over what happened." He rested his hands on his hips, hanging his head. "I'd give anything to go back and get to you both sooner." He sniffed and faced her. "But then I remember. God has a plan. He has a purpose. And—" his voice caught like he was about to cry, "it's better than anything I can imagine."

Tears pricked her eyes. If only she could believe that.

"The Bible says that before we're even born, God has written in His book every one of our days before we live them. He knew how long Matthew had. He planned it."

"So then it's supposed to be fine that those monsters killed him?"

"No." Tiernan rushed back to the chair and sat down, taking Ashley's hand in his. "No, no, no. God hates evil. You remember Matthew's 'like Him' from that Bible verse?"

As if she could ever forget Matthew's last words.

"About God creating us in His own image?" Tiernan's eyes urged her to listen as he gently squeezed her hand.

She managed a nod.

"Well, when He made us, the first people, Adam and Eve, were perfect and there was no evil in them. But then they rejected God."

The apple from the tree. She knew the story.

"Evil entered the world, contaminating everything, especially people. So now people are born into sin. We all do wrong, some more obviously than others. And we'll all be judged by God because He won't let evil go unpunished."

Tiernan stared deeply into her eyes, his own glistening with moisture. "What those men did to Matthew, to you and Frank—they'll be punished for that by God Himself." He brushed his thumb over her hand as he talked. "But God will also use the evil that they did for good."

"How?"

"In many ways I can't see yet."

Figured. She pulled her hand from his grasp.

"But in other ways that I can see."

She looked at him.

"Frank."

That name. So dreadful before. Now the reason Matthew had died.

She picked at the torn afghan.

"Matthew saved him from drowning so God could save him from much worse."

From what? A trial for all his wrongs?

Tiernan leaned forward, as if trying to make her meet his eyes. "Frank is dying, Ashley. The doctors say it's only a matter of days, maybe hours."

She brought her gaze to his face. "Then what was the

point? Matthew didn't know that. And he didn't know what kind of person Frank is, what he—" The growing lump in her throat halted more words.

"Matthew knew where he was going if he died. He did the right thing. Frank didn't know the Lord. If he had died then, he would have been condemned for eternity."

Ashley stared at Tiernan. "Which is exactly what he deserves."

Tiernan leaned back, watching her. "He confessed, you know."

"What?"

"He had the police come to his hospital room and told them what he did to you when you were young, the other crimes he was involved in with Grayson, everything."

She looked at the sliced arm of the couch. That meant Tiernan knew now. All the sordid details.

"Ashley. I am *so* sorry that you had to suffer what you did." He pulled in a breath that sounded shaky. His eyes glittered with emotion. Was it compassion? "I can't even imagine. And I have a hard time not hating him for…doing that to you."

She clenched her jaw. She would not cry. Even if it was the first time she'd felt seen, believed. Understood. She donned a caustic smile instead. "Easy to confess when it's too late to go to prison."

"I was there. It was far from easy."

"I suppose you're going to tell me God will make that good, too, somehow."

"What if that's the truth?"

She glared at Tiernan. "He nearly destroyed me."

"But he didn't."

She stared. "You're saying because of God? That God protected me?"

He lifted his arms out from his sides. "I don't know. I'm not God. But I'm saying look at your life. Think about all the children you've saved from fates like that. Would you have done that without the experience you had?"

She blinked at him.

He leaned forward and took her hand again. "Look, I know that's not enough to..." he glanced away as if the words he wanted were written on the wall, "...make it all better. But God is turning that horrible thing into something good. And He will keep doing that until it's swallowed up in victory."

Swallowed up in victory. The words rang in her mind, sparking something deep within her, like a flicker of a tiny flame.

"Will you go see Frank with me?"

The flame snuffed out.

"He needs to tell you something."

She pulled her hand away again and dropped the afghan on the couch as she stood. "That's why you're here, isn't it?"

Tiernan got to his feet. "I'm here because I won't watch you waste what God and Matthew gave you." His green eyes pierced through her anger, hitting the weak spot in her heart.

"Like him." The pleading on Matthew's face as he'd said those words, the press of his hand on her head—they were as real as if he were there with her right now.

She couldn't refuse to do what he asked...for him.

She closed her eyes. "I'll go."

"I'll be right here." Tiernan's words as they walked down the hallway broke the silence that had hung between them the entire drive to the hospital.

How much had changed. The fear that had terrorized Ashley the last time she'd approached Frank's room had been replaced by anger so strong it might even choke the ache that had squeezed her heart the past six days. He shouldn't have lived.

"In here." Tiernan turned into a room with an open door.

She paused, then followed, her limbs starting to tingle with the fury that burned inside.

Frank lay in a bed as before, hooked up to the noisy dialysis machine as well as other tubes that ran to different monitors and an IV. His face had slightly more color than the last time she'd seen him, unconscious in the water. But he looked unconscious now, his eyes shut.

Tiernan went to the bed and touched Frank's hand where it lay on the sheet, like he was a beloved friend or...family. "Frank. Ashley's here."

The eyes slowly opened, blinked, then found her.

She crossed her arms, clenching her jaw as she dug her fingers into her skin.

"I'm s..." Frank's weak voice faded out so she couldn't hear.

"What?" She didn't try to keep the sharpness out of her tone.

"I..."

Faded out again. She sighed and walked to the other side of the bed, keeping a safe twelve inches between her and Frank.

He stared up at her. "I'm sorry."

"You said that already." She lifted her gaze to Tiernan across the bed. "Is that all he wanted to tell me?"

Tiernan opened his mouth to respond.

"No." Frank reached a hand toward her, but she took a step back. He dropped the hand on the bed. "Matthew..."

The name caught her. What about Matthew? She stepped closer.

"Helped me. I'm...like him now. Jesus...forgave me." He dragged his limp hand to rest on his chest. "Jesus...in here now."

She shot a sharp glance at Tiernan. "Is he kidding?"

"No." Tiernan's eyes were as gentle as the smile that curved his lips. "Jesus forgave him of everything. He saved him."

She stared at Tiernan. "But you said he'd be punished."

"Whoever rejects Jesus Christ will be punished for their

wrongs. But Jesus already took the punishment for the sins of those who believe in Him." Tiernan looked down at the dying man. "Frank believes. He has Christ's forgiveness and righteousness now."

Frank managed to lift his finger. Was he trying to point at her? "You...too."

"What?"

Tiernan glanced at her. "I think he means that you can be forgiven, too."

Her lips curled in disgust as she looked at Frank's pale face. "Arrogant and self-righteous to the last. It was always my fault."

"He's not talking about that."

She glared at Tiernan. "How do you know?"

"I can see it as well as he can." A spark flickered in his eyes as he frowned. "I mean, come on, I just had to drag you away from a pretty pitiful scene."

How dare he? "It's called mourning."

"No, it's called punishing yourself." He met her glare without blinking. "For what? Not for Matthew, I can tell you that much."

Her eyes stung with moisture she desperately blinked back.

A giggle reached her ears. That face—the little angled eyes, the funny nose, the smile. But it wasn't Matthew.

It was her daughter.

Ashley stumbled back.

Strong arms caught her, lowering her into a chair.

Tiernan's face appeared in front of her. "It's okay."

She shook her head, a tear escaping, running down her cheek. "I killed her." Her trembling fingers clutched at Tiernan's arm. "I killed her."

His hand found hers and gently held it. "Killed who, Ashley?"

She took a long, shuddering breath. "My baby." A sob

escaped and then she couldn't stop the flood of tears. She buried her face in Tiernan's shoulder.

His arms wrapped around her, cradling her and comforting her like she didn't deserve.

"Shh. Shh." He stroked her hair. "Give Him those tears. He knows what you've done, and He's ready to forgive you even for that. Why do you think He sent you Matthew?"

She lifted her head, slowly pulling back to see Tiernan's face. Wet tracks lined his cheeks as he met her gaze with nothing but love in his own.

The beeping machine behind him stopped and a long, unending tone sounded.

Tiernan swung around to look at Frank.

"Tiernan?" Ashley got to her feet as rushing footsteps pounded in the hallway.

Two nurses and a man in a lab coat jogged into the room. The man barked out orders that sounded like a foreign language. Someone wheeled in another machine, and they started fiddling with Frank's tubes.

Tiernan stepped back away from the bed, staring at the action as he put an arm around Ashley's shoulders.

"Is he...?" Her heart squeezed as they placed things on Frank's chest and a shock jolted through his body.

The machine still blared in the unending single tone that seemed to ring and echo in Ashley's ears as she watched, frozen.

The doctor stepped back and shook his head.

"No." Ashley ran to the bed. She put her hand over Frank's. There was still warmth in his palm as her fingers curved around the limp hand. She bent down next to his ear to whisper. "I forgive you." A salty tear fell on her lip as she slowly straightened.

Tiernan came to stand beside her, watching Frank with glistening eyes.

The weight Ashley had carried her entire life lifted from her heart. The bitterness, the fear, the shame. It wasn't possible. But she felt the change, as if she'd been pulled out from under the waves once more and could breathe at last.

"*God good.*" Matthew's words echoed in her soul.

Was her little girl saying them with him?

"Is my..." Ashley swallowed. "My baby. Is she with Matthew now?"

Tiernan looked down at her and nodded. "With Matthew and with Frank, in perfect happiness." He gave Ashley a small smile. "Maybe she got to welcome them home."

Ashley reached for Tiernan's hand and held on tight.

Home. Matthew had finally found his way there.

Turn the Page for a Special Sneak Peek of
WINDY CITY WESTONS, BOOK 1

WAYLAID

AVAILABLE NOW

waylaid

Chapter One

Chicago. August 28. 9:26 p.m.

A pop pierced the night.

A gunshot? Spring Weston's stomach clenched as she ducked lower over the handlebars of her bicycle and peddled hard. A shooting wouldn't be a surprise in that neighborhood, but she'd rather avoid a run-in with a stray bullet.

She glanced into the hazy darkness on either side of her as she kept her pace steady, light raindrops mixing with sweat on her face.

Nothing moved in the glow from streetlamps.

A white van waited next to some business with barred windows. The building's sign was a yellow blur as she whizzed by, maintaining her racing speed.

She tapped the backlight on the timer attached to the handlebars. Great pace. Faster than she should be at mile ten. Adrenaline and nerves must be driving her legs.

Drugs. Doping. On *her* team.

The anxiety wadding in her stomach threatened to choke her. She puffed out a breath, willing her muscles to relax as she kept pedaling at the same clip.

She glided through a curve into the headwind. Rain pelted her face.

"Doping? Are you kidding me?" Cliff's denial echoed in her ears, louder than the wind that rushed past. *"I run a clean team. You know that."*

"But I saw Megan…popping pills." Spring had watched her coach, desperately hoping he would offer some explanation she could believe.

"How do you know they were drugs? She takes supplements all the time."

"Megan told me what the pills were."

Cliff laughed. "She told you? That'd be pretty dumb if she was doping, wouldn't it?"

Spring frowned at his jovial grin. "Megan didn't think I'd care. She thought it was expected. She said—" Spring moistened her lips. "She said the whole team is doing it."

"Well, there you go."

Spring raised her eyebrows.

"Obviously, she was just joking. She knows you don't take drugs." Cliff's grin angled sideways. "You know what a kidder Megan is. You gotta learn to lighten up and not take things so seriously."

She stared at him. Why couldn't he be more convincing? Offer some explanation or at least a denial that he was involved?

He had stepped closer to her, his grin softening into a smile that seemed to hide something. "Come on, Spring. Don't you trust me more than that?"

She had trusted him. But she knew what she had seen Megan take, what Megan had said. It wasn't a joke. At least not to Spring.

She shifted her shoulders, trying to relax as she surged through the neighborhood she was moving too fast to see.

The rain weakened, but her tense thoughts pelted her from the inside.

If only it wasn't true. If only she hadn't met Megan for a training run and seen her take those pills.

Spring pressed her lips together, trapping her breath longer than she should. She had no hard evidence to prove doping on the team. Only what Megan had told her. Would anyone believe her if she reported it? She could hardly believe it herself.

But she couldn't knowingly compete on a team that was doping. Every win would mean nothing. And the scandal could come out once she made it to an elite team. Everyone would think she had doped, too.

Lord, give me wisdom. Calm slid through her chest with the prayer, soothing the tension and allowing her to breathe more evenly.

She would have to report what she knew. Whether or not anyone believed her wasn't her responsibility.

Relief flowed to her fingers with the confidence that she'd made the right decision.

Readjusting her position over the handlebars, she focused on pushing her pace back up. A praise song from church started to play in her head, lending a driving beat to her pedaling rhythm.

She sailed into the curve under the overpass, the road wet enough to make her slow just slightly.

She sped into the straightaway.

A rumble behind her.

Ugh. Traffic. Unusual for the area at that time of night.

She drifted closer to the curb to let the driver pass, not slowing her pace.

The rumble grew louder. Why wasn't the car passing?

She glanced back.

A white blur slammed into her bicycle. Catapulted her.

She flew, airborne.

Her breath caught as time stood still.

A concrete abutment waited for her.

She was going to die.

Someone wants to kill her. She wants the killer to finish the job.

Spring Weston will do anything to rise in the ranks of pro cycling and prove she isn't the one failure of the five Weston siblings. Anything except cheat. When she learns of doping on her cycling team, she's determined to uncover the truth. But she can't if she's dead.

Sergeant Torin Cotter may not be the hero the public thinks he is, but he recognizes fear when he sees it. When he takes over the investigation of the collision that landed Spring in the hospital, he's compelled to protect her from whatever danger she's in, even though he knows he might fail. Again.

Spring's faith in God isn't enough to help her face the living nightmare she awakened to after the accident. But neither she nor the handsome sergeant see the greater threat that's coming until it's too late.

If they're going to survive, Spring and Torin will not only have to confront their worst fears—they'll have to find a reason to live.

Shop *Waylaid* at
JerushaAgen.com

She never invites visitors. But visitors sometimes invite themselves.

When a winter storm brings more than snow, May Denver is forced to flee from her home and fight for her life. Can she trust an unwanted neighbor and risk her greatest fear in order to survive?

GRAB THIS ROMANTIC SUSPENSE STORY FOR FREE WHEN YOU SIGN UP FOR JERUSHA'S NEWSLETTER
www.FearWarriorSuspense.com

about jerusha

Jerusha Agen is a Christy Award finalist who imagines danger around every corner but knows God is there, too. So naturally, she writes romantic suspense infused with the hope of salvation in Jesus Christ.

Jerusha loves to hang out with her big furry dogs and little furry cats, often while reading or watching movies.

Find more of Jerusha's thrilling, fear-fighting stories at www.JerushaAgen.com.

The Sisters Redeemed Series

If You Dance with Me
JERUSHA AGEN

If You Light My Way
JERUSHA AGEN

If You Rescue Me
JERUSHA AGEN

JerushaStore.com

www.ingramcontent.com/pod-product-compliance
Lightning Source LLC
LaVergne TN
LVHW032007070526
838202LV00059B/6330